WARRIOR PRINCE

NANCY J. COHEN

Copyright © 2012 by Nancy J. Cohen
WARRIOR PRINCE
Published by Orange Grove Press
Printed in the United States of America
Digital ISBN: 978-1-952886-13-3
Print ISBN: 978-1-952886-32-4
Cover Design by The Killion Group, Inc.
Interior Design by Formatting4u.com

This is a work of fiction. Names, characters, places, and incidents either are the product of the author's imagination or are used fictitiously, and any resemblance to actual persons, business establishments, events or locales is entirely coincidental.

Chapter One

"Hi, I'm Nira Larsen, here for an interview," she told the receptionist, whose solemn stare and black attire would have suited the funeral home she'd visited earlier.

"Please take a seat. We'll be with you in a few minutes." The woman's blunt-cut dark hair swung as she pressed a button on her console to announce Nira's arrival.

Nira glanced at the small waiting area with its threadbare carpet, row of vinyl seats, and musty odor. Why was no one else here? And why did this place appear so seedy, with peeling paint and grime-coated windows? Maybe she didn't want to work for people who treated their applicants with such disrespect.

Nonetheless, she'd like to land a position at Drift World. On her budget, she couldn't afford a ticket to the role-playing adult theme park but getting a job there would solve that problem. Plus, she needed the money for other reasons.

She took a seat, an odd buzzing in her ears. It had started when she walked into the place. But even weirder had been the way the theme park's temporary employment office appeared to materialize out of thin air.

The address specified on the classified ad had taken her next to a popular café on Orlando's International Drive. Maybe she was just tired after her last two disastrous interviews, but she could have sworn this log cabin hadn't been in the parking lot when she'd arrived.

Her thoughts scattered when the inner door burst open, and an attractive blonde smiled at her. "Come in, Miss Larsen. My name is Algie Morar. I understand you're applying for a position as a makeup artist?"

"Yes, that's correct."

Nira followed her into a corridor marked by closed doors on either side. At the far end, the hallway opened into a large room from which low male voices rumbled in a strange guttural tongue. A curtain made of fabric strips obstructed the view.

The woman halted and opened a door, gesturing silently for Nira to enter. But instead of facing a desk and chairs as she'd expected for an interview, she spied a treatment table, sink, and counters' like in a doctor's office. A supply of cosmetics lay spread out on the counter—brushes, eye pencils, powders, and other familiar tools.

"Wait here." Algie turned on her heel and left Nira alone. A moment later, she returned with a burly man in tow.

Nira's mouth fell open. The stocky fellow had oversized ears, a long bulbous nose, and abnormally large hands and feet. His small beady eyes glared at her from beneath bushy brows. He wore a workman's clothes, stained trousers and a plaid shirt.

"Jek is a test subject to see if you suit us for employment. See if you can make him look more normal," Algie said.

Nira stifled a nervous cough. Weren't those huge cauliflower ears prosthetics? "Um, I'm not sure I—"

"Use those supplies." Algie pointed to the counter. "Shadowing, for example, can de-emphasize certain features. You should know what to do."

The blonde sauntered closer. Her porcelain features were so refined, she could have been a model. She leaned inward, her ocean blue eyes shining brightly, her rosy lips parting as though about to confide a secret. Nira couldn't drag her gaze away. Her nostrils picked up a floral scent that held her spellbound.

It seemed so natural when Algie placed a palm on her arm like an old friend.

Nira sprang back as the buzzing sound in her head increased to painful decibels.

Algie's eyes blazed. "How are you resisting me?"

"What?"

"Never mind, just do as I said. Fix Jek to look more human."

More human? Nira shook her head. That annoying buzzing sound must be affecting her brain.

However, it didn't affect her instincts. An inner voice hammered at her to leave. She backed away, but at a simple nod from Algie, the door slammed shut from an invisible force.

"You're not going anywhere until I find out how you're blocking me. Jek, seize her."

The big man's beefy hand clamped onto her arm.

"Let me go." Nira fought to elbow him in the gut, but his strength overwhelmed her. He hauled her toward the treatment table. "Stop, or I'll scream."

The woman's sinister chuckle chilled her blood. "Go ahead. No one will hear you."

Jek thrust Nira against the hard metal table and pressed her in place with his thighs.

Algie sauntered closer. "You're different. You can block my spell. We haven't met anyone like you before. It could be a danger to us." The woman's smooth tone belied the enmity in her eyes.

Nira swallowed against rising alarm. These people must belong to some cult.

Get out while you can.

She stomped on Jek's instep, hoping to dislodge his grip. He merely chuckled and dumped her supine on the table.

"Help! Someone help me!" she cried when he reached for restraints.

Jek had secured one wrist in a leather strap when a crash sounded from outside in the corridor, followed by shouts and loud blasts. The door burst open, and black-clad masked figures poured inside. They aimed weapons at Algie, who repelled their fire by dodging aside in a blur of speed and then vanishing. Air rushed by Nira's ear. Then Jek was gone as well, leaving her at the mercy of these formidable men.

They stood in a huddle, murmuring in low voices. One of the gang slid his gaze her way and pointed at her.

"I'll take care of the woman," he said in a commanding tone. "Algie and her troops have probably vectored out by now but search the place anyway and see what you can find." As the others scrambled to obey, he strode over to where Nira lay helpless on the table.

Wriggling against the strap holding her down, she cursed when it wouldn't give way. Now what? Was she a prize to be claimed by their leader? She cringed when he stroked her cheek.

"Who are you, little one? And how did you resist the Confounding?" His gentle tone surprised her.

"Untie me." She attempted to twist away, but he gripped her shoulder, holding her down. Flat on her back, she gazed into his intense turquoise eyes. She couldn't see the rest of his face, hidden by a hooded mask that covered his head. He smelled like pine trees and peat smoke. Calm trickled through her, quieting the buzz in her mind.

Strange that she didn't abhor this man's touch as she had Jek's. Far from it. She squirmed under his scrutiny, aware that her situation wasn't much better and yet she felt no fear. The stranger in black continued to study her, his eyes narrowed as though he contemplated a decision.

Banging noises sounded from outside as his men searched the building as per his orders. A single lightbulb glared overhead, casting the room into a surreal light. Dust motes floated in the air.

"I will release you, but you must come with us," the man said in a commanding tone.

Ice water sluiced through her veins. She didn't want to go anywhere with these fierce-looking men. "Look, I won't tell anyone what's happened here if you let me go home."

"I understand you are frightened. Be assured no further harm will come to you." He spoke soothingly, as though to a child. "I promise to keep you safe."

"Please, just set me free." She hated the way her voice quavered.

"How about if we make a deal? My men and I will take you home, but then you must listen to my proposal. We could use your help."

She nodded, having every intention of bolting for the door when on her feet. As he untied the strap around her wrist, tingling warmth raced along her nerves. Before she could jerk away, his strong hands grasped her by the waist and lifted her off the table.

Standing, she rubbed her arms, grateful for her mobility. Her glance skittered toward the exit. Unfortunately, the stranger obstructed her route. His tall physique overpowered the room.

"What's your name?" Maybe she could gain his sympathy.

"I am Zohar Thorald. Let us leave this place before the displacement field reactivates." While the man spoke in a soft tone, his authority brooked no arguments.

Nira assumed he must be a foreigner, judging from his stiff manner of speech.

He stalked into the hallway, calling for his comrades to follow. Nira trailed after him, frustrated when she still couldn't reach the main entrance. As if reinforcing her plight, Zohar snagged her elbow while he addressed his men.

"Find anything?"

"It's too late," one guy answered. "They must have taken anything of value before we arrived. It's almost as though they were expecting us."

The wall shimmered, and Nira blinked.

"Everyone outside." Zohar yanked on her arm, dragging her into the anteroom and out the front door. Daylight pierced her vision.

"My sunglasses. I left my purse in there. Let me go."

She twisted sideways but couldn't break his grip. No way would she leave her Coach bag behind. It had been the first designer item she could afford, even if she'd bought it at the outlet store.

Zohar nodded to one of his men, who detached from the group and raced inside. He reappeared in the doorway and leapt onto the pavement just as the entire structure faded before her eyes.

"Okay, that wasn't real. I must be hallucinating." Nira accepted her bag from the man who'd retrieved it.

"No hallucination. You were nearly ensnared." Zohar prodded her toward a parked white van. "This is why you need our protection. Secure her." He handed her off to another masked man before heading toward the driver's seat.

"I have my own car. I can meet you wherever we're going." Nira thought it worth a try.

Zohar whipped around. "Give your keys to Kaj. He will follow us."

"I don't think so. Hey, what are you doing?"

One of the men flashed a pair of stormy gray eyes as he snatched her purse. He fished inside until he found her key ring. Tossing the bag back, he strode toward her vehicle as though it emitted a beacon. Along the way, he ripped off his mask. She got a glimpse of unruly wheat hair, even features, and a taut jaw before he turned his back on them.

"All right, how did he know that's my car?" She held her ground, refusing to budge.

"Your signals are strong, little one. You left your essence on your automobile. Even we are not immune."

Zohar tore off his hood, making her inhale sharply. If kidnappers competed for looks, he could win a spot in *GQ Magazine*.

Deep-set turquoise eyes sat under emphatic brows and above a straight, aquiline nose. A firm mouth spoke of a man who set himself high standards, his upper lip a bit narrower than its fuller bottom. He wore his dark brown hair swept back over a regal forehead like Captain Kirk on the original *Star Trek* show, although his hair was tussled from the mask.

He grinned, transforming his stern expression into one of devilish amusement. An answering coil of warmth rolled through her.

Okay, get a grip. You're trapped with four hunky guys who could easily overpower you, and you have no notion of their true intentions. She had to give them credit for rescuing her, though. Maybe they were undercover agents working with some federal agency on a drug bust case.

"Can we take off our masks, *rageesh*?" another man asked in a respectful tone.

Zohar shrugged. "Why not? The lady is one of us now. Tell me where you wish to go." His deep voice flowed over her like warm honey.

The police station, big guy. Unfortunately, she didn't know where one was located on International Drive.

She gave him her address while the rest of his men tore off their disguises. Crammed inside the second row of the van between two hunks, Nira clutched her precious handbag.

When her friend and mentor, Grace Miller, saw Nira trooping home with a gang of men, she'd probably call the cops herself.

Nira hoped so. Now that she was free to pursue her research, she didn't want anything to interfere.

Her glance dropped to her wristwatch. She'd received the timepiece from her mother as a gift when she lay on her deathbed, along with a confession that Nira had been adopted. This keepsake, left by her biological parents, remained the only clue to her true identity. It ran with no visible mechanism and no battery. She suspected it relied on solar energy.

Once Nira discovered the inscription on its face was runic lettering, she became fascinated with Norse legends. She studied comparative mythology in grad school, hoping to teach after she'd earned her doctorate degree. In the meantime, she meant to trace her origins but lacked the funding to carry out her plans. So far, she wasn't having much luck in finding a summer job.

She couldn't worry about that now. First, she had to get away from these guys.

Twenty minutes later, they pulled up to the curb in front of Grace's house. As the driver of Nira's car joined them outside, the elderly lady meandered into the yard. She wore a loose patterned top with cream-colored pants and not a hair out of place on her teased gray head.

Nira's heart swelled with affection. Grace was a kindly neighbor who'd offered support when her mother died six years ago. After raising her two younger sisters, Nira had moved into Grace's house to save money. While the arrangement suited them both, Nira yearned for freedom, not to mention a measure of privacy. This was another reason why she wanted a job, to afford her own apartment. It would mean leaving Grace alone, though, and the eighty-two-year-old woman enjoyed her company.

"Nira, what happened? I didn't expect you back so early." Grace peered at Nira's companions. "Who are your friends?"

The one with rangy black hair and a beard spoke up. "We are… cousins."

"Really?" Grace propped her hands on her slim hips. "I didn't know you had any relatives besides your sisters, dear."

"No, I, uh—"

Zohar strode to Nira's side and spoke to her in an undertone. "If you need credits, I am prepared to offer you a job."

"Say again?" Leaning forward, Grace cupped her ear.

Nira shot Zohar an inquiring glance. She'd ask him what his remark meant later. In the meantime, she raised her voice so Grace could hear.

"These are cousins on my father's side. Since he walked out on us when I was eight years old, I never knew much about his family. I was quite surprised when they showed up." Glaring at Zohar, she waited for him to contradict her. He grinned back, a gleam of approval in his eyes.

"My word, you must be thrilled. Come inside and have some lemonade and cake." Grace surveyed their attire. "No doubt you'll want to lose those costumes. Your awesome guns add a nice touch, but they might frighten someone. Great choice of props, boys. I hadn't realized a science fiction convention was in town."

"This is Zohar," Nira supplied when he appeared at a loss for words. "Guys, meet Grace. She's a dear family friend."

"Where will you be staying? I know some budget hotels if you need a place." Grace's face lit up as it always did when she offered advice.

A hunk with golden blond hair and a youthful face had been speaking softly into his cell phone, or at least a device that looked like one. Switching it off, he regarded his leader. "Rayne has secured accommodations for us at a local hostelry."

"Oh, that's good. I suppose you'll want to visit the theme parks while you're here," Grace said as the sun broiled Nira's scalp.

Zohar cocked his head. "What is a theme park? Our objective is Drift World."

Grace wagged a finger. "Personally, sonny, I don't see the attraction in adults role-playing their fantasy jobs. Get a real one, that's my opinion."

"Grace, it's too warm out here. I'm going inside," Nira said. She snatched her keys from the carjacker and used the remote to lock her vehicle. Then she wheeled toward the front door, advancing only a few steps before she hesitated. These men seemed friendly, but was it wise to invite them in?

She turned toward Zohar. "Thanks for the escort home. Please don't feel you have to hang around on my account. You must have things to do."

"We still need to talk." A determined look on his face, Zohar gestured toward the house.

Her stomach sank. She wasn't going to get rid of him so easily. Maybe she could figure out a way to ditch these guys after cooling off inside.

Their leader accompanied her, his boots pounding on the hot pavement. The others crowded behind as she resignedly led the way.

Inside the foyer, Nira tossed her purse on a side table. As soon as Grace was out of earshot in the kitchen, she lowered her voice. "Okay, who are you and what do you want? And where are you from? You talk like foreigners."

"Our home is called Karrell." Zohar's eyes smoldered as he regarded her, his height and powerful shoulders making her feel small and feminine.

"Never heard of it. Must be a tiny country." She swept her gaze over their belted tunics, side arms, and tailored trousers. "You could pass for invaders from outer space. Are you sure you're not here for a convention? Or are you actors looking for jobs? Your outfits appear authentic. Or perhaps you're part of a SWAT team?"

"We are here to save your world, not invade it. What is this phrase, swat team?"

"I will research it, *rageesh*." The man with a stubbled jaw, unkempt hair, and killer dimples could have been a double for Josh Holloway on *Lost*. Nira stared at him, wondering if this were some sort of reality show with hidden cameras.

"I told you not to call me that, Paz."

"My apologies." Paz bowed his head, making Nira wonder about his relationship to Zohar.

"What did you want to tell me?" she asked.

Zohar's gaze darkened. "We have much to discuss, but not a lot of time."

"Please, feel free to go and take your friends along with you. Your problems aren't mine, although I do want to thank you for rescuing me from those nutcases in that employment office. Just how did that place vanish, anyway? It was some sort of optical illusion, yes?"

"In a way. Look, you fail to understand the danger. We cannot leave you alone."

"I'm home now, so I am safe. I appreciate your concern, but I'll be fine."

He shook his head. "The Trolleks will come after you. They will follow your scent."

"What scent?" She sniffed the air. "Are you telling me I stink? I may have been running around in the heat, but—"

A grin transformed his face. "You misinterpret, little one. Your skin is fragrant, like purpura blossoms. It is a most pleasant scent and highly alluring."

Her cheeks flushed until she latched onto his other remark. "Trolleks? Who are they? And what did you mean when you mentioned credits outside?"

He raised an imperious eyebrow. "I wish to offer you a position as our local guide."

She gazed at him askance. Whoever these guys were, there wasn't any doubt in her mind that they needed help navigating the locale. Should she accept?

With her track record, it was likely to be the only decent job offer in her future. Her temples throbbed while she debated her response.

Right now, when she could finally search for her birth parents, she didn't need any roadblocks getting in the way. Was it worth tagging along with Zohar and his gang to earn the cash she needed for her research?

Maybe they were tourists from a backwater country, but that didn't explain their raid on the log hut or their assault gear. Something else was going on. Hooking up with them, even as their hired guide, could only spell trouble.

She stood tall, giving Zohar a level glance. "Sorry. Tempting as your offer is, I have to decline."

"Wrong answer." Zohar's jaw tightened as he reached for her.

Chapter Two

"Leave now, before Grace returns." Her eyes blazing with defiance, Nira stepped away from Zohar.

Cursing inwardly, Zohar let his arm fall. He'd failed to convince the Earth woman to accompany his band of men. Now he would have to force her to join them, an action that would not gain her cooperation.

His gaze shifted to her flame-red hair, fluffed on her head as if she'd just come from a windstorm on the Plains of Hyalith. He'd never get used to short hair on a woman. It seemed a sacrilege to their gender, but then, who was he to comment on another culture when he rejected his own?

Her hair framed a perfectly shaped face with dewy brown eyes, a proud nose, and an impertinent mouth. From the determined jut of her jaw, he could tell she'd stand her ground, which would make his task even more difficult.

By the faith, just being near her made it hard to think when a part of his anatomy went hard as well. It couldn't be merely her scent, however strong. Her magnetism drew him, almost as though she exhibited Trollek power.

Impossible. The Trolleks were the reason he and his men were here.

He could still remember his shock when the alarm had sounded on his home world. A dimensional rift had cracked open on Earth, a protected planet whose inhabitants hadn't yet joined the Star Empire. This event didn't coincide with the natural cycle, when the friction between dimensional plates caused the portal to widen. Nor did the rift shut down as it should have after a buildup of cors particles at the event horizon.

As leader of the Drift Lords, Zohar had summoned his troops. It could only mean one thing—the Trolleks planned to invade Earth and enslave the populace. His team's task was to seal the rift and stabilize the space-time continuum.

He'd gotten a brief reading targeting the cors emissions to the area known as the Bermuda Triangle. Then the Trolleks had activated a jamming device, but not before he'd scored a blip at a place in Central Florida called Drift World. This woman served as their best lead to locating the beasts' main portal.

His attention diverted when the older lady returned holding a large brown dish from which emanated a mouth-watering aroma. He moistened his lips, aware his team couldn't afford delays, not even to obtain sustenance. Nira had to leave with them now.

"Aren't you going to introduce the rest of your relatives?" Grace set the platter on a polished wood dining table.

"Only if Nira packs her bag." Zohar scowled at the redhead to induce compliance. "She has accepted our offer to act as tour guide. We need her to accompany us."

"You can't go without tasting my cake," Grace insisted. "Sit down, sonny. Nira can throw her things together after you eat a snack. Boys are always hungry, aren't they? Wait here, I'll get some lemonade." She scurried toward the kitchen.

"Have a seat," Nira said with a smirk. "Resistance is futile where Grace is concerned."

Grace returned minutes later carrying a pitcher and a stack of plastic cups. Unable to think of a way to budge Nira without tossing her over his shoulder, Zohar sank into a chair. He might as well introduce his team members.

"That is Paz." Zohar pointed to his friend across the table. Paz flashed Nira a dimpled grin.

"He can be a bit headstrong, but the ladies love him. And this is Dal." Zohar nodded at the silent, gaunt man. "Dal looks forbidding, but inside he hides a heart of gold. Borius over there possesses a temper, but he also has a reason." The others laughed, while the young man flushed to the roots of his golden hair.

"Kaj lets you think he cares more about his engines than people, but that is untrue." Zohar jerked a thumb toward his tense-faced engineer. "And finally, Yaron writes songs when he is not busy fighting." Zohar indicated the bearded man with dark eyes.

"I'm not leaving with you, so don't get too comfortable." Nira snatched a filled cup from Grace and gulped down the pink liquid.

Zohar cocked his head. "May I have a word with you in private?" He had to convince her to go quietly and not make a scene. Besides, she'd promised to listen if he took her home. He didn't care to be disobeyed in front of his men.

She licked a stray droplet off her lush mouth. "I'm going to use the bathroom and then change into something more comfortable. You can say your piece when I get back."

"She is bathing now?" Yaron shot a puzzled glance at Zohar.

Nira gave him a withering look. "You're kidding, right?" She plunked her cup down. "You can tell they don't get out much," she told Grace. "Too much team spirit, if you ask me."

"No way. You mean… these good-looking men don't like girls?" Grace's eyebrows soared sky high.

Borius drew his dagger. "We are warriors, Drift Lords and Defenders of Earth. Do you dare to challenge our manhood?"

Leave it to the virgin among them to take offense. Zohar's lips curved in amusement. "Stand down, Borius," he ordered in a firm voice. "Nira, pack your belongings at once, or you will forfeit the chance. You will come with us. I shall explain when we reach safe quarters."

She narrowed her eyes. "Safe? You mean from those Trolleks you mentioned? I thought you said they could track my scent."

"We have ways of shielding you, but we must leave this

house. It emits your essence too strongly. Every minute we remain increases the risk of detection."

It wouldn't be long now. The hackles rose on the back of his neck. He sniffed, searching for the chemical marker that preceded a Trollek's vector shift.

Nira swept from the room, leaving him and his mates alone with the chatty older lady. He accepted a piece of cake, chewing absentmindedly. Might as well gain energy before the next battle. Once finished, he scraped to his feet. What was taking Nira so long?

He'd just decided to go after her when he heard a terrified shriek from another part of the house. His nostrils inhaled the smell of burnt filaments.

Pulling his Monix T-6 laser pistol, he fired at the Trolleks vectoring into sight. One of them flung himself onto Zohar's back, hooking an arm around his neck. The Trollek meant to confound him. The spell wouldn't work since Zohar had polarized himself against their power.

With his head forced back, he barely saw the dagger aimed in his direction, hurtled through the air by another beast. Their speed and ability to shift themselves along with inanimate objects gave them an advantage, but he'd been trained to fight their kind. Swirling, Zohar deflected the knife. It caught the Trollek clinging to him instead. With a howl, the creature slid to the ground, the blade imbedded in his spine.

"Get your hands off me, sonny," Grace shouted from somewhere behind. Spinning around, Zohar caught a brief shimmer of light and then emptiness. Oh, no. Grace has been taken.

A surprise bolt of energy ripped the phase gun from his hand. What the—?

He glanced up, stunned to see a disruptor in one beast's grip. Since when did Trolleks carry Class One armaments?

No matter, he had a few tricks of his own.

With a flying kick, Zohar knocked the weapon from his opponent's grip. He didn't have time to catch his breath. Another brute leapt in front of him, teeth bared, muscles bulging. The fellow's eyes narrowed as they sized each other up, circling like prizefighters. He heard the grunts of his mates and Nira's screams echoing down the hallway.

Dodging a blow aimed at his head, he ducked and rammed the beast in the stomach. It felt like a wall. His ears rang.

The Trollek laughed, grasping him under his arms and lifting him off his feet. Thick fingers squeezed into his flesh, causing him to clamp his lips against the pain. He kicked his legs but reached empty space instead of a target.

Fury scalded his blood. He should be enjoying the clear mountain air on Karrell and strolling through the pine-scented woods on his royal estate instead of battling his old enemy. It wasn't the first time the beasts had stolen across the dimensional boundary, but by the great Wise One, it would be their last.

Ignoring the pinching agony in his armpits, Zohar raised his hands. He pressed his thumbs into the beast's eyes. Rage gave him strength. The eyeballs felt like gel-filled globes, but he pushed until he hit solid bone.

Release came instantaneously. The Trollek let go with a yowl and vanished in a flash of light.

Back on his feet, Zohar wrinkled his nose. He'd never get used to the odor of burning circuitry that accompanied the beasts' spatial shifts. Being able to sniff cors particles made him a Drift Lord, so he should be grateful. Not only did it enable him to anticipate their imminent arrival or departure, but it also gave him an edge in sensing when a rift opened.

A loud crash resounded, making him glance at his crew. They were holding their own. So far, Grace had been the only one captured. He cursed inwardly, realizing he couldn't hear Nira anymore either. Could she have succumbed to the Trollek spell? He raced through the house, skidding to a halt when he saw her wrestling with a brute by an open doorway.

Thank the stars. If she hadn't vanished, that meant she resisted the confounding again, since only spellbound victims could be taken. The enemy must want her because she was different. And if they couldn't take her, they'd have one alternative.

The Trollek released her and winked from sight. Grabbing her by the wrist, Zohar lurched toward the front door.

In the dining hall, chairs and china flew through the air where the battle still raged. Trolleks howled and snorted as they fought. Then acting in unison, they glanced at each other, bared their teeth in feral grins, and vanished.

"Lava bomb. Evacuate," Zohar yelled to his companions. "Move out, now!"

Nira tugged on his arm. "Wait, my purse."

The foolish woman dragged him sideways where she grabbed her bag from its perch on a foyer table. His heart racing, Zohar shoved her outside and flung her onto the grass. Shouts sounded from behind as his friends followed suit.

"Grace," Nira cried, her voice hoarse. "Where's Grace?" She rolled onto her back, facing him.

"You can't help her. Take cover!" Zohar dropped on top of Nira just as a deafening blast ripped the air followed by a concussive wave.

He'd covered Nira's body with his own, pressing them both to the ground, but he still felt the jolt through to his bones. His teeth rattled and his head reeled. Debris rained upon them, making him thankful for his lightweight armor.

As he waited for his heartbeat to slow, he became aware of the points of contact between them. Nira wriggled, no doubt attempting to free herself, and the movement only increased his awareness of her softness beneath him. By the moons of Aguilar, she smelled divine. An incredible urge to nuzzle her neck made his senses swim.

"Are you all right?" His assessing glance swept her pale face.

"I'm fine. Get off me."

He leveraged to his feet and offered a hand to assist her. She stood on her own, brushing dirt from her rumpled clothing—a pair of cropped tan pants and a teal top. Then her gaze lifted, and her mouth dropped open.

"Oh… my… God." She stared at the smoldering ruins of her home. "Grace…"

"Is still alive. I saw her get taken by a Trollek before the explosion." Zohar surveyed his men. All were present and accounted for, albeit with minor scratches and soiled uniforms. Sirens wailed from down the street. Neighbors erupted from their homes.

"I-I should talk to the police. They'll want to know what happened." Nira scrubbed a shaky hand over her face. "They can help me search for Grace."

"Didn't you hear what I said?" He gave her a sharp look.

From her dazed expression, Zohar surmised she could barely deal with the destruction of her house, let alone the loss of her friend. Nor did she truly understand what it meant to be confounded. He sighed, aware explanations were overdue.

"We must not linger. The Trolleks may believe you are dead, but they will not be fooled for long. Soon they will pick up your trail again." He took her by the elbow and gently tugged, not wishing to traumatize her further.

"I can't leave. I'll need to explain…"

"About what, the Trolleks? No one would believe you. We will think of a plausible excuse later. People are noticing us. Let us go, now." He couldn't risk his team being detained.

Nira slouched in the front passenger seat of the van beside him while he took the wheel. His men piled into the back rows. They sped down the street past the oncoming emergency vehicles.

"Maybe we should stop at a market along the way. We need to be less conspicuous. Will you help us select proper men's clothing?" He glanced at her wooden expression.

"I suppose."

A shopping excursion might restore the color to her cheeks. Holding the wheel with one hand, Zohar reached into his pocket with the other and withdrew some shiny stones. Most females he knew appreciated glittery objects.

"I understand these hold value on your world. We can use them for money."

Her eyes widened. "Hey, those look like—"

"Diamonds? Yes, they are."

****

"We call them kewa stones on Karrell," Zohar said after they finished their expedition and resumed their journey. "They're worth little where I live."

He'd sold a couple of the gems at a jeweler's shop in Millennia Mall, a dazzling indoor emporium located on Conroy Road. The jeweler had admired the stones' purity while questioning their origins. Zohar said he'd bought the uncut stones in "the islands," hoping this vague reference would pass muster. The proprietor had seemed to accept his explanation without demanding a bill of sale.

Nira wasn't as easy to convince. Her mouth turned downward. "Are you guys from Africa? Those weren't stolen blood diamonds, were they?"

He gave her a patient smile. "You ask many questions, little one. Soon I will provide answers, but not until we reach safety."

Nira folded her arms across her chest. She wore a shirt bought at the Banana Republic, a shop named after a tropical fruit. Zohar hadn't seen any plants in the store so he couldn't imagine how it got named thus. No matter. He and his mates had purchased some fine trousers made out of a sturdy material called denim. Unfortunately, Nira's spirits had failed to rally during their excursion.

What had he expected? For her to become enraptured by a simple barter experience?

The women he knew were more enraptured by his kisses. His thoughts drifted in that direction, tempted by Nira's honeyed fragrance.

Forcing his mind back to the road, he clenched his teeth.

He, of all people, must serve as a role model to his men. He could satisfy his lust, but anything more was forbidden to him.

Otherwise he'd end up the same as their former deranged king—a tyrant who'd spread discontent and chaos throughout the land, all because of his love for a woman.

Zohar would never exhibit such a shameful weakness as his father.

Chapter Three

"Holy guacamole, you picked an expensive resort." Nira gazed out the window as they drove down a palm-lined avenue toward the registration building.

Zohar didn't respond, a frown of concentration on his face. He parked in front of a New England-style structure overlooking a tranquil lake. She remained in the van while he and two of his men dashed inside to collect their room keys.

Her body sagged against the seat that smelled like old leather and dust polish. Too much had happened today for her to assimilate—that weird log cabin, those ugly creatures popping into sight at will, their raid on Grace's house, and the loss of her home and family friend.

She hated having to depend on these guys for protection. Everything was their fault. They acted so strange, like foreign actors from a movie set who'd stumbled off the studio lot. Their fighting skills were real enough, though. They'd saved her life twice now, so she couldn't deny their abilities. Who were they, and why had they come to Orlando? And what should she do next?

If she stuck with Zohar and his team, she could help rescue Grace. Was Zohar correct in his assumption that the older woman was still alive, albeit captured by those nasty beasts? She mulled over their peculiar appearance, considering every science fiction movie she'd ever seen. Were they mutants of some sort? What other possible explanation could there be?

Nira shivered at the thought of Grace being their captive. Nira had to save her, no matter the cost.

She remembered her swell of gratitude when Grace had knocked on her door six years ago after her mother died. What would she have done without the older lady's support? Grace assisted Nira in applying for guardianship of Kristy and Diane, her younger sisters, and aided her through the probate process. A life insurance settlement, along with their pre-paid college tuition plans, had enabled the three girls to finish their education. Once her sisters acquired their own apartments, Nira sold their house and moved in with Grace.

She's always been there for me. I can't abandon her now.

Her attention shifted to Zohar who strode out the exit. Authority rode in the arrogant thrust of his jaw, the determined focus of his eyes, and the erectness of his posture. Glancing at his companions, she wondered if great looks had been a job requirement. Each one of them looked like a warrior god from her comparative mythology texts.

Zohar slid into the driver's seat and started the engine. Doors slammed as the others joined them.

"Our rooms are located in the Nantucket building," the younger man called Borius stated in a soft-spoken manner.

"The accommodations come with two queen-sized beds," Paz noted in a lazy drawl. "At least you got a suite, *rageesh*, although you should have gotten a bed fit for a king."

Zohar shot him a hooded look. "Do not—"

"Mention that word. I know." Paz smirked as though he enjoyed ticking off his leader.

Zohar's lips tightened. He stopped at an intersection, reading the directional signs before turning right. "Nira, you will stay with me. Your safety is my responsibility."

The others chuckled and ribbed each other. "Who will keep her safe from you, captain?" the bearded one asked.

Zohar's jaw twitched. "My mission is my mistress. She need not fear for her virginity."

Nira almost choked on her saliva. At least his remark brought back the blood to her brain and made her feel alive again.

"Excuse me? Just to set things straight, I've been around town a few times if you catch my drift, big guy. I can take care of myself."

"Yes, I see how well you do at keeping yourself from harm." Zohar squealed to a halt in the parking lot beside a three-story unit surrounded by sculpted landscaping and shady oak trees.

Before she could retort, the man with longish black hair and soulful eyes spoke. "Please, we need your guidance, lady. Be patient with our captain." His deep voice had a musical cadence.

"Everyone out," Zohar ordered, switching off the ignition. "Rayne should have stored our gear by now."

The others scrambled to obey. Nira emerged into the hot afternoon sun and helped remove their bundles from the van. Once they separated each person's purchases, they split into pairs.

"Listen, men." Zohar's walnut hair gleamed in the sunlight as he addressed his motley crew. "Deploy your defense perimeter before getting settled. Then check out the environs but keep your guard up if you roam far afield."

"Ease off, sire." Dal, the gaunt fellow with a wiry build, scowled at their leader. His lean face looked as though it never cracked a smile. "You should know us by now. How many missions have we done together?"

Paz slapped him on the shoulder. "Our captain is edgy because he's sharing quarters with a beautiful woman. I would be tempted as well. If you wish to honor the edict, follow his example and maintain a safe distance from any female."

Dal lifted his eyebrows. "You should talk. You never were one for following rules."

"Some rules are meant to be broken." Paz's dimples deepened into a grin.

Zohar held up a hand. "Enough. Let us gather at twenty-one hundred hours in my chamber for a war council. Study our data in the meantime. I will want to hear your analysis."

As one, they bowed before scattering in separate directions.

"Why do they act like that?" Nira stumbled along beside

Zohar with her arms full of packages.

"Like what?" He held the door to the building open so she could pass.

"Like they're your friends, yet there's a certain respect in the way they respond to you."

"I am their commander. It is merely regard for my rank."

She preceded him down the hall, aware of his gaze burning into her back. "If you say so."

The air conditioning cooled her skin but not her nerves. Zohar's confident masculinity overpowered her senses. Soon they'd be alone in a hotel room. A responsive heat swirled within her. She'd yet to thank him for saving her and could think of many ways to show her gratitude.

He owes me answers, she reminded herself. *Focus on your purpose and not on how restless he makes you feel.*

"Rayne will be waiting for us." Zohar's serious tone dispelled her wayward thoughts.

"Is he another of your friends?"

"We are a team of seven," Zohar explained, as though she should understand what that meant.

She paused in front of their door, arms full of bundles. When Zohar squinted at his key as though he didn't know what to do with it, she wriggled a hand free, grabbed his card and swiped it through the slot. Really, these guys seriously needed some cultural education.

Nira pushed open the door and stepped into their suite. "Hello, is anyone here?" Silence met them. "Your pal must not have arrived yet."

Zohar breezed by, brushing her arm. His touch elicited a spark of pleasure. Had he felt it, too?

Evidently not, because he tossed his packages onto a couch and turned away. Facing them were a sitting room and a small kitchenette. Beyond were entrances to the lavatory and bedroom.

"Make yourself comfortable. I will secure the premises." Zohar stomped toward the sleeping accommodations.

"O-kay. I'm going to use the bathroom."

Her face flushed, and she swallowed. This could be embarrassing. Did she really intend to share a hotel room with a stranger? He seemed a decent sort, but still…

She entered the lavatory where her ears picked up the sound of trickling water. Her gaze shifted to the tub shower and to the booted foot sticking out from beyond the curtain.

Her scream brought Zohar at a run. He dashed inside, aiming his weapon. Taking in the situation at a glance, he kicked away the curtain.

A dead man lay face up in the bathtub. Murky water covered his body and dripped over the edge.

"Rayne." Zohar sank to his knees.

"He's your missing team member?" She recognized the fellow's uniform; the same outfit Zohar and his men wore.

Zohar bowed his head, a pained expression on his face. No doubt he'd cared deeply for his friend.

Nira clapped a hand to her mouth, feeling an urge to heave. Dead people had that effect on her.

Zohar must have heard her stifled croak, because he stood and turned toward her. Grief mingled with regret in his eyes.

"I am sorry you had to see this. Come here."

He enveloped her in his arms, and for a few moments, she steeped in the warmth of his embrace. His newly purchased shirt smelled like sandalwood. The scent soothed her until a disturbing thought erupted.

"Do you think the Trolleks got to him?" She sprang back. "If so, we're not safe here. Have you checked the closet, the patio?" Her gaze darted toward the exit.

"Trolleks were not responsible for this crime."

"How can you tell?"

"I smell nothing that heralds a vector shift."

Whatever that means. "Who are these Trolleks anyway? How come they look so weird? And why are they interested in me?"

"I will explain shortly."

Zohar stooped to open the drain. Water swirled from the tub. When the dead man's torso became fully exposed, a charred mark on his tunic became visible.

Had he been shot, and if so, by what sort of firearm?

Perhaps Zohar's gang was working in league with federal agents to track arms dealers who sold advanced weaponry. She'd never heard of a gun before that could do this kind of damage.

"Stand back." Zohar spread a bath towel on the floor and then hauled the dripping body over the tub's edge. He laid Rayne flat and brushed a lock of limp hair off his forehead.

"If the Trolleks didn't kill him, who did?" Her chin quivered. The sorrow on Zohar's face elicited her sympathy.

He stood straight and gave her an inscrutable look. She met his gaze, admiring his stalwart courage. A man of many secrets, he intrigued her more than any guy she'd met. Figures he'd turn out to be a foreigner on a clandestine mission.

His expression softened. "Rayne's wound was caused by a Monix T-6 laser pistol, the same firearm my team carries. It means Rayne's assassin came from Karrell."

"So now what? We call the cops?"

He shook his head, his mouth turning down. "Rayne's death is an internal matter. We must summon the others as witnesses before disposing of the body."

She tilted her head. "Are you sure? Because you're overlooking the obvious: if the killer came from your homeland, one of your own people might be involved. Can you trust them?"

"I trust my men with my life."

"Can you vouch for each guy's whereabouts since you entered the States? Has your team been together the entire time you've been in Florida? Are there more of you here?"

"Just the seven of us. We came on my… the same aircraft." A flicker of doubt crossed his face. "After our arrival, we split up to perform a reconnaissance, but then we converged together on the Trollek site where we met you. Borius spoke to Rayne on his comm unit outside your house. Rayne was still alive then."

"Was he? I'd ask Borius if he spoke personally to Rayne, if I were you. Maybe he just retrieved a message." Or perhaps the young man had lied, pretending to talk to their buddy.

Another thought struck her. When did rigor mortis set in? This guy wasn't stiff by any means. That would help determine time of death, wouldn't it?

They really needed a forensics expert, but from what Zohar had said, he planned to hide the body. Oh great, then she'd become an accessory to a crime.

Could this day get any worse?

Zohar headed out. "We should establish a secure perimeter before we do anything else. I want to be certain no further surprises await us."

"Surprises?" She trailed him into the bedroom, conscious of the body left on the cold bathroom floor.

He tore into the wardrobe, removing several sacks and tossing them onto the closest bed. "At least Rayne delivered my supplies."

Is that all you care about when your friend is lying dead in the next room? She tugged on his arm. His muscle bulged under her fingertips.

"Will you stop for one minute and talk to me?"

Shooting her an oblique glance, he pursed his lips. "I do not believe Rayne was the target."

"Oh, you mean it could have been a robbery attempt, and he got in the way?"

Maybe the bad guy had jumped Rayne and used his own weapon against him. However, there weren't any signs of a struggle, now that she thought about it. Rayne had been shot at point blank range from the front and then likely shoved into the tub. Meaning either one of those Trolleks had leapt out of the shadows… or else he'd known the person who killed him.

Zohar didn't dispute her theory about a robbery. His mouth taut, he rummaged in a bag and withdrew a set of poles. Each one extended legs when he pushed a button.

"These will erect a barricade against vector shifts. Here, take this." He tossed her a small handheld unit. "You can scan for explosives and surveillance devices."

"Explosives?" she squeaked.

Zohar flicked a patronizing glance her way. "Whoever killed Rayne may have left something behind as a gift."

"Like one of those lava bombs?" Her legs quaked. Maybe she should wait in the hallway while he checked the place over for bombs and bugs. Then again, if she went outside his safety net, the Trolleks could vector in and grab her.

She stood frozen with indecision and wonder at the things she didn't yet understand. Trolleks. Bombs. Vector shifts. Laser guns.

Her eyes widened. Lasers? Were those like the phasers on *Star Trek* that shot energy bolts?

Zohar noticed her sudden silence. "You will be fine, Nira Larsen. We shall talk as soon as we finish these tasks." Stepping over, he took her hands in his while his woodsy scent invaded her nostrils.

Heat blossomed from her toes to the top of her head. Lifting her chin, she studied the taut angles enhancing his cheekbones, the dark stubble shadowing his jaw, and the firm lines defining his mouth.

His eyes flared, and he sucked in a ragged breath. Then he dropped her hands and moved away, leaving her oddly bereft.

"Sweep the signal detector over each surface in the room and let me know if a red light blinks." He avoided her gaze, focused on setting up his poles around the perimeter of the suite.

"That sounds easy."

She did as instructed, glad to put some distance between them. Whenever he neared, her senses zoomed into hyperdrive.

Focusing on her task, she scanned the drapes and bedding, even inside each drawer. Meanwhile, Zohar stood two of the poles at the far corners of the bedroom. A heavy silence fell between them as they worked. Nira mentally listed all the questions she wanted to ask when they were done.

Soon she switched to the kitchenette and sitting area. Her rounds produced negative results. Probably the killer had been in such a hurry that he'd left right after gunning down Rayne. Or maybe he'd shot Rayne elsewhere then dragged the body here for Zohar to find. But how would he know Zohar would be assigned this suite?

Idiot, she thought, rapping herself on the head. Of course, he'd realize the team leader would occupy the largest room.

Another thought chilled her. What if Rayne's death had been a mistake? What if the murderer meant to get Zohar instead? Is that what Zohar meant when he'd said Rayne wasn't the target?

She handed Zohar back his device when he joined her. He pocketed it and finished setting up the remaining poles.

"When I activate these rods, our defense grid will prevent the Trolleks from spatial shifting into our location."

He was just about to press the switch when the door burst open and a wild-eyed man charged inside, a curved blade in hand.

Chapter Four

Oh no, it's Rayne's killer come to get us next. With a shriek, Nira jumped back, bumping into the sofa.

Zohar drew his weapon, but the intruder whipped it from his hand with a flick of his sword.

"Zohar, son of Ivar Thorald, do not fight me. I come on behalf of Primer Pedar."

The man had stringy dark hair, fierce eyes, and a definitive jaw, much like Viggo Mortensen's character in *Lord of the Rings*. He wore his hair shoulder length, with two fine braids on either side of his face to keep it from his eyes.

"Pedar sent you?" Zohar maintained eye contact and a combat-ready stance.

"He hired me as your personal bodyguard. I am Lord Magnor of the Tsuran."

Zohar's eyebrows soared. "The legendary tribe? I thought those were stories meant to frighten naughty children."

Magnor sneered. "Not so. We are quite real. I suggest you dismiss your woman so we can discuss certain issues."

"Excuse me, my name is Nira. And I'm not his woman." She scowled at Zohar. "Don't tell me he's another friend of yours."

"No, he is not." Zohar pushed a button on his security device, and the tips of the rods lit green. "You are inside my defense grid, so I hope you have a good reason for being here."

"That is confidential, *rageesh.*"

"Do not call me that. Here, I am merely Zohar."

Magnor inclined his head. "As you wish."

"My men will soon join us for a strategy session. Nira Larsen is acting as our local guide."

"I see." Magnor glanced back and forth between her and Zohar as though suspecting more than met the eye.

Heat suffused her face. "Are you sure this guy had nothing to do with Rayne's death? And where is he from? His accent is different than yours."

So were his clothes. Her glance spanned the man's forest green cloak, clasped at one shoulder with a gold pin, his linen shirt, straight-legged trousers, and the scabbard looped across his hip.

Magnor's hawk-like gaze snared hers. "My kind heralds from the region beyond the Hills of Agoora, where snow can be seen on the distant peaks of the Great Crest." His eyes flared yellow for an instant, or maybe she imagined it.

"What mountain range is that? The Alps, or maybe the Himalayas?" *A source of myth, as in tales of Shangri-La.*

Zohar shrugged. "She believes we are from a country called Karrell."

"Indeed?" Magnor smiled, but his face exhibited no mirth. "What will happen when she discovers the truth?"

Nira turned an eagle eye on Zohar. "Yes, and just when are we getting to those explanations?"

"When my men arrive." Snapping his jaw closed, he retreated to the kitchen. He opened the refrigerator and grimaced at its empty interior.

Male voices and laughter rang from the hallway.

"If I'm not mistaken, here comes the gang now." Nira smoothed her pants, wishing she'd had time to relax. She hadn't even unpacked her new purchases.

How could she, with Rayne lying dead in their suite?

Her throat constricted. She didn't envy Zohar having to break the news to his team.

He deactivated the defensive perimeter, and his men trooped inside. The group halted as one at the sight of the caped man.

"People, this is Lord Magnor of the Tsuran. Primer Pedar sent him for my protection."

"What for?" Dal shot his team leader a sardonic look. "You have us to serve you, *rageesh*, not that you cannot hold your own in a fight."

"Against a known enemy, yes. But against an unseen foe from within our own ranks, perhaps not. I can understand Pedar's concern. Our friend Rayne has fallen victim to this traitor."

His pals dumped the groceries they'd brought onto the counter. Zohar motioned them toward the bathroom. Nira hung back, dreading their reaction but remaining within view. The men cried out in mixed dismay and sorrow as they caught sight of the downed warrior.

Lord Magnor, peering over their shoulders, muttered a curse in a strange tongue. "Brethren of Karrell, protectors of the Drift, allow me to investigate this man's death."

"We appreciate your sentiments, Lord Magnor." Zohar loomed in the doorway. He stood tall, pride shadowing his tone. "But my team will track Rayne's murderer."

"With your permission, sire, I'll obtain a body scan before dissolution." Paz's drawl became more pronounced in his grief.

Zohar gave a curt nod. "So be it."

Nira heard the pain in his tone. Distancing herself from their rituals, she busied herself unpacking the bags of food. She blinked rapidly, her lashes tipped with moisture.

Male voices rose in unison as the men chanted a prayer. One tenor stood out among them, the others falling silent as he sang a poignant solo. A moment of silence ensued, followed by a bright flash of light.

"It is done." Zohar strode toward her with a long face. "We will eat to renew our strength and then begin our council."

Nira had little appetite but she stuffed down some barbecue flavored chicken, potato salad, and cole slaw.

"This meat is tender." Yaron licked his fingers. "It tastes like pamadore."

"What's that?" Nira eyed him. She sat by the desk, using its surface as her dining table. Suspecting he'd been the soloist, she yearned to ask him about his singing abilities. How had he come to be a soldier instead of a vocalist?

"Pamadore is a popular dish on Karrell." Yaron regarded her with curiosity. "We breed the creatures on farms. What do you call this bird on your world?"

"It's chicken. Why do you talk like we live on different planets?"

Zohar forestalled further questions with a wave. "Our meeting will begin. Gather around."

He waited while his men discarded their trash and settled down. They lounged against the wall or draped themselves over the furniture.

Zohar's turquoise eyes pinned her. "We are not from another country. We come from a world in a solar system many light-years from here."

Nira leapt to her feet. "Good joke, boys, but I'm not that naïve. I realize this isn't your home turf, but you must be working with one of our federal agencies: the FBI, CIA, DEA, or maybe the ATF?"

Zohar strode over, clapping a hand on her shoulder, while her mind denied what she'd heard.

"Let me tell you a story." His gentle tone made her quiver. "In the beginning, a race of creatures lived on Earth. When human civilization invaded their natural habitat, they retreated through a dimensional door to another world."

"Whoa." She held up a hand. "Through a *dimensional door*?"

"You are familiar with tales about your Bermuda Triangle, yes? Strange disturbances, unexplained disappearances? This region acts like your San Andreas Fault. It sits on a crack where plates collide, but they are not plates of earth's crust. They are plates between dimensions."

"Oh, man." She sank into her seat. Nothing that happened today jived with reality as she knew it. She'd watched History

Channel shows on parallel universes, but hadn't Zohar said he came from another planet?

She shook her head. "I'm confused. First you say you're from outer space, then you say other dimensions exist. Which is it, big guy?"

He gave her a rueful smile, while his men murmured amongst themselves. Lord Magnor rolled his eyes and leaned against the kitchen counter.

"I realize this is a lot for you to comprehend, little one. But it is essential for you to understand if you are to help us."

"Go on." She swallowed.

He paced the carpet, hands behind his back, an imposing figure with a regal bearing.

"Every few decades, friction between the dimensional plates opens a portal. Those creatures I mentioned… they lived in harmony with nature until mankind encroached upon their territory and chased them through the dimensional door to a world where forests were pristine, and fields were fertile."

"O-kay, so they left Earth. Don't tell me… those creatures were Trolleks."

He beamed at her. "Correct. Over the years, their resentment increased so that during natural rifts, they poured through the gateway to hunt people for slave labor."

"And that accounts for the disappearances in the Bermuda Triangle?" She thought of Flight 19 lost in 1945, and a ship called the USS Cyclops that vanished at sea.

"Indeed." Zohar paused, plowing his fingers through his hair. "These rifts don't stay open for long. Normally, the event horizon produces a substance called cors particles. When their mass reaches critical level, the resultant pressure forces the rift to close. Thus, the portals are self-limiting and seal on their own."

"So how is it different this time?"

"The Trolleks have devised a means to keep the doorways open indefinitely."

"That's not good." Holy guacamole, was she off base. They

weren't foreign agents working with the government. Zohar's team were some sort of vigilantes from another planet. "But why are you here? Why save Earth? What do you care if your world is light-years away?"

"Good question." He tilted his head. "With the portals remaining open, the accumulation of cors particles will breach the point of no return. The dimensional drift will widen, causing a massive shock wave that alters reality in all dimensions."

"Oh."

His expression sobered while his teammates grew quiet, listening. "We are Drift Lords because we have the ability to detect cors particles. We can tell when a rift has opened but not its exact location. Our scanners obtain that data. We had obtained an initial reading at Drift World before the Trolleks activated a jamming device. We must turn it off so we can find the portals through which the Trolleks enter this world."

"So that's why you're interested in the theme park?"

His jaw clenched. "Correct. Locating these gateways is crucial. Then we have to figure out how the Trolleks are keeping the rifts open so we can seal them shut."

"There's more than one place where they're coming in?"

"So we believe, but we will not know the details until we terminate their interference."

"That's just great." Nira sat frozen, trying to assimilate so much information. "These Trolleks, how are they able to jump in and out of sight so fast?"

Please don't tell me Trolleks have supernatural powers. It's hard enough to accept multiple dimensions and heroes from outer space.

"They have discovered how to maneuver vectors within the space-time curve, effectively parallel shifting themselves from one location to another. They can spatial shift inanimate objects, too, which gives them an advantage. In battle, they make micro-jumps to dodge enemy fire and can fling objects from afar."

"You said they capture humans, like they took Grace."

"They can only transport people who have been confounded."

"Tell me again what that means."

Zohar rubbed his chin. "It is similar to a hypnotic spell. Trolleks secrete a chemical substance that directly alters the human brain. They transmit it through touch. Confounding will eventually cause amnesia or madness."

She jumped to her feet. "Oh, no. We have to find Grace before she's too far gone. What can I do to help?"

Zohar's appreciative gaze warmed her heart. "You can act as our guide so we avoid cultural blunders. More importantly, you possess the ability to resist confounding. If we can learn how you do this, it may aid others."

"My ears buzz when Trolleks are near."

His eyebrows lifted. "Just as we are able to sniff cors particles, you may have some unique ability. This buzzing noise may be part of it."

"You think?" She mulled the possibilities. If they could determine what allowed her to fight a Trollek's spell, perhaps a protective agent could be derived to immunize people.

"Get on with it, *rageesh*." Paz stretched his long legs while the others muttered their agreement. "He can be a bit long-winded," the dimpled warrior told her.

Zohar cast him a reproving glance before returning his attention to Nira. "We already know the Trolleks are interested in you. That makes you the best person to act as bait to get us into Drift World."

Chapter Five

"What do you mean, I'll act as bait?" Nira asked after the others left. Her eyes blazed as she faced Zohar in the front parlor. "I don't think I like that idea."

The temptation to stroke her soft cheek made his fingers curl. "You have shown much strength and courage," Zohar told her. "Such is a true warrior's heart. You can do this."

"By offering myself to the enemy? Nuh-uh."

"You won't be alone. We will provide backup. Come now, you have proven your resilience under fire."

"I suppose I could give it a try. After all, I have always been good at rolling with the punches," she added with a shrug.

"You perform in combat?" He looked at her askance before recalling the scene at her house. "I observed you struggling with that beast in your hallway, but I had no idea you were a trained fighter."

"Hey, by punches I only meant… it's an expression."

"I do not understand."

"You know, a colloquialism. It means I can bounce back if I'm struck down… figuratively, not literally."

"Ah, I see." He gave her a lopsided grin. In truth, he saw nothing except the glimmer of her large eyes, the fiery cast of her hair, and the lush shape of her lips. Their rosy hue contrasted to the pallor of her skin. Despite her brave words, the day had taken its toll.

An uncommon surge of admiration swelled within his chest. She had lost her home, her dearest friend, and her possessions, and yet she didn't complain. What more could he ask for from his newest teammate? Recruited with reluctance, she'd accepted the tasks put to her with alacrity.

Stepping behind Nira, he placed his hands on her shoulders. She was tense as a longbow. He examined her neck, its graceful curve tempting him to nuzzle her nape. Her fine reddish hair lifted in short layers that had him longing to plough his hands through to feel its texture.

He squeezed her taut muscles gently, urging her in a low voice to relax even as his own body went hard with need.

"Be at ease, we are safe now," he murmured in her ear.

She pointed toward the sanitation facility. "I-I can't go in there. Can we change rooms?"

"I will see to it in the morning. We need to rest. Close your eyes, and let my fingers work their magic. I am told I have a soothing touch."

His mouth quirked up as she complied and he kneaded her muscles. All right, so soothing might not be the best word his lady friends would use, but that's what Nira needed at the moment. He dug into the sensitive knots at her shoulders. Her low, female murmur of pleasure aroused him further. So did her scent, a floral fragrance that made him want to embrace her.

"That feels so good. Please don't stop."

Her breathy tone almost unraveled his control. When she swayed against him, their body contact set him on fire.

Step away, before your hands slip lower.

Unable to stop himself, he skimmed his fingertips up and down her arms. Her responsive shiver encouraged him more. Not only had it been a while since he'd enjoyed a woman's pleasures, but this Earth woman possessed an allure he couldn't resist.

Giving in to his base urges even while cursing himself for his lack of restraint, he turned her to face him and lowered his head. Just one taste, and he'd clear his brain. Never mind those voices decrying him for his weakness.

Nira didn't protest when he melded his mouth to hers and

pressed her close. Perhaps the heightened emotions of the day had left her craving comfort, because she wrapped her arms around him and returned his kiss.

Rational thought fled. When her lips parted, he thrust his tongue inside her welcoming warmth, savoring her moist heat and minted flavor. His lungs filled with lust-charged air as he heard her raspy breaths. The universe shrunk, until nothing remained except for their beating hearts and their joined mouths.

A glow spread through him, unrelated to the bulge in his pants that strained for freedom. His vision tunneled, and he shut his eyes against a swirling mist. Locked in their embrace, he held tight as the very ground beneath them seemed to vanish and they hurtled into a confluence of time and space.

A beeping sound impinged upon his consciousness, startling him back to reality. He released Nira, breaking their contact and their strange suspension in… whatever that place was. Her dazed expression reflected his own confusion.

"My comm unit is chiming. I should answer." He should also apologize for his behavior, but the words tripped on his tongue.

"Sure. I, uh, I'll get changed. Don't worry about me."

Zohar answered the call in the sitting room to give her some privacy. Paz's lazy drawl came on the line.

"We've begun inquiries into Rayne's death, *rageesh*. It's possible he let his killer in, since your door hadn't been forced open. We're trying to gain access to the security recordings. They may tell us if another visitor from Karrell is present."

And if not, the killer could be one of you.

Zohar didn't voice his suspicions aloud. "Good work. Keep me informed."

"You took your time answering my page. I was getting worried." Paz's voice held a teasing note.

Zohar cleared his throat. His mate's irreverent attitude increased along with his use of slang. As their communications officer, Paz appeared to be adapting to the planet's universal language faster than the rest of them.

"No need. The lady has nothing to fear from me." He spoke in a stiff tone, guilt assailing him for the kiss he'd stolen.

Paz wouldn't let it go. "We'll rejoice when you find a lady worthy of being your queen."

"That shall never happen and you know why. Now set your mind to the task at hand instead of personal issues."

****

Nira kept her thoughts to herself as she drove toward Drift World the following afternoon. She'd spent the morning phoning her sisters and the police to let them know she was okay and retrieving her Camry from in front of Grace's house. She had left her makeup kit in the trunk, so at least her supplies were saved. Losing the rest of her belongings didn't matter as much as losing Grace.

She glanced at Zohar in the passenger seat. His gaze focused out the side window, his profile stern. Dressed in an ordinary T-shirt and jeans, he still managed to look fabulous with his powerful bearing, sculpted muscles, and firm jaw. Her heart somersaulted as he skewed a look in her direction, tightened his lips, and looked away.

He'd barely spoken to her since last night. Claiming fatigue, he'd slept on the couch, leaving her to the bedroom. Had her responsiveness to his kiss turned him off? Didn't he realize she'd siphoned courage from his embrace? She'd craved the comfort and security of his arms? Besides, it had felt so right to kiss him back. Surely, he wasn't put off by her forwardness, especially since he'd instigated the kiss.

No more of that, Nira. Think about your mission for the day and how you'll face those nasty Trolleks.

The memory of those beasts made her stomach churn. Was she nuts for taking on this mission? Walking into the fire didn't seem like the best course of action. Yet she'd committed herself to rescuing Grace, and Drift World was their only lead.

Gripping the steering wheel, she clamped her mouth shut as Zohar paid the twelve-dollar parking fee. Then she proceeded as directed to an empty space in the immense lot. Visitors poured from their cars on either side, but no children were among them. Drift World was restricted to adults aged eighteen and over.

Once on foot, she and Zohar followed the herd to a tram that took them to the front gate. She searched the sea of faces for Dal and Kaj, who'd driven there in the van. Zohar's pals had brought Lord Magnor, who'd insisted on coming, but she couldn't spot any of them. Hoping they had already arrived, Nira veered toward Guest Relations while Zohar got in line to buy a ticket.

"Hi, my name is Nira Larsen." She hoped the attractive brunette behind the glass partition wouldn't notice the tremor in her voice. "I'm trying to get in touch with Algie, one of your staff members. She interviewed me for a job. I lost her business card and don't remember her last name."

The woman's eyes turned glacial. "I'm so sorry, Miss, but we deal with theme park related issues only. The employment office is in another location."

"I'm well aware of where it is… or isn't." Nira's voice hardened. "Look, you can make a simple call for me. Tell Algie I'm standing here. She'll be unhappy if she misses me."

Was this woman a human or a Trollek? If Algie was an example, their females could appear normal. How did one tell the difference?

She glanced at Zohar, who'd secured his ticket and passed through the main gate. Lord Magnor waited by a gurgling fountain with a display of pink and orange flowers. The other guys must be close by as well. Reassured by their presence, Nira twisted the diamond ring Zohar had given her.

He expected them to be separated, but should Nira need help, she could push on the polished stone to activate a distress beacon. She wore it on her right hand, and was aware diamonds were common on Karrell. The ring didn't hold the same cultural significance for Zohar as it did for her.

"Miss Larsen? Algie will meet you inside the entrance." The guest services agent shoved a plastic card into the receptacle. "Take this pass. You won't need a ticket."

"Thanks." Nira snatched the pass then headed for the gate marked Restricted Access.

She entered without a hitch and spared a moment to lift a brochure from the information booth. Her ears buzzed at a low decibel. Wincing inwardly, she fought to ignore the sound.

Zohar sauntered over, pretending to examine a board listing special events. He'd donned a baseball cap, and it helped him blend in with the crowd.

"What is your status?" He barely moved his mouth.

"I'm waiting for Algie. They gave me a pass to get in. Think you could use it elsewhere on site?"

"Maybe. Tell Algie you misplaced it if she asks."

Nira picked up a map, her hand brushing Zohar's as he did the same. She slipped the pass into his palm before turning away. He strode in the opposite direction, while Nira heard footfalls approach from behind. She whipped around, facing her nemesis. Swallowing, she suppressed a quiver of apprehension.

Algie's blue eyes narrowed upon viewing Nira, but she pasted a smile on her face. She looked as perfectly groomed as before, not a hair on her coiffed blonde head out of place, her figure sleek in a low-cut sundress.

"What a pleasant surprise, my dear. I did not expect to see you so soon."

Nira lifted her chin with a show of bravado she didn't feel. "We never quite finished our interview. I reconsidered your offer. I've been wanting to visit Drift World, and this is still my best chance."

"You expect me to believe that?"

"Not really." She curled her hands into fists so Algie couldn't see them shaking. "How about this: I'm trying to find out more about my background. I was adopted as a baby, and I want to locate my birth parents. You may be able to help me."

Algie studied her as though weighing a decision. Before Nira realized her intent, Algie clasped a hand on her arm.

Nira shook her off. "That doesn't work with me, remember? I think we'd both like to learn why. Let's make a deal. I'll answer your questions if you answer mine."

"So you're not really here for a job as a makeup artist?" Algie's scornful glance said she knew that all along.

"It depends. I still need the money." She fell into step beside Algie after the other woman gestured for her to move along. "Are all the employees like you, or are some of them human?" Glancing about, she didn't notice any hulking male Trolleks, but they could be lurking behind the scenes.

Algie's mouth pursed. "How did you learn about us?"

"I'll tell you, if you make my time here worthwhile."

She had to stall long enough for Zohar to do his reconnaissance. He sought the Trollek jamming device, but Nira didn't think it would be so easy to find.

Algie turned right at an intersection while Nira dodged a young couple consulting a directory. A pair of men in overalls strolled past, their eyes straight ahead, their movements robotic. Nira halted, watching them with rounded eyes. A middle-aged woman bumped into her and kept going without an apology in much the same manner. What was wrong with them?

Algie tapped her arm. "Come on, I'll show you our medical center."

"Why there?" Dread filled her stomach. She could imagine lots of reasons for Algie taking her to a clinic, none of them pleasant. Memories of their last encounter rose to engulf her.

"We'll have more privacy. Don't worry, it's one of the venues where guests play out their fantasies. All of our equipment works as it would in the real world, though. We try to make the experience as genuine as possible." Algie's grin reminded Nira of a cat eyeing a mouse.

She gulped. "Maybe we should tour the other stations first. How do people decide what role to play?"

Algie flicked a speck of lint off her dress. "They choose their post during orientation."

"Where does that happen?"

"I'll show you later."

Algie gestured for her to move on. Nira picked up her pace, glad she'd put on sensible walking shoes.

"You said you'd cooperate." Algie gave her an oblique glance, her eyes gleaming in the sunlight. "I'd like to take a sample of your blood when we're in the med lab."

Nira's gut clenched. "My blood? What for?"

"So I can run a few tests to see what makes you so… unique."

She'd like to know the answer herself. Her pulse pounding in her ears, Nira squeaked out a reply. "All right."

Besides, if guests manned the workstations, it couldn't be so bad, right?

Her ears tuned in to the buzzing noise in her brain. Beyond the omnipresent sound rose the splash of water, the droning of an airplane overhead, the flap of a flag in the breeze. Absent were the happy chatter and laughter of families like at other theme parks. Why this struck her as odd, she didn't know. But something wasn't right about this place.

Feeling like a lamb being led to slaughter, she hoped Zohar would gather his information fast so she could bust out of there.

****

"You haven't been through orientation, sir. Please come this way."

Zohar glanced up from the map he was studying in the middle of a plaza to confront the individual who'd accosted him.

"I can manage on my own, thanks."

The speaker gave him a plastic smile. "As a guest, you must make your career choice so we can assign you a work slot. Please come with me."

His eyes had a glassy look, prompting Zohar to wonder if he'd been confounded.

Noting a couple of chunky types gathering nearby, Zohar debated the odds. He could easily subdue these *riffs* but didn't want to initiate a fight. Besides, if he accompanied the fellow, maybe he'd discover an entrance to staff quarters as per his plan. Dal and Kaj were reconnoitering the surface while keeping an eye on Nira, with Lord Magnor as backup.

Zohar frowned, realizing he might be walking into a trap. He couldn't vouch for Lord Magnor's loyalty. Proof would tell in the action.

As for Nira, he hoped she could hang on long enough for him to complete his task. He couldn't worry about her and focus on his job. Nor did he dare think about how he'd tossed restlessly on that infernal sofa last night while burning to join her in bed.

He followed the guide toward an entry labeled Guest Orientation, lustful thoughts consuming him until a handshake jolted him to reality.

"Welcome to Drift World."

An attractive woman in a khaki uniform gripped his palm while horror blossomed in his chest. Chariots of the gods, he'd forgotten to polarize himself that morning. He had just exposed himself to the Trollek spell.

He stared at the female who'd ensnared him. Just like his father, he'd be confounded and have to follow her commands. How could he have forgotten his training so completely? Was his mind so clouded by Nira that she made him lose sight of his goals? Sweat beaded his brow.

The cold-eyed blonde dropped his hand. "Find a vacant console and put on a headset."

Too stunned to respond, he mutely obeyed.

Yet no compulsion overtook him as he sat at a free console facing a blank screen. He'd come of his own free will, hadn't he? Were spellbound victims aware they'd been subjugated by another mind?

He risked a glance at his fellow guests, whose eyes all stared forward while they listened intently. Copying their behavior, he donned a headset while mentally counting the number of male employees in the vicinity. Husky brutes, they wore hats that matched their khaki uniforms but did little to hide their abnormally proportioned features. It would be difficult to give them the slip. If he could, he had an idea that might work.

"Welcome to Drift World," a voice said in his ear, "the place where your dreams come true in a realistic and imaginative environment. Have you wondered what it would be like to be a fireman, police officer, surgeon, or scientist? Now is your chance to experience the job of your choice. Make a selection now."

A series of buttons lit up offering a multitude of careers. Seeing no way to escape until he finished the segment, he debated between an actor, archeologist, athletic star, or TV news anchorman. And those were just the A's. With a wry smile, he pushed the Astronaut button.

Expecting to be directed to the proper venue outside, he raised his eyebrows when a drawer slid open to reveal a set of dark eyeglasses.

"Put these on and your adventure will begin," the voice droned on. "This innovative, interactive technique brings cutting-edge VR into your own personal world. When you are done, you'll be trained for your special role."

What? This was some sort of virtual reality session?

"At the conclusion, follow the instructions of the staff member who greeted you at the door. He is your kabak, and you will obey his commands. He'll supervise your experiences throughout the park.

"When your trainer releases you, you may return home. Tell your friends how much you've enjoyed this experience and encourage them to visit. You'll receive further orders at a later date. Now sit back, relax, and enter the world unfolding before your eyes."

Music played in his headset, but Zohar didn't wait any longer. He ripped it off, scraped his chair back, and stood.

Before the startled eyes of the staff, he headed for the door. "Sorry, I must use the, uh, restroom." He'd almost forgotten the word for a sanitation facility. Silly term. Who rested in there? Emerging outside, he blinked in the sunlight.

"Sir, all visitors must complete orientation." One of the husky fellows blocked his path. He caught Zohar by the wrist. "You are not permitted access to the rest of the park until you're tagged."

"Is that so?"

The brute's grip tightened. "Come with me. Now."

Zohar glanced at the beefy paw and back to the man handler. He still didn't understand why their touch didn't affect him, but he could puzzle that out later. Instead of resisting, he threw an arm over the *riff's* shoulder.

"I shall be happy to oblige, but I really must visit the men's facility first." Maybe the guy would think his brain was addled by his bladder and that's why the confounding didn't work.

The staffer led him around the corner where they ran smack into Lord Magnor who bopped the Trollek out cold with his fist. The beast crumpled to the ground.

"Great Cosmos, what have you done? Have you been touched?" The swordsman's eyes glittered.

"Yes, but it had no effect. I am protected." Let his friends believe he'd polarized himself that morning. He had no other explanation, unless…

"We should collect the others and leave." Lord Magnor swept his forest green cloak behind him.

"Not so fast." Zohar mustered his most authoritative tone. "I have a plan."

Chapter Six

Nira spotted the squat gray building labeled with a red cross and dragged her heels about approaching. Once Algie got her inside, she might be trapped. Was the risk worth it for what she might learn about Grace?

"What's that place over there?" She pointed to a structure with half an airplane sticking from its side.

"That's our aerospace center." Algie lifted her chin in a proud tilt. "One of our most popular choices is being a pilot. See the café next door? Guests work there as chefs. And that auditorium beyond the seal sculpture is a theater for live performances. You can act out just about any dream job here."

Wasn't it all pretend play? She didn't see how guests could be trained so fast otherwise. Could the chefs really cook? Could the pilots manage flight simulators? Could the people acting as doctors know how to suture wounds? If not, how did it seem so real?

While the sun burned her scalp, she glanced at glassy-eyed visitors scurrying past. They didn't speak, intent on their destinations. Uniformed staff members roamed among them. The smell of hot dogs drifted her way from a food vendor. It gave her a craving for potato chips. Salty snacks were both her comfort and her bane during times of stress.

Water sprayed from a nearby fountain. Glancing sideways, she spotted Dal loitering in an alley. A surge of relief swept through her. At least he was around in case she needed help.

Now if only she could eliminate that dreadful buzzing in her head that erupted whenever she came into proximity with Trolleks. Movie theme music burst from a set of loudspeakers, adding to her budding headache. Someone must have turned up the volume. She hadn't noticed it before.

"I'll show you around later. Let's go inside." Algie gave her an irritated glance.

Climbing the steps into the medical center, Nira summoned her courage. She and Algie were both interested in learning the same thing: what made her immune to a Trollek's touch. She'd copy the results later so Zohar's people could use the info.

A receptionist behind a wide counter greeted them. The ponytailed woman appeared to be a human playing an administrative assistant.

Nira and her guide ended up in a treatment room down the hall. A strong antiseptic smell pervaded her nose, reminding Nira of her mother's last days, when she had maintained a bedside vigil. To this day, the sight of IV bags and heart monitors made her pulse race.

After collapsing into a chair, she allowed a technician to approach until she noticed his bulbous nose and ears. He glared at her when she recoiled.

"I thought one of the guests was going to draw my blood."

"It's best not to trust something so vital to untrained personnel." Algie's tone hardened. "Roll up your sleeve, Nira."

Nira forced herself to remain motionless while the tech punctured her vein. When he'd finished, she addressed Algie. "It's time for you to answer my questions. I did what you wanted."

She squeezed a wad of gauze in the bend of her elbow until the tech replaced it with a Band-Aid.

"In a minute. Doctor Sawyer," Algie called.

A man wearing a white lab coat shuffled into the lab from an adjacent room. "Yes, mistress?" He peered at Algie from behind a pair of wire-rimmed eyeglasses.

"Prepare an injection of lythix serum for our guest."

Nira stiffened. "What's that?"

"Just something to help you relax, dear."

"No way." Her pulse accelerating, she surged to her feet.

Algie and the technician exchanged glances. "All right, you've been agreeable so far," Algie said. "Doctor, hold that order."

"As you command." He stood by, a vacant look on his face.

"You'll answer my questions first, Nira. Who sent you?" Algie leaned forward as Nira sank back into her chair. A wavy strand of blond hair curtained Algie's face, hiding her expression.

"No one. I applied for a job through your ad in the newspaper. I need to earn money over the summer."

"Did you know those men who assaulted our station?"

"Not initially." Nira kept her face blank.

"You had no prior contact with the Drift Lords?"

"Never heard of them before yesterday." A spike of worry nailed her. Was Zohar safe? Had he found the jamming device?

Algie studied her as she would an amoeba under a microscope. "We thought at first you must have polarized yourself against us. That's how the Drift Lords shield themselves against our spell."

"Polaroids? What do you mean?"

"Pol-ar-ize," Algie enunciated as though Nira were daft. "We don't know how they do it, but we do know it's painful and leaves an unpleasant result." She snickered. "They're not able to please a woman immediately afterward."

"And you learned this how?" Nira visualized that morning when Zohar had been issuing orders to his team. He hadn't performed any painful ritual, or she would have known about it. Did that mean he'd left himself vulnerable to attack?

Algie's gaze grew distant, her lips parted upon a pleasant remembrance. "We captured a Drift Lord once, many moons ago. Through our persuasive methods, he told us how they defend against our touch, but not how it is done. You could find that out for us."

"Is this why you want to test my blood? Because if I'm not using a similar means to offset your spell, it may be something innate in my breeding?"

"Exactly. You're the first human we've encountered who possesses a natural defense. Further experimentation is necessary."

"Why did your people assault me at home? To capture me or to kill me?"

"Our squadron leader had orders not to leave you in the hands of the Drift Lords. He was to take you unharmed, but we had a misunderstanding." Algie's nostrils flared. "I was most displeased when I heard about the lava bomb."

"How did you know I'd bring the Drift Lords home with me?"

"We have our ways." Her eyes narrowed. "Are you still harboring them? Have you fallen for their lies about us?"

What, that you're hostile invaders who mean to enslave humanity while causing a catastrophic dimensional rift?

Nira didn't think it wise to tell the Trollek female how much she knew.

"I'm not sure what to believe," she hedged. "Tell me more about the Drift Lords."

"Zohar Thorald is their leader. He has his own issues to confront. We were hoping to divert his attention, but the man is dedicated. Stronger means have become necessary to distract him. You would be wise to join us."

"I'll consider it if you tell me what happened to my landlady. Is Grace still alive?"

"Allow us to use the lythix serum. After you've recovered, I'll tell you where we're holding the old woman."

"No." Nira shoved her chair back and stood. Cool air from an overhead vent drifted her way. She rubbed her aching temples, wishing her head would clear.

Algie sidled closer, waves of golden hair cascading to her shoulders. Her soft voice held an undercurrent of menace when she spoke again. "I've researched your connections, Nira. I know there are others who mean a lot to you."

Nira's heart skipped a beat. Not her sisters!

She edged toward the door. "I'd hoped we could be civilized, but this is getting me nowhere."

"Algie, lemme speak to you." The big Trollek drew the blonde aside in such a way as to block Nira's exit. "You should consult the Elders," he said in a low tone that she strained to overhear. "Otherwise, you'll lose this chance to plant a spy among the warriors. Maybe we should offer a better incentive."

"I don't trust her, Gort. Likely she's working for them."

"So? You can play on her sappy human emotions if that's what it takes. With the Coming nearly upon us, we should keep our options open, in case events don't turn out as planned."

"You fool. Be careful what you say. Anyway, I have things covered. Nothing will stop us." Algie's voice rose in pitch. Clearly, she didn't care to be challenged.

"Zohar's men have defeated us in the past." The Trollek scowled. "Do not underestimate them again. If you don't notify the Council, I will."

"All right. Keep her here while I send a message. I cannot imagine General Morar would be happy if we circumvent protocol."

Left alone with Gort and the play-acting doctor, Nira considered her options. She didn't want to hang around, in case Algie's consult went against her.

"So tell me, Gort." She waved a hand in the air. "Who staffs this place? A mixture of spellbound humans and your people?"

"That is correct." Thrusting his chin forward, he folded his brawny arms across his chest.

Nira wondered if she should make a grab for one of those syringes and stab him. But before she could act, a red light flashed on the wall.

"All units report to duty stations," announced a loudspeaker voice. "Unauthorized personnel have entered the grounds."

"I have to go." Gort's ugly face puckered like he'd swallowed a pit. "Dr. Sawyer, do not allow this woman to leave until Algie gives clearance."

"As you command." The lab-coated man moved forward to intercept Nira as Gort swung out through the front door.

Nira surveyed the doctor, wondering how she could gain his support. Although slim-shouldered, likely he'd fight her if she tried to leave.

She pressed a hand to her forehead. If only that incessant buzzing would stop, she might think of a way out of this fix without having to summon help. Maybe if she used the technique she'd learned for headaches?

Closing her eyes, she imagined an open door behind which resided a hive of angry bees. She pictured the door shutting against their swirling mass. The bees, alerted to her effort, became angry and increased their pressure. She pushed harder, squeezing the door shut inch-by-inch until the noise stopped.

Her eyes flew open. Had she truly gotten rid of that sound?

The man in front of her tottered and blinked. What was wrong with him?

"Why don't you let me go?" She gave him a conspiratorial grin. "I'll slip outside, and you can say that I tricked you."

"As you command." He cleared her path.

Impossible, unless… she'd freed him from Trollek mind control. Another theory arose to choke her.

Could she possess the same ability as her hosts?

"Open the door," she commanded to test the notion. "Tell me how to escape the park undetected."

He flung the door wide. "Head toward the food court in the rear. Look for an exit marked Staff Only."

Afraid to ruminate on her newfound power, she wiped sweaty palms on her pants. Maybe she could gain some information from this guy.

"Tell me, where do the Trolleks go after the park closes?"

Silence.

She rephrased her question into an order. "Talk to me about where your employers go after hours."

"They retreat to the village."

"What village? I mean, describe this place. Tell me where it's located." She had assumed the beasts spatial shifted back to their dimension.

"I am not privy to that information."

"Then describe your living quarters."

"I go home at night."

"All right, listen up." She clasped her hands for emphasis. "The Trollek spell will no longer work on you, even if you are touched again. You will be immune. You're in the Drift World theme park. Go home and don't ever come back."

His eyes popped, and he turned to dash outside.

Nira hastened in his wake. She nearly collided with Dal and Kaj coming around the corner. Uniformed staff members bustled about, but they blended in thanks to their stolen khaki uniforms and hats.

"Where's Zohar?" She craned her neck to look beyond them but didn't see their leader's imposing figure anywhere.

"We have not seen him nor Lord Magnor." Kaj jerked a thumb toward the main entrance. "We are to rendezvous at the van, but the exit is blocked by a cadre of Trolleks."

"I know another way out. Follow me."

They scurried in the shadows from building to building until reaching the rear wall. Unfortunately, a couple of employees stood guard in front of the staff door.

Noting her companions tense for a fight, Nira held up a hand. "Wait, let me try something first."

As soon as she'd stepped outdoors, the buzzing in her mind had resumed. Now she imagined the mental door again and pushed against it. More effort was required this time, and her body trembled as she fought the pressure.

"Listen up, you guys," she called to the confounded humans. "You will let us pass and then you'll forget you saw us. Open the gate and stand aside."

To her new friends' astonishment, the two men did exactly as ordered. She and her pals strode forward, finding themselves in an employee parking lot.

"How did you do that?" Kaj gaped at her.

"I'll tell you about it later. Let's find your van and see if Zohar made it out okay." She didn't understand why his safety mattered so much, but it did.

"When the alarm sounded, I thought we had tripped an alert, but it must have been the captain." Dal, wearing his perpetual scowl, led them across an embankment toward the guest parking lots.

Nira hurried to match his pace. The ground was soft, still moist from a recent rain. "Can you call him?"

"Negative. He ordered radio silence." Kaj, striding beside her, peeled off his khaki shirt but didn't discard it. He wore his own clothing beneath.

"Then where is he?"

They reached the van, but neither Zohar nor Lord Magnor were anywhere in sight.

****

Zohar and Lord Magnor crept along a utility tunnel located beneath the theme park. An entire underground maze consisted of corridors where staff members prepped for the day, received training, and dispersed provisions. Also located here were supply depots. Pipes stretched overhead, competing with wiring, while valves hissed at various intervals. Generators hummed in the background, while the scent of cleaning fluid pervaded the air. Florescent lighting provided harsh illumination.

Wary of security cameras, they proceeded cautiously. It had been Zohar's plan to access the employee areas while Nira scouted the tourist sites, and the pass she had given him made it easy. After accosting a second guard, he and Lord Magnor had donned a couple of staff uniforms before slipping through a door marked Private.

They'd barely explored two of the tunnels before an alarm sounded. Weaving their way to the surface, they ended up in a shop. Zohar glanced outside at the people streaming past, the food vendors selling treats, and the theater players handing out tickets. Water danced at a plaza fountain, spraying passersby.

Which way to the entrance?

Hoping his sense of direction would hold, he signaled for Lord Magnor to follow. They strode through the open doorway into the street.

"You there!" A staff member gestured to him. "Identify yourself."

When Zohar hesitated, the man muttered into a wireless device hooked to his ear. Everyone stopped, humans and Trolleks alike. As one unit, they wheeled in his direction. The confounded individuals had hostile expressions.

Zohar's muscles tensed. He'd prefer not to hurt spellbound victims who lacked control over their actions.

"I can hold them off." Lord Magnor drew his sword. His strange attire had attracted merely curious glances. Other guests must have believed him garbed for his fantasy role.

"I do not run from battle." Zohar reached for the dagger in his boot. He'd left his phase weapons behind.

"My job is to protect you. Remember whom you serve."

"I serve—"

"This way!" A man wearing a white coat waved at them.

Without a backward glance, Zohar raced after the man. Magnor followed on his heels. The fellow led them through a twisting series of alleys between buildings, up a flight of stairs, and onto a flat rooftop.

"Here's a low area where we can jump over the outer wall." The man paused, bending forward to catch his breath. "They don't electrify it until after hours."

Zohar scrutinized him. He appeared to be in his right mind. "Why are you helping us?"

His face reddened. "My name is James Reefer. I don't

remember much except some flame-haired lady telling me I was free. This place is cursed. I'm never coming back."

"Tell me about this woman," Zohar demanded, his pulse speeding. "Where did you see her?"

"In the clinic. She told me to get out. I don't know if she escaped."

Zohar dropped over the wall. His legs folded as he broke the fall. He rolled to his feet, the uniform collar rubbing against his neck.

"Thanks for your help," he told the fellow before parting ways. He and Lord Magnor headed for their rendezvous.

All he could see in his mind's eye were Nira's soft brown eyes, her impertinent nose, and her tantalizing smile.

Zohar shook his head—since when had her well-being become so important?

Chapter Seven

"You are a brave woman, Nira Larsen. I would have chosen another path than putting you at risk, but you played your part well." Zohar flashed Nira a smile from the passenger seat of her car.

She beamed with pride, her eyes on the road. "Thanks. I'm just glad we made it out okay."

She drove to the new hotel where Borius had secured rooms. After collecting their keys, they wolfed down a meal in the resort restaurant and exchanged news.

"I got you a room suited for a king," Borius told them after the debriefing. He sat across the table while chewing on a chunk of bread. The youngest team member, he had a voracious appetite, ordering two appetizers before his main meal.

"What does that mean?" Nira asked innocently, wondering why the men wore broad grins.

It meant their suite this time had a king-sized bed. Unfazed since Zohar would claim the sofa, Nira didn't protest. She was just grateful they wouldn't have to stay in the same place where Rayne had died.

Once in the privacy of their suite, she left Zohar to set up their safety perimeter and headed into the bathroom. Questions hovered on her tongue, but right after she emerged, Zohar dashed inside. If she didn't know better, she'd think he was avoiding being alone with her.

Her immediate intentions disintegrated when he strolled out twenty minutes later wrapped in a towel with moisture glistening on his skin. She stood by the dresser, brushing her hair. As he sauntered over, she put down the brush, examining his broad shoulders and muscular chest in the mirror. Talk about eye candy. Oh, man.

He cleared his throat. "I realize you would prefer to have your own space. Once Borius finds us a house to rent, you will have your own quarters. I regret that our actions have forced you into our protective custody."

She whipped around, ignoring her rapid pulse in his presence. "It's not your fault. The Trolleks grabbed me in the employment office. If not for you, I'd still be their prisoner."

His scent drifted her way, clean soap mixed with a hint of spice. She breathed it in, aware of his gaze traveling her length. Suddenly conscious of her bare legs under her nightshirt, she felt her cheeks heat under his scrutiny.

Backed against the dresser, she posed the first question in her mind to distract herself from his overwhelming masculinity.

"Tell me, how does this defensive perimeter work? It keeps the Trolleks from jumping into range via their spatial shifts?"

He nodded, his eyes glittering. "We can block their shifts, but we have been unable to determine the technology they use to create them."

She pointed to the poles he'd placed in the four corners to prevent the Trolleks from vectoring in. "Is that how you protect yourself against confounding? By creating a personal shield?"

His brows folded. "Where did you hear this?"

"Algie said you guys polarize yourselves, whatever that means, and she'd like to know how it works. She also said the method is painful and leaves an unpleasant side effect."

The corners of his mouth turned down. "We must subject ourselves to an electric current. The change in polarity renders us temporarily unable to perform certain manly functions, but it protects our skin from absorbing the substance secreted by Trolleks."

"You forgot to do it this morning, didn't you?"

His lips compressed, his eyes guarded. "I was distracted."

She knew what he meant. Risking a glance south, she noted the blatant tent in his towel. Oh, my. Why did he sound so displeased?

"Is being near me such a bad thing?" she asked in a small voice.

Like it or not, Zohar served as her anchor in this crazy universe. As though he were made of iron, she felt drawn to him like a magnet. She took a tiny step forward, wanting to stroke his face and ease his concerns.

His gaze dropped to her parted lips. "Quite the opposite. I want nothing more than to sweep you into my arms and steal a kiss. Duty insists that we perform an experiment."

"What?"

She'd heard nothing except how he wanted her. A compulsion to plow her fingers through his slicked-back hair assailed her. She wanted to mess up his hair, mess *him* up. He took things too seriously. The Drift Lord captain needed to relax, and she had just the prescription.

Her breasts tingled, her nipples peaking in anticipation. Having sex wouldn't compromise their working relationship. If anything, getting over that hurdle would ease things between them. She craved comfort between the sheets, if only for one night, and his towel-clad body only fueled her desire.

"I kissed you last night." His voice gruff, he peered down at her. His gaze fixated on her taut bustline.

"I remember." She lifted her chin, feeling the fabric against her skin like sandpaper. Resisting the urge to tear off her nightshirt, she waited to see what else he would say.

"Trolleks touched me today, and it had no effect. I suspect it had something to do with our mingling."

"Mingling?"

"Tasting each other. You are immune to their spell. Possibly you passed that immunity to me."

"Really? So this experiment, do you mean to try it again?"

"I do." His eyes smoldered with desire, his voice deepening to a husky tone.

"Then what's the problem?"

"I must restrain myself."

Afraid of losing control, are you? That's just what you need, big guy.

She rose on her tiptoes to whisper in his ear. "Don't worry. I'm sure a strong man like you can keep his cool."

"Cool? This room has grown exceedingly hot. Only one remedy presents itself. We must initiate the experiment at once." Bending his head, he brushed her lips lightly in a teasing caress.

His warm breath fanned her cheeks. Wanting more, she leaned forward, parting her mouth.

Still he did not oblige by going deeper. His tongue darted out, tracing the outline of her lips while molten heat pooled in her belly. Nira yearned for him to take her into his arms but Zohar made no move to draw her closer.

Without shifting his hands, he trailed nibbling kisses from her mouth to her ear.

She raised up on her tiptoes, tilting her face, tempting him to take her to the heights of passion. Was this all he intended, to give her the briefest of kisses as his so-called experiment?

Maybe that was the real test, to see how far she'd be willing to go. Or perhaps people on his world mated like this. What did she know about alien customs?

Nira did some testing of her own to find out.

When he slanted his mouth over hers again, she licked him, probing with her tongue until his lips, firm and warm, responded with more pressure.

Triumph surged through her. She'd feared their attraction wasn't strong enough, that he rationalized their kiss as an experiment. But perhaps he wasn't testing her at all. Maybe he fought to maintain his own self-control, the warrior in him fearing to yield to lust.

Now that she suspected what kept him reined in, she grew bolder.

Returning his ardor, she imprinted her hunger on his mouth. Excitement spiraled through her as his control loosened. He grabbed her by the shoulders and crushed his lips to hers in a bruising, demanding kiss.

She moaned as her body responded, melting into submission. Her arms snaked around him, drawing him closer. Craving his embrace, she yearned for him to protect her from the evils of the world. She'd never felt safer nor more feminine than when in his presence.

He ground his hips against her. Only her nightshirt and his towel remained as blockades between them. Sliding her hands to his chest, she splayed her fingers over his muscular ridges.

"I cannot resist you. Tell me to stop," Zohar muttered.

"No, the experiment hasn't gone on long enough."

To demonstrate her willingness, she nudged him toward the bed. Mindless sex would be a welcome release from the tension of the day. Backed up against the mattress, she kept her mouth attached to his.

With an agonized moan, he rolled her onto the bed and swiftly followed, gluing them together in another embrace.

She pressed her swollen lips to his and opened to him, playing a tactile tongue duet that left them both breathless.

His toweled erection pushed between her thighs. Heat coiled in her core, seething toward eruption. Impatient to feel her skin against his bare flesh, she reached down.

****

Zohar brushed her fingers away and slid on top of her. Elevating himself on his elbows, he peeled Nira's nightshirt over her head while she watched him with passion-glazed eyes. Then he flung away his towel.

Raised above her, he grinned as a flush spread across her lovely face. She lay exposed before his hungry gaze. He did a slow perusal, enjoying how her chest expanded with each breath.

He tweaked her pink-tinged nipples, pleased when she squirmed in response. His fingers played with her, alternating between a light pinch and a circular stroke until she moaned with need.

He filled his hands with her soft flesh. His arousal escalated as he slid his gaze southward. What mysteries awaited his explorations there?

His pulse pounded erratically. He couldn't remember the last time he'd felt such heat for a woman.

"You are beautiful, my *carona*." The endearment slipped from his tongue.

Was he mad, yielding to her charms so easily? Could he already be turning into his father, a weak man who'd been seduced by a Trollek female into betraying his people?

Nay, this was merely an experiment to see if the Earth woman could convey her immunity to him. But oh, what a sweet task it proved to be. He hadn't meant to go this far, but with her so willing, how could he stop? As long as he maintained control, he'd be all right.

Chariots of the gods, it would take all his strength.

Zohar clenched his jaw when she opened her legs, inviting him to discover her female secrets. Rationale slipped when she snaked her hand down to direct him.

"Not so quick, little one." He gently pried her wrist away. "Allow me to show you what happens when you bed a Drift Lord."

Edging along her body to kiss her breast, he engaged her nipple with his tongue while his hand titillated her other peak. Twisting beneath him, she cried his name. Satisfied to see her eyes darken with passion, he suckled one side before changing over. Sampling her wares only made him crave more.

Holding his need in rigid check became an exercise in stamina. His blood fled his brain, swelling his lower regions. He gave a final peck to her rosy areolas, then kissed his way down her sweet skin, past her flat belly to the nest of hair between her thighs. She gasped, her legs stiffening.

He brought his hand into play, exploring the nether folds guarding her slick entrance. His heart beat a rapid staccato. Soon he'd join with her, blending their bodies, feeling her tightness close around him.

Of all the Earth women he might have encountered, he'd lucked out by finding this one. He admired her tenacity, her courage, and her devotion. Once she set a goal, she didn't deviate from her path.

What would it be like to be the object of her affection?

Wanting to find out, he increased his pressure, stroking her until she lifted her hips to meet him. His mental shackles broke away. Lost in a consuming lust, he bent to kiss her private parts.

Her body jerked, her responsiveness driving him mad. As he breathed in her musky essence, his abdomen tightened. He wouldn't be able to hold out much longer.

"Omigod, you're killing me." She moaned when he licked her secret place. "Please… don't stop."

Fulfilling her wish, he discovered her tiny bud of flesh, circling his tongue around the sensitive nub before shifting his mouth to discover the entry she so generously offered.

As she quivered with a beginning spiral toward release, he kissed her one last time before pulling back.

"Are you certain?" he asked in a husky tone.

"Oh yes," she half-cried and half-laughed.

His blood surged. Aligning his length over her, he thrust into her welcoming warmth.

He felt as though he'd come home.

Nira's pupils dilated as she adjusted to his fill. She folded her legs around him, pressing him closer, body to body, flesh to flesh, until they fit as one.

Reason fled his mind. His vision receded, until nothing remained except her face with its luminous frame of red hair on the pillow, wide dewy eyes, and trembling lips. He crushed his mouth to hers, driving himself deeper, until his self-control imploded.

****

Nira thought she'd come when his mouth feathered across her sensitive southern region and his tongue plunged inside her wet heat. Her pulse quickened, and her hips gyrated on their own accord. But before the race to the finish barely started, he raised himself above her and joined their bodies in one swift push.

The crescendo resumed, propelling her toward a crest that rocked her in its intensity. With the spasms that followed, her vision tunneled, and her mind flew beyond the normal plane of existence to a place of light and warmth and swirling mist.

Zohar cried out as his body jerked over hers. Vaguely, she remembered protection but too late. Maybe men from Karrell didn't bother with such things? Or maybe getting impregnated by an alien was so far removed from reality that she should forget about it. Their species were different, right?

Worry about it later.

Eventually, he removed his weight, rolling onto his side. She relaxed as a languorous warmth stole into her limbs. Sweat coated her skin, but she felt sublime. For a while, she lay with her eyes closed, listening to his steady breathing and waiting for her pulse to regulate.

Sounds filtered into her consciousness: the tick of a clock, the hum of an air-conditioning unit, and the muted drone of traffic from outside.

Zohar's shadow crossed her eyelids as he leaned over to brush a kiss on her mouth. She opened her eyes. A smile curved her mouth at his tender expression. She'd only had sex a few times, and mostly with her latest boyfriend, but it had never been this good.

"I did not mean to go so far, my *carona*." His voice held a note of apology.

"Don't be sorry. I wanted it as much as you."

"I merely intended to test my theory."

"Well, if you're looking for excuses, remember that it takes two to tango."

"Tango?" A frown creased his forehead. "Is that not a dance form in your world?"

"A mating dance, in this case." A kernel of hurt invaded her, and she tapped him on the mouth. "Not to worry, captain. We don't have to repeat your experiment."

"It is not for myself that I test my hunch. If you can transfer your immunity to the Trollek spell, we might be able to synthesize a compound to help the populace."

"Of course. Why else would you want me?" She looked away.

"Do not mistake me, Nira Larsen." His voice softened. "I feel the spark between us. Your scent drives me wild. It clouds my mind and distracts me from my purpose."

"Oh. So what's the problem?"

"We may enjoy the mingling, but a permanent bond between us is impossible. That is why I kept my distance from you last night. I do not wish to start something I cannot hope to finish."

"I see. Well, don't concern yourself." She kept her voice even. "I realize you have to leave at the end of your mission."

Did he have someone waiting for him back on Karrell? Was that why he tried to rein in his impulses? Or did his people frown upon interspecies bonding?

She stole a glance at him. A look of relief crossed his face while she swallowed her disappointment.

"I am glad you understand. I would not want to hurt you."

"I'm a big girl. If I sleep with you, it's my choice."

"About that…"

"What?"

"How do I know it was actually my decision to join with you and not your influence?"

"What do you mean?"

"You tempted me."

"So?"

"I lost my sense of reason."

"What are you getting at?" She yanked the sheet up to cover herself and leaned on one elbow.

Turned sideways, Zohar regarded her squarely. She didn't like the doubt in his eyes.

"My father was seduced by a Trollek woman."

That did it. She hopped from the bed, tangling herself in the sheet. "You're comparing me to a Trollek?"

He had the grace to look embarrassed. "Not really. I only meant—"

"May I remind you, Mr. Drift Lord, that you started this stupid experiment. You're the one who gave that sad excuse when you really just wanted to jump my bones."

"Jump your…?"

She almost laughed at his confusion, but her throat closed.

Turning away so he couldn't see the moisture in her eyes, she strode to the bathroom and slammed the door.

Inside, she twisted on the shower faucet, tossed aside the sheet, and proceeded to drown her tears under the spray of water.

How dare he insinuate she had anything in common with those nasty beasts? They'd stolen her life, her mentor, and her home. And if *she* hadn't been so beguiled by Zohar, she'd have remembered why she got entangled with him in the first place.

Her goal was to rescue Grace and then move on with her life. Deciphering the rune on her wristwatch would help her discover the past.

Her true parents had abandoned her for a reason, one that did *not* include an intimate connection to the Trolleks.

Chapter Eight

Zohar slid between the sheets after his turn using the facilities. Nira, with the quilt pulled over her nightshirt-clad body, slept with her back to Zohar. How could he lead his team when desire for this woman clouded his mind?

Thinking one taste of Nira would satisfy his craving had been pure folly. Now he only wanted her more, his nose sensitive to her scent, his nerves fired to her presence. All the cold showers on this planet wouldn't wash away his lust for the lovely redhead.

She'd surprised him around every corner. Her willingness to bed him had caught him unawares. Not many females on his world, except those who sold their charms, accepted him to their bosom without wanting something in return.

But then, Nira didn't know his true rank, the one he fought so hard to deny.

He dared a glance at her. She slept peacefully, her short layers of hair fanning the pillow, while he imagined the glorious lengths she could grow them to if she followed the customs of his people.

His gaze traveled over her luscious curves. Her body tempted him to snuggle closer and enfold her in his embrace, but he reined in his longing. Weakness lay in that direction. Weakness and insanity.

She'd mumbled something about discussing their plans for tomorrow but had fallen asleep too quickly for talk. Her input had been useful during their debriefing earlier, especially in terms of Earth customs, and he wondered what she'd meant to add.

Better to get some rest so he could think with a clear head in the morning. But as he closed his eyes, all he could see were Nira's plump lips and naked form. Twisting restlessly, he found himself staring at her back and the curve of her neck.

Is this what his father had felt in bed with that witch who called herself his stepmother? A driving lust that obliterated all rational thought?

Clenching his teeth, Zohar tamped down his desire. Tomorrow would be the ultimate test if she conferred her immunity to him. If it worked, he'd face the decision whether to continue their therapeutic mingling to protect himself, or to apply the polarization technique regardless of the painful side effects.

And if the test didn't work, the decision would be irrelevant. His mind would be lost to a Trollek kabak.

Time would tell. The potential for salvation through Nira's blood was too great to ignore, almost as great as his fear of being confounded.

****

"I want to make sure everybody knows what to do," Zohar told his men during their breakfast meeting in the resort restaurant. He scooped a forkful of scrambled eggs into his mouth, chewed, and swallowed. "First, to reiterate what we learned yesterday, humans are being confounded at Drift World and sent home to recruit more victims. They are told to wait for further orders."

"Further orders for what?" Paz asked in his customary drawl. The communications specialist gulped down a sip of orange juice.

Zohar shrugged. "This is what we need to find out. I am concerned that Drift World may be only one of such recruitment stations."

"We won't know for certain until we kill that jamming device." Paz stabbed a potato onto his fork and ate it.

"I found no sign of such a device in Drift World."

"What about that village I heard mentioned?" Nira, who'd

been relatively quiet while his men discussed their tasks, piped in. She hadn't said a word about their mingling last night, and Zohar wondered if she regretted their act.

"Following up on that lead is our job." His voice came out gruffer than intended.

"That's not until after work hours."

"Right. In the meantime, you and I will visit the real estate office Borius contacted yesterday. They require your signature on the rental contract for a furnished house."

"And how are we supposed to pay for it?" She jabbed a finger in the air. "Grace's insurance won't kick in until the claim is processed."

"We can stop at a jeweler to cash in another one of my kewa stones." Zohar turned to the stony-faced swordsman at his other side. "Lord Magnor, you will act as our personal backup."

He harbored doubts about that plan but didn't voice them. The security footage of the corridor outside the suite where Rayne died had been erased. Now they'd never know who had entered with the intent to murder the Drift Lord leader. Zohar knew without a doubt that he had been the intended target. But until he had proof otherwise, he would extend his people the benefit of his doubt. An outside assassin could still exist. Either Lord Magnor would watch his back, or Zohar would have his enemy close at hand.

"Dal, I am concerned about the disruptors the Trolleks used against us. Those are Class One military use restricted armaments, meaning someone in Imperial Space Command might be supplying them to our enemy. See if you can trace the route."

The demolitions expert nodded. He cracked his knuckles, a forbidding look on his lean face as though he'd like nothing more than to uncover the traitors and demolish them himself.

Nira shifted restlessly beside him. She'd eaten a muffin and some fruit, nothing more. Hungrier than usual, Zohar sliced into a chocolate chip pancake with vengeance. He couldn't resist ordering them after tasting Grace's cake. He had developed what Nira teasingly referred to as a sweet tooth.

"Paz, you will shuttle back to the ship to coordinate communications. While there, you can analyze the scan you took of Rayne's body."

"Let me help." Borius's blue eyes shone with zeal. "I have more training with the science modules."

Zohar gave their youngest crewmember a stern glare. "You will remain planet-side to investigate other leads in Rayne's murder."

Kaj and Yaron, across the table, bumped fists.

"We get the easy assignment." Yaron gave his mates a broad grin. "After you and Nira get the keys to our house, we shall go shopping to obtain provisions."

"After you set up a full security perimeter," Zohar reminded them. This was not a game they were playing. Sometimes he felt like a father to a bunch of children. He supposed he should be pleased his team tackled tasks with such enthusiasm.

"I need to go shopping, too." Nira took a sip of the brew called coffee. It had a bitter taste, but Zohar liked the mental kick it gave him. "We need to get a computer so I can check my email and register for fall classes." She hesitated. "And there's one more thing."

All eyes turned in her direction.

"Algie took a blood sample from me yesterday. We need to obtain the results."

"What? You did not mention this earlier." Half-rising from his seat, Zohar scowled at her in accusation.

"You've been dominating the conversation." Her sarcastic tone challenged him to reprimand her.

"Let me explain something to you, Nira Larsen. As a member of our team, I expect you to be forthcoming with information. Do not withhold data that can be critical to our mission or you endanger us all."

Her chin lifted. "I agreed to let Algie test my serum when I went with her at the theme park. You want to know why I resist confounding, right? Perhaps there's a component in my blood, you know, like an antibody. We need to steal the analysis."

"She's right." Paz shot her an admiring glance. "If the Trolleks find the component that renders her immune, they could synthesize an antagonist."

Zohar sighed. "We shall add this to our objectives for the day. Everyone clear on what to do? We can rendezvous later at the safe house. Paz will send you the coordinates. Good hunting."

Inside their suite, Zohar stuffed his belongings into a sack while Nira touched up her lipstick in front of the dresser. He read the taut lines around her mouth.

"You are angry. What is troubling you?" He hoped it wasn't their lovemaking last night that bothered her. She had been more than willing to fall into his arms.

She whirled to face him. "I'm worried about you. You're exposing yourself to their touch. What if yesterday was a fluke? You may have had some immunity left over from your last polarization. Maybe it wasn't me at all."

"You are concerned for my well-being?" Clearly, this Earth woman remained a mystery to him. Did she not realize his duty included her protection, and not vice versa?

Her face flushed. "Of course I am. You're a born leader, Zohar. Your men need you. It isn't worth the risk."

Disappointment weighted him. He'd hoped to hear her say that she needed him. Fool. She had only fallen in with his troop because she'd had no choice—her survival depended on him.

"Let me worry about the risk." He ploughed stiff fingers through his hair. "Once we enter the theme park, we will head straight for the medical building. We can find a place to hide in there until the park closes."

She tilted her head. "What about those solar calculators you said were being shipped to an underground mail room?"

"I did not have time to learn more, but the quantity of devices far exceeds the administrative use for them. It is another mystery we have to investigate."

"Too bad we can't slip in there like that guy." She pointed to a lizard scurrying up the wall toward the window ledge.

"Curious creature." Its color allowed the animal to mimic its surroundings. He watched the long tail dart from view behind the blinds.

They finished packing their things and then hit the road in Nira's car. After a visit to the jeweler to cash in another precious stone, they headed for the real estate office to sign off on a rental property. He radioed Paz the address to pick up a set of keys. Zohar requested that he have copies made for the rest of their team. Next, Nira insisted on shopping for more clothes and necessities. They stopped at Grace's insurance agent to fill out papers and continued on until he felt like a heckled husband.

The comm unit on his wrist chimed just after they exited a drugstore. With a sense of relief, he tapped the activation key. "Zohar here."

"This is Borius. We have a situation."

"What now?"

"Lord Magnor has been injured."

"How is that possible?" Zohar had cut him loose while he and Nira ran errands. The swordsman had wanted to pick up some supplies of his own.

"We set a rendezvous so I could update him on your itinerary in person, but he changed the site. I found him unconscious in an alley."

"Any sign of Trollek activity?" He stood aside as Nira unlocked the car.

"No, sire. Shall I summon Yaron?"

The woodsman acted as their team medic. "Not yet. Is Magnor's condition critical?"

"I cannot say. The Tsuran's physiology may be different than ours."

"I will join you. Let me know if his status changes before I get there."

"What happened?" Nira tapped his arm after he'd signed off.

Her mere touch electrified him. "Magnor is down. Borius is with him."

He opened the driver's door for her. After she'd taken her seat, he strode around to the passenger side and slid into the hot interior. He wore a loose-fitting shirt over his denims and reached down to retrieve his phase gun. He'd left it on the car floor in case the stores had metal detectors. Now he tucked it into the waistband of his pants.

"What else did he say?" Nira turned on the engine. A welcome blast of cooled air blew from the vents.

"Borius and Magnor had set a meeting, but for some reason, Magnor changed the location. Borius found him there, senseless on the ground. That is all I know."

Nira cast him a sharp glance. "Wasn't Borius the last person to talk to Rayne?"

"What is that supposed to mean?" His spine stiffened.

"Can you trust what Borius says?"

"Borius has been on my team for years. I do not doubt his word." He glared at her. "You will not spread suspicion among my crew."

"All right, if not one of your men, then who?" Nira backed out of their space.

He compressed his lips. "An assassin from my home world is the most likely culprit. It's possible he learned Magnor is here to guard me and tried to take him out. But if Lord Magnor dies, Primer Pedar will merely appoint another in his place."

Nira braked in the exit lane, watching traffic roar past. A bus belched fumes while Zohar shook his head at the pitiful modes of transportation on this world.

"Did you check with this primer guy to see if he even sent a bodyguard?" Nira wagged a finger at him. "You're too trusting, Zohar. You take too much at face value."

He glanced out the side window, his throat too clogged to respond. What did she know about his warriors? They'd fought together, trained together, and sometimes died together. He'd give his life for his men, and vice versa. Nira had no right to judge them… or him, for that matter.

Fires of Agathorn, she'd only strengthened his resolve. He may have accepted her into his circle, but he'd never allow her entrance into his heart.

****

As she wound through mid-morning Orlando traffic, Nira cursed Zohar's arrogance. If he weren't too obstinate to see beyond his nose, he'd suspect Borius of being in league with his enemy. And what enemy was that? Other than the Trolleks, who did he suspect had sent assassins after him?

Despite their physical intimacy, she hadn't made any inroads regarding his emotions. Maybe he'd let her into his band of merry men, but he sure hadn't let her into his confidence. Zohar's personal background remained a mystery. For all she knew, he could be married on his home world, if they even followed that custom.

She attempted to ease the tension between them. "So tell me, where did you guys learn how to drive? Do you have cars and trucks like this on your world?"

His jaw tightened. "We have been dirtside on your planet before. We appropriated some of your land vehicles during that excursion."

"It must have been a brief visit." They sure hadn't learned much in the way of cultural practices. As for language barriers, he'd admitted they used implanted translators.

Fifteen minutes later, she took exit 68 off I-4 toward Lake Buena Vista. "You said the address Borius gave you is off Palm Parkway, right?"

He nodded curtly while her glance skipped over his broad shoulders to his corded forearms and powerful legs. Those jeans fit him like a second skin. If only he'd look at her with the same smoldering glance he'd given earlier.

Likely he was too worried about his companions.

Borius, or any one of his other teammates, could have been

compromised. True, Lord Magnor had shown up right after Rayne's death, but she didn't read him as a killer. Zohar relied more on the fellows he'd known for years, which made one of them the best target for corruption. Or maybe Zohar's suspicions were correct, and an outside assassin had targeted him. But then why had Lord Magnor been taken down? Because he got in the way?

She stopped at a traffic light with a hotel entrance on the left and a shopping center on the right. A row of chain restaurants tempted diners on either side. Tropical foliage softened the commercial feel. Green palms, flowering red hibiscus, and colorful pink bougainvillea bordered the sidewalks.

After a right turn onto Palm Parkway, she followed the winding road past a series of hotels. Peering through her sunglasses, she searched for the shopping plaza where Borius said to meet him.

"There it is." Zohar pointed to a turnoff.

Nira veered into the crowded parking lot and lifted her foot off the accelerator. A steakhouse was on the left and a pizza place sat on her right. Across the parking lot, she could make out a hair salon, a Cuban restaurant, and an India eaterie.

"I see him." Zohar's voice rose in excitement.

She spotted Borius in front of an expresso bar across from the pizza place. He waved at them.

"What could have brought Lord Magnor out here?" She pulled into a parking space and shut down the engine.

"Good question."

"Maybe someone contacted him offering information," she suggested. "That could be why he changed the rendezvous."

"Information on what?"

She shrugged. "Who wants you dead, maybe?"

His mouth thinned. "I knew there was a reason I brought you along. You could be right. Let us see what Borius has learned."

Blond hair askew and dark circles under his eyes, the young man looked ill when they confronted him. "I have bad news, *rageesh*. Lord Magnor has vanished."

"What?" Zohar's narrowed gaze swept the environs.

"I came out curbside earlier to see if you had arrived yet, and when I returned, he was gone." The young man's voice wavered. "I should not have left him."

"Any evidence of cors particles?"

"No, sire. I do not understand what happened. Let me show you where I discovered him."

Nira trailed after them, annoyed that Borius hadn't even spared her a greeting. He led them into an alley behind the shopping strip where air-conditioning units provided a steady drone. Water from an early morning rain ran in rivulets along the asphalt. Bordered on one side by a concrete wall and on the other side by shady trees, the alley appeared deserted.

In the summer heat, garbage from a series of Dumpsters lent a ripe smell to the area.

Nira wrinkled her nose. "Say, how do you know Lord Magnor wasn't confounded? Did he get touched by any Trolleks at Drift World?"

Zohar lifted an eyebrow. "I figured he had his own means to resist their spell. I did not care to delve too deeply into Tsuran secrets, but maybe I was wrong." He stroked his jaw. "Borius, what made you think he had been injured?"

Borius snorted. "You mean, other than him lying on the ground unresponsive? His pulse was weak and erratic, and his skin color was grayish."

"Any obvious wounds?"

"None visible. Could have been disruptor fire on a stun setting."

"What's that?" Nira asked.

"A weapon that disrupts the neural pathways." Zohar's eyes glittered in the midday sunlight. "It has two settings: stun and kill. Disruptors cause a more profound effect than the stun setting on our laser pistols."

While he performed a scan with a portable device at the spot Borius indicated, Nira surveyed the weeds growing through cracks in the asphalt and the empty beer bottles discarded on the ground.

"You are correct. No sign of Trollek activity." Zohar pocketed his instrument.

"What happened to Lord Magnor?" Nira's scalp prickled. They should move on. She had a bad feeling about this place.

"Perhaps he was only lightly stunned, roused himself, and left." Borius pressed his lips together. "Do you doubt me? I thought he was dead until I felt a faint pulse."

A nearby door crashed open, forestalling their debate. Eight men with shaved heads and tattoos burst out.

"This will be fun." A thug with a nose ring swung a metal chain. "As least you're not wearing a stupid costume like that other guy. Whadja do with his body?"

Zohar thrust Nira behind him and pulled his weapon. Borius took his back, with Nira sandwiched in between. The young warrior had drawn his laser gun, too.

Zohar aimed at the gang member with the chain. "If you are being paid, I can pay you more. Tell me who hired you," he demanded.

"No deal, buddy. We got our reputations to maintain."

A guy with a bandana tied around his head brandished a knife. "Yeah, but we didn't count on no skirt bein' here."

"She'll just make it more fun, Curt. Don't worry, we'll all get a piece."

While his words made her shudder, Nira realized Zohar must be their target. He'd been set up. The thugs surrounded them.

"Stand down, I do not wish to hurt you." Zohar's voice held a clear warning.

Chainman flicked his wrist and whipped the gun from Zohar's hand.

"Odds are eight against two." Borius's weapon clattered to the ground, too. They'd been flanked on both sides.

"Nira, get down." Zohar yanked his dagger from his boot and launched himself at the nearest attacker.

A flurry of kicks, grunts, and punches ensued. In the midst of the fight, Nira stood by uncertainly. What could she do to help?

One of the thugs staggered back, and she saw her opening. She whacked him on the head with her handbag.

The guy spun and backhanded her across the mouth. She flew into a wall and sank to the ground, her cheek stinging. Her hand grappled for her handbag a few feet away. Surely, she had something inside to use as a weapon.

The same man grabbed her by the hair before she completed her plan. Her scalp burned as the brute dragged her sideways.

"Come with me, bitch. I get you first."

Her glance fell on Zohar's laser gun lying a few feet away. Would she know how to fire it? Only one way to find out.

Gritting her teeth, she reached over her head, clamped onto the guy's fist, and yanked back his pinky finger.

"Ow!" His grip loosened.

She flipped around, scrambled to her knees, and then stood. Using the momentum, she hit him on the jaw with her elbow.

A satisfactory crunch met her ears.

Cutting free, she pounced on the weapon and aimed.

Her assailant growled, a murderous look in his eyes. He sprang forward just as she squeezed the trigger.

The beam caught him midair. His eyes widened in shocked surprise before he crumpled into a heap, a scorched mark on his chest. The smell of burnt flesh made her want to gag.

Oh. My. God.

She had killed a man.

He wasn't the only one down. Borius fought a single attacker, having knocked his other assailants to the ground. As the guy thrust a knife at him, Borius deflected the strike with his arm. Baring his teeth in a derisive grin, the warrior smashed a frontal kick into the thug's groin. With a howl of pain, the man toppled over. A brutal stomp finished him off.

Zohar had two guys left. He bobbed and weaved so they couldn't get a straight bead on him. Nose Ring swung a chain at the Drift Lord captain. Zohar ducked and lunged to punch him in the stomach. Grunting, the guy bent over. Zohar chopped him on the neck, and he went down.

Nira raised her weapon with both hands, her entire body trembling. She could take out the remaining man, but sweat dripped into her eyes, blurring her vision. Her sight cleared in time for her to see Zohar kick his remaining attacker in the torso and follow up with a side smash to the guy's temple.

His chest heaving, Zohar strode to her side. "Are you all right? Did that *riff* hurt you?" He pried the gun from her stiff fingers.

"I'm okay." She gulped, swallowing a rise of bile in her throat. Her body quaked like a leaf in a storm, and her veins filled with ice, but she quelled her reaction. Zohar needed her to be strong. "You?"

"Some minor scratches. You fought well, little one." A grin lit his face, slick with sweat and blood. "I will tell the rest of my men of your courage in battle."

His words filled her with pride. "Thanks… I think." She drew in a deep, steadying breath. "We should get out of here."

"She is right." Borius retrieved his weapon. He didn't look any the worse for wear except for a torn shirt.

Zohar stooped to yank his dagger from one of the victim's chests. He wiped it on the guy's shirt before tucking it back into his boot.

Sirens sounded in the distance, giving Nira a discomfiting thought. "I-I shot one of them. We won't… I mean, can the cops link us to the crime?"

The last thing she needed was to be hunted as a criminal, even if she could claim self-defense. She'd already stopped off at the police station to fill out a report on the explosion at Grace's house. How could she possibly explain her involvement in a gang war, which is how this would appear?

Zohar and Borius exchanged a glance. "Stand back." Zohar changed a setting on his firearm.

"What are you doing?"

"Getting rid of this scum. There will be no witnesses left to tell tales."

"Wait, *rageesh*." Borius held up a hand. "Let me get a scan. I can analyze it later."

"Good thinking. Go ahead."

Borius withdrew his portable device, punched a couple of keys, and swung it back and forth. With a satisfied nod, he slipped the instrument back into his jeans pocket.

Zohar aimed at the bodies strewn on the asphalt and fired. One by one, they vanished in a burst of light.

Nira regarded Zohar with horror. He'd vaporized them, just as he'd done with Rayne. Yet what other choice did he have?

This had been a trap. By luring Lord Magnor here, possibly under the pretense of offering information, Zohar's enemy had waylaid him, knowing Zohar would be summoned.

On the other hand, Borius claimed he'd set a rendezvous with Magnor who changed it at the last minute. Was he telling the truth, or had he set this up to make himself appear innocent?

Very likely the thugs didn't even know who'd hired them. And they hadn't expected Nira to accompany Zohar. So it couldn't be the Trolleks after her again.

No, Zohar had someone else who very much wanted him dead.

Chapter Nine

Zohar exulted when they slipped into Drift World without a hitch later that afternoon. It had been a tumultuous morning, with Lord Magnor's disappearance and the ensuing ambush.

He couldn't fathom how Nira insisted on completing their errands afterward. She'd been rattled by her first kill but rebounded swiftly, to his admiration. He had barked orders to his crew via his comm unit before parting from Borius. Then they each had resumed their tasks. Nira hadn't once requested time to rest. He suspected she didn't care to reflect on what she'd done or her composure might unravel.

His team had hung onto the outfits they'd borrowed from the staff at Drift World. After checking into their safe house earlier, he'd donned the khaki uniform. He gave Nira an employee badge to wear on her outfit. Then they had breezed inside the staff entrance using the pass she'd given him. Fortunately, it still worked. He hoped that was an oversight and not a lure.

Nira stood patiently beside him around the corner from the medical center. Wisps of short hair teased her face. A sprinkle of freckles scattered across her complexion. It had been hard to keep his hands to himself while accompanying her all day, but now he edged closer, unable to resist her draw.

Cursing his weakness, he dragged his gaze from her lush mouth to focus on their surroundings. Guests crossed the plaza, bustling to their posts. Some of them nibbled on a confection called a funnel cake. The sugary aroma made his mouth water. He also smelled the snack called a hot dog, although the elongated meat had nothing to do with the domesticated animal.

His pulse accelerated when a couple of Trolleks marched into view, their ugly features making his skin crawl.

"What now?" Nira slunk back against the wall.

"Wait until they pass."

"We have to get into that clinic to find my blood sample, or at least the lab report. I'll ask one of the guests who works there, but we have to get by the receptionist first."

"A confounded human will be under orders to sound an alarm if we're not properly tagged."

"Trust me, Zohar. I know what I'm doing." She shook her head. "Damn, I hate this buzzing sound in my ears. I get it whenever I'm near the Trolleks."

"Remember our main objective is to follow them to the village where they retire each night."

"Yes, but if they do a vector shift to get there, we'll be left in the dust."

"We shall see." He peered around the corner. "The entrance is clear. We may proceed. Stay with me."

His hand itched to hold a weapon, but he forced himself to approach the door with an air of nonchalance. Pretending to be a staff member, he'd claim to have been sent here under orders.

And if he met a Trollek face-to-face? He'd have to hope Nira's immunity transferred to him.

They had no backup now. His teammates had their own assignments. This mission rested on his shoulders.

Pushing open the door, he allowed Nira to precede him. A receptionist greeted them from behind a wide counter.

"Hello, comrades. How may I help you?"

Zohar assessed the dark-haired woman. Trollek or human? Unlike the males, Trollek females showed no overt physical traits, and he lacked the ability to detect their pheromones. The only way to tell the difference was by the cunning in their eyes and the irresistible allure of their beauty.

"We're here to pick up a lab report." Nira maintained a bland expression.

"Your ID card?" The woman peered at her staff badge.

Nira presented her pass instead.

"Down the hall, around the corner, third door on the right."

Restraining a grin, Zohar trailed Nira down the sterile corridor with open doors leading into different treatment rooms. She stopped halfway, peering into a room holding chairs, metal instruments, and various other medical paraphernalia. For a pretend theme park, it looked real enough to send a chill up his spine.

"Here's where they took my specimen." She grimaced. "I hope we don't run into Gort."

"Who?"

"He's the Trollek technician who drew my blood." She bowed her head when a white-coated man emerged from a door ahead.

"Hello, I'm Dr. Dibell. May I help you? Are you hurt, injured?" He consulted his clipboard. "I've finished my roster of patients for the day. We're just getting ready to close. But if it's an emergency…"

"We're looking for the lab." Zohar kept any inflection from his voice. "We have orders to retrieve the results from a test done yesterday."

"Ah." The human's impassive face showed little emotion. "This way, please."

"He's role-playing a doctor," Nira whispered as they trailed the man.

Zohar nodded. "After orientation, he would have been assigned this position to enhance his experience. He'll go home and tell everyone how real it felt."

They followed the guy into a room strewn with lab equipment including racks filled with vials of blood. Zohar squinted at them. Surely, there were too many here just for practice. And if a Trollek tech obtained them, that refuted the role-playing aspect. Were the beasts collecting specimens from the general human populace for some other reason?

He glanced at Nira, who might have been sharing the same thought from the look of concentration on her face.

"Do you know the test subject's name?" Dr. Dibell stopped at a computer console.

"Nira Larsen," she replied, meandering to the counter to peer at the specimen labels.

"I'll check the database." A pause. "Sorry, that name isn't registered. Please spell it for me."

He still came up empty, while Zohar hoped he wouldn't summon his kabak for instructions. Nira, her lips pinched, rubbed her forehead as though the strain of their subterfuge gnawed at her.

"What do you do with these vials?" Zohar pointed to the racks. There must be dozens of them.

The false doctor shrugged, still engrossed in his role from the glazed look in his eyes. All the better to get answers from him, Zohar thought.

"We run them through our routine tests. Depending on the results, specimens are either destroyed or sent out."

"Sent out where?"

"I'm not given that information."

"Where are the samples from yesterday?" Nira's voice sounded strained. "I mean, tell me where I can find yesterday's specimens."

"They've been processed by now, mistress."

She turned to Zohar. "We have to find my results."

"Move aside." Zohar lifted the man out of the way, plopped into the chair, and began typing. Cracking encryptions had never been his strong point, but he might find something useful.

"You're violating protocol." The doctor backed away, his gaze darting between them. "I'll sound an alert."

"No, you won't." Nira advanced toward him, a determined gleam in her eyes. "You will obey me." Her forehead creased as though it took an effort to speak each word.

"As you command." The doctor snapped to attention.

"You'll tell no one about our inquiries. The receptionist is aware of our presence, so inform her we left empty-handed through another exit."

Zohar gaped at her. "Why does he listen to you?"

"He's in a suggestive state."

"If you say so." It sounded logical. Frowning, he glanced at the monitor. "Here's a database that might be relevant, but I need Paz to interpret it."

"Copy everything."

Zohar grunted his agreement. She made good suggestions, thinking outside the box. So far, she'd been a beneficial addition to his team.

Focusing his attention away from her riveting eyes, he withdrew a crystal from a pouch on his belt.

"This can hold the data. Do either of you know how to transfer it from this antiquated machine?"

Nira addressed the fake doctor. "Tell me if this computer has wireless capability."

"Yes, it does."

"Can your crystal receive the signals?" she asked Zohar.

"It will receive a targeted transmission if this computer recognizes it as another drive." The doctor's responsiveness baffled him. Confounded humans shouldn't act so malleable when ordered around by another human.

"Copy the file and then forget we made this request," Nira commanded. The fake doctor complied.

Zohar heard voices from the corridor. Uh-oh. It appeared a Trollek was coming to shut down the hospital for the evening.

"Hurry," he urged.

Several heart stopping minutes later, he and Nira pushed out a rear door, scurried across an open square, and dipped into a shadowed corner of the theater complex.

"Are you sure that man won't sound an alarm?" He backed against a wall, listening for sirens clanging an alert.

"He'll obey my orders." She sounded confident.

"If he describes us..." Zohar stared pointedly at her recognizable hair color. Most inhabitants on this planet possessed shades of brown, black, or yellow. Red indicated a less widespread genetic disposition.

She pursed her lips, changing his focus to her mouth. His body responded instantly as his blood surged south.

Her gaze flickered beyond him toward the plaza. "Look. The guests are leaving."

Twisting his neck, he confirmed her observation. All remaining guests streamed toward the exit to the main parking lot. Waiting to see what would happen next, he swiped his forehead. Although the sun descended, the early evening heat made sweat bead on his skin. Spotlights flicked on as the darkness progressed.

Staff members had yet to exit the park. If his theory was correct, they'd enter the underground complex to change before going home. He had every intention of being among them.

Minutes ticked by at an interminably slow pace. Spotting their chance when a uniformed couple strode by, Zohar tapped Nira on the shoulder. "Let's go."

They fell into place behind the pair. Washing his face of emotion, he followed them down a flight of steps, through a maze of utility corridors, and into an employee locker room.

A dozen or so other humans congregated inside the cramped space that smelled of old socks. Gray walls and harsh overhead lighting added to the institutional setting. An oppressive silence prevailed as the staff members shed their uniforms and dumped them into a laundry bin before donning street clothes.

Zohar pulled open an unlocked cubicle and tore off his uniform, switching his belt to the black trousers he wore beneath with a dark shirt.

Oh, no. A beefy Trollek arrived to stand just inside the door. The ugly brute wasn't one of the usual staffers judging from his back-country attire and the laser carbine slung across his shoulder.

Zohar's eyes widened. Was that a RAD-4 Special? Those were conscribed to military troops for restricted use.

His blood ran cold. At their last encounter several years ago, Trolleks had still preferred their old methods of knives, axes, and the occasional shell shedders. The fact that they'd progressed to military-grade energy weapons so rapidly concerned him. This confirmed his notion of a leak in imperial supply lines. Deeper worries consumed him until he noticed the Trollek's gaze had shifted in his direction.

Zohar bent over and pretended to fix his boot while his heart pounded, and his throat closed. When he risked a glance up, his instant relief that the fellow was no longer looking at him changed to consternation.

The Trollek shook each person's hand as they left. Extra insurance to make certain their confounding hadn't gone awry?

His hand hovered over the dagger tucked inside his boot.

No, he'd have to take the chance. This would be the ultimate test to see if Nira had conveyed her immunity to him.

Her fingers brushed his arm. "Zohar, do you see that? He's touching everyone."

"I know. If I... if things go wrong, you must complete the mission. Go to the village and look for the jamming device. It must be deactivated. Then use your ring to summon my men."

He turned away, willing his countenance to go vacant.

Joining a row of other humans, he shuffled toward the exit mimicking their robotic movements.

His heart jumped when the Trollek grasped his hand, beady eyes seeming to rip into his soul.

"Good job," the large fellow bit out in a gruff voice. "Remember, tell no one about your work here. You may rave about the guest experience and recommend a visit. Act normal. Return tomorrow at the same time."

"As you command," Zohar murmured, keeping his head low.

He heard Nira's subdued voice as she followed behind, repeating the words after being issued the same instructions.

"Wait."

The Trollek's command made Zohar freeze. He spun around, prepared to fight. The Trollek grasped Nira by the elbow.

"You are different." Twisting her arm, the Trollek surveyed her skin. "Ah, you have the mark, chosen one. You're intended for the village. Move ahead then."

The village? Even while Zohar breathed a sigh of relief and hustled onward, he wondered why humans were being sent there.

Catching a moment when they wouldn't be observed, Zohar steered Nira away from the trail of exiting staff members and into a corner.

He rolled his shoulders. Tension made his muscles taut and his neck ache. "Either that Trollek will spatial shift alone, or he will join others of his kind. My plan is to jump in on their vector after them."

"Oh, great idea. As soon as we land on the other side of wherever, we'll get taken."

"What did he mean, you are marked for the village?"

"How should I know? He noticed the needle stick mark on my arm from yesterday. When I took the Band-Aid off this morning, I noticed a red circle penciled there. The tech must have done it, but I don't remember." Her mouth parted. "The Trollek's touch had no effect on you."

Zohar's lips curved. "Apparently not."

"That's terrific." She beamed at him, eyes sparkling in the harsh overhead lighting.

"Indeed." Her scent entered his nostrils, compelling him to edge closer. "I'd better get another dose of immunity."

Stealing a kiss, he stifled a moan of pleasure when she responded by wrapping her arms around him. Chariots of the gods, she drove him mad. Their universe shrank, and his mind hurtled into a netherworld of warmth and longing and light.

Encroaching footsteps broke the spell. He flattened himself against the wall, drawing her with him, still feeling the imprint of her soft body and the plush fullness of her lips.

Focus on your mission, not on the effect she has on you. What kind of leader are you if you fail your men?

A fallen warrior like his father, who'd succumbed to a woman's wiles until she stole everything that made living worthwhile.

Fighting Trolleks was nothing compared to the battle that raged in his heart. More than lust was involved here. How could he protect Nira from harm when he had to guard her against himself?

Clenching his jaw, he listened to a set of heavy footfalls recede down the corridor. The Trollek from the locker room lumbered toward a section off limits to humans. Did the beasts collect there to spatial shift en masse? Or did they use more mundane means of transportation to reach their village?

He'd have to risk discovery to find out.

Signaling Nira to remain close behind, he zigzagged from wall-to-wall, keeping a safe distance behind the Trollek. He stopped when he saw the beast enter a room and heard a murmur of voices from within. Shouts of greeting and laughter told him this was their gathering place.

Waiting until the voices quieted, he ventured forward, Nira at his heels. When he reached the room, he halted in surprise.

A raised platform stood at the far end under a pavilion supported by four posts. One of the columns held a control panel. No one was inside.

A low chuckle sounded from behind them, followed by another person's hearty laugh.

Grabbing Nira's arm, he hauled her behind a stack of sealed cartons just as a couple of Trolleks stomped into the room.

Say, weren't those boxes similar to the ones he'd seen in the mailroom? Scanning the labels, he sucked in a breath. Could these solar calculators be destined for the village? And if so, why would the Trolleks be sending them there?

Nira nudged him. "Watch what they do."

He pulled out a small telescopic device from a compartment

on his belt and aimed it at the Trollek fingering the control pad. He caught the series of numbers before the two fellows stepped onto the dais and vanished in a flash of light.

Shoving the scope back into its pouch, he grinned at Nira. "Fortune is with us. This device must act as a mass transporter."

"Through a dimensional rift?" Her eyes shone in the enclosed space.

He sniffed the air. "I smell cors particles, but I detect them any time a Trollek shifts vectors, even from place to place on this world. It does not always mean they are jumping between dimensions."

"So their village could be somewhere on Earth?"

"That is correct. We should go through before someone else comes along."

She stood her ground, looking thoughtful. "Could this be one of the rifts where they enter our world? Large numbers of them could arrive here through this portal."

It couldn't possibly be this easy to locate one of their gateways. "We can study the markings on the control panel later. Once we destroy the jamming device, our sensors will be able to detect all the rifts."

She tilted her head, regarding him. "Tell me something. Why would these beasts call this tourist attraction Drift World if they knew you would zero in on the name?"

"Because they wanted us to find it."

"Why? To lure you into a trap?"

"Perhaps. Or else to distract us from the real point of entry. There remains one other possible explanation." He paused. "They named it thus to flaunt their superiority. We have defeated them in the past, but they have grown stronger. This could be their way of challenging us."

"Oh. Like, they're thumbing their nose at you."

"Their nose? They cannot sniff our presence like we can theirs. I do not understand this reference."

"Never mind. It's another slang expression."

"Come, we waste time." When she still didn't budge, he snorted in exasperation. "Now what? If we tarry, we might miss our chance."

"W-What if we can't get back?"

He pressed his lips together. "We shall deal with that problem as it arises."

"Right. Worry about it later." She gave a wan smile.

"You can choose not to go. In that case, return to our safe house. I will radio Kaj to look after you."

"No, you need me to protect you. I'm going."

Her words spread a warm glow through him. "Very well. Then prepare to spatial shift."

They stepped onto the platform, and he pressed the keys on the control panel as he'd observed. His nerves tingled. His hair lifted.

Then his vision blurred and all went black.

Chapter Ten

Nira blinked and opened her eyes to a forest glen with scrub brush and moss-draped trees. She stood on a platform similar to the one they'd just left at the theme park except this canopy was under the stars. Dusk spread its fingers overhead. Broad strokes of tangerine bled into navy.

Taking a deep breath of air redolent with the earthy aroma of wood and humus, she attempted to get her bearings.

Some sort of structures vaguely showed through a gap in the trees. Moonlight glinted off a lake in the distance.

"Are we still on Earth, or did we shift to the Trollek world?" She stepped off the dais.

Zohar, chin thrust forward, sniffed the air. His nose wrinkled with obvious distaste. "I am uncertain. I can take a reading on my PIP later, but we should not linger here."

"Your what?"

"My personal data device or Portable Intel Platform. Come, let us find the village." He gestured for her to follow him.

She rubbed her temples. Her head throbbed from that incessant buzzing noise. Could she mute it? Scrunching her forehead, she pushed against the mental barrier, but the effort only intensified her headache.

"What's wrong?" Zohar, on the path ahead, halted to glance back at her. His turquoise eyes gleamed in the fading light.

She couldn't keep her gaze from roaming away from his handsome face to his broad shoulders and then his trim hips. Her breath hitched as need spiraled through her. He looked magnificent with his regal bearing, muscled body, and stubbled jaw. His hair fell casually across his forehead, making her pulse pound. She liked his mussed look. It made him less stiff, more approachable. Not to mention sexy as hell.

"Nothing, I'm fine." She moistened her lips.

Her feet took her to a dirt trail strewn with leaves, twigs, and roots. Humidity hung in the air, similar to a Florida summer night. Wait a minute. Was that a cabbage palm?

"Zohar, do they have palm trees on the Trollek world?"

"Theirs is a more temperate climate." His gaze sharpened. "This looks like the terrain we just left."

"Exactly." She spotted a sign and scurried forward. "I don't believe it. We're in Turkey Lake Park."

"You know this place?"

"It's in Orlando. How is that possible?"

His mouth compressed. "We just did a short spatial jump. As for why no one else can see those buildings among the trees, the Trolleks must have screened it from human view."

"What does that mean?" An insect whined past her ear.

"They've shifted their village to another phase. It's here, but no one else can see it or hear anything. If someone walked over, he'd pass straight through that place as though it didn't exist. You and I are out of phase as well. That portal did more than just a spatial shift. It put us into the displacement field aligned with the village."

Gesturing for her to follow, he resumed his pace.

Nira didn't understand but trailed after him anyway. Perspiration pricked her brow. The sun's descent had done nothing to cool her skin. Night might arrive late on the wings of summer, but the air remained warm. Crickets chirped, adding to the clamor in her ears. Swatting a mosquito, she considered they had bigger creatures to confront than insects.

She'd only been to this park a couple of times before but remembered walking trails and picnic tables. At the other end of the park would be a swimming pool, lake, and boathouse. Yet the profile had changed, as though a village from the Middle Ages had been plopped into modern-day times. Because that's what she saw when they neared the buildings.

A village square stood dead ahead, intersected by dirt roads lined with buildings. Structures made of logs with thatched roofs predominated. People bustled about, both humans and Trolleks. The humans hauled buckets and carried boxes and wielded construction tools. Everyone wore a blank expression.

"Mind slaves," Zohar muttered. He'd paused behind a thick tree trunk to survey the scene.

"Looks like they're being used as a labor force, but to what end? Why would the Trolleks set up a base here?"

"That is what we must discover." He clapped a hand on her shoulder. "Listen, if anything happens to me, head back to the portal. Punch 3-5-0-10 on the control panel."

She wouldn't leave without him but didn't say so aloud. "Do you think the jamming device is here? Or could this be a staging area for something else?"

"Your guess is as good as mine." His brow wrinkled as though he contemplated their approach.

It could be a trap, Nira mused, wishing she'd worn long sleeves to guard against bugs as something stung her skin.

Did the Trolleks truly name their tourist attraction to lure the Drift Lords there? Capturing the warriors would remove a serious threat to their plans. Or were they merely, as Zohar had suggested, demonstrating their arrogance?

He removed his hand from her shoulder, and she felt bereft of his touch. How long would Zohar remain immune if captured? Biting her lower lip, she fought against a rising sense of dread.

Algie said they'd snagged a Drift Lord once. The man hadn't told them everything they'd wanted to know but he had talked. She supposed he'd been trained to resist interrogation, even when confounded. But still they'd gotten to him. She didn't want to imagine what means they had used.

Zohar needed her protection, and if necessary, her bargaining power. She was valuable to the Trolleks, who still had knowledge important to her. What did her blood analysis show? Did it reveal anything about her parentage? Where was her landlady?

Remembering her goals only frustrated her. She wouldn't get anywhere by doing nothing.

"Let's go. Grace might be here. She's too old to haul stuff, but she could be employed as a house servant." Nira spoke in a hushed tone, aware their voices might carry on the night breeze. "Look at that large residence at the far end of the street. A Trollek must live there. I'll bet he uses humans to wait on him."

Zohar's appreciative gaze swept her face, making a thrill leap through her. She liked how he valued her opinions. Her glance dropped to his mouth, so perfect in its chiseled contours. His lips applied just the right pressure when he kissed her.

She flushed and glanced away. Distractions could prove dangerous.

Zohar indicated a group of laborers. "Note how they bring crates into that building? I would like to see what is inside."

"We could split up. You look for the jamming device. I'll search for Grace. Meanwhile, keep your eyes open for people who have a mark on their arm like me. I don't understand what it means. Do they test everyone, or just certain people? And why would a blood test or some other trait determine if you're sent to the village?"

"Maybe they want only healthy individuals as laborers."

"Possibly." The beasts might be screening humans to obtain the most robust specimens for their heavy chores.

Or they might be taking blood samples for another purpose. Having seen enough horror movies, she didn't care to consider the alternatives.

An anguished wail pierced the air. The cry repeated, escalating into a series of screams that made her blood curdle. God Almighty, what was happening?

Zohar yanked her back several feet. "Fires of Agathorn, who is making that hideous noise?"

"It sounds like someone's in terrible pain." She cringed in empathy. "Can these people not hear it?" The workers went about their business as though nothing was amiss.

"They are confounded. Their minds are not their own."

The last scream got abruptly cut off. Activity in the village continued without disruption.

"That was horrible." Her feet, heavy as lead, remained rooted to the spot. Her heart pounded in her chest. Her stomach knotted. What was going on in this place?

She remembered the brawny Trollek strapping her to a table in the employment office, and a shiver racked her spine. If either she or Zohar fell into the hands of those creatures, they could be the ones next howling like a banshee.

"Are you sure you do not wish to remain by the portal?" Zohar's eyes glittered as he regarded her solemnly from the shadow of the trees.

"Not if I have a chance to rescue Grace."

She glanced at the town square, lit by lanterns on posts. The Trolleks may prefer natural resources for their construction materials, but they didn't skimp on electricity. Too bad. She and Zohar could have used darkness as a cover.

Torn between going with him and fleeing into the woods, Nira forced her feet to advance. She needed answers, and this place offered their best lead.

"Wait. You need to cover your hair. It is too distinctive." Zohar retrieved a bandana from a pocket and tossed it to her.

"My, you come prepared." She tied it on her head. "What else do you have secreted away?" His pants fit his hips as though molded to his contours. As she looked her fill, the fabric stretched tauter.

"I will be happy to show you later," Zohar promised in a husky voice. "Meanwhile, please refrain from paying me undue attention. The Trolleks will notice your interest."

Arrogant lout. "Look, there go some likely prospects. We can fall in with them."

A couple of men plodded along the edge of the road, carrying a bucket between them.

"It is time." Zohar sped off to join them.

Nira scurried after him, casting her gaze about for an object to snag so she could blend in. She snatched an empty carton standing by the roadside. Her glance swept the label. Solar calculators. Isn't that what Zohar said the Trolleks were collecting at the theme park?

They passed a pair of other workers lugging a trunk-sized crate. Nira stuck the box in front of her face and assumed an impassive expression. Trollek sentries stood at various inter-sections directing traffic. Anyone who strayed got poked with some sort of stick that made them shriek.

Bile rising in her throat, she lowered her head as she and Zohar accompanied the two guys into a timbered structure. Inside, stacks of crates and cartons were piled high. An interior door led to another room. She deposited her box just as a sentry stuck his head inside.

"Woman, come here."

Me? She glanced side to side, but she appeared to be the only female in the vicinity. Hoping Zohar wouldn't betray them, she bowed her head and obeyed.

"The Grand Marshal tires of his selection. Your species is too frail for his taste. Perhaps you can amuse him. Follow me."

Amuse him... how? Alarm flared along her nerves, making her muscles tense. She didn't dare refuse, or punishment would be swift. Zohar still had a chance to finish his mission if she complied. After shooting him a warning glance, she shuffled along in the Trollek's wake.

****

Zohar watched Nira follow the sentry from the building. Gods, how could he let her go? Who was this Grand Marshal, and what did he want with her? What would happen if they discovered her identity?

His fists clenched until he realized the other fellows were stealing glances his way. It wouldn't do to show emotion or he'd be taken next, and then he'd have no chance to save her.

He made a show of straightening a couple of crates then ambled outside. He saw her slender figure retreating down the street behind the burly guard. Striding forward, he stumbled when somebody whacked him on the head.

"You there." A Trollek, with jowls that could sweep the floor and a shock stick in hand, blocked his view. "Where do you think you're going? Get back to work."

Without argument, Zohar dodged back int the stockroom. Anxiety pitted his stomach. How would he reach Nira now?

Stacking a series of crates kept him occupied while he cursed his luck. As time passed, he'd lose his chance to pursue her, but then he rallied. Until the route was clear, he could at least investigate this building. Nira was resourceful. Surely, she could hold her own until he found her.

He waited until the other slaves had completed their tasks and filed out before ducking into the next room. Enough lamplight streamed through the window for him to see without turning on the lights.

Dozens of mirrors, in various assortments of frames, leaned against each other. One end of the room held a worktable where it looked as though the mirrors were pried from their frames. Broken pieces of wood splintered the sawdust-strewn floor. Strange. What did the Trolleks want with mirrors?

Returning to the anteroom, he peered at one of the crates. It had been shipped to an address in Windermere before arriving here via the portal. That location could be useful. Pulling out his PIP, he scanned the label.

So the Trolleks were shipping solar calculators to Drift World and mirrors elsewhere before bringing both items here. Were the calculators being disassembled also? What happened to the resultant parts?

He had to discover their plans.

Peering outside, he was glad to note street traffic had lessened. At least the Trolleks allowed their slaves to rest. If only he could snap one of these people out of their spell long enough to get some answers, he'd be a step ahead.

Nira had better luck at it. That pretend doctor had listened to her earlier as though she were his kabak. The man had done exactly as she ordered. How was that possible?

An unhappy thought leaked into his brain. Could she be part of an elaborate ruse to derail his team?

He thrust the notion aside as soon as it entered his mind. How dare he doubt her loyalty? Trolleks had attacked her house, abducted her landlady, and nearly killed her. She'd risked her life to distract Algie while he surveyed the theme park.

Ashamed of himself, Zohar blamed it on his father's influence. That betrayal had cut so deeply, it left him with an ever-festering wound that refused to heal.

Aiming to find her and absolve his guilt, he slipped around the corner of the building and headed down an alley, passing by several residences inhabited by Trolleks being served dinner by their slaves.

This was merely a meal break. He wondered if work resumed through the night, or if the people were done until sunrise. Whoever dropped with fatigue could always be replaced. Was this why these particular people were chosen, because of superior physical stamina?

A large hand clamped on his neck, delaying any further speculation.

"Hold, human." The hand squeezed. "Tell me why you are out beyond curfew."

Zohar cast his gaze downward and slumped his shoulders.

"I was told to bring order to the storeroom. I was just on my way to my quarters."

A painful jolt struck the side of his thigh, and his legs crumpled. He fell to his knees.

"Proceed to your bunk. If I see you out again, I'll send you to Tent Ten."

Having no idea what that meant but aware it represented a threat, Zohar struggled to his feet. His muscles quivered from the shock. "As you command," he mumbled between spasms.

Shuffling off in what he hoped was the right direction, he rounded a corner before breathing a sigh of relief.

He'd only progressed a few feet more when he glanced down. A trail of rust discolored the packed dirt road.

No, not rust. Dried blood.

Chapter Eleven

Nira preceded her escort into an imposing two-story residence belonging to the Grand Marshal. Instead of a thatched hut, this wood-frame building had a beamed ceiling along with painted walls, glazed windows, and polished plank floors. Electric sconces illuminated a series of comfortable rooms decorated with upholstered furniture.

Past the foyer, she glimpsed a dining room with a long rectangular table. It held a golden bowl laden with fruit and a set of chinaware. Her gaze flew to the gray-haired woman polishing a silver candelabrum.

Hope kindled in her chest that it might be Grace but when the woman turned, she suppressed a groan of disappointment. Still, her mentor might be employed elsewhere as household staff. Would this Grand Marshal keep records of the slaves who came through the transport device?

"Upstairs." The burly Trollek prodded her in the spine.

She trudged up the steps, realizing she knew next to nothing about the Trollek lifestyle. This could provide an opportunity to learn more about them—assuming she survived whatever they had planned for her.

The guard shoved her toward a bedroom opening off the upstairs hall. Inside, a beefy Trollek sat cross-legged on a rumpled bed that faced the door. His nose was so long it curled inward toward his thick lips. Tufts of hair sprouted from his pate, almost obscured by his large ears.

Nira stifled a giggle. He reminded her of the Ferengi on *Star*

Trek: Deep Space Nine. Did these beasts like their ears rubbed, too?

"Who does she belong to?" The Trollek's nostrils flared as his derisive gaze scanned her.

"No idea, Your Eminence. Thought you might like a young one even if she is a bit too thin."

"She isn't marked for Tent Ten, is she?" The Grand Marshal favored her with a scowl. "I don't mess with the experiments."

"I didn't see no tag. Ask her yerself about her kabak."

Her guard wasn't particularly respectful, making Nira wonder if the Grand Marshal's post was considered civilian or military. Remembering how Algie had argued with the med tech, she made a mental note to discuss this defiant attitude among their ranks with Zohar next time she saw him. Where was he? Was he safe?

"Tell me who commands you."

She glanced up, startled. The Grand Marshal glowered at her.

"Algie," she blurted, before realizing that might get her into more trouble. What if this guy summoned her nemesis? She doubted Algie would be so blasé about their next encounter.

His gaze flickered, as though that name meant something to him. "Remove that scarf from your head so I can see you better."

Was she supposed to obey any Trollek in the village? She complied, hoping a bulletin hadn't been sent out matching her description.

The ugly brute studied her, his eyes narrowed, his breaths raspy. His eyes gleamed as though she were a bird he'd like to swallow whole. "You don't look like you'll last long, but we'll see. Leave us." He waved at her escort. "And shut the door on your way out."

She willed her mind to blank, so he wouldn't sense her apprehension. He beckoned her closer. Tiny quills of hair dotted the blemished flesh on his face like mini antennae.

It took an effort not to grimace as she approached. How

could she turn this situation around to get information on Grace? There must be a database somewhere in this house if His Eminence truly was the administrative authority.

She halted before him and pressed her lips together as he stroked her arm. Schooling her features to hide her distaste, she searched for weapons in the periphery of her vision. It wouldn't do to kill the village leader, but perhaps she could disable him long enough to escape.

She hoped Zohar was having better luck and didn't do anything foolish to save her. Finding the jamming device was infinitely more important than one human life. If his team couldn't shut down the portals and stop the dimensional drift from expanding, it meant curtains for everyone.

"Tell me, human, has your mistress taught you how to please a male of my caliber?" The Grand Marshal sneered while a dribble of drool leaked from his wide mouth and ran down his chin.

She shuddered inwardly. "I understand you like your ears massaged." Leaning forward, she applied herself to the task. Ugh, they felt patchy like eczema. *Don't throw up*, she told herself. *Focus on your mission.*

While he rolled his eyes in pleasure, she surveyed the room. A nightstand held a key ring, one of those sticks all the Trolleks carried, and a leather belt. The wall sconces precluded lamps, but that wooden chair might come in handy. She didn't spot anything else that could be useful.

"Enough. Show me what else you've learned." The Grand Marshal's eyes gleamed in anticipation as he lay back on the pillow.

"Um…" She froze, unable to think what to do next.

"Never mind. I will instruct you. Strip off your clothes and then undress me."

"As you command."

She slipped off her tank top while frantically searching for a means out of this mess. When none came to mind, she stalled by offering a generous view of her cleavage. The beast licked his thick lips, watching her with beady eyes.

Steeling herself, she reached for his plaid shirt. His body odor made her itch to wrinkle her nose, but she resisted. Her fingers trembled as she unfastened his shirt, afraid he would become impatient. A hairy chest revealed itself, scarred from old wounds.

Tossing aside the shirt, she hesitated. No way could she undo his pants. His crotch bulged, showing his physiology in that department to be larger than a human counterpart. His endurance might last a lot longer, too.

Her throat went dry. This charade had to end now.

"Why do you delay? Get on with it, or perhaps you need an incentive." Rolling to his side, the Grand Marshal reached under his bed to retrieve a whip with serrated metal tips.

If you were confounded, you'd show no fear. Do not react.

"I only wish to perform the huggabear ritual." The words popped into her brain. "It is so much more enjoyable."

"I have not heard of this practice. Describe it." He flicked the whip lightly against his palm.

"Well, you remove your pants and lie face down on the bed." She forced herself to stroke his abrasive jaw. "Then I mount you from behind. You will have to see what happens next, but it's incredible."

"Hmph." He dropped the whip, reaching up to fondle her breasts while considering her offer.

She bit her lip, lifting her face to stare at the wall. She should snatch that whip and wrap it around his neck. If Princess Leia could strangle Jabba the Hutt, she could do it, at least enough to shut off his air and render him unconscious.

"You did not obey my order. Remove your clothing. I will not tell you to do so again, human."

She swallowed, afraid she'd have to comply or he'd realize their spell didn't work on her.

Her thoughts racing, she slid out of her pants, flushing under his lecherous perusal. If only she could ask questions, she'd at least gain information while seducing him. But slaves did not question their masters.

She didn't blink when he rubbed her breasts through her bra and dipped his pudgy fingers down her cleavage. Instead, she swallowed against the bile rising in her throat and the nausea churning her stomach.

Snorting in triumph, he leapt to his feet and stripped off the rest of his garments while Nira gritted her teeth. He flopped himself onto the bed on his stomach. His buttocks showed not one ounce of flab, making her wonder how much strength would be required to subdue him.

"Pleasure me, woman."

Nira reached for his belt, curled on the nightstand.

"Wait."

Her hand froze. When she realized he was about to roll over, she pretended to be tugging off her panties.

"Your scent is… unusually arousing. We'll do it my way first." He yanked her down across his body.

"No." Panic seized her. She'd kept it at bay, but now hysteria threatened to erupt. Her breaths came short and fast.

He grasped her panties, and she knew that once he ripped them off and flipped her onto her back, the game would be done.

"Now you'll see what a real male can do," he crowed.

No, I won't.

She pushed against the mental barrier in her head, seeking to diminish that incessant buzzing so she could fight him. A resistant force countered her efforts. She pressed against it, forcing the noise into a mental closet with an agonizing effort that left her breathless. With a final push, she shut the door.

A sudden silence ensued, during which the Trollek's sweaty body went flaccid.

Nira thrust him away and hopped from the bed. *Quick, before he rouses himself.* She grabbed her clothes and yanked them on, uncertain about what had happened. Did it matter? This gave her a chance to get away.

Then she spared a moment to glance at him.

Her face blanched. Oh, no. His chest wasn't rising.

She checked his pulse. His skin felt clammy. No rhythm beat beneath his wrist.

As realization hit, she recoiled in shock. The Trollek hadn't merely passed out. He was dead.

And she had killed him.

****

Zohar glanced at the shuttered building nearest the stain on the ground and wondered at its purpose. Unlike the tradesmen's shops he'd spotted along the main street, this place held no sign swinging from an overhead post.

Instead, its front door displayed a *No Entry* type of symbol. It wasn't a wooden door like the others in town, either. He knocked, and his knuckles hit metal.

Curiosity compelled him to take a closer look. He pulled a tool from his belt and used it to jiggle the lock until the latch clicked. The noise sounded loud in the night air. Hoping no one would chance upon him, he twisted the knob, swung the door open, and slipped inside.

A coppery odor assailed him. He grimaced, unable to identify it and yet recognizing its familiarity. His nerves hummed with unease.

From another pouch, he whipped out a thumb-sized dazlite and flashed it around the perimeter. Good, no sign of a silent alarm system. Just to be certain, he took out his PIP and did a scan. Clear. The Trolleks must feel secure that unauthorized persons would be unable to gain access.

After shoving the PIP back into its holder, he flicked the light around the large room. Built into all four walls were rows of tiny numbered boxes. Strange. What did they keep in there?

Stalking over, he slid one open. A data crystal met his glance. Several more drawers revealed the same contents.

This was some sort of filing system? Figuring he'd check out what they contained later, he pilfered a couple of crystals and stuffed them into a pocket.

Halfway back to the front door, he aimed his light at the ground by chance and noticed an uneven surface. Crouching, he traced a geometrical outline with his fingers. Rectangular in shape, it appeared to be about six feet long and located in the exact center of the room.

Something was there, but how to get it to reveal itself?

He straightened, casting his light along the walls, careful to skip past the shuttered windows. The beam hit a button by the doorframe. He'd assumed it was a light switch, but maybe not.

Just to be on the cautious side, he peeked out the front door, making sure no one was present before slapping his hand on the button. He shut the door and whirled as lights flooded the interior.

In the center of the room, a rectangle of packed dirt slid away, and a metal table ascended on hydraulic legs. The table was rimmed with grooves and had a blackish discoloration.

His gut sinking, Zohar pulled out his PIP again and thumbed the keys. The resultant reading confirmed his suspicion.

Chariots of the gods, this room was some sort of extermination chamber. The reading indicated phase weapons fire set to dissolution. Bodies were being vaporized, and from his quick analysis, they were human.

A muffled cry made his head jerk up. It came from outside. A louder series of wails followed in a rising crescendo.

Jabbing the button to squash the lights and retract the table, he weighed his options. At this point, he didn't think he would find the jamming device here, but he'd sure like to know what caused those horrifying sounds.

After making certain he'd left no evidence of his incursion, he eased the door open and slipped outside.

He hoped it wasn't Nira issuing those screams. Rushing around a corner in the direction of the noise, he collided with someone speeding from the opposite direction.

"Nira!" He glimpsed her untidy clothes and frantic expression. "Thank the stars. What happened to you? Are you all right?"

"No, I'm not." Her eyes went wide in a pale face. "I mean I'm fine physically even though he tried to… you know. I couldn't help what happened. I-I had to stop him…" Her lower lip trembled. "Let's talk about it later, okay? We have to get out of here."

"Did you hear those screams? Something bad is going down in this village."

"No kidding." Another wail pierced the night. "What are they doing to these people?"

"Let us go see, and then we can leave." Assuming he and Nira made it to the gateway, and assuming the portal worked in reverse.

Nor could they just walk into the park named after a fowl. They were out of phase with their reality and wouldn't have any substance there. The only other possibility might be to wait for a power fluctuation, which could cause the displacement field to crash.

Zohar didn't voice his concerns. Weaving a path toward the bungalow from which the cries emanated, he slowed to a cautious pace. Light streamed from within between cracks in the logs. As the windows on this structure were shuttered, that allowed their only opportunity to peer inside.

"The widest crack is too high for either of us to reach," Zohar whispered. "I'll have to lift you on my shoulders."

"Are you sure I won't be too heavy for you?"

"Huh. Try me." He was glad to note the color returning to her cheeks along with her sardonic tone. "Up you go." He held his clasped hands out for her.

Muttering several colorful expletives, she stepped onto his proffered base and boosted herself onto his shoulders. While he struggled to maintain his balance, she stretched toward the gap. He raised his hands to steady her, clamping onto her legs.

"Good God, there's a lab inside. A girl is strapped to a

table." She spoke in a low, tremulous voice. "They have an IV attached to her, and a Trollek is injecting something. Two aides are present, making recordings."

A cry of pain issued forth from inside, then it cut off.

"She's convulsing. Oh no, Zohar. I think… I think… she's gone limp."

He'd heard enough. "Get down. We cannot do anything for her."

The breeze picked up, tossing hair into his face. It smelled like rain. Thunder rumbled in the distance, confirming his impression. But that wasn't what made his nape prickle. His feet picked up a vibration underfoot. A patrol headed their way.

He herded Nira back toward the village and the gateway at the other end, but they hadn't gone far when the streetlamps brightened, illuminating the night. A siren clanged, and sentries poured into the streets, cutting off their exit.

"Uh-oh, they must have found…" Her voice cracked.

He didn't ask what she meant. No time.

"Get inside." He tugged her into the storeroom where they'd started their exploration. "We have to wait until things quiet down." Neglecting to share his fear that they might get caught before that moment arrived, he flattened himself against a wall.

She brushed a lock of hair off her face. It shone like fire in the moonlight from the window. Afraid they'd be discovered, he gestured for Nira to follow him into the adjacent room. His boots kicked up a swirl of sawdust on the way.

"What are all these mirrors doing in here?" she asked when he'd shone his dazlite around the four walls.

"Good question. I noticed them before."

She spied a worktable. "Curious. Why would they be removing the glass from the frames?" Before he could venture a guess, she peered into a nearby upright mirror. "Ugh, I'm a mess." She pressed a hand to her temple.

"What is it?"

"I have a headache, but it'll go away. What's in there?"

"Where? This is as far as it goes."

"No, it isn't. Behind this crate is another door."

"Let me see." Hearing voices from outside grow nearer, he examined the outline on the wall. Pressing his hand against its edge, he gave a gratified exclamation when a latch clicked and a door swung open.

"Someone's coming." Nira pushed past him.

As soon as he joined her, the door slid shut from behind, enveloping them in darkness.

She shrieked, bumping into him.

"Remain calm." His light reflected from dozens more mirrors stacked several deep against the walls. "There may be another exit."

"Or not. I can't even tell where we entered."

"Right there." But he found no telltale outline on the wall nor was one evident when he shifted several heavy frames. "Or was it on that side?"

Intent on finding their entry point, he lost sight of Nira and ended up in a twisting aisle lined with mirrors.

"Nira, where are you?" He panicked when he couldn't find her.

"Over here." Her voice sounded muffled.

His reflection bounced back at him from scores of mirrors as he searched for her. Where could she have gone? This place didn't appear that large from the outside.

He rounded a corner and heaved a breath of relief when he spotted her slim figure.

She appeared engrossed in examining a gilt-framed mirror. Her mouth hung open as she reverently traced the edges of the ornate frame.

Then she touched the glass.

With a flash of light, the mirror sucked her in, and she vanished.

Chapter Twelve

Nira tumbled onto a spongy surface, at first aware of the sun gleaming overhead and a warm breeze kissing her skin. Night had turned into day, but that wasn't the only change. Instead of the earthy smell of woods, she sniffed the sea: a fresh salty tang that cleared her brain and chased away her headache.

Waves crashed onto a shore and birds twittered overhead. Then those sounds receded as a loud thump shook the ground beside her. Zohar had plunged to the earth, knocking her in the hip.

"Hello, Alice. Welcome to Wonderland." Leaning on an elbow, Nira scanned their surroundings.

They'd landed on a carpet of moss overlaying a rocky precipice. Black rock, to be precise, that ended at a cliff. The plateau stretched to a tropical forest at the base of a mountain range.

"Where are we?" Zohar drew a knife from his boot and rolled to his feet, a wary look on his face. His muscles tensed as he assumed a fighting stance.

"I'd say we're not in Kansas anymore."

"Kansas? What is that?"

"Never mind. Relax, there's no one here. You can put that thing away."

Standing, she brushed dried moss from her pants. If she'd looked a mess before, now she must be worse. She smoothed her hair, her trembling hand betraying her uncertainty. "Any idea where we are?"

His eyes scrunched. "We must have passed through another gateway. This cannot be good. If the Trolleks did not orchestrate it, the vector shift represents a spontaneous crack in the space-time continuum."

"Meaning?"

"The rate of dimensional drift is exceeding my prediction."

"Oh." Refusing to grasp the portent of cosmic implosion, she focused on her own reality. "On the good side, we've escaped the village."

"True. Do you recognize this place? I presume we have spatial shifted again to another location on your planet."

"Those palm trees and the humidity indicate a tropical climate, but Florida doesn't have mountains." Her gaze rose to the green-covered peaks in the distance. "Could we have passed the dimensional barrier into the Trollek world? Or maybe we're in another galaxy. Do spatial shifts occur between star systems? Surely this phenomenon isn't confined to Earth?"

"Since Earth is the spearhead for the Trollek invasion, I would assume we are still here." Edging toward the overhang, he peered below. "Note the black sand beach. This plain looks like it came from a lava flow. See if you recognize any landmarks."

She peeked over the edge. Waves ebbed and flowed onto a pristine beach fringed with coconut palms. The sea melded from aqua to deep cobalt blue, the horizon stretching to infinity with no ships or other bodies of land in sight.

"Many Caribbean islands are volcanic," she said. "So are Hawaii and other places in the Pacific Ocean. Considering the time change, it's more likely we're there."

"Let me see if I can get a fix on our coordinates."

He pulled his scanner from a pouch inside his belt while she studied him. A lock of hair rode his forehead, creased in concentration. He cut a manly figure with his broad shoulders, sinewy muscles, and taut abdomen. Her glance roamed south to his sexy hips and long, lean legs.

He fiddled with his instrument. A second later, his

expression brightened. "You guessed correctly. We have traveled to one of the ley lines in the Pacific basin."

"The what?" She shaded her face with her hands, wishing she had her sunglasses.

Zohar gave her a broad grin. "The dimensional faults underlying your planet fuel an energy grid that intersects at twelve distinct geographic areas. These points, known as Vile Vortices, are sites of anomalous activity. The lines connecting these points are termed ley lines."

"You mean, places like the Bermuda Triangle are vortices?"

"Indeed. They act as doors between dimensions when rifts occur. As I explained earlier, just as Earth has tectonic plates, dimensional plates exist on a cosmic energy level. These plates are usually in alignment except for occasional drift."

"And that's when strange phenomena occur in these regions?"

He nodded, his eyes gleaming as he warmed to the topic. "When the drift is wide enough, vector shifts can occur between dimensions. This is how Trolleks harvested human slaves in the past. The rifts close naturally when cors particles, produced at the event horizon, reach critical mass. The resultant pressure forces the gateways to shut."

"Except now, since the Trolleks have forced the process, the drift is widening to disastrous proportions," she clarified.

"True, and I fear these random shifts will increase in frequency." Zohar paused, his brow folding. "Did you sense anything strange when you came through?"

"A momentary flash of disorientation. Why do you ask?"

"I felt as though a force pulled me down… toward another place."

From his sudden glower, she surmised it hadn't been a pleasant experience. "Nope, that didn't bother me. Maybe your ability to detect cors particles is affecting you."

"I do not think so. It was unlike that plane I visit when you and I, when we…"

"Yes?" Facing him, she tilted her chin upward, wanting to

experience the otherworldly sensation that happened when he pressed his lips to hers.

His gaze shifted to her mouth. He stepped closer, his eyes darkening, desire written on his features.

A raucous cry from above dispelled the mood.

"We have company." He reached for his phase gun, but it wasn't there. "*Has 'pute*," he muttered, drawing his dagger.

A winged creature dove at them. It had sharp talons, a spear-like beak, scales, and a long tail. More cries joined its war whoop. Three additional silhouettes circled on the horizon.

"Pfrells! Make for those trees." Zohar set off at a run.

Nira charged toward the vegetation. Would they reach it in time?

She raced ahead, reaching the perimeter of the trees just as one of the flying beasts sideswiped her. The impact sent her sprawling onto a layer of dead leaves. Her face ate the ground, dirt clogging her nostrils. She coughed, spitting out grime.

Zohar hauled her to her feet. "Keep moving."

At his prodding, she staggered past clusters of bamboo, curtains of vines, and prickly-trunked trees until the sunlight muted and the only sounds were rushing water and occasional bird songs. The overhead canopy provided protection from the swooping predators, but it meant she and Zohar could not return to the open plain. Would they find another route home?

She stopped mid-trail, panting. Hot, thirsty, and tired, she refused to budge another inch without a plan. "We must be safe from those things now. What are they?"

Zohar, his face haggard, allowed his shoulders to slump. "Pfrells are a hunter species native to the Trollek world. The creatures must have passed through the rift. This is a bad omen."

"Great. What do we do now?"

"Search for water. We will drink and then find shelter until we can summon aid."

They trudged through a lowland rainforest, crunching over dried leaves, skirting tree roots, and brushing into cobwebs. Nira was sorely tempted to yank off her increasingly tattered top and use it to swat insects. Sweat dripped between her breasts and down her spine. She swallowed, her throat dry. As the sound of gushing water grew closer, she increased her pace.

"Look." She pointed to a stream tumbling down a rocky slope to a pool below. Eager to reach the water, she half-tripped, half-tumbled down the ridge.

"Careful, we are not sure it is safe." Joining her by the pool, Zohar deployed his scanning device. "It appears free of contaminants."

"Good, I'm dying for a drink." Crouching, she cupped her hands, dipping into the clear stream to drink her fill.

Her thirst quenched, she sank onto the rocky ledge and observed the pool where it emptied into another waterfall. They'd been climbing uphill without realizing it. Her stomach growled, while post-adrenaline fatigue sapped her strength.

"I'm starving." She pressed a hand to her middle.

"Me too. We should search for something edible." He compressed his lips, his usually proud posture slouched, but the stoic warrior never once complained.

Her nurturing instinct fueled her energy, and she pushed to her feet. Batting aside prickly ferns and broad leaves, she hunted for food until she spied a clump of banana plants. Summoning Zohar, she instructed him to gather an armful of ripe fruit. They returned to the water's edge.

"Bananas are tasty." Zohar smacked his lips after taking a bite once she'd shown him how to peel the skin. He downed several bananas in succession then gulped down a drink of water.

Nira ate her fill, a languorous warmth stealing into her limbs once she'd satisfied her stomach. She perched on a rock, absorbing the sun's rays, grateful for the momentary peace.

"Peculiar shape, is it not?" Zohar held up a banana, a sexy grin on his face.

"Yes, Captain, I get your drift."

He raised an eyebrow.

"O-kay, that was a pun. A play on words. You know, Drift Lord. Dimensional drifts. Oh, forget it. My hands are sticky. I need to wash." She scrambled to her feet.

Zohar's teeth shone white. "You have many demands, little one. I can think of another."

"Yes?" She swallowed, aware of where his thoughts led.

"Let us cleanse ourselves, and then I will show you."

"Fine." She glanced around to ensure they were quite alone. Feeling bold, she divested herself of her soiled garments. His heated gaze followed her as she padded naked from rock to rock until reaching a grassy area. She slipped a toe into the water, testing the temperature. Delightfully cool, the clear stream showed nothing to fear in terms of marine life.

Taking the plunge, she jumped in, deciding quick action would be best. She splashed around, until her body adjusted and the water felt warmer. Overhanging trees and trailing vines produced a shady awning, while wild orchids provided a palette of color among the greenery. Water gushed and trickled down the rocky waterfalls, obliterating any other sounds of the jungle.

"Join me." She gestured to Zohar, who'd stripped and stood proud by the grass-covered bank, showing off his muscular build.

Her gaze feasted on him, admiring his broad shoulders and powerful chest. She let her glance roam southward, past his taut abdomen to where his arousal jutted like a flagpole. A coiling warmth sprang from her belly.

"Are there… fish in this pond?" His face reddened, while she wondered why he hesitated.

She dragged her gaze to the crystal-clear water and its pebbled bottom. "I don't see any, unless they're hiding among those tree roots." Mangrove-like trees edged the secluded pond, but there didn't appear to be much wildlife.

"O-kay," Zohar said, imitating her favorite expression. "Here I come." He gingerly stuck a foot in the water.

"Don't tell me, big guy, that you're afraid of swimming with the fish?" A smile curved her mouth.

"I do not care to share my space with slimy creatures of the deep."

"Oh, for heaven's sake, you don't mind battling flying reptiles and terrible trolls, but you're scared of little fishies? Give me a break."

"I am a warrior of the Drift Lords. Nothing fazes me."

Thrusting his shoulders back, Zohar strode forward until he was thigh deep in the water. Then he dunked himself all the way, reappearing with his hair dripping and a big grin on his face.

"You have made a man of me, my *carona*."

She pointed at his blatant arousal. "Oh no, I think you've done that quite well on your own."

Diving underwater, she swam to him and tickled his privates. Surfacing, she laughed while water droplets cascaded around them.

Zohar's agile hands slipped to her breasts. "Think you can tease me, do you? I can play this game."

She gasped when he tweaked her nipples, sending a shock wave to her core. Her knees weakened, and she leaned into him.

His other hand crept down her belly and farther south. When he touched her *there*, reason faded. His strokes increased, bending her to his will, suspending her rationale until passion overwhelmed her.

****

Zohar wrapped his arms around her pliant body as he lowered his mouth. He kissed her, his tongue probing her contours until she parted her lips and allowed him entry. He couldn't believe her responsiveness and how she unleashed his wildest desires. Her soft curves imprinted on his hard body, maddening him to the point of wanting her to be closer still.

A tiny warning light blinked in his brain, but he ignored it. She'd never harm him. Besides, he wasn't weak like his father. He could control his lust, but just not now.

The current caressed their bodies as they wound together, mouths glued in a never-ending kiss. When he couldn't breathe, he came up for air. Her eyes, glazed with passion, enticed him to further heights.

Unable to wait any longer, he lifted her onto his shaft. She slid onto him, sheathing him in her silken heat. With a needy groan, he rocked against her, rejoicing in their unity.

Their surroundings dissolved as he hurtled into a zone of warmth and light, conscious of nothing except her incendiary murmurs and her womanly scent. Lost in a haze of passion, he fastened his hands on her buttocks while she rode him like a *wigonk*—or canine—in heat. Flames consumed him, driving him toward a channel of molten fire, and then he erupted, spilling into her while she convulsed her climax.

Once their shudders subsided, she withdrew from him. She stroked his jaw with a gentle finger as they stood waist deep in the water. Droplets glistened on her luscious breasts.

"That was amazing." She rested her hands on his shoulders.

"It is always amazing with you." He brushed her lips lightly with his own.

He couldn't deny the hold she had on him. It was more than just the transference of her immunity to the Trollek touch. He needed her to satisfy his soul, to bring him home, and that set off his internal warning alarms more than anything.

They belonged to different worlds, and even if he wanted to be with her, a permanent bond between them would never happen. Should it be necessary for him to take a wife, he'd long ago vowed to play no part in choosing his queen. Not that his people would ever let him make the same mistake as his sire.

For now, he had to be satisfied with sex. That's all she could mean to him. He felt like a *riff* for using her, even though she didn't ask for anything in return.

"We should get dressed." His voice brusque, he ruffled her short hair. He didn't want to hurt her. She was brave, determined, and resourceful. She deserved someone better than him with whom to spend the rest of her days.

Careful of his footing over the slippery stones, he retreated to the grassy slope where they'd left their clothes.

Once presentable, he withdrew his PIP. "I will tell Paz to retrieve us in the shuttle."

"Oh, yeah?" Nira had donned her clothes and stood air combing her hair. Her skeptical look told him what she thought of his idea. "See if your signal goes through from here."

Her caution proved correct as Paz didn't respond, nor did his teammates. "I will try again later. Perhaps we should go toward higher ground."

Tall trees provided a shady canopy as they trudged through the jungle. Smaller plants grew in the undergrowth, their leaves wide to catch the dappled sunlight. Ferns, vines, and parasitic air plants embellished the tree branches. Bamboo arched overhead like crossed swords. A cluster of purple orchids drew his gaze, while nearby, a bright green bird took flight. Further along, they spotted a large brown and white animal drowsing under a tree.

"Do not wake it." Zohar urged her forward, dodging layers of dead leaves that might make noise and creeping past a grassy swathe.

After they'd hiked for several hours in the afternoon heat, Nira paused to wipe sweat from her brow. "I can't go on. I'm too tired." Dark circles rimmed her eyes.

He gave her a reassuring pat on the arm. "If we climb to that ledge over there, I might be able to get a signal through." But when he tapped his comm unit from the higher vantage point, again he got no response. "Forget it. Something in the composition of this mountain must be interfering. I should have made contact down by the beach."

"We were too busy dodging those creatures. We'll figure something else out."

Zohar nodded, his brain too fogged with fatigue to think straight. Insects buzzed by his ear, while he scratched at a bite on his arm. At this pace, they'd be covered with itchy welts by the day's end.

After a brief rest, they shoved onward. Smells of animal droppings mingled with the earthy scent of decay. Sheened in sweat, he yearned for a cool breeze or another dunk in a stream.

"Daylight is waning. We should try to reach a higher elevation before nightfall."

She slapped at a bug. "I agree. Hey, what's that? I see something up ahead."

Low-hanging fronds and leafy plants battered him as he took the lead through the brush.

When he spied the crumbling ruin between the trees, he raced forward. This island wasn't totally uninhabited after all.

Broken walls stretched like supplicating arms toward the sky. Their absent tops had long since given way to the elements, except for one structure up a flight of stone steps that still had its roof intact. Moss grew in the cracks, widened by vines seeking new outlets.

"I think it's a temple." Nira gestured toward a faded mural on one wall depicting a battle scene with a fierce woman on a winged horse flying above a troop of warriors. "And that's obviously a shrine."

She indicated a display of reddish clay spires backing a ledge with an assortment of goblets, bowls, jugs, and even a corroded metal kettle. Seashells were strewn about the ledge as were green papayas and some kind of lumpy purple fruit.

Alarm frissoned up his spine. "This sector must be inhabited. We should leave." Narrowing his eyes, he surveyed the forest for hints of movement.

"Wait, look over there."

Nira sped to a stone monolith with a broken top. Engraved on its sides were carved symbols. She sank to her knees, splaying her fingers over the cold stone. Then she glanced at her timepiece with dawning astonishment.

"What is it? What have you found?"

"These markings are similar to the ones on my watch. This could be runic writing."

She lifted her face to regard him with sparkling eyes.

"Don't you understand what this means? Our arrival here may not have been a coincidence. I was meant to find this place."

Chapter Thirteen

"What do you mean these symbols match your watch?" Zohar crouched beside her in front of the stone column.

Nira pointed to the monolith. "You see these markings? Their vertical strokes are characteristic of runic inscriptions. I've been studying this type of writing for my doctorate."

"You are studying to become a doctor?"

"No, I'm going for my graduate degree in comparative mythology." Nira gritted her teeth. Had he not been briefed on their educational system? "I study legends of the Norse gods."

He glanced down his nose at her. "I do not see how this is relevant."

"Look." She showed him her watch face with its unique marking. "The writing on the column exhibits strokes like these. My birth parents left me this watch. I assume it means I have Scandinavian blood. My red hair could have resulted from intermarriage if another ancestor came from the British Isles."

"Those lands are distant from here, yes?"

"That's right." She sucked in a breath, about to reveal a secret she'd kept for six years. "I only learned the truth about my birth when my adoptive mother lay dying. She told me I'd been abandoned on a church doorstep as a baby. This watch was found inside my blanket."

"And this is why you study old legends? To learn about your true parentage?" His brow wrinkled in puzzlement.

She tapped the wristwatch. "My professor told me this symbol is runic in origin. It's derived from a variant called Elder

Futhark. If you're familiar with Earth history, the runic alphabet predates Christianity."

"You are saying your watch contains ancient lettering?"

"Correct. Unfortunately, Professor Mulligan has been unable to interpret this rune. They're difficult to decipher because the lettering can be combined into many different forms."

"Have you sought help elsewhere?"

"I haven't had the time before now." Or the funding, she added silently. Pursuing her studies plus her research required more money than her budget allowed.

He tilted his head. "You scour old legends to find a key to this language?"

"Yes. This symbol on my watch could be important."

"How so?"

"The root word for runes means *secret*. In the old days, people believed the runes were of divine origin and that the writing had magical powers. Only oracles could interpret their meaning."

He shrugged. "If you say so. You should let Paz have a look. He's our linguistics expert."

She held out her hand. "Can I use your scanner? I'd like to record these markings before we leave. This could be the reason why we ended up in this particular place. We were meant to find this inscription. It might be connected to my past."

An arrow twanged into a nearby tree. She lifted her head.

A bald man, his nostrils pierced by two feathers, aimed a bamboo bow at them. A necklace made of animal teeth encircled his thick neck. Horns and seashells adorned his body, naked except for a loincloth. His face, painted with fierce black streaks, grimaced as he let loose another arrow.

"Run." Zohar prodded her.

"I can't leave until we record this writing."

"Do as I say. This man is merely a scout."

Zohar grabbed her hand and dragged her toward the jungle.

A tremor shook the ground.

"What's that?" she asked, startled.

"Who knows? If this island has volcanic origins, perhaps one of the craters is still active."

She scanned the horizon. Mountains blocked their view, but was that a cloud in the distance or a spurt of steam? One of the ranges did appear to be more angular. She liked the looks of the other gentler, nature-tamed slopes better. Which way should they go?

Bloodcurdling whoops turned her veins to ice. A herd of tribesmen tramped into view. Their murderous expressions and pointy spears made the choice for them. Sprinting past another ledge that held bowls filled with fruit, she cursed herself for ignoring the signs earlier. She should have realized worshipers still lived here; meaning she and Zohar had trespassed on a sacred site.

They crashed through the brush, gaining distance from their pursuers. However, it soon became evident that they'd made the wrong choice in terms of direction when the ominous rush of water sounded ahead.

Nira halted as the woods ended at a wide chasm. It stretched across a gorge where gushing water tumbled through the narrow channel. The only way to cross was on a rickety suspension bridge. Its bamboo underpinnings looked none too secure, gaps showing where pieces had decayed.

"I can't go on." Her heart skipped erratically, and her feet froze. Heights had never appealed to her.

Zohar squeezed her elbow. "We have no choice. You go first. You weigh less."

"It won't hold. We'll fall." Her hands gripped the railing, but she couldn't bring herself to step onto the first rung.

"Nira, you must do this." He ducked as a flurry of arrows were launched at them.

Air whooshed by her ear. "I'd rather get killed by a spear than be crushed on those rocks below."

"We will make it across the ravine. I promise."

"I'll hold you to those words." She swallowed, her throat tight.

"We must complete our mission. Go on."

A terrifying war cry came at their heels. Her pulse hammering, she forced her feet to step onto the swaying bridge.

Her hands, slick with sweat, grasped the wood rail. She concentrated on putting one foot in front of the other. Her knees shook so badly she stumbled several times. Zohar steadied her from behind.

Please, please, let me reach the other side.

She focused on their target and avoided looking down. The bridge swung with each step. Her heart pounding, she progressed at an interminably slow pace.

When she finally reached the opposite bank, she took a deep, shuddering breath and pried her tight knuckles from the rail.

An urge to fall to her knees and kiss the earth evaporated when she noted the half dozen shrunken heads on poles. Her spirits sank. No wonder the natives hadn't followed them.

"I assume this means there's a rival tribe on this side. They can't be friendly either."

Zohar gave her a reassuring pat. "Follow the water upstream. We need to reach higher ground."

An iguana scurried by, pausing to glare at them before vanishing into the brush.

Fortunately, they encountered no other creatures, human or otherwise, as they climbed. Rocks morphed into boulders. Slopes extended into mountainsides. Mahoganies and rosewoods gave way to cedars, oaks, and beeches. The air grew cool, making her shiver when they finally stopped to rest. Mist permeated the air, adding to the dampness.

"You are cold, and it is getting dark." Zohar faced her under a pine tree. "We should find shelter for the night."

She lifted her chin. "I disagree. We should keep moving if there's any chance of rescue tonight."

"You are limping." He pointed to her grime covered shoes. "Are you injured?"

"No, but it feels like I have a blister. Don't worry, I'm fine, all things considered."

From his look of doubt, she knew she must look a mess: her hair tossed, her clothing torn, her skin smudged.

Closing the distance between them, he stroked her cheek. "You are very brave."

Her heart swelled at his tender touch and his admiring glance. "That's only because I have no choice. I didn't ask for this trouble. It all started with that stupid job interview."

"It was not chance that brought us together, little one. You said so yourself. Our fates are entwined."

That's not all I'd like to be entwined, she thought, gazing up at him. His eyes were the clearest, most brilliant turquoise she'd ever seen. She could lose herself in them—if Zohar returned her regard. But whenever they made love, he kept part of himself in reserve. Did he view her merely as a member of his team with whom to spend a few hours of pleasure?

She couldn't blame him for guarding his heart. While she yearned to determine her birthright, she feared what she might find. There had to be a reason why the Trollek spell didn't work on her. What if her bloodline traced back to those creatures? Did Zohar already suspect as much?

The Trolleks kept humans for slaves and used women for bedmates. Did offspring occur from such couplings?

Maybe she was one of them.

But even as this chilling thought surfaced, she realized it didn't matter. Zohar's world waited for his return, same as hers. Regardless of his feelings for her, he'd leave in the end. And she'd had enough of being left in the lurch. It wasn't only her adoptive father who'd deserted their family—her birth parents had also abandoned her. She would not form another emotional attachment, only to be cast aside again.

****

Zohar dropped his hand, the imprint of her soft skin on his fingers. Nira was without doubt the most baffling female he'd met. One moment, she looked as though she wanted to kiss him, then in the next instant, her lips pinched and her eyes chilled.

Clearly, she blamed him for her predicament. *I have no choice,* she'd said. He had dragged her into this quagmire, and since then, she'd become an essential part of his team. He couldn't let her go, not only because he still needed her, but also because she remained a target for the Trolleks.

Their lives truly were twisted together, whether she liked it or not. As for their personal desires, those had no place on a mission. His job was to quell the enemy, not seduce an ally.

In the meantime, it was just as well for Nira to be wary of him. Nothing permanent could come from their union. While Zohar might marry someday, it would be a political match. His people would stand for nothing less, and neither would he. He'd learned long ago to limit passion to the bedroom, and to remove it from his heart.

Wondering why he felt so lost when she turned away from him, he strode after her toward the summit they'd spotted ahead.

Dusk deepened the sky as he halted at the crest, awed by the vista before them. The sea sparkled far below a rocky cliff. Their piece of land was a sizable island divided by green-covered mountains, at least on this side. The peaks marched into the distance where a cone-shaped mountain towered over them all. Jungle covered the interior.

"It's beautiful." Nira stood at his side, a stiff breeze whipping hair into her face.

Zohar resisted the urge to fold her into his embrace. His duty was to find a way off this island, not be distracted by her soft curves. That mental sinkhole was the very thing he needed to avoid.

"I don't see any electricity or other signs of modern civilization. This place must rarely get outside visitors." He swept an arm in a wide gesture encompassing the trees. If they hadn't met the natives, he'd have assumed the place to be uninhabited.

"Look in that direction." Nira jabbed her thumb. "Do you see smoke?"

"Indeed." He could barely make out the vaporous trail drifting upward from the forest. "More primitives on the prowl?"

"Possibly. We should investigate. I'm starving. If it's an encampment, we could steal some food."

"All right, but first let me see if I can get a signal through to Paz on the ship."

She always came up with the best ideas. How could he ever let her go free when he… when his team needed her valuable input?

He triggered his comm device but static answered him. "*Has'pute*, I still can't get through."

"What if I use the ring you gave me for emergencies?"

"That will not work. It uses the same frequency as our comm units. Forgive me."

She faced him squarely, her eyes large and luminous. "For what, Zohar?"

"For failing you." Her scent drifted his way, tantalizing him. It took a force of will not to drag her into his arms. "I have not done my duty in protecting you. We may be stranded on this island."

Nira studied him, her head tilted. Whatever she read on his expression made her gaze soften. "It's not your fault. I'm the one who touched that mirror and landed us here."

He didn't deserve her compassion. Nay, he didn't want it. Caring about what she thought made his task more difficult.

"We should go see what's causing that smoke." Despite her words, she remained facing him, her gaze drifting to his mouth.

His southern region responded with a strong jolt. He leaned closer. Her seductive scent compelled him to taste her wares. The succulence of her lips drew him near. He could almost inhale her sweet breath.

No! Disengage. This is not the time.

He stiffened and turned on his heel, berating himself once again for his weakness.

"Let us move on. Follow me."

Realizing he'd sounded curt, he advanced, listening for her footsteps in his wake. He wove between the pines and tall oaks, bending his knees as their descent steepened. The light dimmed the farther they went into the lowland forest.

He slowed his pace when they approached the source of the curling smoke. "Do you smell that?" The aroma of roasting meat flooded his mouth with saliva.

"I smell a barbecue all right. Let's hope it doesn't belong to a cannibal tribe."

His heart rate accelerated. "Proceed with caution." Drawing the dagger from his boot, he crept forward.

A twig cracked underfoot. He froze, waiting. When no answering shout came from nearby, he resumed his steps. With practiced stealth, he dodged from tree to tree in a half-crouch, until he reached a clearing.

He parted a couple of branches to get a clear view. An old man sat before a campsite fire, his white beard and hair illuminated by the flames. Focused on the fire, he roasted a wild rabbit over a makeshift spit. Bowls of fruit spread around him as well as several water jugs.

"Where did he come from?" Nira nudged Zohar from behind as she jostled for a view. "Maybe he's willing to share his meal."

"Or not."

Zohar didn't miss the large staff leaning against a tree within easy reach of the man's grasp, nor his powerful frame under the canvas robe he wore. Nonetheless, he stuffed the knife back in his boot, hoping to negotiate without the use of force.

"You can come out from your hiding place." The old man lifted his gaze to peer directly at them. "You've nothing to fear. Join me at my evening meal, my friends."

Zohar took Nira's hand, and they emerged together. Somehow, he felt more secure holding her, as though she gave solid substance to his soul.

The old man's world-weary eyes regarded them from under furry white brows. "It's about time you found me. I'd about given up, what with all your chasing around the island and exploring the hills."

"You were expecting us?" Zohar regarded the fellow with astonishment.

Nira elbowed him and spoke in a hush. "I told you we were brought here for a reason. Maybe he's part of it." She addressed the stranger. "I'm Nira Larsen, and this is Zohar Thorald. May we sit with you?"

"Please do." The man made no move to alter his comfortable perch. "You may call me Askr. Here, you may want to wear these to keep warm."

He yanked a sack from behind the tree, rustled out a couple of woolen ponchos, and tossed them to Nira and Zohar.

They ate in silence. Zohar tore into the roasted leg the old man gave him and followed it with a cluster of sweet berries and a drink of water. His stomach satisfied, he pulled on the cloth wrap. Warmth seeped into his limbs as he relaxed cross-legged before the fire.

He glanced at his companion. Nira had finished her meal, looking like a cat that just finished a bowl of milk. She huddled in the poncho, her eyes half-lidded. This day had taken its toll on them both.

He might as well start the conversation. "We were hoping to find a way home before nightfall. Do you know a way off this island?"

"That depends." The old man studied each one of them in turn. "Gather your strength. You will need it in the coming darkness."

"Yes, it's getting dark. Soon we won't be able to see the path." Zohar shifted impatiently.

"I don't think that's what he means." Nira pinned the old man with her keen gaze. "Tell me, what exactly is coming?"

"You will learn the answer during your journey." His

malachite eyes swung toward Zohar. "It is your duty, son of Thor, to protect this woman." He reached inside his robe and withdrew a shiny object. "Take this amulet. It will keep you from harm."

"What did you call me?" As Zohar's hand closed on the pendant hanging from a gold chain, his palm heated.

"You are a descendant of Thor, born of the Aesir, dweller of Asgard, the great celestial palace."

The old man spoke nonsense. Perhaps he had been confounded. Had the Trolleks touched him and driven him mad?

His hope plummeted that they'd find an easy route home. At least Askr had given them a decent meal and warm clothing. As for the gift, he could always barter it if they met more hostiles.

He strung the chain around his neck. As he flipped it inside his shirt, the pendant flashed as though reflecting the fire. He flinched when its warmth penetrated his flesh. What type of metal produced this effect? Surely not pure gold.

The man pointed a wavering finger. "The charm will protect you, my son. Do not remove it."

Nira skirted the fire to kneel by Zohar's side. "Show me that necklace." Her fingers grazed his skin, stoking an ember of desire he hadn't realized he'd left smoldering.

Lifting the pendant on its chain, she rotated it back and forth in her hand.

"I know this design. I've studied it in history class. This looks like Thor's hammer."

"Who is this Thor you both mention?"

"Thor was a warrior god of Norse legend. He carried a magic hammer, holding it with iron gloves. The hammer returned like a boomerang when thrown. He called it Mjollnir. A dwarf forged it, like so many other magic objects owned by the gods."

"A dwarf." Skepticism dripped from his tone.

"I can tell you many stories of Thor's bravery, but not now." She turned to their host. "Why do you call Zohar a son of Thor? He's not even from… he comes from somewhere far distant."

"I can only tell you what is written in the stars, Nira Larsen. Or should I say, in the runes."

She sat up straight. "You know how to read runes?"

"I do not." The old man tilted his head.

"Then how—?"

"So it is foretold. So it comes to pass."

"You speak in riddles." Zohar's fatigue made him snappish. "What we really need is to find a way home. I repeat my earlier question: how do we get off this island?"

"Be patient. I have more to say." The old man stroked his beard, his gaze fixed on the fire. "Remember, son of Thor, it is your duty and that of your brethren to protect the daughters of Odin. You must combine your powers to defeat the coming darkness."

"How did you get here?" he persisted, annoyed by Askr's avoidance of the issue. "Do you have a boat we can use?"

Nira put a placating hand on his arm. "I do not think he speaks of nightfall. Hear him out."

"You are correct." Askr smiled at Nira, but his eyes didn't show any mirth in the dancing light from the fire. "A permanent night will overtake us should you fail."

"Algie mentioned something about a Coming being nearly upon us. What did she mean?"

"You seek answers, Nira Larsen. If you wish to find them, you must drink from the Fountain of Wisdom."

"Excuse me?"

"The Fountain flows from a well deep within the sacred forest. When you taste the water, you will be able to read the runes." Askr gathered a handful of dirt and sprinkled it on the fire to douse the flames.

Without the fire to provide heat, moisture curled into the clearing on wispy tendrils. It thickened into a mist that swirled around, embracing branches, caressing rocks, and obscuring trails.

Zohar's head turned when he heard a loud fluttering overhead. His pulse leapt. The pfrells couldn't have found them here, not this far from shore. A blur of red flashed in the trees. Whew, not a pfrell then. His nerves had made him jumpy.

"It's a cardinal." Nira scrambled to her feet, brushing dirt off her clothes. "A type of bird," she added for Zohar's elucidation.

Zohar stood, his eyes scanning the trees. The bird flitted from branch to branch. Overhead, the sky bled with navy. Soon it would be too dark to go anywhere. They'd have to spend the night here.

Meaning to demand a response from Askr regarding the use of a boat, Zohar spun to address him.

Empty space met his astonished gaze.

The bearded man had vanished into the mist.

Chapter Fourteen

"Where did he go?" Nira stared at the spot where the old man had sat. A lizard scampered over a rock then performed a similar disappearing act into a tangle of roots.

Zohar scratched his head. "We just looked away for an instant."

"Could he have vector shifted like a Trollek?"

Zohar's brow folded. "I do not smell cors particles. Perhaps he just vanished into the forest. This mist makes it hard to see past the boulders."

"I suppose." Nira watched the cardinal soar overhead and alight on a branch. It twittered a song and then flew a few feet to another limb. There it cocked its head, as though trying to communicate. "You know, I think that bird wants us to follow it."

"Have you taken leave of your senses?" Zohar quirked an eyebrow. "First the old man talks gibberish, and now this?"

"Call it a hunch, if you will. And I don't believe Askr spoke nonsense. His words made a weird kind of sense." The bird hopped to the next tree. "Let's see where it goes."

"We should head to the coast, try to pick up the old man's trail. I'll wager he has a vessel hidden somewhere."

She propped her hands on her hips. "I beg to disagree. You hired me as your guide, remember? Let's follow my instincts this time."

The bird flitted through the branches. They followed up an incline to a higher elevation where the trees thinned and a stiff wind blew. Despite her poncho, Nira's teeth chattered. The air had grown colder, and she was exhausted.

Her muscles quivering, she scrabbled for a handhold on the solid rockface. A curse escaped her lips when her fingers slipped, but she managed to get a grip and boost herself to the next level. A short roll over a protuberance brought her onto a flat plateau. She heaved in huge gulps of air, waiting until Zohar caught up. She could barely see in the dark. The rocky edges blended into each other.

The bird hopped onto a ledge, warbled, and then flew into a shadowy crevice between two boulders. Great, they'd reached a dead end. But maybe their climb didn't have to be a total loss. That gap might lead to a cave where they could spend the night.

"Sorry, I guess I was wrong." She scrubbed her face, so tired she wanted to find a patch of moss and curl up on the ground. "We'll head for the coast in the morning. Meanwhile, let's see if that space leads to shelter."

As soon as she stepped between the two towers of rock, blackness enveloped her. Lacking a sense of orientation, she lost her balance and toppled over. She flailed her arms but reached empty air as she fell into a void. Pinpricks of light swirled in front of her, making her head reel and her stomach somersault.

Then her teeth clanged together as she landed on a soft surface. Zohar's grunt indicated his arrival next to her.

She lay there, stunned. Her consciousness registered a canopy of stars in a night sky. Branches rustled in a warm breeze.

"Holy guacamole." Her eyes rounded as she discerned the boathouse outline in the dark. "I think we're back at Turkey Lake."

Zohar, rubbing the back of his neck, leveraged himself to his feet. "You mean, this is where we first entered the Trollek village?"

"That's right." She scrambled upright, peering into the dark. A bird warbled a familiar song then went silent. She didn't observe the cardinal anywhere. "The village is probably still here but we can't see it. We're not in that spatial displacement field like before when we came from Drift World."

He sniffed the night air. "That means we fell through

another spontaneous tear in the space-time fabric. I smell cors particles. Moreover, I felt that same heavy pressure as before when I entered the rift." His eyes gleamed in the moonlight.

"We should get out of here. I don't want to meet any more bad guys tonight. And you should be able to call your team, now that we're back on home turf."

Zohar whipped out his device and keyed it on.

"Where have you been, *rageesh*?" Paz demanded in a loud tone that Nira could hear. "I have been unable to raise your signal. We feared the worst."

"Nira and I are safe, but we need a ride home. Take my coordinates and send Dal to pick us up."

"At once, sire."

"Schedule a debriefing for the morning. Meanwhile, Nira and I are exhausted. We must rest."

"Understood." A pause. "Dal is on his way. Paz out."

Too tired to speak, Nira comforted herself with listening to Zohar's steady breaths as he wrapped his arms around her, and the cocoon of the night enveloped them.

****

Zohar awoke early, alert, and aroused under a light quilt. Nira slept on her side next to him. Layers of red hair fanned the pillow. Her long-lashed lids made half-crescents against her unblemished skin. Her chest rose and fell with each breath, the sensual outline of her breasts making his blood surge.

Resisting the urge to wake her and satisfy his lust, he climbed out of bed to head for a cold shower. He wanted to consult with his men before she joined them.

Lingering to gaze upon her bared neck, he shook his head to clear away the haze of desire. By the faith, he wanted to crawl under the covers and bury himself in her until the sun reached noon. But duty called and so did many unanswered questions.

Still, he couldn't help himself from planting a kiss on her

soft cheek. She stirred, shifting her position. The sheet slipped off one shoulder, and her sweet scent beckoned him.

Cursing his weakness, he turned away. He had much to discuss with his men. Voicing the main thing on his mind would not be possible, though, because he could never admit how Nira occupied his thoughts and seared his soul.

He headed into the sanitation facility. As leader of the troupe, he occupied the master suite with its king-sized bed, armoire, mirrored dresser, and nightstands in a polished cherry wood that pleased his regal eye. More importantly, the room came with a private lavatory.

Fifteen minutes later, after he'd dressed in a clean pair of denims and a pullover shirt promoting a local ale, he sat around the dining table with four of his teammates. Paz, linked from the ship, completed his crew.

Originally, the Drift Lords had dozens of members from different worlds. During the Great Purge, a seventeen-year span in which their league was outlawed, their numbers had decreased until only nine remained. Two were lost during the last Trollek incursion, and now Rayne. That left one team of six, Zohar's unit. The genetic variant that allowed them to sniff cors particles was a rare occurrence. With such great losses, the Drift Lords had become a dying breed just when they were needed the most.

Drinking the strong, dark brew called coffee, Zohar regarded his team. They sat at the opposite end of the house from where Nira slept.

"We shall begin with the investigation into Rayne's death. Paz," he said on an open speaker to his crewmember on the ship, "have you completed your analysis of Rayne's body scan?"

"Aye, Captain. It confirms death from phase weapon fire, a Monix T-6 laser pistol, to be precise. As for estimated time of death, that requires a more extensive forensics assessment."

"Never mind. We have more pressing matters at the moment. Borius, did your investigation planetside yield any results?"

The young man scraped a hand through his blond hair. "I

tried to restore the image on the hotel security footage, but someone did a thorough job of erasing the data. My retrieval efforts came out too fuzzy to be of much use."

Zohar tapped his finger on the table. "The wound was not self-inflicted, nor were there any signs of a struggle. Did Rayne let in someone he knew?"

He'd address the problem of the weapon later. It bothered him that this was the same gun his team carried. And if it wasn't one of them, who else had access to Imperial armaments?

"The killer could have been waiting for him." Borius waved a hand. "I interviewed the staff responsible for our floor, plus the registration people. The only item of interest was a call asking if our party had checked in yet."

"Did you trace it?" Kaj, wearing a thoughtful expression, leaned casually back in his chair.

Zohar, when grabbing a quick bite earlier, had complimented their engineer on his provisions: not only food, but also more clothing, computers, and other necessities. Kaj had also made sure their security net covered the perimeter. There wouldn't be any surprise vector shifts into the house.

He missed Borius's reply. "Say again," he ordered.

"I suspect the caller may have been Lord Magnor inquiring about our arrival." The youngest team member fidgeted under his commander's scrutiny.

"Has anyone heard from Magnor?"

At his team's negative response, Zohar frowned. "Whether or not Rayne's death and Lord Magnor's disappearance are related remains to be seen." He sipped his coffee. The bitter taste reflected his disappointment at their lack of progress.

"Rayne was killed by a laser pistol," he went on, "but the Trolleks used disruptors at Grace's house. Possibly Lord Magnor got hit by disruptor fire, also."

"You think the Trolleks took Magnor?" Paz's voice issued from Zohar's comm unit, where it sat on the table.

"I did not detect any cors particles."

"Then who?"

"Perhaps the assassin sent after me." Zohar leaned forward, clasping his hands in front of him. "If you recall, at our previous encounter, the Trolleks still relied on shell shedders." Their term for old-fashioned projectile weapons. "Now they use Class One armaments that are supposedly restricted for military use. It is my theory someone is selling them these newer weapons, perhaps the same person who took out Lord Magnor."

"We did not confirm Lord Magnor's death," Borius reminded them. "Those *riffs* who ambushed us were just as surprised to find him gone. There's still a chance—"

"I know," Zohar cut in. "My point is that the person who masterminded the ambush might be the same man who murdered Rayne."

"Then the assassin could be the one supplying arms to our enemy?" Dal raised his eyebrows. As their demolition specialist, the lean man was best qualified to tackle the investigation into potential arms smuggling.

"Yes, that is a strong possibility." Zohar drummed his fingers on the table.

"*Rageesh*, your devotion as leader of our team goes without question." Paz's lazy drawl became more pronounced. "But we know factions on Karrell would be happy if you never returned home. If you're looking for a connection, any one of their supporters could have sent an assassin. This same man could have forged an alliance with the Trolleks."

"I agree this smells of treachery. But surely you do not believe my political enemies have supplied the Trolleks with arms just to take me down?" He barked a harsh laugh. "I can hardly credit the beasts would open a rift for that reason alone. They have their own agenda."

"Nonetheless, we cannot ignore the broader implications." Dal jabbed his finger in the air. "Suppose we defeat the Trolleks and seal the rift. You must still face your opponents."

"Let me worry about that."

Zohar clenched his jaw. Had the assassin been sent to eliminate him in case the Trolleks couldn't do the job? In which case, need he look any farther than his own team? While they'd all passed stringent background checks, that had been some time ago. Since then, any one of them might have become a target for corruption.

Despising himself for suspecting his friends, he decided to make subtle inquiries. It wouldn't do to leave any stone unturned. But how to convince them meanwhile to focus on the greater threat posed by the Trolleks?

"I agree with critics who say our empire is archaic." Head bent, he spoke in a low tone. "Our system of government hasn't changed in years. Not only did my father nearly destroy our world, but he set back our progress by decades. That proves how too much power in one man's hands can be dangerous."

"Precisely why you must take your rightful place, *rageesh.*" Yaron's melodious voice held a soothing note. "Faced with our rapid pace of change, the people need constancy. They need you as their ruler."

He stiffened his spine. "I would never take the risk of ending up like my father."

"You are too hard on yourself." Dal pointed at him for emphasis. "You can resist the beasts' power. A Trollek female would never weave her spell on you."

No, but a feisty redhead can scorch me with a mere glance. While his mind might be strong, his loins responded whenever Nira walked into the room. He could not risk betraying his people the same way as his sire.

"This argument is old. Dal, use your resources to find the trail for illegal arms trade."

"Aye, Captain."

He tightened his mouth. "Regardless of who is out to stop us, we must focus on our primary mission. Nira and I found a portal at Drift World that vector shifted us to a Trollek village, screened from view in a local park."

A memory threaded into his mind, causing a sense of unease. It had to do with their time in the clinic and Nira talking to a theme park guest. But the thought wouldn't surface, so he pushed it aside. He did remember the vials of blood, however.

"The Trolleks are collecting solar calculators and mirrors for some obscure purpose. They are also taking samples of human blood. I do not know what they intend with these specimens, but I did obtain a copy of their computer data."

He handed the crystal to Kaj. "Take the shuttle and transport this to the ship. Paz can analyze it. Nira had a sample of her blood drawn yesterday when she accompanied Algie. Tell him to search for her file."

He reached into his pouch, withdrew two more crystals, and gave them to his engineer. "I lifted these from a building in the village." He described the place. "I'd like to know what sort of data they contain. Not a word to Nira. She does not know of my find."

"Did I hear my name?" Nira, yawning, sauntered into the room. She'd tossed on a pair of drawstring pants and a tank top.

His body stirred at the sight of her tousled hair and sleepy eyes. "Yes, we have started our debriefing. Get some food if you wish. Kaj stocked the refrigeration unit."

"Oh yeah? All I saw in there last night was a bucket of fried chicken, two six-packs of beer, and a bag of grapes. Don't you guys know how to shop?"

"We stocked up at the local supermarket." Kaj pocketed the crystals, keeping them hidden from view. "I didn't notice anything super about it. The produce lacks vibrancy and has no smell. Meats are cut and wrapped into tiny, unrecognizable portions. Cider comes in plastic jars, not jugs. Do you not have any natural food marketplaces on your world?"

Nira rolled her eyes. "Put grocery shopping on the agenda for this morning. I don't eat chicken for breakfast."

Zohar grinned at her. "Try the cookies. Look on the counter by the heating unit. And bring some out here, will you?" He'd developed a taste for those chewy brown rounds with the chocolate chips.

She returned with a platter and a glass of water a few minutes later.

Kaj stood to give her a seat. He went to lean against a wall.

"What did I miss?" she asked, while Zohar's gaze zoomed to her cleavage as she sat across from him.

Did she have to reveal her assets so blatantly to his men? He'd have to teach his woman to dress more modestly.

His woman. He couldn't help feeling possessive of her—even if he knew he shouldn't.

"I mentioned how you and I got from Drift World to the Trollek village. There we noted crates of solar calculators being stored along with mirrors. The mirrors are first shipped to an address not far from here. Kaj, check it out."

Kaj dutifully scribbled down the location.

"What about the jamming device?" Yaron stroked his dark beard while regarding his leader.

"Unfortunately, we found nothing relating to the jammer." Disappointment colored his tone. "Then we got separated and Nira ended up in the Grand Marshal's residence." He swung his gaze in her direction. "I am still not clear on how you escaped. Relate to us what happened."

Her skin flushed, and she cleared her throat.

"I'd hoped to gain information on Grace but I didn't learn anything new. When I left the Grand Marshal's house, I heard a girl screaming. That's when Zohar and I ran into each other."

Zohar could tell the topic made her uncomfortable from the way she squirmed and avoided his glance.

The Grand Marshal must have upset her since she couldn't talk about it. He'd seen her disheveled appearance and knew there was more to her story than she'd admit.

"Nira, we are your friends." He spoke in an encouraging tone. "If anything happened that requires retribution, tell us now and we shall take care of it."

Chapter Fifteen

"The Grand Marshal intended to use me for his pleasure." Nira glanced away, unable to look the men in the eye. "I was brought to his chamber."

"Did he… did you…?" Zohar gave a convulsive swallow, as though choking on his words.

"No. He didn't get too far. I, uh, grabbed hold of a lamp and cracked him on the head."

"You knocked him out?" Dal, his wiry body shirtless, displayed a physique any woman would admire. His incredulous tone made her bristle.

"She rocks with the punches." Zohar puffed out his chest. "I am not surprised she fought her way to freedom."

"Thanks, big guy, but it's roll with the punches, not rock. And I was lucky I found a servant stairway when the guard outside wasn't looking. I got clean away before they discovered me missing."

"Your flame-colored hair is distinctive. This Grand Marshal will have reported your visit." Dal gave her a reproving glance.

I doubt it. Dead men don't talk. However, his henchmen might mention how they found their boss dead in bed with no visible marks on him.

"Maybe so, but they don't know how I left the village."

"I agree." Zohar addressed his men. "I do not believe they are aware of the rift in their own storeroom. Nira's falling through the mirror allowed our escape."

"What do you mean?" Yaron's soft-toned voice strummed through the air.

With his soulful eyes and heartthrob black hair, he'd make an appealing vocalist. Nira resolved to ask him to sing for her one day. The mournful song he'd offered for Rayne had teased her with his talent.

"One minute we were at the village in the middle of the park, and in the next instant, we found ourselves on an island." Nira's stomach growled. Cookies didn't constitute a satisfying breakfast. "It appears one of those mirrors contained a rift. I touched it, and zap. We were transported."

Zohar explained his theory about a spontaneous tear in the space-time continuum allowing for their spatial shift.

"This isn't good." Borius shook his head of blond hair.

"At least I was able to fix our location in the Pacific basin along one of the ley lines. But that is not all." Zohar gave them a twisted smile. "When I crossed the rift, I felt something pulling me down."

Nira cut in, remembering something else they should mention.

"You forgot about that screaming we heard in the village. We discovered a hut where the Trolleks were holding a girl prisoner. She was strapped to a table and had an IV line. One of the beasts injected a substance into her. She convulsed and then went still." Nira's throat clogged at the memory.

Kaj stroked his bristled jaw. Wearing a black shirt and pants, the team's engineer looked ready for a secret ops mission. "Are you implying that not all humans sent to the village are being used as slave labor?"

"Yes, and listen to this. You know how Algie got a tech to draw my blood when I was there yesterday? One of the guards at Drift World looked at my arm. I hadn't even noticed the red circle drawn around the needlestick point. He said I was marked for the village."

"Meaning what?"

Zohar answered, his face solemn. "We noticed a lot of blood samples in vials in the clinic at Drift World. This may sound far-fetched, but what if they are screening people for something specific?"

"Like a gene or antibody?" Paz's voice came through the speaker.

"Right, and when they find this factor, they send those guests to the village for further testing."

"Ugh." Nira shuddered. "Add that to the list of things we have to investigate. And I still have no idea if Grace is alive or where they might be keeping her."

"Tell us about this island where you ended up. It cannot be a coincidence that it rests on one of the ley lines." Dal got up to pace, giving her an enticing view of his powerful back muscles. They rippled as he moved, stealthy as a cat.

Zohar saw her looking and scowled. She gave him a smug smile in return. What right did he have to claim her? Just because they'd been intimate didn't mean he intended anything permanent. He'd leave as soon as he defeated the Trolleks.

"We met primitives who chased after us." Zohar folded his arms across his chest. "Then we encountered an old man who gave me a golden amulet." He showed the gift while the others murmured in appreciation.

Nira pushed back her chair and stood. "You're leaving out the most important part."

"Which part was that?" He gave her a smoldering look that let her know where his memories led.

Her cheeks warmed as she envisioned the tropical pool where water gushed over a rocky cascade and his hands explored her body. "In the jungle, we found an old temple ruin with a column that has carvings similar to the lettering on my watch."

Nira explained how she'd been left as an infant on a church doorstep with the watch as the only keepsake from her true parents. Her professor in comparative mythology had identified the markings as runic in origin but she'd been too busy raising her younger sisters to research the subject before. Now she had the time, and that had been her goal before she met Zohar.

"If you hadn't abducted me, I'd have found a job by now and none of this would have happened."

"I did not abduct you." Zohar's mouth thinned.

"You shoved me into your van. I didn't have much choice."

"If I recall, you willingly accepted my offer to act as guide."

"Yeah, about that. When do I get paid?"

His eyes chilled. "We will speak of this later. You cannot blame me for the Trolleks's interest in you. They attacked before we even arrived on the scene."

"Well, there is that."

Zohar turned toward his youngest crewmember. "Borius, as our xenobiologist, you should take a look at those ruins. That is, if we can find the place again, and if we can subdue the hostile natives."

"Tell them about those flying monsters." Nira meandered to the window and glanced outside.

Their house was located in a decent suburb with one-story homes and sculpted landscaping. The morning sun gleamed off white tile rooftops. It looked to be a scorcher, barely any clouds in the sky.

"Ah, yes. We got attacked by pfrells. If they can pass through the dimensional rift, who knows what else may follow?"

"How did you get off the island?" Yaron's curious tone drew glances his way.

"We followed a cardinal, a red bird." Nira heaved a deep sigh. "That's after we met the old man who gave Zohar that pendant. One minute the old guy named Askr sat by his campfire, and in the next he was gone. Vanished."

"How?" Kaj sat up straight. "Did he spatial shift?"

"I did not smell cors particles. He may have just slipped into the woods." Zohar's tone said he believed otherwise. "Nira recognizes the shape of this amulet. Tell them," he commanded.

Nira's passion ignited for her favorite topic. "It's Thor's hammer. I'd always been hooked on mythology, but I became interested in Norse legends when my professor said the symbols on my watch could be a runic inscription. Runes are an ancient form of writing thought to have magical properties."

Zohar's head lifted in pride. "The old man called me a son of Thor, who was a Norse warrior god. He said it is my duty and that of my brethren to protect the daughters of Odin."

"Who's Odin?" Paz's drawl pronounced the name as oh-din.

Nira took a sip of water. "Let me start with the creation myth so you'll get the whole picture. These tales derive from the Edda, an epic of Germanic origin. It says a great void stretched between the land of ice and darkness in the north and the land of fire and light in the south. When warm air met the ice, water formed, and the drops produced the first Giant, Ymir, along with a cow who fed him."

Dal's mouth curved in disdain. "We are supposed to believe this?"

"It's a myth, okay?" Nira paced back and forth while the legend spilled from her tongue. "While the Giant slept, a male and female grew from his armpit. They were Frost Giants who had human form and supernatural powers."

"Can you give us the short version?" Kaj, standing by the wall, shot her a sardonic glance.

"Hold on and listen. The cow licked the ice and brought forth a man named Buri. Buri's son married a descendent of Ymir, and they in turn produced three sons. These offspring became the Gods, including Odin.

"Odin and his brothers killed Ymir and used his body to create Midgard, the middle land, from the void. Then they made the oceans and the earth, the heavens and the stars, and the cycles of night and day."

"Are these deities still worshiped?" Borius, the team's xenobiologist, soaked up her words with a rapt face.

"No, of course not." She glanced at Zohar to see if he wanted her to continue. At his nod of encouragement, she plunged on. How she yearned for a classroom, to teach this subject to a roomful of eager students.

"The Gods split into two families, the Aesir and the Vanir. Odin and Thor belonged to the Aesir. They were warriors, while the Vanir became farmers and merchants. Odin ruled over them all as king of the Gods. Thor was a great warrior who carried a magic hammer."

"What destroyed belief in these legends?" Borius inquired.

She smiled at him in appreciation. At least he showed an interest in history and culture. "Christianity swept through the land. However, let me finish the story. It ends with a great battle."

Dal flexed his biceps. "Now we get to the good stuff."

Finally, some aspect of her tale appealed to their explosives expert. "The Aesir Gods lived in Asgard, a celestial palace. A rainbow bridge connected Asgard to Midgard. Odin created humans to occupy Midgard. That left Niflheim below for the Giants to inhabit."

"The Underworld," Borius murmured, his eyes bright.

"As the first living creatures," Nira continued, "the Giants were angry when the Gods expelled them from their rightful place. They gathered their allies and attacked the Gods who fell in defeat. This great battle was called Ragnarok."

"The Trolleks are like these Giants, forced from their homes." Zohar's deep voice resonated throughout the room. "They, too, gather their allies."

"That's right. You see the similarities?" Pleased by his remark, Nira kept going, not that she could stop now. "The Giants didn't live alone in Niflheim. Remember the first Giant, Ymir? After he died, Dwarfs formed from the maggots in his flesh."

"Dwarfs?" Kaj coughed the word out, his doubt evident in his expression.

"They lived in Niflheim, too. The Goddess Hel ruled over them in this underworld."

"Is this where the concept of Hell derived?" Borius's gaze lit. "I thought it was a pit of eternal fire for damned souls."

Nira shook her head. "In Norse mythology, Hel's realm was a peaceful place, even though it was called the Land of the Dead.

She lived in a palace like the Gods. It wasn't considered a punishment to end up there."

"So this saga does not include a demon or devil like the biblical version of a creation myth?" Borius persisted while the others exchanged amused glances.

She tapped her chin. "Well, there is Loki. He used to be a companion to the Gods, but he caused much mischief. He had the ability to shapeshift and delighted in causing trouble.

"Eventually, the Gods banished him. I suppose you could call him a demon, although not in the fallen angel sense. More like an evil spirit who relishes chaos."

Zohar pointed a finger at her. "Did not the old man say you should drink from some fountain? What did he mean?"

Nira spread her hands. "Askr said if I took a drink from the Fountain of Wisdom, I'd be able to read runes. Hey, wait a minute."

Retrieving her purse from the bedroom, she rummaged inside. The flash drive she always carried held her backup computer files. She took it to the study and stuck it in the laptop Kaj had acquired. The men drifted in to crowd around her.

"Okay, I forgot to mention the World Tree from the legends. It's an ash tree that connects all three realms of the Gods. Look, here is my reference to Mimir's Well."

"What's that?" Zohar stood at her back, peering at the monitor over her shoulder.

She could almost hear his teeth grinding in exasperation. They'd come no closer to discovering the jamming device or Grace's whereabouts, and yet she felt these stories were important to their mission in some way.

"The ash tree is fed by three sources of water under its roots. One of these is the Fountain of Wisdom, guarded by the god Mimir. According to legend, Odin sacrificed an eye to drink from this fountain. That's how he gained his powers of prophecy."

Zohar clapped a heavy hand on her shoulder. "I hope you are not planning to search for this fountain. It would be a waste of time. Askr might have meant something else entirely."

"You think he was off his rocker, don't you?"

Zohar frowned at his pals. "What is this word, rocker?"

Borius lifted an eyebrow. "A rocker could refer to a type of chair, *rageesh*, or to a popular musician."

Nira rolled her eyes. "Come on, it's just an expression. You know, off his rocker. Out of his mind. I think his advice would make sense if we understood these things better."

Further research brought no new answers. She retrieved her thumb drive and stood, brushing a hand over her face.

"Now what? We need more leads."

Zohar followed her into the living room. "We have the data crystals… crystal to examine, and the shipping address in Windermere to investigate."

"What about looking for that island?" She spun to face him. "Send Borius to get a reading of those carvings when you find the place. If he's got a phase gun, those natives won't be a threat. And while you're at it, check the other ley lines for signs of Trollek activity."

"We cannot do so with the jamming device activated." Zohar glanced at a lizard scurrying along the air-conditioning unit by the window.

She followed his line of vision. The creature skittered away into a crack. "You don't need to scan for cors particles. If the Trolleks put Drift World near the Bermuda Triangle, maybe they have gateways near other Vile Vortices. See if you can locate a place where lots of people go, like a casino or another theme park. Maybe that's where they've hidden the jammer."

"Good idea." Zohar beamed at her. "I'll have Paz use the ship's sensors to scan those regions."

"Meanwhile, I have my own things to do. Let's meet back here later to exchange reports."

"You cannot go alone. I will accompany you."

"Not this time. I have your diamond ring. If I need help, I'll use it."

She considered how little the ring meant to him. Did lovers

give such tokens to each other on his world? Had Zohar ever wanted a woman so much that he'd pledged himself to her?

Realizing how little she knew of his background didn't make her any happier. It only widened the gap between them and brought home the fact that he'd leave her someday.

Zohar regarded her with a stern expression. "Promise you will summon me should you gain news of Grace. You are not to attempt a rescue on your own, understand?"

"Yes, sir. Or should I say, *rageesh*. What does that mean anyway?"

Yaron sauntered inside. "It means our captain is—"

"Their commanding officer," Zohar finished, giving him a warning glare.

Despite all she had done for him, Zohar still didn't trust her. So be it. She'd search for Grace while he pursued his mission. And once it was done, he'd leave and she'd never see him again.

Good riddance. The man disrupted her life, distracted her from her goals, and played havoc with her hormones.

As the men huddled to discuss their plans, she slung her purse strap over her shoulder and headed for the front door.

Chapter Sixteen

Zohar gathered his team to review their assignments. While they draped themselves over the chairs and sofa in the living room, he swallowed the bitter taste of remorse. Despite her defiant words, he shouldn't have let Nira depart on her own like that. Her absence left him feeling hollow. It took an effort to drag his thoughts away from the fiery redhead.

Washing his face of emotion, he addressed his crew. "Dal's assignment is to learn how the Trolleks acquired Class One armaments."

"Consider it done." Dal stood by a bookshelf, his body tense with restrained power. "I will contact military command to see if they report any discrepancies in their inventory. The trail may originate there."

"Good. Meanwhile, Borius will track Rayne's movements."

He swung his gaze to the young man who'd flicked on the screen called a television. Zohar didn't see how anyone could find those flat images entertaining.

"Your wish is my command, rageesh." The blond man's gaze remained focused on a sports game.

"Kaj, I will accompany you to the ship. I have some encoded messages to send from our secure channel." Zohar had another reason for wanting to go onboard. He planned to give Paz a sample of Nira's hair for DNA analysis. "Do not forget to bring the crystals I gave you."

Kaj, reading messages on his PIP, waved in acknowledgement.

"Finally, Yaron, you will stay here and scan the ley lines for signs of congregated activity like Nira suggested. Look for theme parks, visitor attractions, and religious meccas. Like Drift World, these may be recruitment centers for mind slaves. The Trolleks may have opened gateways in their vicinity. Paz will scan the surface with our ship's sensors for the same purpose."

"Is Nira going shopping?" Yaron gestured toward the kitchen. "We need more food if I am to remain."

Zohar snorted. Leave it to his men to worry about their stomachs. "One of us will restock the pantry. As for me, I will take a shuttle from the ship and revisit the Trollek village. I did not have a chance to fully explore the last time."

Dal flexed his powerful muscles. "Allow me to accompany you, sire. You should not go alone."

Zohar bristled. "Do you question my decisions?"

"Of course not, *rageesh*, but I do question your motives. Why did you allow Nira to go off alone? She is a target for our enemy, and so are you."

"The Trollek female, Algie, took Nira's blood sample. That may be all she wanted. Nira might not be of interest to them any longer."

"All the more reason for them to destroy her." Kaj stood and faced his leader with steely gray eyes. "I agree with Dal."

Zohar strode to the opposite end of the room. A puff of air brushed his face, as if another presence crossed his path.

He glanced out the window, but Nira's car was gone. Had he been wrong in allowing her some privacy? He missed her already, even though they'd barely been apart.

Tempting as it was to join her on her errands and learn more about her life, it would be futile. Why get deeper involved when they'd only hurt each other down the road? She belonged here with her people, while he had his own demons to quell.

"The lady wished some time alone." He lifted his nose. "I was only respecting her needs."

"You like her," Kaj stated in a flat tone.

"Who would not? She is attractive, determined, and resourceful." His mouth curved up as he pictured her intelligent eyes and resolute chin. "The woman has a body like a goddess and a wit as sharp as a blade."

Dal folded his arms across his chest. "Why did you not give her a comm unit?"

"She has the ring for emergencies, and while she slept, I implanted her with a locator beacon."

"Wise move, but if you ask me, rageesh, you choose to avoid our lovely associate because you care about her."

Zohar's face heated. "You and Kaj are reading things into our relationship that are not there."

Yaron stroked his beard, a teasing gleam in his dark eyes. "She would make a worthy queen."

Zohar's blood surged at this sore subject. "Should I ever accept the throne, which I have no intention of doing, I will allow the Primer to select my bride."

"You are entitled to happiness, sire."

"I am only entitled to what serves my people."

"The people would be served best if you took your rightful place." Yaron stood and met his gaze squarely. "They would trust you to choose a proper wife and would rejoice with you."

Like they'd rejoiced with his father? That road had led to weakness and destruction when the Emperor became the tormented puppet of his bride. Zohar's stepmother may have hidden her true nature until she became queen, but it soon became evident. No one would forget the pogroms and other horrors that followed.

"I cannot risk falling for the wrong woman."

"Some of us have already done that." Kaj's tone rang with bitterness. "You are smart to be cautious."

"Nonetheless," Yaron persisted, "you might consider Nira for the role. She has many admirable qualities, and you have feelings for her."

"Thank you for your insights." Zohar squared his shoulders.

"Now, you each have your assignments. Get to them. I need another cookie."

"Bring me a glass of that orange juice, would you?" Dal asked without any regard for Zohar's rank. "I am plagued by thirst. The food on this planet has too much salt."

"I can get it." Borius strode toward the kitchen. "I would like a smack myself."

"A snack, Borius, not a smack," Zohar corrected with a grin.

They meandered toward the dining room. Zohar grabbed another cookie from the nearly empty plate. He savored the treat's gooey center while Borius returned with a glass of juice for Dal. Kaj disappeared toward his bedroom, and Yaron aimed for the study.

Shaking his head with fond affection for his crew, Zohar leaned against the table to mull over his thoughts. Rolling the melted confection on his tongue, he compared its pleasure to sex. No contest there. He'd give up a dozen cookies to lie with Nira, to stroke her smooth skin, and to hear her soft pants of delight.

What if he did consider her as a possibility for his bride? How would she feel about it?

She expected him to leave at the end of his mission. That meant she held no hope of a future for them. Likely she'd only bedded him as a release valve and to share her immunity. Once she regained her sense of order, she wouldn't need him anymore.

Not that she needed him now. How had she escaped from Algie during their first foray into Drift World, and again from the Grand Marshal in the village?

Until he knew the true answer to those questions, he would do best to restrain his feelings for her. That was another reason why he wanted to revisit the village. Nira claimed to have hit the Grand Marshal on the head with a lamp, but she'd been reticent to provide details. Was he right to be suspicious, or was he so colored by his father's faults that paranoia ruled?

Perhaps if his father had been more wary, he would not have succumbed to the witch he called his wife.

Losing his appetite, Zohar finished the cookie and retreated to his room. He spent the next fifteen minutes preparing for the tasks ahead. Wishing he could wear his uniform tunic, he'd just secured his weapons when a loud crash sounded from the living room.

His pulse pounded as adrenaline flooded his veins. Had the Trolleks broken through their perimeter defense?

Drawing his laser pistol, he raced down the hallway. When he rounded the living room, he skidded to a halt.

Dal lay face down on the carpet, still as a corpse.

****

Midday traffic on I-4 moved at a decent clip as Nira drove east toward Winter Park. She regretted leaving the guys behind. Despite their bravado, the Drift Lords acted like Old West gunslingers arriving wide-eyed in the city.

Refusing to think about how Zohar's attempts to fit in with society touched her, she gripped the steering wheel. He hadn't wanted her to go off alone, being concerned for her safety, but he'd graciously allowed her freedom. A rush of gratitude swelled within her, mixed with longing for his company.

Had it been only twenty minutes since she'd left him? It seemed like forever. Already he had imprinted himself upon her mind and upon her heart. She'd never met a man who treated her with such tenderness and respect. He considered her an equal, both as a teammate and in bed, and she appreciated his esteem. Too bad nothing else could come from their relationship other than great sex.

Worry about it later.

That's right, she should just enjoy him for now and forget about the future. They wouldn't have one if the Trolleks won.

Nira didn't know if Algie would still be interested in her or not but she wasn't taking any chances. She'd phoned her sisters to meet her for lunch. This might be her only chance to warn them of possible danger.

Tamping down her sense of urgency, she found a parking lot in downtown Winter Park on a shady side street. She pulled into an empty space, shut off the engine, and glanced around to make sure she hadn't been followed. The coast clear, she exited to the street and headed toward Park Avenue.

Home of fashionable boutiques and bustling cafés, Park Avenue was a popular thoroughfare. Nira had sampled at least half the restaurants there and loved to shop in the Farmer's Market on Saturday mornings. Across the street was Central Park, with its bandstand at one end and a rose garden at the other. As she strolled along, a train whistle tooted in the distance.

She dodged a woman walking a white poodle with a rhinestone collar. The café Nira wanted should be on the next block.

After locating the place, Nira claimed a seat at an outdoor table to wait for her sisters. She'd just taken a sip of water when Kristy arrived.

"Hey, Nira. What's up?"

The twenty-four-year-old leaned down to hug Nira, who gave her an extra squeeze. Kristy dressed casually in white shorts with a turquoise tank top, long beads, and flip-flops. Sterling silver earrings dangled from her ears.

"I'm good. Thanks for coming." Nira's glance rose to Kristy's layered hair. "I see you've added red streaks to your blond this month."

"Let's not get started on my hair, okay?" Kristy plopped into a chair. "Where's Diane?"

"Here I am," called a singsong voice. Their younger sister tripped into view, dipping to give each one an air kiss. Her curly brown hair framed a face with modest makeup. "Nira, have you lost weight? You look thinner."

"I haven't weighed myself lately, but I'm fine. Really. I want to catch up on all your news."

The waitress came to take their orders. After she left, Nira made desultory small talk until their food arrived. The inane chatter almost made her feel like life had returned to normal. She picked up her fork and dug into her trio of tuna, shrimp, and chicken salads on a bed of lettuce.

"There's a reason why I wanted to see you both." She swallowed a bite then took a drink of water. "What I told you about the explosion at Grace's house wasn't the entire truth. You can't repeat to anyone what I'm about to say. It wasn't an accident."

"How could it not be an accident?" Kristy jabbed a finger in the air. "What else would cause an entire house to blow up? And where's Grace? You said she's okay but missing. How do you know she wasn't inside?"

"Because I was there. Listen, I've taken a job as a local guide with some guys who do dangerous work."

"What kind of work?" Diane's brown eyes narrowed.

"They're agents from another country here to stop a group of terrorists. It's all very hush-hush."

A gaggle of teenagers strolled by, chatting as they window-shopped. Two mothers pushed strollers in tandem while a group of men in suits brushed past them all at a brisk pace. Traffic picked up as the corner light turned green.

"How did they hook up with you?" Kristy, taking a drink, glanced at Nira over the rim of her iced tea glass.

"We sort of ran into each other by accident." Nira raised her voice as a motorcycle zoomed past with a belch of exhaust.

"Another accident, huh? What are you, a lightning rod?" Diane's mouth tightened. Dressed for work in a skirt and blousy top, she could easily be taken for the oldest among them, and often she acted like it, too. As marketing director for a non-profit group, she had a more regular schedule than Kristy, a magazine photographer.

Nira twirled her water glass. "Actually, I had an unfortunate encounter with the bad guys, and Zohar rescued me. He's the team leader."

Diane and Kristy exchanged concerned glances.

"Are you aware the cops interviewed us?" Kristy dabbed at her mouth with a napkin.

Nira's jaw dropped. "What? When was this?"

"After the explosion. Your car was parked at the curb, and a neighbor saw you drive off in a van with a bunch of guys."

"I spoke to the police and gave a statement," Nira said. "I needed the police report to file an insurance claim for Grace."

"They'd like to speak to your friends." Diane chewed a bite of her sandwich.

"What for? The cops are the ones who proposed a gas leak as the cause of the explosion. I was on my way out when the house blew up. The impact tossed me onto the lawn."

"What were those men doing there?" Diane tucked a strand of curly brown hair behind her ear. "And why are the cops interested in them? Have you thought about the possibility that they're the terrorists?"

"That's ridiculous. The police would have said something." Or not. Perhaps she was a person of interest to them, too.

Lava bombs didn't leave residues, did they? Oh gosh, she didn't need the police on her tail in addition to the Trolleks, not to mention any confounded humans they might control.

"I'll tell Zohar to get in touch with the authorities. He'll straighten things out."

She signaled the waitress for the check, suddenly conscious of their exposure. She'd thought meeting her sisters in a public place would be safe, but she could be wrong.

"Listen, I brought you here to warn you. You may be in danger. Believe me or not, those bad guys Zohar is after… they're trying to stop him from exposing their operation. His team was with me in the house when it blew."

"Are you saying the crooks tried to take him out?" Kristy scoffed.

"Yes, and I've been threatened—"

"You?" Diane raised her eyebrows. "Come on, Nira. Do you really expect us to believe this?"

"I know it sounds far-fetched, but the baddies regard me as a member of Zohar's team now. By association, you could be on their hit list, too. You have to leave town until this is over."

"What happened to Grace?" Diane persisted.

Nira scraped a hand through her hair. "She's alive but in their custody. Don't worry, I'll find her."

Kristy raised her hands. "Nira, you're usually so sensible. Ever since Diane and I moved out on our own, you've been acting strange. And now you come to us with this wild story."

Nira's muscles tensed. She'd never mentioned what their mother had told her privately on her deathbed. Perhaps confession would cleanse her soul.

"I suppose this is as good a time as any. I have more news. This will come as a shock."

She grabbed the check when the waitress brought it and threw down her credit card.

"What now?" Diane pursed her lips, her expression guarded.

"Mom spoke to me as she lay dying. We had enough to deal with after her death: making funeral arrangements, sorting through her things, deciding how to manage financially. It slipped away from me and then..." Her throat closed.

"Don't keep us in suspense." Diane's voice dripped with sarcasm.

Nira swallowed beyond a lump in her throat. "Mom and Dad adopted me when I was a baby."

"What?" Kristy stared at her in disbelief.

"My real parents left me on the church doorstep with nothing except this watch." She showed it to them.

"You're not really our sister?" Kristy squealed.

"Sshh." Nira didn't know who might have listening devices aimed in their direction.

For all she knew, the cops could have put her under surveillance since the bombing. She'd been so beguiled by Zohar and focused on the Trolleks that she hadn't noticed anyone else paying attention to her. That didn't mean they weren't there. She'd have to alert Zohar, but now more pressing matters took priority.

She leaned forward, folding her hands on the table. "I am your sister in every way that matters. However, I want to discover my ancestry. That's why I took time off from grad school this summer, so I could earn some money. I need it to conduct my research."

Diane cocked her head. "Why didn't you tell us sooner?"

Nira glanced away. "I was afraid you… we'd lose our close relationship. I guess I've made that happen without any help from you."

Kristy grabbed her hand. "Nira, you'll always be our sister, no matter who your parents are."

Diane added her handclasp. "All for one and one for all." She repeated their favorite phrase from *The Three Musketeers*.

They sprang back, grinning.

Nira sobered. "I meant what I said about you leaving town. I'm involved in this mess and now by association, so are you. I won't rest until I know you're safe."

Kristy's eyes filled with concern. "What about you?"

"I have Zohar's team to cover my back. We don't know how far the tentacles of this terrorist organization reach. Meanwhile, I'm attempting to interpret this symbol on my watch. It may be a runic inscription, and somehow this relates to things in a manner I can't explain."

"What will you do now?" Diane threw a surreptitious glance over her shoulder.

"I'm going to Cassadaga to see if one of the psychics there can answer my questions. Maybe a reading will point me in the right direction."

"Cassadaga." Diane shook her head. "Nira—"

"I know this sounds nuts. Just humor me and heed my warning, okay? Otherwise, the consequences could be bad, and I'd never forgive myself if anything happened to either of you."

Chapter Seventeen

"Dal, what happened?" Zohar rushed forward, his heart thumping. He crouched and rolled Dal over. Thank the Creator, his friend still breathed but his face looked ashen.

"Stomach." With a moan, Dal curled his legs up and clutched his midsection.

Zohar glanced at the broken juice glass on the floor as the others charged into the room. "We have to get him to the ship." His mind made quick calculations to alter their plans.

Yaron knelt, performing a quick examination. "No time. It must be something he ingested, perhaps an allergic reaction. He needs his stomach pumped."

"Should I call 911?" Kaj's dark eyes lacked their usual scorn, reflecting concern instead. "It is the local code to summon assistance." Yanking out his comm device, he glanced at Zohar for approval.

"Do it."

Kaj complied. They all heard a woman's loud response: "Hello, do you need police, fire, or medical?"

Kaj's startled glance met theirs. "My friend is sick."

"How sick? What are his symptoms?"

"He is lying on the floor, clutching his stomach."

"I will dispatch medical and police." She noted their address. "Did he ingest something?"

"We ate the same things for morning repast, but he drank some fruit juice."

"What kind of juice?"

Kaj's brow furrowed. "It is orange colored."

"Is he allergic to citrus, maybe?"

"Not that I know."

"I'll relay your info to the paramedics. They should be there within minutes."

"Thank you." Kaj rang off and loped to the front window to watch for their arrival.

Zohar took Yaron aside. "Will the doctors detect anything different in Dal's physiology?"

"No, sire." Yaron spoke in a subdued tone, his face somber. "We are as human as the earthlings in terms of our anatomy."

"Security will be a problem." Zohar surveyed his fallen teammate, whose unhealthy pallor made his heart wrench.

He didn't want to lose another man, not after Rayne. Dal was one of their strongest fighters. That he could fall so quickly concerned him, not only because of the possible causes but also because his loss would reduce their numbers even further. His fingers curled. Dal had to survive.

"I can stay with him." Borius hovered nearby, wearing an anxious expression.

Hadn't he been the one who'd brought Dal the fruity beverage? Borius had been the last person to talk to Rayne, too. And he'd been at the scene of the ambush where Lord Magnor had disappeared.

"I think it best if Yaron supervises his care as team medic." Zohar's commanding tone dissuaded any arguments. He turned to the bearded man who still knelt by Dal's side. "Make sure he gets the best treatment."

Yaron punched his fist to his chest. "As you wish, sire."

Kaj, waiting by the door to let in the emergency personnel, interrupted. "Yaron, did Dal polarize himself this morning?"

"I believe so. As did I," Yaron said, reminding Zohar he had neglected to perform that duty.

"Then you will both be protected while Dal receives aid off premises." Zohar straightened his spine. "As soon as he is out of danger, transport him to the ship. Kaj, you will accompany me to the Protector as planned. You can take a second shuttle back down to patrol the ley lines. See if your sensor sweeps pick up anything unusual. I will give the data crystals to Paz."

"Yes, my liege." Kaj bowed.

"Do not bow to me. I am not your king."

"Aye, Captain." Kaj gave him a broad grin, a rare occurrence for the young man stung from a failed love affair.

Zohar ached inside for his fallen comrade. It fell to him to give orders, so he steeled himself against his emotions. It would be a disservice to his men if he lost focus. He'd already done so, forgetting to polarize himself that morning. He shouldn't rely on Nira's immunity, especially with another trip to the village on his list.

By the faith, he hoped he hadn't done her wrong by allowing her to go off alone. If anything bad happened, it would be his fault. He would call her later to make sure she was all right. Besides, he needed to tell her about Dal.

Outside sirens whined, brakes squealed, and doors slammed. Kaj threw open the front door. Men in uniform jumpsuits grabbed equipment from a shiny red vehicle and advanced toward them.

He hoped no one noticed the poles outside the house. Kaj had set them up to appear decorative, like garden accessories. When active, they'd sound an alarm for human intruders in addition to acting as protection against vector shifts. He'd shut down the perimeter before Nira left.

After the medics took Dal away on a stretcher, with Yaron going along posing as his brother, Zohar rallied his troops.

"Borius, forget tracking Rayne's movements." He faced his two remaining crew in the living room. "I want you to take Yaron's job and use the computer to search the ley lines. Locating the jammer is still our priority. Once Dal is in the clear, Yaron can join the hunt."

"What about Dal's assignment?" Kaj flicked a lock of wheat brown hair off his forehead.

Dal was supposed to track the supplier of energy weapons to the Trolleks. Zohar would have to handle that task himself.

"I will begin inquiries. That is not as important as deactivating the jamming device." Zohar's lips thinned. "We still have to pinpoint the Trolleks' entry points, determine how they maintain the rifts, and shut them down."

He couldn't afford to get sidetracked, and looking for the traitor who sold weapons to their enemy would do just that. It might lead to the person who'd sent an assassin after him, but he could deal with that problem later.

Zohar retreated to his room and obtained a sample of Nira's hair from her comb for a DNA test. He felt traitorous doing it, but she had been in the kitchen earlier. That gave her the perfect opportunity to put poison into the juice carton. The same could be said for the rest of them, but there was also the matter of how she'd escaped from Algie and the Grand Marshal.

He should wait until the doctors made a diagnosis on Dal before jumping to conclusions, but he had other reasons for checking on his team as well. If his enemies wished to terminate him, what better route than to corrupt one of his most trusted circle?

Maybe that tainted juice had been meant for him. So what if it killed his colleagues too? The assassin wouldn't care.

His blood ran cold. Bad enough that the Trolleks would stop at nothing to obstruct his mission, but to have to deal with political insurgents at the same time strained his patience.

Action had always proved a balm for his problems. From a sack in his closet, he withdrew the set of electrodes that had become part of his routine. Anticipated pain made him bare his teeth. It would cleanse his mind and prepare him for the difficult path ahead.

After stripping off his clothes, he fastened the nodes on his upper arms and thighs, leaving the final one for his forehead. When he'd pulled that strap tight enough to crimp his skin, he grasped the switch in his hand. Applying the mouth guard was the last step.

Zohar lay flat on the carpet, sucked in a breath between clenched teeth, and pushed the button. A jolt of energy snapped through him, contracting his muscles in painful spasms as his body's electrical resistance responded to the charge.

His teeth clamped down on the mouthpiece. Nerve endings fired. Focusing on a singular object on the wall as he'd been taught, he endured the agony until the prescribed interval passed. It was the price he had to pay to be a Drift Lord. The polarization would last twenty-four hours, protecting him against the Trollek touch.

He sat up, his limbs trembling, and ripped off the electrodes. "For duty and country," he pledged for the umpteenth time, thumping his fist on his chest.

When his legs steadied enough for him to stand, he rose and dressed quickly.

Zohar piloted the shuttle to the Protector while Kaj rode in the copilot's seat. Their Class IV Fomian gunship, cloaked from planetary sensors, maintained a high orbit. Paz greeted them with a wide grin in the hangar bay.

After a brief exchange of news, Kaj headed off to begin his assignment. Zohar retired to his cabin and dialed Primer Pedar on his private comm channel. As Regent, Pedar ruled in Zohar's stead.

"*Rageesh*, I am glad to hear from you." The white-haired man's eyes shone with relief on the video monitor. "When my man failed to check in, I feared something bad had happened."

Zohar tilted his head. "You mean Lord Magnor? So you really did send him to keep an eye on me?"

He cursed the time lag that delayed communications while he waited for a reply. Paz was working on a secret project in his spare time, hinting it would boost the relay system and allow for real-time dialogue. For various reasons, he had to guard his research, even from his friends.

"I felt the Tsuran swordsman would benefit your team," Pedar said at last. "Things are not going well here. It seemed wise to send you extra protection while you fend off the Trolleks."

"Tell me, old friend, what has gotten you so disturbed?"

"Demonstrations have become increasingly violent. A common thread exists among the dissenting factions these days."

"Oh?" Zohar sat up straight.

"I believe the malcontents are being herded under one leadership. We have our agents out, and they confirm the attacks are better coordinated."

Zohar knew the downturn in the economy had made people angry, but rebels had been stirring up trouble ever since his father's death. They called for a republic and an end to the empire. Zohar had half a mind to join them until they started harming innocents in the name of their cause.

"What are you doing about it?" he asked his regent.

Primer Pedar gave a weary sigh. "Our enforcers are working overtime, but we are headed for civil war unless you come home. Sire, you are the only person who can sway public opinion."

He snorted. "I am the last person my people want. Father made sure of that. Our royal line is despised. Why should I be any different than him?"

"As captain of the Drift Lords, you have proven your worth. You are stronger than our former king, more resistant to outside influences. You must come home and assert your birthright." Pedar's voice softened. "The people will love you as I do when they see what kind of man you are. Zohar, please have more faith in yourself."

"I cannot leave yet. The Trolleks are jamming our cors particle detectors so we are unable to locate their rifts. We have no idea how many gateways they have activated. Meanwhile, they are confounding humans and infiltrating society to the extent of which we have yet to learn."

"Your team has met their challenge before."

"Not on this scale, and our problems have only just begun. Since the rifts will not shut down via their natural cycle, the dimensional drift is widening. Already there are tears in the space-time fabric.

"So far this has resulted in spontaneous spatial shifts here on Earth. Further shifts could potentially expand to other worlds, other dimensions. If this process continues, a great cataclysm will result, and reality as we know it will cease."

Primer Pedar chuckled. "You have always been a doomsayer. It cannot be your mother's genes. Alythira was a ray of sunshine in our eyes."

His heart squeezed. He'd barely known his mother before she died, just enough to remember her laughter and the songs she sang to him at bedtime. The king, not yet crowned emperor, had mourned her loss deeply, distancing himself from his son as though Zohar increased his pain.

Zohar had hoped his father's mood would brighten once he remarried, although he disliked the woman Ivar chose for his new bride. Yetta's smile seemed too cloying, and her eyes were chips of ice. As it turned out, his instincts were correct.

"My duty remains here." He firmed his lips, aware that if he shirked his role on Earth, the repercussions would destroy all they held dear. "Once we have forced the evil beasts back to their domain and sealed their gateways, then you and I can continue this discussion on Karrell. Until then, I rely on you to maintain control."

"As you wish, sire." The old man signed off with a heavy sigh.

Shifting restlessly, Zohar made another call to a childhood friend who now worked in State Security. After they exchanged pleasantries, he stated his purpose.

"It pains me to ask you this, but I need a discreet background check on the members of my team. Examine their recent contacts, see if anything in their lives raises suspicion. You know, like large credit deposits, unpaid debts, illicit affairs, that sort of thing."

"You want me to dig for dirt?" Tog's voice rose with disbelief. He knew the stringent requirements for acceptance into the Drift Lords' cadre.

"One of them may have succumbed to blackmail. An

assassin has targeted me, and Rayne was killed in my place." Zohar described the circumstances.

"How do you know this Lord Magnor is on the level? Just because the Primer sent him doesn't mean you should trust him."

"It is irrelevant; he is lost to us." Zohar told Tog about the ambush.

"Nonetheless, I'll put out feelers for him as well. Anything else?"

Rubbing his neck, he instructed Tog to follow through on Dal's assignment. Tog would know whom to contact about missing military grade armaments.

Feeling a sense of accomplishment, he hung up on Tog, then made a quick call to Yaron. Dal's condition had stabilized, so at least one thing was going in their favor. However, the doctor wanted to admit him until his toxicology results came back.

Zohar switched his unit off, stood, and stretched. Calling Nira was on his mind, too, but first he needed to consult with Paz.

Paz was on the bridge deck monitoring the propulsion systems when his captain strode through the hatchway. He turned his stubbled face toward Zohar and threw him a two-fingered salute.

Zohar's shoulders sagged as he greeted their communications specialist. "Paz, I appreciate you manning the stations while the rest of us run ourselves ragged dirtside."

"No problem, as long as you let me join the fight when the time comes, sire." Paz regarded him with a twisted smile. "I found something on a quick analysis of that data crystal from Drift World."

"What is it?" His pulse accelerated.

Paz pointed to a display at the science station. "See this? Nira's blood shows an anomaly. I'm not sure what it means yet. The Trolleks tagged her file."

Zohar compressed his mouth. He felt unfaithful, doing tests behind Nira's back. "Do any of the other samples show similar results?"

Paz's eyes darkened. "Some of them are marked, but I need to study them further. You should have Yaron take a look. He has better training in the science modules than I do."

"Yaron is busy. We had a situation. Dal is down." He explained what happened.

Paz shook his head. "First Rayne, then Magnor, and now Dal. I don't like the implications."

"Neither do I." He handed over Nira's hair sample and the additional data crystals then rattled off his instructions. "Report to me when you have more definitive answers. Our first priority is still to send the Trolleks back home and seal the rifts, but Nira's connection might hold the key."

With the redhead on his mind, he commandeered a shuttle and programmed his destination for the park at Turkey Lake.

Chapter Eighteen

Nira drove northeast from Orlando on I-4 while mulling over the conversation with her sisters. Vastly relieved they hadn't rejected her after learning she'd been adopted, she swallowed. If anything bad happened to those girls… She cut off the thought as pressure built behind her eyeballs.

Hopefully Kristy and Diane would listen to her advice and leave town. She'd done her part in warning them. Now she could concentrate on finding Grace.

Glancing at the empty passenger seat, she felt a pang of regret that Zohar hadn't come along. She could use his company. Relying on him had become second nature in such a short time that she didn't want to think about what it meant.

All she knew was that she missed him, and they had only been apart for several hours. Did he feel the same way about her? Did he miss her conversation? Her companionship? Or did he merely view her as a means to an end?

She hadn't really believed he'd let her roam far on her own. The Trolleks might still pursue her. How could he leave her unprotected? Sure, she had the ring, but how quickly could his men arrive in case of trouble?

Stow it, Nira. It's up to you, now. You'll do just fine on your own.

Turning off the highway at exit 114, she followed her GPS directions onto Dr. Martin Luther King Jr. Beltway and then onto County Road 4139. The narrow two-lane route reminded her of old Florida with its hilly terrain and wooded slopes. Driving alone on roads like this always made her nervous. What if her car got a flat tire? She didn't have a mechanic's bone in her body, and who knew how long it would take the auto club to come?

Gripping the wheel, she glanced in the rearview mirror. An old Subaru bumped along behind her. From its rattling noise and faded paint, that car was likely to break down before hers.

Hoping for the best, she reviewed what she knew about Cassadaga. A man named George Colby founded the settlement in the late nineteenth century. During his early adult life, he communicated with spirits and traveled around conducting seances. Then his spirit guide told him to go to Florida and file a homestead claim on a patch of government land.

Eventually he deeded the territory to the Southern Cassadaga Spiritualist Camp Meeting Association. That was the town's formal title, and it was listed in the National Register of Historic Places.

She passed a sign indicating a congested area ahead. Expecting to come to a bustling town center, Nira gaped in surprise when five commercial buildings framed the main intersection.

This was it?

The sparse traffic made her speculate about the inhabitants. Did they prefer to be as invisible as the ghosts they summoned? Evidently so, because she didn't see many people out and about.

Probably it got more crowded on weekends, when visitors arrived. Regardless, Nira hoped consulting a medium wouldn't be a problem. She wanted to learn about her origins and maybe find someone who could read runes. Tarot cards, runes, tea leaves—all were methods of divination. There must be someone here who could help.

Pressing on the brakes, she eyed the village bookstore and the Cassadaga Hotel. The former might be the best place to start. She might find texts on runic inscriptions different than the ones in the UCF library.

The Subaru squealed to a halt behind her. Was that occupant another desperate soul seeking a reading? Or perhaps a mourner who sought to communicate with a dead loved one?

Dishonest psychics could easily prey on people. How could you tell which ones were valid? Then again, that's why she'd come to this place. Supposedly, Cassadaga mediums were certified. She assumed that meant they'd passed some vetting process to get approved.

Deciding to park in the hotel lot, she drove across the street and onto the gravel surface.

She gave the hotel a cursory exam upon emerging from her car. A two-story building with a cream facade and red awnings, the lodge dated from the 1920's. A covered porch invited exploration, but it could wait. The bookstore beckoned her.

As she stood by the curb, a warm breeze stirred the hairs on her arms. Humidity hung heavy in the air, as though an afternoon thunderstorm brewed. The Subaru rumbled past, kicking up dust. It turned a corner and disappeared from sight. Tension eased from her shoulders. She hadn't realized she'd been anxious about being followed.

Wearing a frown of concentration, she headed for the bookstore, a squat structure needing a fresh coat of yellow paint. Once inside, she hesitated, allowing a spicy scent to enter her nostrils. Bookshelves lined the interior, along with display cases offering jewelry and assorted gifts.

Trying not to appear too clueless, she strolled around, squinting at incense sticks, metal balls in boxes, stones painted with odd symbols, and other strange items.

She meandered toward the cashier, a middle-aged woman wearing huge dangling earrings.

"Excuse me, but how do I find someone to do a reading?"

The woman glanced up from the eBook reader in her hand. "The next room over has a chalk board, hon. It lists all the available mediums for today. You can use the phone to see who has an opening. Or, the hotel across the street has psychics on call. Was there a particular specialty you're looking for?"

"I'd like someone who can read runes."

The woman's brow folded in thought. "That would be

Reverend Hazel Sherman. She lives past the house on the hill at the end of Stevens Street. You can walk from here if you're up for a stroll. That is, if she has a vacancy."

In a lucky break, Nira got an appointment with the recommended psychic. She wondered what to expect as she strode along a series of shady residential streets toward the given address. A woman with gypsy eyes wearing long earrings and a caftan? Incense burning in the background? New Age music playing while the Reverend read her fortune or summoned ghosts from her past?

Reality intruded when she stopped at a quaint blue cottage on a quiet side street. Nira cast a glance over the jasmine hedge, flowering pink bougainvillea, and sculpted landscaping. Unlike some of the other dilapidated properties she'd passed, this yard appeared well tended. Her estimate of the occupant climbed a notch.

Her eyes widened when a friendly brunette opened the door. "Hi, I'm Reverend Sherman. Please call me Hazel." With a smile, the woman stood aside so Nira could enter.

In the foyer, Nira assessed the Reverend's lavender blouse, black pants, and pearl jewelry. She looked like the average businesswoman, especially when she led Nira into a furnished home office. What, no crystal ball?

Her gaze took in the large wood desk, office chairs, bookshelves, and filing cabinets. A half-filled mug of tea sat on the desk, which also held a laptop computer, a disorderly array of papers, and a framed photo of two gray cats.

"We can record our session, if you like." Hazel sat behind the desk and regarded her with an encouraging smile.

Cradling her purse in her lap, Nira sat in the spare chair while inhaling a pleasant vanilla scent. "That won't be necessary. I'm here for a specific reason. The lady in the bookstore said you might be able to help me."

Hazel tilted her head. "What can I do for you, dear?"

"First I'd like to know if you can interpret this symbol on

my watch. I'm a grad student in mythology at UCF, and my professor says it's a runic inscription."

"May I see that?"

Nira unsnapped the band and handed over the watch. She rubbed her wrist. Her exposed skin itched. It showed white from lack of sunlight, a telltale strip the width of her band.

Hazel put on a pair of eyeglasses for a closer look. "This has the same vertical structure as runes, but if these are letters, they've run together. Or else they are backward. Runes can be read from left to right or from right to left, sometimes both on the same artifact. They're usually found on stones, weapons, or jewelry. Where did you get this?"

"From my birth mother. I was adopted, and I'm trying to trace my true parentage."

Hazel clutched the watch against her chest and stared into space. "You're on a quest, seeking to learn more about yourself. You will find answers, but you may not like them. Call upon the strength within you. Your power will emerge when the need arises."

Goosebumps rose on Nira's flesh. Was Hazel referring to strength of will or Nira's innate power?

Hazel continued in a flat, rapid voice. "You search for someone dear to you. She is not yet lost. Persistence will lead to reunion but not without cost."

Nira sucked in a breath. Did she mean Grace?

"My friend, is she okay? Where can I find her?"

"Continue on your path, and the way will be revealed." Hazel scrunched her forehead. "I see someone else at your side. It's hard to tell who it is. The shape flickers and changes…"

"It could be the guy I'm working with. Zohar has his own mission, but we've teamed up and—"

"No, not him." Hazel's eyes skewed toward hers. "This entity lurks in the shadows and is evil. Beware, it watches you." She thrust the timepiece back at Nira. "Here, I can do nothing more."

"What about my rune?"

Hazel's lips pursed. "I am not well versed in rune casting, but I know someone who is. Edith doesn't get out much and abhors visitors, but you can give her a try. You'll have to drive there, though. She's got her own place in the woods."

"Edith?"

"Edith Marsh." The psychic leveraged to her feet. "She used to make a living doing readings until she came across something that frightened her. I wonder…" Hazel's face grew pensive, then she shook her head. "Anyway, you can ask her your questions, if she'll let you in."

Nira scraped her chair back and stood, her knees trembling. Bewildered by Hazel's remarks, she fastened her watch on and secured her purse.

After accepting payment, Hazel guided her to the door. Just before she let Nira go, however, she touched her arm.

"Be careful, dear. And be warned. Your companions may not be all they seem."

Nira swallowed. "Thank you. I appreciate your time."

She watched her footing over the cracked pavement outside, sniffing a cloyingly sweet scent as she made her way downhill toward the lake below. Tall, leafy trees shaded the street, interspersed with splashes of color from flowering plants. Thunder rumbled in the distance, confirming her earlier impression of a coming storm.

A storm was coming all right, in more ways than the weather.

What had she learned from Hazel, other than Grace was still alive and unharmed? She took reassurance from that belief, but what about the warning regarding her companions and the mention of her inner strength?

A bottomless morass opened before her. Unanswered questions swirled within, spiraling deeper into the unknown. The more she learned, the less she knew. Where would it end? When would she go back to the routine she'd known before the fateful job interview that had changed her life?

She yearned to earn her doctorate and qualify for a teaching position at the University. Then she would make enough money to buy a townhouse and get a good camera. She'd always liked photography but never had the time or equipment to pursue it. People fascinated her. She wanted to capture the expression on a person's face during an instant that would never occur again.

But that was before Zohar and the Trolleks, before she understood that tracing her origins was more than an adopted child's desire. And forget her travel plans. The only Norway she'd be visiting was their pavilion at the local theme park.

She hadn't even considered losing Grace so soon. Perhaps later, after an illness, or as the result of old age when Nira would have time to prepare. But not now, and not because of her foolish wish to visit Drift World.

Guilt assailed her. She turned the corner, her shoulders slumped. Weeds grew between cracks in the sidewalk, reminding her of the dimensional rifts, ever widening. Like the Trolleks who would destroy their world, roots encroached, threatening to break apart the pavement. The roots needed to be cut back and the weeds eradicated.

"Nira Larsen?"

Her thoughts scattered, and she snapped to attention. She stood in front of the village bookstore. A man leaned against a car in the hotel parking lot across the street. The vehicle was the same Subaru that had been behind her on the way into town.

The fellow waved at her. He had peppery hair, craggy features, and a sledgehammer torso judging from the taut fit of his trousers. He wore a dress shirt and tie that seemed incongruous with his pudgy appearance.

"Yes, that's me." Her muscles tensed. Damn, she'd forgotten again to ask Zohar for a weapon. Should she use the ring to summon help?

Wait and see what he wants.

He strode over and unfolded a wallet. "I'm Detective Dan Carlson, from Orange County." He flashed a badge. "Do you have a few minutes? I'd like to ask you some questions."

Orange County? He'd come all the way from Orlando just to interview her? He must have picked up her trail in Winter Park where she'd met her sisters.

Her pulse accelerated. "Is it normally your routine to follow suspects so far from home?"

"Who said anything about you being a suspect?"

Oops. "Then what is this about?"

"The explosion at your house. Your landlady's death."

"Grace isn't dead."

"No? Then where is she? No one has seen or heard from her since the incident. Her car was parked in the garage."

"Did you check with her son in California?" Something she should have done, Nira realized.

"Grace Miller has not contacted her son. He was disturbed to hear of his mother's disappearance. What can you tell me about the explosion, Miss Larsen?"

"It's in the police report. I'm sure you've read it by now."

"A neighbor saw you on the lawn outside just afterward. You had friends with you, and you left with them in a white van."

She adjusted her sunglasses. "I'd just arrived home with the guys. They're, uh, cousins from out of town. One of the men smelled something funny, and we ran out the door. Then the house blew up. The cops figure it was a gas leak. Do you have a problem with that?"

"I looked up your records. You don't have any other known relatives besides your sisters."

She lifted her chin. "My statement stands. Read it again."

He folded his arms across his chest. "I gather you wanted the police report to file a claim for Grace's insurance."

"She'll get the money when she returns. I am just as keen to locate her as you are."

"Are you aware of the provision in Mrs. Miller's will?"

Her stomach sank. "What provision?"

The detective's eyes became two ice orbs. "Where she leaves her house and all her personal possessions to you?"

"What? Why me and not her son?"

"He gets the rest of her assets." Carlson stepped closer. "Who were those men with you? Names, addresses, occupations? And how come we got a report of a van with a similar description in the vicinity of Lake Buena Vista?"

She swallowed, feeling her face drain of color. "What are you talking about?"

"Someone heard shouts coming from an alley behind a shopping center. By the time officers arrived on the scene, no one was present, but they found traces of blood on the pavement."

"If your witness saw a van, it could have belonged to anyone. Now if you don't mind," she said, tapping her watch, "I've got to run. This conversation is finished."

"Here's my card." He handed one over. "If you think of something I should know, call me." His voice lowered to a deceptively soft tone. "I'm aware of how good girls can fall in with the wrong people. They make you do things you wouldn't ordinarily do. Be aware, though, that being an accessory to a crime comes with stiff penalties."

"Thanks for sharing that information." Nira stalked to her car, giving up her plan to scour the bookstore for resources on runes. She beeped her remote and opened the driver's door.

"Did the psychic provide any comfort?" Carlson persisted, following in her wake.

"What do you mean?"

He moved his face to within inches of hers. She recoiled at his radish breath.

"Were you able to communicate with Grace from beyond the grave, to tell her you're sorry?"

"She's not dead." Nira glared at him.

"Then prove it. Where is she?"

"I wish I knew. I'm searching for her myself."

"Tell me how to reach your friends. Their van is rented, you know. They paid cash in advance."

"Did they?" One foot inside the car, she paused, startled by a new thought. Had he looked at her credit card transactions? Because if so, he could follow the paper trail to their safehouse. She had to tell Zohar.

Sliding into the driver's seat, she fumbled to fit the key into the ignition. Her fingers shook. How dare he insinuate that she'd killed Grace for her own gain.

"Goodbye, Detective. This interview is over." She slammed and locked the door.

Even if he had tracked her credit card charges, Carlson could be biding his time until he figured out what Nira's associates planned.

She drove from the lot and headed out of town. At a stop sign, she peered into the rearview mirror. So far no sign of the Subaru, thank goodness. She dug into her purse, retrieving her cell phone. Her fingers punched the number Zohar had given her. One of these days, she'd have to learn how to use voice commands.

"Nira, it's good to hear from you. Is everything all right?" Paz asked in a concerned tone.

"Yes, I'm okay. I need to reach Zohar."

"He took a shuttle for a mission and is on radio silence. Do you need assistance?"

"No, but the police are on my tail about the explosion at Grace's house. You guys have been spotted in my company. They may be watching the house."

"No problem. The defense grid is in place."

"Our people might be followed from there. The cops are on to the van." Her shoulders ached. She rolled her neck to ease the tension.

"All right, I'll tell Borius. He's the only one home right now. Are you returning?"

"Not yet. I'm going to see a woman who might be able to read runes."

"Good fortune, *sira*. I will pass your message on to our captain when he checks in." He hesitated. "You should know. Dal has taken ill."

"What happened?"

"Stomach pains. Yaron accompanied him to the medical facility."

"Couldn't you take him to the ship? I mean, your sick bay is probably better equipped than our hospitals."

"His condition was too critical for transport."

"Oh, dear. I'm sorry." She winced as an unpleasant thought surfaced. "Warn Yaron about the authorities. They might use this opportunity to question him, perhaps even to arrest him if they have evidence of arson."

Detective Carlson hadn't mentioned his findings at all. She'd done most of the talking. Fool. She should have tried to interrogate him in turn.

"Consider it done. Take care, Nira Larsen, and stay out of trouble." Leashed tension strained his voice.

It must irk him to remain on the ship while the others took action. Nonetheless, his post was important. With everyone dispersed, he became the glue that held them together.

Worried about Dal's condition, she forced herself to focus. The sooner she finished her business here, the quicker she could get back to Orlando.

A sense of power flowed through her. She hadn't realized how much of a victim she'd become. First, her parents abandoned her as a baby. Next, her adoptive father deserted his family. Then her mother died, leaving Nira to care for her sisters. Finally, the Trolleks sucked her into their quagmire.

Well, no more. She'd take matters into her own hands hereafter. She'd already killed people. She'd fought against terrible beasts. She would survive like always, just not in the same way. Knowing she possessed special abilities gave her the confidence she'd never had before.

She glanced at the directions Hazel had scribbled on a piece of paper. Just ahead was the signpost where she had to turn left. It led her to a dirt road. Her Camry bumped along as the trees closed in and overhead branches blocked the sunlight.

Would this be another dead end, or would she finally learn the meaning of the symbol on her watch?

Chapter Nineteen

Nira braked in a cloud of dust in front of a one-story Florida cracker house with a steep hipped roof, shaded porch, and stone chimney. From the neglected yard, peeling paint, and rickety wood steps, the place appeared deserted. But as she approached, after locking her car, she noted a figure scooting behind a window shade.

"Hello?" She climbed a short flight of stairs onto the covered front porch. "My name is Nira Larsen. Reverend Hazel Sherman sent me." She dodged a crooked floorboard before knocking on the door.

"Go away. I don't want no visitors," a woman's voice yelled.

"I need your help. Please."

"You got something wrong with your ears? Leave now, before I shoot you." A weapon cocked.

Zohar, you really should give me one of your ray guns. "If you're Edith Marsh, I need your help interpreting a rune."

"I'll give you one last chance, missy." Footsteps neared.

Refusing to be intimidated, Nira stood her ground. "I inherited a watch from my birth mother. There's lettering etched onto its face. My professor says the symbol is runic in origin, but the letters are all jumbled." Desperation edged her tone. "Please, you have to help me."

The footfalls stopped. "You inherited a watch, you say?"

"Yes, from my parents. I was adopted as a baby and never knew my real mother. My life is at stake." She didn't stint on the melodrama. "I must know what this rune means."

The door swung open, and a gray-haired woman stood firmly in her path. Shrewd green eyes regarded her from over a prominent nose. A sense of recognition startled Nira. Those eyes reminded her of moss in a pine-scented forest and fires blazing in the night, of low voices murmuring and twigs cracking, of days long ago like the Vikings she'd studied. This woman had the same strong features as the Norsewomen who wore long shift dresses covered by linen tunics.

Good God, for a moment, she almost felt transported through time. Had the Trolleks messed with her mind, or was this a side effect of her newfound power? She blinked to sharpen her focus.

Edith, shotgun in hand, leaned around Nira to survey the grounds. "Did you come alone?"

"Yes. May I come in?" Her scalp prickled. She was too exposed with her back to the woods. It couldn't totally be her imagination if she felt eyes watching her, could it?

She swept inside at Edith's invitation and experienced a jolt of relief when the old woman shut the door and slid home the bolts.

Edith propped her weapon by the door then led Nira into a great room in the center of the house. Bedrooms jutted from three of its corners with a kitchen dining room combo facing the rear. It was a basic but workable plan. Wood flooring, upholstered furniture, and table lamps gave the place a comfy feel. Nira's nose clogged, probably from those dust bunnies along the wall.

"Take a seat, missy." Edith sank into a wing chair with a grimace. "My bones ain't what they used to be, but now that you're here, I'll be able to rest."

"What do you mean?" Nira claimed a seat on the sofa.

"I've been waiting for you, and my sisters before me, to give you the message."

Her heart pounded. Hadn't that old man in the forest said something similar?

"What message? You didn't know I'd be showing up at your door."

"The prophecy said so." Edith tilted her head. "You have no idea, do you?"

"I'm sorry." Nira spread her hands. "No idea about what?"

"Who you are. Your destiny."

"It's related to this symbol on my watch, isn't it?" She held out her wrist.

Edith nodded, her eyes gleaming. "Yes, that is the key."

"To what?" Nira shifted impatiently.

Edith glared at her. "To saving the world. All that came before will come again. You must stop it."

"You sound like a man I met on an island. Askr lived in the woods, too, and told me strange things."

"Others have been waiting, like me. Our job is to guide you. What did this fellow say?"

"He called my companion a son of Thor and said it was his duty to protect the daughters of Odin." Nira leaned forward. "Odin and Thor are figures from Norse mythology. What do they have to do with anything?"

Edith's gaze sharpened. "There's truth in his words. Did he speak of a coming darkness?"

"He did." A chill crawled up her spine, and the hairs on her arms lifted.

"You study these legends, don't you, missy? You feel compelled to learn your history."

"How do you know that?"

"I know many things. You have heard of Ragnarok?"

"Of course. Ragnarok was the big battle between the Gods and the Giants. It didn't end well."

"It marked the world's destruction. The Gods met their defeat." Edith spoke with conviction, as though the stories rang true to history.

"Not everyone died. The survivors started anew and repopulated the earth."

"And now Ragnarok comes again. There's only one thing that can break the cycle: the six daughters of Odin must join with the six sons of Thor to utter the ancient words."

"What words?" She wished these old folks would stop speaking in riddles.

"The spell that will vanquish your foe."

"O-kay. Where do I find this spell?"

Edith shrugged. "That secret is not mine to keep. I only know you and your sisters have the key."

Nira stood and unsnapped her watch. "Look, can you interpret this symbol or not?"

Edith accepted the timepiece and squinted over it as though she needed reading glasses. "I cannot interpret this rune. Only you will be able to decipher it."

"The old man we met in the woods said I should drink from the Fountain of Wisdom to gain that knowledge."

"Good advice." Handing back the watch, Edith nodded vehemently.

"Maybe so, but how am I supposed to find this magic water?" Not that she was buying into the whole legend thing, but it could explain a lot. Nira snapped the watch back on her wrist and resumed her seat.

"I will consult the stones."

With a grunt, Edith rose. She left the room and returned a few minutes later holding a piece of fabric and a leather pouch. After spreading the white cloth on the coffee table, she sat, and then selected certain rune lots from the pouch. She cast them onto the table.

"This one represents your past, this here is the present, and the last one that's face down shows the future." Edith pursed her lips as though expecting Nira to doubt her.

"Go on." Nira held as much faith in rune casting as in Tarot cards or crystal balls. Then again, she shouldn't discount the ancient form of divination, not with all the other weirdness in her life right now.

Edith tapped the first stone. "Your past displays innocence, before you became aware of your destiny. Sadness and pain touched you, although family and friends provided support."

She indicated the next rune. "Now you are awakening, becoming more powerful, but you must choose the right path. If you select the wrong one, all will be lost. Listen to your teachers. Learn from your guides. Look to your heart for the light of truth."

As Edith turned over the last stone, she gasped. "By the Norns…"

The Norns? Nira had read about the three goddesses who represented Fate: Urdh—the past, Verdhandi—the present, and Skuld—the future. Just like the ghosts in *A Christmas Carol* by Charles Dickens. So Edith was casting the Norns for her reading instead of using another method. Was there a particular reason why she'd chosen this technique?

Edith gathered the stones and thrust them back into the sack, pulling the drawstring so tight it burst apart. Rune lots scattered over the floor.

"See what you've made me do, child." Hands shaking, Edith bent to scoop the stones into the bag.

"What's wrong? What did that last one say?"

"You don't want to know." Straightening her spine, Edith hobbled to a bookshelf where she stuck the pouch into a lidded jar.

"But you expected me. Remember, you had a message to deliver?" Nira didn't understand what could have made her so upset. Did the old lady really believe that those stones, inanimate objects etched with mysterious drawings, could foretell the future?

In any event, her interview was over. She rose, brushed off her pants, and thanked Edith for her time.

Halfway out the door, she paused when Edith spoke in a low rasp. "The last rune tells of the one of whom we do not speak. He stirs, using his instruments of evil until he can rise again."

Nira spun around. "What do you mean?" This sounded like a rerun of Harry Potter.

Fear shone in Edith's moss green eyes. "Heed my words, missy. The future of all mankind lies in your hands. Choose wisely, or you'll be doomed to spend eternity in his dominion."

****

Zohar patrolled the field in Turkey Lake Park where the Trollek village remained screened from view. He'd found it purely by scent, using his ability to sniff cors particles, and had stood by while attempting to devise a means of entry.

He had thought about entering through Drift World again but quickly discarded that idea as foolish. No sense risking capture there when they might have put out an alert for him.

Hours passed as the sun blazed toward the west. His stomach rumbled with hunger, and his tongue dried with thirst. He pretended to be a naturalist studying plants in case the villagers could see him. His one chance would come if the displacement field went down during a power fluctuation.

His hope surged when the air shimmered and the village materialized like a blurry mirage. Taking advantage of the momentary lapse, he thrust his hand through the rippling curtain. When nothing bad happened, he stepped all the way through. The scent of burning filaments intensified. He emerged inside the village perimeter, presumably with the screening back in place. Now to steal some slave clothing so he could roam free.

He waylaid a poor soul hauling a water bucket and donned his clothes. Hefting the load, he trudged onto the main street toward the Grand Marshal's residence at the far end. Questions singed his mind, but one was more urgent than the rest.

His head lowered, he approached the sentries barring the double front doors.

"I brought fresh water for you to drink," he mumbled, staring at their scuffed boots.

"Bring it here," spoke the guard with a nose like a carrot stick.

"As you command." Zohar offered him the ladle.

"Who is your kabak?" The other guy rubbed his large ear-lobe.

"I was house servant to the Grand Marshal until recently.

Then I was reassigned to Yunis Barack, a minor official." He hoped they bought his story.

"I wonder why Heris Raggo didn't retain you when he became temporary Grand Marshal." Carrot nose passed the ladle to his friend.

Heris was their honorarium for a landowner. Zohar remained silent, wondering how to loosen their tongues.

"Heris Raggo probably figured this one could be more useful hauling buckets, Yorg. Look at his muscles. Better he should work in the yard than the house."

Yorg ribbed him. "No wonder our former leader liked him. He enjoyed sampling both kinds, eh?"

Big Ears snickered. "His Eminence squandered too much human flesh and thought with his wonk instead of his head."

"That won't be a problem anymore." Yorg scratched his groin. "Heris Raggo is better at the job. I hope he gets a permanent appointment. Production is up twenty percent since he took over."

The Trolleks spoke as though Zohar weren't there, but then slaves often were treated like pieces of furniture.

"Were you still employed in the house when the human witch was brought before the Grand Marshal?" Yorg asked Zohar.

Did he mean Nira? "No, sir… er, master." He had a quick moment of panic, hoping they didn't notice his slip.

"Algie put out an alert for a woman with her description," Yorg told his friend, "but the Grand Marshal must have been so eager to bed the witch that it didn't register."

Big Ears finished sipping from the ladle and tossed it back into the bucket. "His Eminence got what he deserved, but I'd like to know how he ended up dead in his bed without a mark on him. What did that woman do to him, and how did she escape?"

What? Zohar's heart lurched. Nira claimed she'd cracked the official on the skull with a lamp.

Had she deliberately lied to him?

Yorg poked the other guard. "You know what I think, Wick? Algie wanted to get rid of the Grand Marshal because he opposed her operation, so she sent the human female to seduce him. Then whammy, the witch kills him with a Nid Rune."

"Come on, there's no such thing as a magic curse."

"Is so. We're just not allowed to talk about it."

"Don't you start getting all weird on me." Wick lowered his voice. "Bad enough our king acts possessed."

"Shut your mouth. You'll get us in trouble."

They both looked at Zohar who stood rigid, his head bowed.

"Get back to your duties." Yorg pointed to him, a mean scowl on his face. "And speak of this to no one, not even your new kabak, understand?"

Zohar bowed. "As you command."

Lifting the bucket, he turned on his heel and scuttled out of sight. Around the corner, he dropped his burden, deciding to scrap the rest of his mission and search for the jamming device.

Then he had to warn his crew about Nira. She'd lied to them about the Grand Marshal. What else did she hide?

****

Nira slammed on the brakes when a fallen tree branch obstructed the narrow country road. Great, just what she needed. Tired and thirsty, she yearned for a cold lemonade, but she'd been too eager to escape the pesky detective to linger in town. Now she wouldn't make it back to Orlando before rush hour unless she could budge that chunk of wood.

She put the car in Park and got out, hoping to swing the log to the side of the road. But her straining muscles made few inroads on moving the obstacle. She kicked it in frustration. She'd have to call for help.

Brushing off her hands, she trudged to her car. Sweat dribbled down her back and between her breasts. At least the thunderstorm had drifted away. Clouds dotted the sky, but the rain marched west.

She'd just pulled out her cell phone when another engine approached. She spun, and her stomach somersaulted.

Oh no, don't tell me. Detective Carlson was back on her tail. He must have waited until she visited Edith and then picked up pursuit again. Still, she was glad to see another driver. Either he'd have to assist her, or he'd be stuck, too.

He squealed to a halt behind her car and shut off the ignition before getting out of his wreck of a vehicle. He'd rolled up his shirtsleeves and looked every bit as weary as she felt.

"Still following me, huh?" She planted her hands on her hips. "Well, see if you can lift that branch, buddy."

"You didn't do this on purpose to annoy me, did you?" Taking a handkerchief from his pocket, he wiped his brow.

"Oh, sure. I love waiting in the heat like this. Can you move it or not?"

Carlson shrugged his shoulders. "Let's find out."

Positioning himself by the branch, he bent his knees and wrapped his hands around the bark. He heaved. He shoved. He grappled the wood and yanked, his face turning red. Nira hastened to help him, but their combined efforts yielded the same result.

"I give up. We should call road service." Letting go, he huffed to catch his breath.

A piercing wail came from the hill beyond.

Goosebumps rose on her flesh. "What's that?"

"Sounds like a child." Shading his face, Carlson squinted at the grassy slope. "I'll check it out. Could be some kid who wandered from home and got lost." He ambled up the hill toward the woods beyond.

Nira opened her cell phone, and the low battery signal beeped. Uh-oh. She'd left her car charger home after cleaning out her vehicle. She'd better make good use of her remaining time. Her instinct to summon Zohar won out.

Paz answered again.

"Isn't Zohar back yet?" Irritation colored her tone.

"The captain still hasn't checked in. What's the problem?"

"I need his advice." She didn't want Paz to think her a helpless female who summoned a man over car trouble. "Please have him contact me as soon as you hear from him."

"You got it." Paz clicked off.

The guy probably thought she was a nuisance, interfering in his team's affairs. Longing for their leader stole into her. If Zohar were here, he'd vaporize that log with a single shot. But apparently, the man didn't need her anymore.

Was he out searching for the jamming device? He should have taken her with him. At the very least, she could neutralize the confounding spell on any human foot soldiers he encountered.

Feeling like used luggage, she tossed her cell phone onto the car seat after it went dead. So much for the warriors from outer space, or the auto club for that matter. She'd have to rely on Detective Carlson.

She locked her door with the purse inside. As she climbed the hill, her rubber-soled shoes sank into the soft earth. At the slope's summit, she stopped to scan the line of trees ahead.

"Carlson, where are you?" She didn't spot him anywhere.

"This way." The stocky detective stuck his head out from behind an evergreen and waved. "We can probably reach the kid before road service arrives. How long before they get here?"

"Uh, about that…" She reached him just as a piteous whine sounded from deeper in the forest. Dense undergrowth and a tangle of vines decreased visibility into the interior. She shuddered, reluctant to trek farther without letting anyone know their whereabouts. "We need to use your phone. Mine died."

Carlson yanked it off his belt, but when he looked at the screen, he frowned. "No service. Sorry."

"Let's go back to the road. It'll work there."

"Not without helping that kid." His feet crunched on dead twigs as he turned inland.

"How do you know it's a child? It could be an animal."

"Animals don't cry like that unless they're hurt. You can

wait here if you're afraid. I have a Labrador and two cats at home. Whatever this is, it's in pain."

She admired his compassion but not his stubbornness. If nothing else, she'd get insect bites and scratches from battling her way through the branches, not to mention tangling with cobwebs.

The alternative, waiting alone by the roadside, appealed to her less. She could walk back to the nearest residence, but the heat sapped her energy. Her best chance was to stick with Carlson.

Dead leaves crunched underfoot as she hastened after him. He might dress like a city slicker, but he knew how to blaze a trail. He forged ahead, swatting plants out of his path and skirting rocks.

"I'm thirsty. Don't suppose you have any water?" he said in a gruff tone, his neck ringed with perspiration.

"Nope, sorry." She listened for the sound of a trickling stream, but heard only occasional bird cries, rustling leaves, and those pitiful wails. Ugh. It reminded her of the horrible cries in the Trollek village, except this sounded inhuman.

"It can't be much farther." Carlson mopped his brow.

Nira paused beside a moss-draped oak. "I hope you know the way back." Light ebbed as the trees closed around them.

"We'll be fine. I've been breaking branches along the way so we won't get lost. Keep going forward."

Steering clear of some prickly-spined plants, she moved on, her trepidation growing.

This was a bad idea. We should have stayed by the roadside and waited for help.

Nearly colliding with a cobweb, she ducked past and sped ahead. She bumped into Carlson who'd come to an abrupt halt.

"There," he said, pointing. Triumph brightened his face, reddened from exertion.

Nira spotted the cave and stepped back. "Oh no, I'm not going inside, and I don't advise you to do so, either. It could be a bear making that noise."

"Hello?" Carlson's voice boomed in the clearing. "Can you hear me? We're here to help."

"I don't think it's a child." Her blood curdled when a series of sniffling cries issued forth. Carlson could be right. It sounded like someone in pain.

Carlson picked up a large stick. "Wait here." He approached the darkened gap. "Too bad we don't have a flashlight."

"I have an emergency light on my keyring."

He took it from her and flicked on the blue LED light. His way lit, he disappeared inside the yawning gap. A moment later she heard him holler.

"It's a dog. Someone left it tied up in here."

She edged into the narrow space which widened a few feet further into a small cavern. Sure enough, a rangy mutt was secured to a rock by a gold-colored cord. Its coat matted with grime, the small creature wagged its tail at the sight of them, straining on the leash looped around its neck and body.

"Poor thing is too hoarse to bark." Careful not to scare the animal, she advanced slowly.

He looked half-starved from his scrawny body and his dry tongue hanging out between panting breaths. Sad brown eyes regarded her as he gave a low, pleading whimper.

Detective Carlson didn't budge, his features wary. "I don't know. This whole setup doesn't seem right. Maybe we should—"

"Untie him, of course." Nira sprang forward.

"Wait!"

But it was too late. She'd unlooped the cord from the rock and undid the knot. *Strange.* The leash felt more like a ribbon than a rope. Why hadn't the creature broken free before? Surely this silken bond wouldn't be enough to hold him, even in his weakened state.

Unease rose the hackles on her nape. Had she judged wrong?

Released from its restraint, the dog leaped forward, its eyes glowing in the darkened interior. As she froze, its body fattened and elongated. Its ears stood up and its fur lengthened. Rows of incisors flashed in a feral grin, as it morphed into a much more dangerous animal.

A wolf.

"Get out," Carlson yelled.

She didn't need his words to spur her. She'd already taken flight.

Nira had just cleared the cave entrance when a snarl sounded from behind followed by a scream. Nira spun, and her stomach dropped. Oh God. The beast had pounced on Carlson.

Quick. Grab a rock.

She snatched a weighty specimen and hurled it at the wolf. The rock hit his nose. He howled, his eyes glowing with fury. Its powerful jaws snapped at Carlson's throat. The pair rolled, one over the other, a tangle of arms and legs and sinewy limbs.

A spurt of blood flooded the dirt. Carlson's body jerked once, twice, then grew still.

Nira's bones turned to ice as she stared in fascinated horror. The wolf, who'd expanded to monstrous proportions, opened its huge jaws and engulfed its victim in one swallow.

Nira's mental freeze snapped, and she shrieked.

The animal swiveled toward her, its yellowish eyes gleaming.

One flying leap, and it would be over.

Would the beast tear her limb from limb? Or would it swallow her whole, like Carlson?

She had a last, fleeting thought that someone would find their cars and report them missing.

She faced her death head on, wondering if Zohar would care.

Chapter Twenty

"What are you waiting for?" She met the wolf's predatory gleam with a lift of her chin.

"I owe you my thanks."

Nira stumbled backward. "You can talk?"

The beast cocked its head. "You released me from the magic chain no one could break."

"I-I… yes, I did. I freed you." Maybe she could bargain for her life.

"I will make your death painless in return." He bared his fangs, dripping with blood from his dead prey.

"Wait." She held up her hand, palm forward. "I know your name." In fairy tales, saying a sorcerer's name aloud often neutralized his power.

"You do not." A low growl tore from the wolf's throat. Drool slobbered from his mouth as he stood poised to strike.

So far everything she'd encountered related to Norse mythology. Her face lit as she remembered the appropriate tale.

"You're a Fire Giant in disguise. You bit off the hand of the God, Tyr."

The beast snarled. "Tyr tricked me. They all tricked me. You will pay, human. Just as I crushed Odin before, so shall I crush his descendants."

According to legend, the Gods attempted to restrain the great wolf but nothing would hold him. Not wishing to kill the creature, they begged the Dwarfs, makers of magic, to create an indestructible chain.

The Dwarfs wove a magic ribbon, and the Gods challenged the wolf to a contest to see who could tear it. Averse to being called a coward, the wolf agreed to prove his prowess if one of the Gods stuck his hand in the wolf's mouth during the ordeal. He wasn't a fool and realized this might be a trap.

The God, Tyr, volunteered, remaining stoic while the Gods tied the monster with the indestructible ribbon. When the wolf realized he could not break free, he bit off the God's hand in his wrath. Tyr became the God of Law because he respected the contract and sacrificed his hand rather than go back on his word.

"Look, the Gods spared your life. They're the ones who imprisoned you. I had nothing to do with it, so why don't you show me the same mercy? I'm worth more to you alive."

"I do not deliver mercy to the daughter of my enemy. Prepare to die." The ferocious beast leapt.

"Fenrir," she yelled, "that is your name."

"Arrgh!" It dropped to its haunches, fur glistening on its powerful body. "Never fear, human, we shall meet again. When I have joined with my brethren, nothing will stop me: not saying my name, not your puny magic, not any arguments you offer on behalf of mankind."

Letting loose a chilling howl, Fenrir loped into the woods and vanished.

Nira fell to her knees, shaking violently.

Oh man, that was close, so close. And Carlson, dear heaven. He'd only wanted to help some lost child.

Tears trailed down her cheeks as she rocked, hugging herself, until her terror ebbed and her energy dissipated. Devoid of strength, she barely managed to push to her feet. A glimpse of Carlson's blood on the ground made her stomach heave.

If she'd doubted her beliefs before, this encounter had brought clarity to her mind. Events truly were repeating themselves. What had Edith said? *All that came before will come again.*

She quaked at the notion that Ragnarok loomed in their

future. In the legends, portents heralded the great cataclysm, many of which existed today: armed conflicts around the globe, corruption running rampant, hunger, and pollution.

In the first Ragnarok, the skies went black. The earth grew cold and withered. Perpetual winter descended upon the world. Fires, earthquakes, and tidal waves swept the land, and all life extinguished. Could this explain why the dinosaurs vanished?

Destruction would find them again unless… *the six daughters of Odin joined with the six sons of Thor to utter the ancient words.*

Her purpose firm, she accepted that her encounter with Zohar had been ordained from the start. Ditto regarding her passion for Norse mythology and her quest to discover the past.

She glanced at her watch. Edith said the symbol etched on its face was the key. She might be no closer to finding the Fountain of Wisdom to interpret it, but at least now she understood her role.

If this was her destiny, she'd embrace it. *Better than a boring life full of bill payments, meal planning, and laundry, huh?*

Running a finger under her collar, she realized the sun had begun to wan. Sweat and grime coated her skin, making her itch. She smacked her lips, so dry they hurt. But how could she think of her own discomfort when Carlson was dead?

Needing to do something to honor his memory, she mumbled a quick prayer for his departed soul. With no body to bury, she kicked dirt over the stain on the ground instead. A gleam caught her eye. Her keyring lay in the grass where Carlson must have dropped it. She scooped it up, shaking the dirt off her keys.

One last errand remained. Summoning her courage, she darted inside the cave to snatch the golden ribbon. The magic cord might come in handy someday. Stuffing it into her pocket along with the keyring, she emerged from the gap between the rocks. Except for the matted grass, the clearing appeared tranquil.

Looks can be deceiving.

True. She shouldn't forget what she'd learned.

Wary of letting her guard down, she ruffled her hair to get rid of cobwebs. She must look a mess, but who cared? Glad to be alive, she inhaled a deep breath of earth-scented air.

Time to summon assistance. She fingered the diamond ring. Would Zohar come if she activated its alarm, or would he send one of his men? Fear fluttered in her chest. She'd introduced him to her culture, and now the warrior from outer space had no further use for her. She'd been abandoned again.

Nonetheless, she pushed on the faceted stone and sent the emergency signal to summon him. Despite her doubts, they had more important concerns, like saving the world from myths come alive. She and Zohar were bound together to save humanity, if only she could convince the Drift Lord captain to believe her.

****

"Zohar here," he answered his page.

"*Rageesh*, where have you been?" Paz's voice came through loud and clear over their comm channel.

"I escaped the Trollek village through the portal in the mirror. I am on the same island, but this time I summoned my shuttle. Our frequency works from the beach."

He surveyed the sandy stretch, strewn with sun-bleached shells and seaweed. Salt air teased his nostrils, while a light breeze ruffled his hair.

No sign of any pfrells, thank the Creator.

"I received an emergency signal from Nira. How do you want me to respond, sire?"

Fear for her safety surged until he remembered his recent findings about her deception. His jaw clenched. "How is Dal?"

"His condition has worsened. He's been moved to what they call an Intensive Care Unit. Yaron stays with him."

"And Kaj?"

"He's patrolling the ley lines as you ordered. Borius is still searching online for signs of Trollek activity around the globe. He's found a number of possible hot spots and wants to know if he should check them out in person."

Zohar cursed inwardly. "That would spread us too thin. If we get the jammer out of action, our sensors would locate the gateways. That remains our priority."

"True, but the jamming device could be located at one of these sites."

"All right. Send Borius out with Kaj. They can follow up on the leads together. I will track Nira's signal."

He swallowed hard. Gazing into Nira's alluring eyes and smelling her enticing scent was just what he'd been trying to avoid.

"Did you discover anything new in the village?"

"Yes, but we will discuss it later." He signed off, reluctant to confront Nira but realizing the necessity. Unlike his father, he would not condemn a person without a trial. She deserved the chance to explain.

He landed his cloaked shuttle north of Orlando at the given coordinates. She sat on a hill near where her car was stalled, or rather blocked by a large tree branch. Had she been hit by that car stuck behind hers? An accident might cause her to huddle into such a small figure, knees bent, hands covering her face. She looked so tiny and helpless that he raced forward.

"Zohar! Where did you come from?" She leapt to her feet when she saw him.

His heart lurched at the hope and joy that sprang into her eyes. "Paz relayed your signal to me. I took my shuttle here. What is wrong?" He wanted to maintain his distance from her but her delicate features and forlorn figure battered his resolve.

"I can't move that branch."

He stared at her. "For this you summoned me?"

She drew herself upright, nose in the air. "I also want to share what I've learned. That is, if you're still interested."

Her eyes flashed and her full lips pursed. He thought she'd

never looked sexier. His caution blown, he yearned to sweep her into his arms and turn her eyes dark with passion.

"Where is the driver of that other vehicle? Has he gone for aid?" He curled his fingers. It took all his restraint not to touch her and feel the silky smoothness of her skin.

"He's gone, all right, but not for help." Her lower lip quivered. Clearly something had agitated her.

"Stand back." He drew his T-6 and set it to vaporize. Soon the log no longer blocked the road. Zohar kicked the residue, and the powdery ash scattered on the breeze.

"Do you think… you could get rid of Carlson's car like you did the tree branch?" Nira asked in a small voice.

"Why?"

"I'll explain later."

That you will. "All right."

After she moved her vehicle safely beyond the traffic lanes, she joined him by the roadside where he'd finished his task. He waited under the shade of a moss-draped oak tree.

"Thanks, I'll be all right now." She averted her gaze so he couldn't read her expression. "Let's meet back at the house."

He tilted her chin so she had no choice except to look at him. "You may not leave yet. First tell me what happened." Intent on getting her to divulge her secrets, he lost himself in her chocolate brown eyes.

"We shouldn't hang out here. It isn't safe." She moistened her lips. "Carlson is dead, and I nearly got killed, too."

"What do you mean? Who is Carlson? Talk to me, Nira."

His glance rose past her stubborn nose to her brows, arched like two crescent moons. His loins tightened. Chariots of the gods, how he wanted her. Suspicious of her motives, wary of trusting her, he still wanted to drop her on a bed of grass and make wild love to her.

"I'll tell you later. I'm just so glad you're here."

Her voice cracked, and that unraveled him. For whatever reason, she needed comfort, and he was only too glad to offer it to her. Just a quick kiss, he told himself, but when he dipped his head, the touch of their mouths set him afire.

Her hands pressed his chest, lightly as though she meant to push him away. But when he deepened the kiss, she sighed against him and her hands clutched his shirt. He darted his tongue out, ready to explore, his exaltation swelling when she joined him in a duet. Never had he met a woman who gave herself so generously without any practiced airs. Nira delved wholeheartedly into her passions with a sweet naïveté that beguiled him.

Supporting her nape, he changed the angle of his mouth, wanting to devour her. With his other hand, he held the small of her back, where she yielded to his pressure to draw nearer. Their bodies folded together. When her arms snaked around to hold him, he let out an animalistic moan.

"See what you do to me?" He ground his hips against her. It took all his strength of will not to toss her to the ground and rip her clothes off. "When we are apart, all I think about is our mingling. When we are together, I am on fire. I cannot think straight."

A warning bell clanged in his mind, restoring his reason. Had he forgotten what he'd learned in the village? She'd killed a man without leaving a mark on him. Worse, she had lied about it.

Lowering his arms, he stepped away. "We have things to discuss. Let us return home and talk there."

"O-kay." Her face flickered with disappointment then firmed into determination.

Glancing at his chronometer, he noted it was six-thirty, local time. Soon it would be dark. An insect buzzed his ear. He swatted it away, pausing when another sound wafted on the wind: a melody, in a high, clear voice.

The compelling notes rose and fell, attuned to the breeze whistling through the trees, the worms crawling through the soil, and the birds soaring overhead. Such music could steal one's soul.

"Do you hear that?" He cocked his head.

"Hear what?"

"A woman's voice. This way." Grabbing Nira's hand, he yanked her toward the woods bordering the roadway.

"Stop, Zohar." Panic inflected her voice.

"We have to find this person who sings with such glory."

"I've been through this already. Let go of me." She dug in her heels, resisting, but he dragged her along. "You don't understand. We heard noises earlier, too. Carlson wanted to investigate. He thought it might be a lost child."

Her words gushed like a waterfall, consonants tumbling one after another. She wasn't making sense.

"Who the devil is Carlson?"

"A police detective who followed me from Orlando. He questioned me after I saw the psychic in Cassadaga."

Forging through a tangle of vegetation, he followed the sound. Water joined into the mix, a gurgling noise that grew louder with each step. Branches lashed his face, but he ignored them, pulling Nira in his wake despite her protests.

"Keep talking." Zohar sniffed, wondering whether her caution had merit. He didn't detect any cors particles, just an earthy scent with a pleasant, spicy note.

"We found a scruffy, starved dog tied to a rock in a cave. Except it wasn't a dog. It morphed into a wolf. A wolf from the legends, Zohar. They're all true."

Her words bounced off him, so intent was he on his goal. They were getting closer now, he could tell because the singing rang clear on the evening air. Through a stand of spindly tree trunks, he spotted the girl.

She sat on the slope of a meandering stream, her bare legs stretched out beneath a cotton sundress. She wore no shoes and her golden hair twisted into two braids.

"Look, there she is." He increased his pace.

Nira kicked him in the shins. "Wake up. You're not behaving rationally."

His knee folded, and he lost his grip on her. "What's wrong with you?"

Nira broke free and staggered back. "Don't you see? This could be a trap, and you've fallen for it. That girl is luring us here, just like the ancient sirens called to sailors."

"The singer may be a child, but her voice is fabulous. Stop acting so paranoid. Hello there," he yelled to the stranger.

The girl gave them a startled glance. "Oh, hello. Please help me. I've injured my ankle." She wiggled her toes, wincing as if to demonstrate her pain.

"I'm telling you, this is a set-up." Nira's voice hardened. "I won't fall for that ploy twice." She snatched his phase gun from where he'd tucked it behind his waistband. "Give it up, Fenrir, or I'll shoot."

Zohar regarded her, open-mouthed. She'd aimed at the child, using both hands that shook visibly. Was she out of her mind? "Put that down. Can you not see this girl needs our assistance?"

"Yeah, right. I'm damn tired of fighting today. Stand aside, Zohar, so I can have a clear shot."

"I mean you no harm." The girl regarded them with wide green eyes. "My name is Sylvia."

"What are you doing here, Sylvia?" Nira demanded. "Why are you alone in the woods?"

Before the girl could answer, Zohar spun in a crouch and kicked the weapon from Nira's hand. He caught it in mid-air.

Exchanging a glance with her, he felt smug satisfaction at her angry glare.

"I was gathering herbs, but I tripped on a rock and gashed my leg." Sylvia pointed to a red slash on her skin. "I'll be okay if I can get that plant on the other side of the stream. It has healing properties and will ease the pain so I can walk."

"Are you from Cassadaga?" Nira asked, as though that would explain everything.

"I live nearby, but I'm not a member of the camp if that's what you mean."

"Your parents let you go into the woods by yourself?" Nira scoffed.

"I come here all the time." The girl's voice rose and fell in a melodious cadence. "When I hurt my ankle, I got scared and started to sing. That's what I do to calm myself."

Nira tapped Zohar's arm, her gaze compelling. "Let's go. We can call 911 from the road."

The little girl attempted to stand but collapsed with a whimper. "Don't leave me. Please just pick a few stems of that plant. See the ones with yellow flowers? They'll heal my wound so I can stand. My mother wouldn't want outsiders to treat me."

"I'm heading home," Nira said in an undertone. "If you want to play her game, do it without me." With a suspicious glance at the girl, she turned away.

"Wait," Sylvia cried. "I have something valuable for you if you help me. It will aid you on your quest."

As Nira hesitated, Zohar narrowed his eyes. When someone offered gifts, he proceeded with caution. He'd learned his lesson from a silver-tongued salesman on Marresh Station. He had been fighting a stomach virus, and the slick-haired fellow had provided a remedy. In hiding from the empress's troops and weak from dehydration, Zohar had accepted the brew, actually a drug to disable him.

The purveyor had turned him over to state forces. Those lost hours were a dark blur in his memory, but he remembered endless questions about his colleagues' whereabouts and his nerves screaming with pain. He'd broken free when a disagreement between his jailors diverted their attention.

His men never spoke of the incident, even after he'd submitted himself for recuperative counseling. It hadn't affected his leadership of the Drift Lords, but the experience had only increased his self-doubts in terms of ruling the land.

He regarded the girl, assessing her. Had her music so bewitched him that he'd let down his guard with such ease?

Stepping forward, he intended to offer his assistance if only to allow Nira to escape.

"I will give my gift only to you." Sylvia pointed to Nira, who had turned toward them. "It will take you where you want to go."

Zohar's blood chilled. Nira had been right to warn him. He shooed her away.

"Go on, I will handle this." Could Sylvia be a Trollek? Usually, they didn't send their young through the dimensional gate, nor did they confound human children, but it's possible they'd made an exception this time.

"Why do you not just give me your gift?" Nira waved at her. "You probably cut your own leg and are perfectly capable of getting to your feet."

"Please believe me." The girl pressed her palms together. "I truly need your help. You search for knowledge of your past. Get me those plants, and I will tell you where to find the answers you seek."

"Oh, for God's sake, more riddles." Nira stripped off her shoes and threw them on the ground. Then she stooped to roll up her pant cuffs.

"What are you doing?" Zohar glanced at her askance.

"I'm wading into the stream. You wait here. It'll take me a minute to pick those stalks."

"No, you stay, and I will go." Maybe those stems oozed poisonous sap. He wouldn't allow her to take the chance.

Zohar approached the gurgling brook. Crystal-clear water swirled over a sandy bottom strewn with smooth, round rocks. It looked gentle enough. Across the bank, yellow flowers swayed gently in the warm summer breeze. Hopping first on one foot and then the other, he yanked off his boots.

"I didn't finish telling you about Carlson." Nira passed him and dipped her foot in the water.

He shook his head in exasperation. "All right, go ahead, since you insist."

Her face turned grim. "The detective followed me from Cassadaga. He drove the car stuck behind mine. We heard cries coming from the woods, and he thought it might be a lost child. Instead, we found a dog tied in a cave. The dog changed into a wolf and ate him."

"Say again?" He gaped at her.

"The cute little dog was Fenrir, a Fire Giant in disguise. He's a shapeshifter who takes the form of a huge wolf." She gave a brief recap of the legend. "That's why I don't believe Sylvia is an innocent little girl who needs our help. However, I'm willing to give her a chance if she'll provide some answers."

His hackles rose. Instinct urged him to flee while they had the opportunity.

Nonetheless, Zohar submerged his toes. If Sylvia could help them in their quest, it was a risk worth taking.

Chapter Twenty-One

"Let's just grab those flowers and get out of here," Nira muttered to Zohar. Cool water swirled about her ankles, reminding her of fond memories from her youth.

Her adopted mother had often taken the girls on lakeside picnics. They'd pack a cooler with cold chicken and homemade potato salad and juicy plum tomatoes. Then they went swimming, without worrying about the many dangers that ruled the news these days. Those were simpler times, but they brought peace and love.

With a bittersweet smile, she watched Zohar enter the water. She appreciated his effort to take charge so she could remain safe. Usually she took care of everyone else. His solicitous attitude made her feel special.

As though reading her mind, he gave her a dazzling grin that set off a coiling warmth within her. She could get used to having him around. His presence radiated comfort and security. His broad shoulders and tall stature provided strength. His commanding air demanded respect and made her want to earn his regard. And what for? So he could leave her in the end?

Dismissing her wistful fancies, she focused on their target. At the opposite bank, the yellow wildflowers swayed in the breeze. A honeyed fragrance drifted her way. All she had to do was skip across the rocks and pluck a few plants.

She skirted a slimy stone and stepped onto the sandy bottom, her feet sinking into the moist granules. The water rippled as it dodged rocks and danced downstream. She advanced a few paces, dipping into a deeper zone where her legs sank to mid-calf level. Zohar, maintaining his balance by wind-milling his arms, tiptoed across the rocks toward her.

Meanwhile, Sylvia had climbed the ridge to watch from a higher vantage point.

Nira gave her a sharp glance. She had thought the girl's sore leg hobbled her. That must have been a ruse, as she'd suspected.

Sylvia's voice carried as she began to sing, the words indistinguishable on the wind.

Nira looked down. She'd sunk lower, where the water frothed and spun as though resenting the intrusion. She glanced back at Zohar, who'd almost caught up to her. He wore a puzzled frown.

They'd better hurry to the opposite bank, but when she glanced at their objective, her breath hitched. The flowers seemed more distant, the opposite slope smaller in perspective.

Impossible. She'd been halfway across.

A faint roar droned in the background, competing with the girl who chanted her song in a rising voice. With each high note she sang, the crescendo got louder. Nira glanced upstream, where the brook disappeared around a bend surrounded by dense foliage. The hills rose on either side, forming a wedge.

Uh-oh. It had rained last night, too.

She'd heard of tumultuous tides and flash floods, but never in Florida. Yet as her eyes widened, water catapulted between the two steep ridges. White-capped, fomenting waves charged in their direction as though propelled by demons.

She shouted a warning to Zohar just as the rushing rapids licked at them with an advance wave. Then the full force arrived to snap at her knees and uproot her into the frothing deep. In an instant, the brook became a raging river.

Nira sucked in a quick breath as her feet lifted. She submerged, flailing her arms for balance. The strong current swept her along, smashing her into rocks and sharp-edged reeds. She gasped each time her head broke the surface, bruised but still breathing, her strength rapidly ebbing.

An eddy pulled her under again, and she tumbled into a tangle of weeds, panicking when her ankle snagged.

No, she wouldn't die this way.

Her lungs burning, she untwisted the vine to free herself. She burst to the surface, inhaling a large breath of air. Zohar's head bobbed up—then he vanished. The current pushed her along, forced her underwater again. Opening her eyes in the murky depths, she noticed a vine trailing from above.

Old advice for dodging undertows came to mind. *Swim parallel to the current until you break free. Don't fight against it.*

She kicked her legs to propel herself diagonally, using a large rock as a lever. Inch by inch, she advanced toward the fibrous vine. Resisting the urge to open her mouth and gasp like a dying fish, she grabbed the vine just as Zohar's body crashed into hers. He seized her by the waist to secure a hold on her.

She tugged on the vine to show him what she intended. He nodded, his cheeks puffed and his lips pursed like a great trout. His big hands clamped over hers. Together they hauled on the vine, kicking toward the surface to gain a breath of lifesaving air. Smashed down again, they held on tight.

Progress took minutes but it seemed like hours. Once her feet touched bottom and her head broke the surface, Nira sucked in huge gulps of air. Coughing and spitting water, she crouched until her lungs cleared. Finally, she could breathe without long shudders. She crawled onto the sandy bank, scraping her knees. Too exhausted to climb the slope, she collapsed on her stomach.

Zohar landed on his back, his arms splayed out like a human sacrifice. He gasped for air beside her until his respirations slowed. Then he rolled sideways to regard her with bleary eyes. "Are you all right?"

She warmed to his concern. Drenched and tired, he still thought of her welfare first. His body heat radiated toward her, lighting her inner furnace and igniting a low fire in her belly.

"I'm fine." She resisted the urge to press her mouth to his to raise their body temperature. "You?"

"Good enough. You were right. Sylvia tricked us. She must be working for the Trolleks."

Nira sat up abruptly, her sodden hair causing rivulets of water to stream down her face. "Where is she? I don't see her."

"She's gone?" Swearing, Zohar struggled to his feet.

"Over here." Sylvia waved from their side of the river. She stood at the top of the slope, golden hair loose and blowing in the breeze. "Please complete the task I have given you, and the path to enlightenment shall be yours."

As though attuned to her singsong voice, the rapids subsided with her words, until nothing remained except for the pleasant meandering stream.

"Are you confounded, girl?" Zohar demanded. "Do the Trolleks command you?"

"Stand aside, soldier of the stars. This is not your trial."

Nira stood in her sopping clothes and squeezed out the excess water. At least the air was warm so they'd dry off quickly. Dusk would come soon but the temperature should stay in the eighties.

"Those flowers you wanted are right behind you." Nira pointed to a spot beyond Sylvia. "Since you can walk, pick them yourself."

"My injury still exists." Sylvia turned her leg to show the gash. "It will not heal unless you fulfill our bargain."

"Then move out of my way."

Her limbs trembling with fatigue, Nira plodded up the hillside. Zohar might be right. Sylvia could be confounded. Or she could be a Trollek herself, although Nira's brow didn't ache like it normally did in the beasts' presence.

"Only those pure at heart shall succeed." Sylvia stepped back, making way for Nira with an encouraging smile.

Was she an ally or an enemy?

"Whatever." Nira could figure out the riddles later. Reaching the summit, she plucked a handful of yellow blossoms. "Here." She shoved them at the child as Zohar reached her side.

Sylvia beamed with approval. "You have done well." She accepted the offering, broke a stem in half, and dabbed the sap onto her wound. Her flesh began filling in instantly until she bore smooth skin with nary a mark.

"See? You possess powers beyond your comprehension." Sylvia's wise eyes regarded Nira with the knowledge of the ages. "When you have need of them again, these flowers will reappear."

"That's good to know. Now what's this reward you promised?"

"You can have my shoes." Sylvia slipped off her black leather pumps.

Hadn't the girl been barefoot earlier?

Nira took them with a doubtful expression. The shoes had shiny gold buckles that added style. Actually, they looked a lot like the pair of very expensive shoes Nira had seen in a high-end catalog recently. Could the girl have read her mind?

She slipped her feet inside. No big surprise. They fit perfectly. Was this her reward? A new pair of shoes?

"You nearly killed us for footwear?" Zohar put a protective arm around Nira's waist. His incredulous expression said he'd expected something more.

The child gave him an angelic smile. "Did I not say my gift would take the lady where she wants to go? Simply think of your destination, and you are there."

Nira glanced at her askance. "You mean, I just visualize a place, and these shoes will take me there?" Did she have to click her heels together? Or would wishing be enough?

"You will be transported, along with anyone holding onto you. Try it, and you'll see I speak the truth."

Nira hesitated. What if this was a trick and they ended up on the Trollek world?

"Fires of Agathorn, I grow tired of these games." Zohar nudged her. "Let us return to our vehicles."

She dug in her heels, refusing to budge. "Aren't you forgetting something? We'd have to cross that stream again."

His nostrils flared. "What choice do we have? My boots are over there, and I lost my weapon in the river. We are improperly equipped to carry on."

She touched his arm. "I understand your concerns, but I have to pursue this opportunity. You should return home. Your men need you."

"You need my protection." His eyes glimmered. "I will not leave you alone."

"Then let's see where these shoes take us."

"How about Orlando? Consider it a test to see if this gift truly works." He glared at Sylvia as though challenging her to refute him.

"Tests," Nira muttered. "Why is everyone so keen on tests?"

Zohar gestured to the shoes. "Note that small crystal set inside the buckle? It could be an energy source. Paz knows more about those things. He's involved in a private research project involving crystalline structures and the comm networks."

How nice for him, but he's not here now.

"You mean these shoes could be a transport device, like the Trollek technology that allows them to vector shift?"

She lifted her head to query the girl but saw only the yellow flowers waving in the breeze. Pine trees towered in the near distance. The waning sunlight cast shadows on the hillside. "Sylvia has disappeared."

Zohar glanced up. "Look what has shown up in her place: my boots and my T-6. Dry as a bone," he mumbled after retrieving his footgear and his gun.

Their clothes were drying rapidly as well. Nira had given up on trying to figure out how things worked anymore. The rules of her universe had changed.

"Please, Zohar. I have to reach the magic fountain, if it's real. I-I'd like you to come along."

"Would you now?" His low, sexy tone had a purring quality.

Aware of his restrained power, she gazed into his deep turquoise eyes. "I promise we'll go home afterward."

His lips curving upward, he raised his arms toward heaven. "Very well. Imagine us at this place where you drink from the well of knowledge."

Snaking her hand into his, Nira shut her eyes. She imagined the freshwater spring feeding the great World Tree.

Her senses reeled as though her motion sensors had gone haywire. When her brain settled, she opened her eyes, clutching Zohar as if her life depended on it.

They stood beside a small brook, much like the one they'd just left, but the vegetation beyond had changed from pines to tropical foliage. The sounds of trickling water and rustling leaves met her ears, but the noise of civilization had abated. No airplanes. No muted drone of traffic. A bird warbled high in a tree, the only sign of wildlife.

"Where are we?" Zohar dropped her hand and pulled his personal scanner from its waterproof pouch.

"I was hoping you'd tell me."

He fiddled with his instrument. "This does not work here."

"Could we have landed on one of the ley lines like that island?"

"I doubt it. My scanner does not register anything." With a snort of dismay, he replaced the device in its slot.

Her nape prickled. "Is this what the Trollek dimension looks like?"

"Negative. I would be able to get a reading." He sniffed the air. "No cors particles. I wonder…"

"What?"

"I have heard of the space between dimensions but never thought it real."

"This looks real enough." Nira's gesture encompassed the palm trees, broad-leafed plants, red anthurium, purple orchids, and huge trees that stretched toward the bright blue sky. Mountains surrounded them, effectively corralling the peaceful valley. Definitely, they'd left Florida behind. "It feels real, too." She kicked at a stone.

Fruit hung heavy on banana plants and papaya trees. At least they wouldn't go hungry.

"What now?" Zohar scratched his head.

"We may be in the right place." A warm, sweet-scented breeze ruffled her hair.

He drew his weapon. "Then where is your magic fountain? I am prepared to battle the creature guarding its sacred water."

"Put your gun away. We don't want to offend Mimir."

"What manner of monster is he?"

"He's not a monster." A gust of wind sent leaves fluttering to the ground. She lifted her gaze to the branch overhead, and her eyes rounded.

Nearly hidden by the shrubbery was a huge wall of bark. It reached up and up until it vanished into a haze of light.

"Remember I told you about Yggdrasil, the great World Tree that connects the mystical lands of the Gods?"

His gaze speared hers. "Indeed. What of it?"

She pointed to the huge growth. "Behold one of its roots."

"That is a root? It is enormous." He tucked his pistol into his waistband.

"And imagine, it's only one of three."

"What do you mean?"

"Three roots anchor the wondrous tree, and each has its own source of water."

Zohar panned the area. "So where is the source for this one? I see no fountain. What does the legend say?"

Nira leaned against a tree and folded her arms. "We're looking for the Fountain of Wisdom, guarded by Mimir. The Urd well, or Fountain of Youth, is protected by the Norns, Goddesses of Fate. Their root supports the tree at Midgard, so they rule the destinies of men.

"A dragon named Nidhog guards the third spring and gnaws on its root. When Ragnarok approaches, rot will weaken this wood and Nidhog will succeed in chewing through it."

"And why is that bad?" Zohar cocked his head, a curious smile tilting his lips.

At least he's listening, Nira thought with a surge of gratitude.

"Because then the branches will break and fall. Three years of endless winter will follow with howling winds that blow the great tree down. It's happening again. That's the coming darkness Askr predicted."

She told him about her interviews with Edith and the psychic in Cassadaga. "They're repeating the same messages."

"In the stories of Ragnarok, what happens next?" His tone held a note of skepticism.

"Fire consumes Midgard, and all is lost."

"Sounds to me like the end of the world scenario predicted by many of Earth's religious doctrines."

Nira shrugged. "You'll find similarities in all the tales. According to the Bible, God created Adam, the first man, and from Adam's rib, he created woman. In Norse legends, the Gods formed a man and a woman from branches of an ash and an elm tree. Rubbed together, the hard and soft woods produced fire."

"Like how a man and woman rub together to produce children? I like this parallel." Zohar grinned at her, his teasing smile stirring embers deep in her core. "However, precious time wastes while we discuss these fanciful histories. Let us remember our purpose."

Nira's ardor cooled at his easy dismissal, and she turned away. A cluster of flowers shaped like tiny bells tinkled in the breeze. The soil where they grew appeared rich and loamy. Perhaps the water came from beneath?

She approached the woody column that appeared more like a tree trunk than a root. Its grayish-brown bark was striated with grooves reaching upward in a vertical pattern. Her glance skipped from tree to tree and to a juncture where they all met overhead. The basic root had given birth to other roots that sprouted their own branches, providing a canopy that let in limited sunlight to the valley floor.

"How will we ever find Mimir?" She swept her hand at the tangle of vegetation. "He could be anywhere."

A low chuckle sounded from behind. She spun around, her heart skipping a beat.

"Who comes to see the son of Bolthorn and the uncle of the mighty Odin?" A deep voice boomed at her elbow.

A couple of gnarly bumps on the nearest piece of bark blinked open to reveal a set of eyes. After she got over her shock, she noticed features that could apply to a mouth and nose as well. That moss hanging down even looked like a beard.

"You… are you Mimir, the wise one?"

He gave a roar of laughter that shook the branches. "Call me Mim for short."

Zohar rushed to her side, his shoulders hunched, and a scowl of menace on his face. She grabbed his arm with a warning squeeze to stand down.

"My name is Nira Larsen, and this is Zohar Thorald. We need your help, Your Honor." How did one address a god?

"I know why you have come, human."

Nira lifted her chin. "I need to drink from the magic fountain so I can interpret the runes."

"How did you find me?" Mimir's face protruded from the wood. He didn't look at all friendly from his deepened furrows.

Nira glanced at Zohar, gaining reassurance from the proud gleam in his eyes. "These shoes brought us here."

The gaps that were Mimir's eyes darkened. "You dare to wear Loki's magic shoes? Be gone, I will not stand for trickery." His features retracted, melded into the tree.

"Wait, I didn't get them from anyone named Loki. A child, Sylvia, gave them to me as a gift."

"You lie." Mimir's loud voice loosened a barrage of nuts from a nearby tree.

Zohar stepped forward, gun in hand. She hadn't even seen him draw it. "Do not threaten my woman, or I will have your head for it."

His woman? Nira stared at him. She'd barely registered his words before Mimir's roar made the ground tremble and shake.

"My head is all I have left." Mimir's face protruded again. "Do you foolish mortals not know? The Vanir beheaded me eons ago."

Chapter Twenty-Two

"You have brought us to the wrong place," Zohar said, standing beside Nira under a branch of the great World Tree. "This must be the land of the dead." His pitch rose. He couldn't help it. He'd rather face an enemy soldier than a supernatural god.

"Put your weapon away and calm down." Her soft brown eyes implored him. "I'd forgotten my history. Mimir is correct. When he was taken hostage in the war between the Aesir and the Vanir, the Vanir cut off his head. They sent it back to his people. Odin, with the knowledge he'd gained from drinking the sacred water, embalmed Mimir's head and gave him back his power of speech."

"You are already wise." Mimir's bark-like features moved with animation. "However, I suspect you are blind to the truth. Beware the trickery of Loki. Those are his shoes you wear."

Zohar's brain spun with all the names. Aesir and Vanir? Loki? The pair of them spoke as if these mythological beings were real. Then again, who'd ever heard of a talking tree? Giving Mimir the benefit of his doubt, he tucked his phase gun out of sight.

"Our concern is with the Trolleks," Nira told Mimir. "This symbol on my watch holds the key to defeating them."

"Nasty creatures." Mimir coughed, rattling branches and scattering leaves.

Nira held out her wrist. "See this marking? Can you interpret it?"

The great tree-face huffed. "I only guard the well. Those who drink from it gain the knowledge they seek."

Zohar couldn't stop Nira from moving closer. "Then please, tell me where to find the fountain."

Mimir chuckled, a low, throaty sound. "Think you it is easy? The universe must retain its balance. Every gain comes with a cost."

Zohar leapt in front of Nira, remembering her tale of how the mighty Odin gave his eye to drink from the fountain.

"I will not allow you to be harmed. This has gone on long enough. We shall find the well on our own."

"You need to learn patience, traveler from the stars," the god's voice bellowed. "I have but a simple request."

"What is that?" He straightened his spine.

"I am tired of being stuck in this wood. Resting here for so many years, my head has petrified. Retrieve for me the golden hairpin from the elves, and I shall reveal the spring to you."

"You must be joking." Nira lifted on her tiptoes to regard Mimir whose expression showed no mirth.

"Give nothing, take nothing." Mimir's voice taunted them.

Zohar grasped her arm. "We leave now. You can find another means to read the runes. We have wasted too much time already."

But as he hauled her away, the god's mouth pursed, and a great wind arose. Branches lashed at his face. Dust clogged his nostrils. Debris stung his eyes. Strong gusts snapped tree limbs and whipped dead leaves off the ground. The frenzy increased into a roar that hurt his ears.

Nira stumbled as the earth shook, and he lost his grip on her. The wind howled. An ominous cracking sounded above them.

"Incoming." He shoved her away just as a heavy limb crashed to the ground.

He'd learned his lesson. You don't defy a god.

"All right." Whirling around, he raised his palms toward Mimir, whose fury showed on his craggy face. "We will do as you ask. You have demonstrated your power."

The tremors subsided, and the breeze died.

Some warrior, he berated himself, curling his fists at his side. Yet how could he prevail against magic? Ragnarok was merely another name for the catastrophe that would happen if he and his men failed to close the dimensional rifts. Yet unlike their previous encounters with the Trolleks, this time a new element had entered the equation.

He'd sensed it whenever he made a spontaneous spatial shift, like going through that mirror in the Trollek village. A dark presence tugged him downward. Could the feeling of dread it engendered relate to Nira's tales?

If so, darker forces were at work here, and he needed Nira to defeat them. But what of the prophecy that said the sons and daughters of ancient gods must unite to chant some spell? If he and his men represented the sons of Thor, who were the daughters of Odin besides Nira?

"Where do we find the golden hairpin?" Nira addressed Mimir in a weary tone.

Her shoulders sagged, but her eyes shone with determination. She needed a respite but never complained and refused to back down. Pride swelled his chest. She'd make a worthy mate, facing adversity with defiance on her lovely face and devotion in her heart. What man would not be blessed to have her permanently at his side?

More than his pride swelled. By the faith, her bravery alone was enough to engage his lusty response. He resisted the urge to bury his fingers in her fiery hair and turn her mouth toward his to claim her lips.

"You must journey to the realm of the elves." Mimir's knobby brows lifted. "Obtain for me the magic hairpin that restores youth to the wearer. It will make my body whole. But beware: Do not join the dance, or you will never see the sun again."

What those parting words, Mimir's face folded into the surrounding bark. The tree solidified, and the forest quieted.

Zohar turned to Nira, intending to offer support. But when

she moved into his embrace, he groaned with repressed need. Lowering his head, he brushed his lips against hers, unable to stop his flow of passion. She might be courageous, willful, and fiercely independent, but she was still female. Every woman needed succor now and then.

Her body, soft and pliant, melted against his hard form. She parted her lips, allowing his tongue to plunder her depths. He groaned deep in his throat. How he yearned to feel her womanly curves beneath his fingers, to peel off her clothes and feast on her beauty, but he still needed answers.

How had she killed the Grand Marshal? How did she influence the confounded guest playing a doctor at Drift World?

He broke apart and glanced away from her puzzled frown.

"Time to move on." Best to find this blasted hairpin and let her drink from the fountain. Then they would return home and he would demand answers.

Nira's expression shuttered, long lashes shading her creamy skin. Despite his doubts, he credited her words about the mythology coming true. They needed each other, in more ways than one. He pushed his personal issues aside to deal with the most immediate concern.

Grasping her hand, he gave her an encouraging smile. From the way her eyes frosted, it must appear more like a grimace.

"Take us to the land of elves," he commanded.

****

Nira gripped Zohar's hand, closing her eyes and wishing herself to the elven realm. A disorienting sensation hit her, and she cartwheeled through mental corridors until her vision steadied. She blinked, clearing away the cobwebs, and scanned the environs with a critical eye.

Woods at their back, they faced a lake as the sun descended to the western horizon. Insects flitted in the pine-scented air, while her skin felt the caress of a cool breeze. The temperature had dropped from their last location, telling her their locale had radically altered.

"Where are we?" Zohar dropped her hand as though it sizzled.

She glanced at his profile: solid jaw, stubborn nose, and suspicious gaze. How had he gone from a solicitous and tender lover one minute to cold warrior the next? She didn't understand why he'd kissed her and then thrust her away. The Trolleks weren't here for him to need her immunity as protection. What had prompted the kiss and his subsequent action? Did he deny his feelings for her? Or did he resent her interference with his mission and blame her for his failure?

Swallowing, she answered his question. "I assume the shoes brought us to a place where the elves live. It's still daylight. They don't come out until after dark."

He peered at her, scrutinizing her face in a manner that made her skin flush. "Tell me about these creatures."

"I only know what I've read. They're luminous beings who live in the water, woods, or mountains. They like dancing and gambling. A king rules over them."

He frowned. "Like the Trolleks."

"Oh? Are you familiar with their system of government? We have time to kill while the sun goes down. You can tell me more about them." Maybe it would thaw the sudden freeze in their relationship.

She pointed to a boulder big enough to seat two, and they sat at a comfortable distance from each other. Hoping it wouldn't get any colder, Nira drew her knees up and wrapped her arms around her legs.

Zohar stared at the lake, a thundercloud expression on his face. "Trollek society is divided into classes. The ruling class consists of royalty and clan chieftains. The king is elected by a Council of Elders made up of chieftains. It is not a hereditary position… like some other cultures."

She shifted her position, aiming for a better perch. To the west, tangerine colored the horizon where the sun descended.

Something in his tone told her politics was a sore topic for him. She gave him a searching glance. His thick hair hung in damp waves below his neckline. Stubble shadowed his chin. Never had she met a man with such an authoritative air who exuded sexuality from every pore. Just looking at him made her want to kiss his frown away and soothe those worry lines on his brow.

"Go on." She swatted at a mosquito. These woods reminded her of the northeast, with maples and oaks mixed with evergreens.

His shoulders hunched. "Landowners come next in the hierarchy. The clan chieftains, landholders themselves, appoint Grand Marshals to govern their villages. The Grand Marshal acts as local judge and administrator."

"Who's under the landowners?"

"The working class: warriors, farmers, merchants, and skilled craftsmen. Slaves and outlaws fall at the bottom of the scale."

He turned toward her with hooded eyes. "That reminds me. After Dal got taken to the medical facility, I took a shuttle from my ship and returned to the Trollek village."

She touched his arm, regretful of her thoughtlessness. "How is Dal? When I spoke to Paz, he told me Dal had fallen ill."

"Dal took sick after drinking some fruit juice."

"Was he allergic?"

"Nay, I suspect he was poisoned." He leveraged to his feet, meeting her gaze squarely. "You and Borius had both been in the kitchen. It would have been easy to put a toxic substance into the pitcher."

"You're accusing me?"

She stood to confront him. After all she'd done, the lout didn't trust her? No wonder he'd thrust her aside like used goods after kissing her.

His eyes blazed. "You have not been truthful. How did you manage to—"

She cut him off. "No one knew who would drink the juice.

It could have been you lying in a hospital bed instead of Dal." Her jaw dropped. "Do you think—"

"That it could have been another assassination attempt? The thought crossed my mind." His mouth curved downward. "Dal will recover, but I had to reassign everyone's task. I should check in, if my signal works from this location. Paz may have news."

****

Relief flooded him when Paz answered his hail.

"*Rageesh*, I was worried. You missed your last call."

"Sorry, I was unable to get a signal through before. Nira is here with me." He hoped Paz wouldn't reveal anything sensitive in her presence. "Have you news of Dal's condition?"

"He improves, but Yaron fears to leave him. What are your orders?"

Zohar considered their options. While Borius and Kaj patrolled the ley lines, no one tracked the illegal arms shipments to the Trolleks except his off-world friend. Should he pull Yaron from Dal's bedside to work on that problem? He didn't want to leave Dal vulnerable to attack.

"Let Yaron stay with him for now but have him move Dal to the ship as soon as possible. Yaron can figure out an excuse to transfer him from the medical facility."

"Acknowledged. We may have another snag, sire."

"What now?"

"I cannot raise Kaj on his comm frequency."

"*Has'pute*." The Karellian curse slipped from his lips. "He could be out of range. See if you can track his shuttle."

A sense of hopelessness glued his feet to the ground. He should be there with his men, not here chasing some fool's errand.

His glance slid to Nira, whose crown of red hair shone like burnished copper in the fading sunlight. Ever since they'd met, his life had become more complicated.

"Have you gained anything from your analysis of the data

crystals?" he asked Paz. They still needed to learn why the Trolleks were collecting human blood samples. Nira's record might hold the answer.

"Nothing conclusive yet."

Did Zohar detect a note of evasion in his communication officer's voice? "All right. Keep me informed."

"When do you estimate returning to the ship, sire?"

He glanced at his chronometer. "In the morning. It is nineteen hundred hours local time." That is, if they were back in the real world again. They had to be back, since his comm unit worked.

"Understood. Signing off."

Nira remained standing, a wary expression on her face. "I'm glad Dal is better."

"Me, too." He cleared his throat. "Before you changed the subject, I told you I had returned to the Trollek village."

"I changed the subject? Excuse me? Would you rather I not care about what happens to any of you?" She stomped her foot. "What's going on, Zohar? Spit it out."

"My mouth is clean. I have nothing to spit."

"Oh, for God's sake. It's another colloquialism. Tell me what's on your mind and why you're acting so damn strange."

He spread his feet, arms folded across his chest. "You lied to me. The Trollek chieftain was not knocked out with a blow to his head. You killed him."

Nira's mouth opened and closed like a gupper fish in the Sargosi Sea. "I can explain."

"Then do so."

She bent her head. "I was brought to his room. He put his hands on me, and I pushed him away." Her voice hitched. "I-I don't mean physically. I just, sort of, closed a mental door. I meant to, like, block him out, you know. The next thing I knew, he wasn't breathing."

Zohar stared at her in horror. "You murdered a powerful Trollek chieftain with a mere thought?" His voice rose on the last words.

Her gaze lifted, pleading. "Please don't condemn me. I don't understand how it happened."

"You are worse than a Trollek." He backed away. "Is that what happened to the detective who followed you? You wished him out of your way?"

Her face drained of color. "I already told you how he died. A wolf attacked us and swallowed Carlson whole. The wolf was really Fenrir, a Fire Giant in disguise."

"Where is your proof?"

Her eyes welled with moisture, and he felt a surge of guilt for interrogating her so ruthlessly, but he had to be sure of her loyalties.

She reached into her pants pocket and yanked out a cord. "Here, see if you believe me now."

"What is that?"

"The magic ribbon that bound the wolf." She repeated the fable, told him about a conversation with her sisters, and reiterated what the psychics had predicted.

When she finished, the sun had drifted lower on the horizon. "So you have all negatives to report," he concluded. "The police are watching our safe house. You released an ancient beast bent on vengeance. Doomsday approaches, and you have a power that you cannot explain or control."

Nodding, she grinned, her face transforming as he appeared to accept her story. "Look at the positives: Grace is likely still alive. Dal will recover. My power, whatever it means, is part of my destiny to stop Ragnarok from coming to pass again."

Zohar's face split into a wide smile. "I like your attitude, little one. You do not accept defeat."

"As long as we're laying all our cards on the table, you have a few things to tell me." She brushed a stray hair off her face.

His gaze followed the movement then roamed south to her mouth. As the moon rose, so did his desire for this woman who wouldn't be intimidated. "I do not possess any cards. Do you think they would be useful when we meet the elves? The tree god said they like to gamble."

She rolled her eyes. "It's another expression, big guy. It means, spill it out, or tell me what you're hiding. As in, what does *rageesh* mean? You don't like it when your pals call you by that title."

He sank onto the boulder, his fingers splaying on its cool surface. Would revealing his identity change the way she felt about him? Did he care if it did?

"*Rageesh* is an honorary title, used to address the crown prince of the Star Empire."

She gaped at him, while he admired the tawny lights in her eyes. "You're joking, right? I thought you were leader of the Drift Lords."

He patted the seat next to him, and she sat. Her womanly scent drifted into his nostrils, making him fight an urge to slide closer. "So I am. I choose to serve my people in this capacity."

"But what happens… when your father dies? You go back to Karrell and assume the throne?"

"My father is already dead. I have appointed a regent to rule in my stead." He paused. "I should also confess I brought Paz a sample of your hair to verify your DNA. I'd wondered about your influence on the guest at Drift World."

Her lips pursed. "That's another manifestation of my power. Remember how I get a buzzing sound in my head when I'm around Trolleks? When I push against that mental door to shut out the noise, I break the spell on confounded humans. Or at least, then I can command them."

"You can command confounded humans?" A chill crept up his spine at her admission.

"It means I can free them from their Trollek kabak." She thrust her chin at a defiant angle. "That's a good thing, Zohar."

"Ack." He made a choked sound. Her talent was still too close to Trollek mind control to make him comfortable. Worse, she could kill someone with a mere thought.

Yet if they discovered what gave her such a unique ability, maybe they could create a vaccine or an antidote to the Trollek touch.

"There is one more thing." He leaned forward, gripping his knees. "When we were in the village the first time, I came across a sealed room used to… to vaporize people."

"What?" Her round eyes reflected the moonlight.

"It appeared to be a crematorium of sorts, using energy weapons. Records were being stored there as well. I swiped a couple of data crystals for Paz to decipher."

"Do you think this relates to the experiments the Trolleks are conducting?"

"It is likely the method they use to remove evidence."

"You mean, when test subjects die."

He nodded, his throat constricted. They had too many mysteries to solve, and meanwhile, his team was being decimated. He needed to get back to them.

Sounds of laughter reached his ears. He shot to his feet, listening intently. Nira sprang up at his side.

Singing ebbed and flowed on the breeze. It came from behind a line of trees edging the woods, away from the lake.

Zohar took several steps forward then stopped when a luminous glow lit the forest in front of them.

Chapter Twenty-Three

"We may have found the elves." Excitement caught Nira in its grip, and her concerns about Zohar slipped away.

Almost. What about his bombshell about being crown prince of a star empire? No wonder he acted so imperious. It just brought home the fact that one day he'd leave her world to fulfill his duties elsewhere.

Never mind that now. She had to complete her quest, return to Mimir, and drink from the magic fountain. Then she had to find Grace and figure out a way to get her home.

She stood to her full five-feet six-inches. "Let's go."

Zohar's eyes gleamed in the moonlight. The moon cast diamond sparkles across the lake. "Do we have a plan? How do you expect to get this golden hairpin?"

"How should I know? We'll play it by ear."

"What is wrong with your ear?" He peered at her head with a worried expression.

"Oh, for God's sake. Come on, Zohar."

She winced each time one of them scrunched on a pile of dried leaves or stumbled on a root. Shadowy figures moved among the trees ahead.

Would the elves scatter if humans made an appearance?

"Hold out your necklace, the one Askr gave you." She tapped Zohar's shoulder.

"Why?"

"He said it would protect you. Maybe showing it will work in our favor."

"Good point."

From the expression on his face, she could tell the mythology baffled him, but that was okay. She could handle it, as long as he fought by her side.

With Zohar in the lead, they broke through the cluster of thin trunks framing a pastoral clearing. Fireflies flitted about, their lights blinking on and off, but that wasn't the only source of illumination. A campfire burned. Around the flames, small beings crouched with glowing auras ringing their bodies. Other elves danced and sang while a musician played a flute.

"Humans," someone screamed.

Chaos ensued, as dozens of pairs of eyes turned in their direction. Cries of panic resounded through the night.

A mist swirled into the meadow, tendrils curling and licking like flames. It filled every hollow and every corner, narrowing visibility. One by one, the elves faded into the gray curtain.

"Do not flee. I bear the symbol of Thor," Zohar announced in a hearty voice. "We seek friendship and aid."

Fine particles of moisture entered Nira's nostrils as the mist tickled her face. It crawled up her legs, circling her body, reducing her vision. A multitude of voices murmured, seeming to surround them.

The mist tingled as though alive, probed at her temples, snaked around her head. She forced her mind to relax. Only the glen remained in her consciousness along with her physical form and Zohar's presence.

As quickly as it had come, the mist receded.

She took a deep breath, not realizing how she'd frozen with rigidity. Her muscles relaxed. When the veil dissolved enough for clarity of sight to return, she gasped.

A ring of small people, their features delicate and angular, stood staring at them. Their wispy eyebrows rose up on a diagonal, accentuated by pointy ears and sharp noses. Their eyes, glimmering with curiosity, showed watchfulness as well.

Nira spread her hands. "We did not mean to disturb your peace, but we need your help."

A broad-shouldered elf shuffled forward from the shadows, his hefty body encased in a fur-trimmed cape. A leafy crown adorned his mustard-blond head. His long hair, tied at his nape, was pierced by a single gold pin with a knob of quartz on top.

Nira's gaze fixed on their objective. How would they ever win this from him? And why did she feel guilty for coveting it?

Maybe because your aims are selfish. You need the pin to satisfy Mimir so he'll let you drink from the magic well.

Nonetheless, she felt bad for even thinking about stealing the elf's possession. Maybe they could obtain it through some other means.

"I am Jadlok, liege of the lakes region." The elf surveyed her and Zohar in turn. "We don't usually let humans pass, but for you, we'll make an exception. You wear the symbol of Thor, the great warrior god. Why do you seek us?"

Zohar straightened his spine. "We have been commissioned to obtain your golden hairpin. I should like to make you a wager."

Nira glanced at him in surprise. What did he have in mind?

"Would you now?" Jadlok exchanged amused glances with the other small folk. "What could you possibly offer us?"

Zohar jerked his thumb at Nira. "She has a magic leash that can hold anyone it ties. Show him."

As comprehension dawned on what he planned, Nira withdrew the cord. She hated to lose it, but they needed something valuable as a bargaining chip.

Jadlok's opalescent eyes widened. "Is that what I think it is?" He stepped closer, his cape sweeping the ground.

"It held the wolf beast, Fenrir. You've heard of him?" Nira spoke in a soft tone so as not to startle the elves.

"Who hasn't? Don't tell me you freed him?"

She winced. "It was a mistake. He tricked us by taking the form of a rangy little dog."

"And you, puny humans that you are, could not see through his deception. Why am I not surprised?"

The elves muttered amongst themselves in a disapproving clatter.

"It wasn't intentional. But now that you know the value of this item, we can discuss Zohar's offer." She and Zohar both knew the elves liked gambling, but how could he win against them? "Maybe we should just do a trade instead."

"By the fires of Muspel, I don't think so. A contest is much more fun." With a look of glee, Jadlok clapped his hands. "What's your wager, impulsive young fool?"

While Nira stuffed the golden ribbon back in her pocket, Zohar answered Jadlok. "I bet that I can out- dance you."

Alarm skittered up her spine. "No, Zohar. Mimir warned us against dancing with them."

"Do not worry. This charm protects me, remember?"

"It protects you how? Maybe it only guards against the Trollek spell."

He grasped her arm, his warmth penetrating her skin. "I will be fine."

The elves expanded their circle, while Jadlok signaled to Zohar. "Come into the center. Our womenfolk will compete against you."

"Not you, Liege?"

Jadlok regarded him with a bemused glance. "I am two hundred and fifty-six years old. My dancing feet need a rest."

Three shy-looking females glided into the middle, their slim bodies reassuring Nira. Surely Zohar had more stamina than this trio. They wore short skirts and bands of woven fabric around their chests, leaving their arms and legs bare along with their feet. The cooler night air didn't seem to bother them.

Zohar divested himself of his heavy belt and handed his weapon surreptitiously to Nira, who stuck it in her waistband. She hoped his boots were as comfortable for dancing as they were for trekking through the woods.

A bevy of musicians came forth and set up their instruments. They began to play a compelling tune that soon had her tapping her foot. Realizing she could easily get caught up in the beat, she made herself go still, watching Zohar instead.

One of the women grabbed his hands. With fancy footwork, they went round and round while the other two females bounced from foot to foot and clapped. Then they joined the circle, keeping time to the rhythm.

Zohar introduced a series of steps he must have learned on his home world. His feet scuffed and tapped an intricate pattern. Nira's blood heated while she watched his lithe form. Impressed by his gracefulness and the aura of power he projected, she resisted a strong urge to join him.

The beat increased, tempting her. Sweat beaded her brow. She swayed, taking little steps side to side. It was impossible to stay still with music so enticing. Her entire body yearned to jump and leap.

The three elves kept up the pace, their motions effortless, smiles on their petite faces. Their arms waved. Their bodies bent like willow branches in the wind. Their legs blurred. Mesmerized by their quick-footed movements, Nira didn't realize she was keeping time to the rhythm until her breath came short.

"Dance, dance," exhorted the crowd.

They pushed her into the center where she faced Zohar, whose red face told her the exertion took its toll. How many minutes had passed? Glancing at her watch, she was shocked to note the hour hand nearing two o'clock. When had they started? Around ten? Good God, four hours had gone by without them noticing?

"Zohar, this has to end." Her lungs hurt. She wanted to stop but the music pounded in her ears, making her feet move and her body jump. The tune was just so catchy.

Zohar kept going as though he didn't hear her, a glazed look in his eyes. The tempo increased, faster and faster.

Nira's feet flew over the ground. She couldn't last much longer. Her muscles ached in protest, the pain growing. Her heart raced. Her pulse drummed in her ears. She felt as though she'd explode out of her skin if she didn't stop.

Across from her, Zohar wheezed in short, gasping breaths. His eyes took on a wild, frantic look. His face got blotchy.

They were nearing collapse, while the three temptresses pranced in tune, their elven faces smug with triumph.

Nira clamped her lips together as a plan formed in her mind. *If this is a game, it's time to play my trump card.*

Turning away, she skipped over to where Zohar had left his belt. Bending her knees, she scooped it up in one quick motion. The heavy belt weighted her arm, but she managed to sling it over her shoulder.

She danced toward Zohar and rubbed against him back to back. Reaching behind, she took his laser gun and transferred it from her waistband to his.

Her pulse pounding in her neck, she spun around and grabbed hold of him. She waltzed him toward Jadlok, who stood on the sideline clapping his hands.

Nira plucked the hairpin from the king's wiry hair, closed her eyes, and wished her shoes to whisk them back to Mimir's realm.

Darkness closed around her. Blinded, she didn't know if she'd succumbed to the dance or if the magic shoes had worked. Air rushed by, thwacking her, tumbling her to the ground.

The solid ground. Still, silent, and unmoving.

Her ears beheld the silence with awe. While her heart rate slowed and her respirations returned to normal, she huddled on the earth, curled on her side.

Then sounds trickled into her ears: water gurgling, branches rustling, and the steady rasps of someone breathing.

Zohar.

She rolled over. He lay beside her on his back, his chest heaving. The night sky greeted them above, stars twinkling in the heavens, as the humid smell of the jungle invaded her nose.

"Are you all right?" She trailed a finger down his sturdy arm. Muscles bulged under his skin.

"My strength returns. Good work." His insolent grin made her teeth clench at his arrogance.

"Idiot. What were you thinking to make that stupid bet when you'd been warned?"

"The elves like dancing and gambling. It seemed logical."

He rolled to his feet and lifted his belt from the ground where Nira had dropped it. Buckling it around his waist, he adjusted his laser pistol in the process.

Tremors shook the ground. "So, humans," Mimir's voice boomed, "have you succeeded in your task?"

Nira lifted her head and peered into the night. She could barely make out the god's face protruding from the nearest trunk.

"Yes, we have your prize." She dragged herself upright.

"Pierce my bark," Mimir instructed.

"Where?" She approached, ducking under an overhanging branch. A bird squawked nearby, while something slithered under a pile of dead leaves.

"Doesn't matter. Just do it."

Grasping the quartz knob, she stabbed the pin into the bark beneath what looked like his lower lip.

A startled look entered the depressions that signified his eyes. The great face grimaced, its mouth working grotesquely. Pieces of bark felt away and branches cracked.

Underfoot, the earth shook and rumbled.

Nira cast an alarmed glance at Zohar, who gave her a steady smile in return. The amulet still rested against his chest, its golden hue shining in the moonlight. She warmed toward him, reassured by his company, pushing aside the notion that one day he'd leave this planet, and she'd be alone again. In the meantime, she wanted to be with him as much as possible.

His smile broadened as though he'd read her thoughts, but her attention diverted when a bearded man emerged from the tree with a loud grunt. As the bark popped back into place, Mimir strode ahead, shaking off bits of debris. He was stark naked and in full virile form with a reddish beard and hair.

"By the ice caves of Niflheim, I cannot wait to cleanse myself." He strutted forward as though oblivious to their presence.

Nira stared in awed wonder. If this was what a god looked

like, Zohar wasn't far behind. The prophecy rang in her mind. Could she and Zohar really be descendants of the ancient beings who had ruled Earth in the days before time? She might find out if she could read the symbol on her watch.

"Ah, Mimir, you are going to let me take a drink from the sacred fountain now, right?"

Mimir halted by a clump of thorny bushes. Ignoring her question, he bent from the waist, giving them a clear view of his buttocks. "It should be right here."

Zohar scowled at Nira. "Stop ogling the fellow."

"Why should I? He's pretty good-looking for a god."

His warrior's teeth gleamed white in the moonlight. "You want to see a naked man? I can oblige." His hand went to his jeans' zipper.

"Stow it." She held up a hand. "I'm only interested in clinching our deal. Where's this magic well?"

"It has been covered through the ages. Come, assist me." Mimir shoved aside a fallen palm frond.

They helped him clear away a blanket of jungle growth that obscured the site. By the time the sun's rays breached the horizon, they'd forged a channel through to a tropical pool by a gushing waterfall. Foliage provided a natural camouflage. Roots stretched down from overhanging branches, reaching deep below the water's surface.

"Behold, the Fountain of Wisdom." Mimir beamed at his guests. "Nira Larsen, I grant you one sip of the sacred water."

On a glistening rock rested a wooden dipper. As Mimir knelt to retrieve it, Nira's face flushed. She wished he'd put some clothing on, or at least find a bunch of leaves to serve the same purpose.

"Guard your knowledge wisely." Mimir offered her the dipper. "Do not fall prey to those who would use you for their own gains."

"Thank you, I'll be careful."

She grasped the handle, then picked her way carefully over

a series of rocks to the water's edge. Spray from the waterfall wet her face. A moment's trepidation rocked her. Remembering what had happened during their adventure with Sylvia, she crouched down to complete her mission before the water level rose to swamp them.

A ray of sunlight pierced the breaking day. As she got a clearer look at the pool, she gasped. An eye floated on its surface.

"Is that…?"

"Odin's eye? Yes, it is. Hurry, child. I long to dive in and wash off this debris."

Without further hesitation, Nira sank the dipper into the water, brought it to her lips, and filled her mouth. She swallowed, tasting a faint mineral residue.

"Well? You feel anything?" Zohar faced her, his legs spread apart in a combat stance. He, too, wasn't trusting their safety.

"No." She put the dipper on the nearest rock. "Is that it?" she asked Mimir, who readied himself to leap into the pool.

The fierce god wrinkled his brow. "Look at your watch, girl, and go home. Your task here is finished."

She glanced down, moving her wrist at an angle to catch the fledgling sunlight. Ah, there. She studied the symbol that had been incomprehensible before. As she squinted at it, the markings rearranged into decipherable letters.

"Zohar, listen. I can read it. It says, *one of six*." Her voice trembled with excitement.

"One of six?" He frowned. "That is it?"

"There's a phrase here too, but it doesn't make sense. I think it's incomplete. Remember the prophecy: the six daughters of Odin must join with the six sons of Thor to utter the ancient words. Maybe I'm one of the six, and the ancient words refer to a spell. This phrasing could be part of an incantation."

"What kind of spell, against the Trolleks? We do not need magic to defeat them. The Drift Lords have brought them down before."

She shook her head. "There's more at play here this time.

And if I'm descended from Odin, you must be from Thor's line." Her words tripped over themselves in her eagerness to explain.

Zohar regarded her with a grim face. "If what you say is true, we are each of us one of six. My team has lost Rayne. That leaves me, Kaj, Dal, Yaron, Paz, and Borius."

Her eyes widened. "You're right. Six of you remain. Perhaps it was Rayne's destiny to die."

"Perhaps."

He didn't sound convinced, but another, more compelling notion induced Nira to grip his arm.

"Hey, if your team has six guys, where's the rest of my equation? I'm *one of six*. That means I have five sisters, not necessarily blood related, but other women who have the same powers as me. We have to find them."

Chapter Twenty-Four

Zohar heard a splash before a cascade of water dumped onto him. Mimir had dived into the pool. Time for him and Nira to go home before the god emerged and found them still there. They didn't want to provoke his anger.

Nira's hand still gripped his arm. He placed his large palm over hers and squeezed. "Use your shoes to get us out of here."

"You got it."

She shut her eyes, concentrating, and his vision whirled. When he could see clearly again, they stood by her motor vehicle parked on the roadside just where they'd left it.

The rising sun heated the asphalt and made his shirt stick to his back, reminding him he could use a good shower and a change of clothes. Moisture hung in the air, wafting an earthy scent into his nostrils. From the cottony clouds gathering overhead, rain appeared imminent.

"I'll drive my car from here." Nira let go of him, weariness invading her face. "You can take the shuttle, but I'm afraid the safe house might be compromised. Where should we meet?"

"I must return home to retrieve my equipment. Let us rendezvous around the corner from the house. You can whisk us inside without anyone noticing." His head tilted. "Perhaps you can pick up some provisions along the way? I like those round cookies with the sweet dark chunks."

She swatted his arm. "Bad idea. Someone's probably reported Carlson missing by now. If the cops know he was following me, they'll have put out an alert for my license tag. I should ditch the car in town."

"Leave it here and take the shuttle with me."

"No thanks." She blew a stray hair out of her eyes. "I've had enough excitement for one day."

The local authorities are not the only people interested in you, my carona.

Zohar might be shielded by the charm he wore, but why hadn't the Trolleks made another attempt to grab Nira? Were they truly done with her? Was the blood sample Algie's only reason to want Nira?

He may have thought so before, but perhaps Algie merely waited to see what Nira discovered. Now that she could read runes, she'd be more valuable to them. Since he couldn't drive with her, he must offer some means of protection.

While she foraged in her pocket for her car keys, he slipped the pendant off his head.

"Wear this." He held the necklace out to her.

Her large eyes regarded him with astonishment. "Why? The amulet is yours. You need it to ward off evil."

He snorted. "It didn't help much with the elves. You need it more. The Trolleks could still vector shift in at any time to assault you. I have polarized myself. I shall be fine."

He didn't add that his last session had been yesterday morning. He was due for a renewal, but if he and Nira had a moment alone in the house, he'd rather lose himself in lust before immunizing himself. Her flowery fragrance made him wild with wanting. After all their exertions, he craved an hour or so of mindless lovemaking. Burying himself in her would provide the only true comfort he'd ever known.

That thought discomfited him, so he told himself he really wanted to wipe the exhausted look from her eyes and change it to passion. That's all it was, a diversion from stress. She knew it. He knew it. It couldn't be anything more.

"I can defend myself against the Trolleks," she reminded him in a quiet voice as he held out the medallion.

"The Trolleks do not have to confound you. They can take

you by force. I would rather you wear this charm. We do not know how it works. It may provide some sort of energy shield against them."

"O-kay." She put it on, then patted her pockets. "Oh no. I've lost the magic ribbon, Zohar. It must have fallen out when I was dancing with Jadlok's people." Dismay etched her face.

"Do not distress yourself. That may have been the elven king's intention all along."

After watching her drive off, Zohar hiked to the spot where he'd left the shuttle. Decloaking, entry, and liftoff took minutes. Putting the flight plan on automatic, he hailed Paz.

"It's good to hear your voice, *rageesh*."

"Nira and I are headed for the safe house. Have you any news?" Anxiety for his team pitted his stomach.

"Kaj's locator beacon still does not show on our monitors, sire. Nor does he answer his comm signal. And there's one more thing." Paz's voice sobered. "Borius found his shuttle, abandoned on a remote island in the Pacific."

"Any evidence of external damage or a malfunction?" Dread sank like a lead weight to his toes.

"Nay, sire."

"What of Dal? Has he been moved to sickbay?"

"Not yet. He reacted adversely to a medication and remains dirtside in the hospital."

Has'pute. Zohar couldn't afford to lose another one of his friends. Gazing out the viewscreen as his shuttle flew toward Orlando under full cloak, he rubbed his neck.

Maybe that was the plan. Eliminate the Drift Lords one by one. If so, it was working all too well. Forget about the prophecy's six sons of Thor. Until Dal rallied, only Yaron, Borius, Paz, and himself were left from the original team of seven. Nor did he have any trainees in his back pocket he could summon from the Academy.

He swallowed. "Did Borius have anything to report?"

"Nothing unusual. He's wondering if Kaj discovered something significant, so he is repeating Kaj's patrol vectors."

"Good idea." He considered asking for an update on those crystals he'd given Paz to analyze but it would have to wait. He'd almost arrived at his destination.

"Did you and Nira have any success, sire?"

"Aye, she gained the ability to read the symbol on her watch. We will have a debriefing later." Zohar signed off, scraping stiff fingers through his hair.

Fortunately, he and Nira made it safely home without attracting undue attention. He met her at the assigned place, and she used her magic shoes to whisk them inside the house.

She had managed to stop for food stores along the way despite her earlier protests, reminding him if Dal had been poisoned, they should throw out whatever remained from before.

Alone in the house, they ate a quick meal with chocolate chip cookies for dessert. Then Nira headed for the sanitation facility. Hearing the shower run made his loins tighten as he imagined her naked beneath the spray. Standing beside the bed, he stripped off his clothes down to his briefs.

He headed for the bathroom, as she called it, like a bee homing in on a flower.

"What?" she yelled upon his knock.

"I have waited long enough." Zohar pushed open the door.

"Eek! What are you doing?"

He stepped onto the cool tile, kicked his underwear off, and slid the glass door aside. "Make room. I will scrub your back."

Her gaze dropped to his proud member. "Um, I don't really need help…"

"I insist." He stepped inside the narrow space, the evidence of his arousal like a flagstaff between them.

She stood frozen, cloth in hand, staring. Her nipples peaked under the stream of water. How he wanted to lap up the droplets on her skin.

He plucked the washcloth from her fingers. Replacing her under the spray, he allowed the steamy flow to flatten his hair and cleanse the day's cares from his body.

His pulse hammered as he regarded her from under hooded eyes. She smelled like sweet purpura blossoms. He inhaled deeply, soaking in her essence like his skin soaked in moisture. Damp ringlets framed her face. He itched to smooth them back and kiss the tender spots on her temples.

Spurred on when her eyes darkened with desire, he soaped the cloth and approached her with a determined gleam.

So they were destined to be together, huh? Their meeting was the result of fate, not chance? What it meant for their future didn't matter now. All he cared about was erasing those lines etched around her mouth and taking her to that ethereal plane of light and love.

No, not love, a mental voice chided. *It's only a momentary pleasure.*

Yet when they were in the throes of passion, he felt so much more than lust. He felt as though he'd come home.

Weakness lay in that direction, his inner demon said. *You'll lose much more than your seed between her legs.*

Growling, he spun her around and lathered her back until reason fled. After letting her rinse off, he bent to kiss her shoulder from behind. That simple act unraveled him as he nibbled his way to her neck. Her skin was so soft and pliant, and her low moan of pleasure drove him wild. He had to join with her, flesh to flesh, body to body.

His fire ignited, and he yielded to the conflagration.

****

"Brace yourself against the wall."

Zohar's husky rasp sent thrills along her nerves. Her heart pounding, Nira obeyed. He adjusted the faucet to allow a trickle of lukewarm water from overhead. Moistening her lips, she sighed with delight when he reached around to fondle her breasts.

Oh yes, touch me there.

His hot breath tickled her ear while she considered her folly.

She shouldn't let him seduce her like this. She'd wanted time alone, to think about what she must do next. But now she couldn't think at all.

His fingers roamed south to tantalize the sensitive folds between her thighs. She moaned as his fingers explored her. Heat pooled in her belly, gathered strength, fomented like a kettle of lava boiling toward eruption.

"Don't stop." She pressed against him, his stiff organ prodded her juncture.

"You wish for completion?" His low, sexy tone turned her knees weak and her bones to jelly.

"Yes. Now."

"Not yet. Turn around. I will wash your front."

As she complied, he soaped her body from neck to toes, stopping now and then to brush his lips against hers. Leaning inward, she yearned for more. Instead, he increased the force of the spray so she could rinse herself.

"Now do me." He handed her the cloth with a wicked grin.

Intending to give him the same sweet torture, she scrubbed his chest in a slow circular motion, enjoying the feel of his hard muscles beneath her fingers. His soft hair wove from his chest past his taut abdomen to a nest at his privates.

Resisting the urge to grasp what protruded below, she knelt to lather his legs. She didn't neglect his feet, well formed with straight, strong toes and a firm arch. Stroking his sinewy calf with the cloth in one hand, she used her other hand to tickle him along the inside of his leg in an upward sweep.

He sagged back against the shower wall, his face a study in agonized pleasure. His male organ hovered so near her mouth, she could almost taste him. Her fingertips brushed his sex, and it jerked upright. Hard and soft at the same time, his flesh pleaded for her attention. She flicked a thumb across the cleft, pleased when his belly clenched in response.

Sweat broke on his brow. "Chariots of the gods, you drive me mad, woman." He swatted her hands away. "That's enough."

After a quick stance under the spray to remove the suds, he drew her close.

The washcloth dropped from her hand as he captured her mouth. Her lips parted, and his tongue slid inside to claim her heat. No teasing kiss this time. His mouth moved hungrily, insisting on her surrender.

The universe receded except for the trickle of water and the crush of their mouths. If all the Drift Lords made love in this manner, they were masters of much more than the space-time continuum.

Then he broke off and spun her around to face the wall.

"I wish to take you like the wild animal you make me."

He thrust into her from the rear, holding her by the waist as he plunged deeper. Her consciousness ebbed as she joined his rhythm, aiming toward a release so sublime, reality faded. Light and serenity swirled around her as she convulsed, endless spasms sending her to a distant plane. Finally, she floated to the ground ever so gently.

"That was incredible." Her breathing slowed to normal, and she turned toward him. "It's more than just great sex. Don't you feel something different when we're together?" Searching his eyes, she was dismayed to see his ardor dim, replaced by a cool aloofness.

"Indeed." He gave her a quick peck on the mouth before shutting off the faucet. "But let us not dwell on it now. We have work to do." He stepped out and grabbed a towel, tossing one to her. "We have a plan to formulate, people to contact. Get dressed."

Toweling herself off, she stared at his naked butt as he retreated toward the bedroom. What was up with him? He'd disregarded their lovemaking as though it had been another chore on his list.

Her lips compressed. Didn't he see anything in their future together? Then again, did she? Her place was here, with Kristy, Diane, and Grace. Zohar had an empire to run once his Drift Lords completed their mission. A universe divided them. They both knew this and had silently acknowledged that sex was all they could share. Would it be enough?

A hollow feeling inside gave her the answer.

****

"Zohar, we have to talk." Nira strode into the bedroom, a towel wrapped around her womanly curves.

"Talking is the last thing on my mind." Zohar glanced at her exposed cleavage. He burned with the desire to strip that piece of fabric away, to take her again, and to lose himself in her yielding body.

Going down that road would lead to insanity. Soon he'd be like his father, craving her heat, breathing in her essence, fulfilling her every whim. His cock reacted, ready for another round. What did she want to talk about? It was never good when a woman said those words.

Clamping his jaw, he whirled toward the dresser to get his clothes and froze. A red scribble marred the mirror.

"Omigod, what's that?" Nira's voice rose in pitch.

"It was not here when we entered the shower." With an alarmed glance at the doorway, he grabbed his T-6 from where he'd tossed it on the bed. "Get some clothes on."

They dressed in haste, speaking in hushed voices.

"I recognize the symbol. It's a runic death knot."

"Meaning?" He fastened the zipper on his denims, remembering he'd forgotten to set their defense perimeter. His obsession with this woman already undermined his caution.

"See the way those three triangular shapes overlap?" She adjusted her cropped pants and short-sleeved cotton top. "It's called the Valnott. Odin's followers wore this emblem, and they had a tendency to die violently."

"*Jor'ked nok tong.*" His native language slipped from his tongue.

"Talk in English, please."

"I said, how fortunate for us."

An intruder might still be present. Was this how the orange juice became tainted? But which enemy from his home world possessed knowledge of the ancient runes? And how did the villain enter their house?

Zohar didn't sniff cors particles, so no one had vectored in. It had to be someone skilled in the art of stealth.

Watching a lizard scurry from behind the drapery, run along the baseboard, and disappear toward the hallway, he formulated a plan to catch the miscreant. The person might be just as elusive as that reptile, but Zohar would expose him.

Shortly thereafter, he and Nira pretended to take a nap under the sheets, with the drapes drawn and the lights dimmed. He'd considered stuffing the bed with towels and lurking in the shadows, but whoever had watch on them seemed attuned to their movements. It was a chance they'd have to take, hoping the assassin wouldn't shoot them where they lay.

He had to catch the fellow. His team, ever diminishing in numbers, must focus on the Trollek problem and not on political pressures from home. This had to end now.

The window curtain fluttered although the air-conditioning hadn't cycled on. He gripped his laser gun beneath the covers.

Nira lay half-smothered under him for protection. It was all he could do to regulate his breathing when he wanted nothing more than to mingle with her. Her breasts pressed against his chest, torturing him with the urge to cup her softness.

A scratching noise sounded from out in the hall.

Going rigid, he held his breath, before remembering he was supposed to be sleeping. He breathed in and out, cracking his eyes open a slit. A shadowy figure crept toward him.

Zohar thrust the sheet aside and raised his weapon, only to see two shadows collide.

No, not shadows. Two men battling each other.

One bearded with an age-lined face. One strong-armed man wearing a forest green cloak and brandishing a sword.

"Askr. Lord Magnor. What is the meaning of this?" Zohar's aim wavered between the two of them.

Nira popped up, her eyes wide. "Magnor, you're not dead."

"No, my lady." The Tsuran swordsman flashed a fierce grin. "I have been watching over our rageesh to protect him from vermin like this." His sword point caught the old man at the throat.

"Hold it, I'm on your side." Askr held up a hand. "I can explain."

Magnor maintained his stance. "I've been using my invisibility shield. How did you gain entry?"

Zohar slid off the bed, still gripping his phase gun. "You have been following me?"

He didn't know the Tsuran could make themselves invisible. How? Did Magnor's cape hold the technology, or was it an innate ability of their race? He knew so little about them, only rumors meant to frighten children.

Magnor dipped his head at Zohar. "Aye, I have been on your trail ever since the ambush in the alley. I lost you last night, until you reappeared by your shuttle. I expected another attempt on your life, but I did not anticipate so feeble an opponent."

Zohar snorted. "Rayne is dead and Dal has been poisoned. Treachery comes in all shapes and forms."

"You are correct, son of Thor, but you've got it wrong." Askr's voice firmed. "Rayne is the one who plotted against you."

Chapter Twenty-Five

Zohar gaped at the old man. "You slur my friend's honor. I have no reason to trust you, especially when you invade our safe house." He turned toward Lord Magnor. "And you, we thought were dead. Explain."

The dark-haired swordsman bowed. "I set a meeting with Borius to review your itinerary. En route, I received a message offering information on dissidents from Karrell."

"Who sent this message?"

Zohar glanced at Nira who'd risen to stand against a wall, arms folded in front of her. Her narrowed eyes darted from Askr to Magnor as though she didn't know which one to trust.

"The text appeared on my comm unit with no way to trace its origin. I gave Borius the new rendezvous point. When I arrived, I was set upon by a gang of local *riffs*."

"Borius found you unconscious in the alley. He said you'd been injured."

Magnor's eyes glimmered. "That is true. I activated my shield so I could heal on my own."

"What is this shield?"

The warrior's lips curved. "Some secrets must remain with the Tsuran, my liege."

"You knew I'd be ambushed, and yet you left?"

"I figured between you and Borius, you could handle them. Besides, I wasn't far if you needed assistance."

Zohar's brow creased. "Were you here when Dal drank the tainted fruit juice?" If Magnor had been invisible, he could have poisoned the beverage. Or, perhaps he'd seen the guilty party.

Lord Magnor studied a speck of fuzz on the carpet. "I'd prefer to discuss that later, in private."

Who did Magnor want to guard his observations from: Askr or Nira? Zohar would press him for answers at another time.

Uncomfortable continuing their conversation in the bedroom, he gestured for his companions to head into the dining room and be seated at the table.

"Old man, tell us your story." Zohar couldn't wait to hear his tale, although he hoped the fellow would speak more clearly than in their previous encounter by the campfire.

Askr's robe spread on the floor as he sat with a dignified air. "I am Askr, last of the Gatekeepers. We are guardians of Earth whose task is to protect humans during Trollek incursions. It is a duty passed down through the generations."

Askr stroked his white beard. "We and our allies also may act as guides to the Drift Lords. I have been aware of your destiny for some time. I've been keeping watch on you."

"You, too?" Zohar's gaze flickered to Magnor sitting across from him. Even with his legs crossed in a lazy pose, the Tsuran exuded power.

Askr's brows furrowed like wispy clouds. "I have the ability to change my form. You may have seen me as a lizard. Disguised thus, I entered your hotel suite shortly after your first successful engagement against the Trolleks."

Nira hunched forward. "You mean, after Zohar and his team rescued me from the theme park employment office?"

"That is correct."

"Are you the person who called the front desk to see if Zohar had checked in yet?" She tapped a finger on the table.

"I did." Askr nodded.

"Were you in the suite when Rayne came by?" Zohar snapped. Something didn't jive here. How had Askr learned where they'd be staying?

"Hear me out. I observed Rayne tampering with your equipment, captain. Upon realizing he meant you harm, I removed the threat."

Zohar shoved his chair back so quickly that it toppled over. "You killed him?" Standing, he tensed.

"I merely carried out the sentence for treason."

Zohar curled and uncurled his fists, resisting the urge to smash the old man in the face. How dare he take justice into his own hands?

"That explains why there were no signs of a break-in." Lord Magnor's eyes gleamed. "We figured Rayne let in someone he knew, but you were already inside."

"He was shot by a T-6 laser pistol." Zohar, gripping his own weapon, held it up. "These are restricted military class armaments."

Askr lifted aside his robe, showing a similar weapon strapped to his thigh. "Gatekeepers and Drift Lords have been working together since the beginning. Your predecessors gave us an earlier model. We have updated it with minor variations."

"But you say you're the last of your kind?" Nira's brown eyes reflected mingled confusion and dismay.

"It is so." Askr's shoulders slumped. "Things were peaceful until the Trolleks forced open the dimensional door. They sent pfrells to attack before we could rally. The beasts massacred my brothers. I, alone, escaped their assault."

Zohar righted his chair and sat down with a heavy heart. The Trolleks had targeted the Gatekeepers for extermination just like the Great Purge, when the Empress had condemned the Drift Lords to death. But were the Trolleks capable of such cunning?

Certainly, they'd advanced rapidly since his last skirmish with them. Was that due to their own lust for power, or was someone else urging them on, not to mention supplying their armories?

He eyed the old man. Did he speak the truth? Askr claimed the Gatekeepers kept people from harm and aided the Drift Lords during previous rifts, yet Zohar had never heard of them before.

Dread prickled his spine. Who could he trust?

Lord Magnor was reluctant to reveal what he'd seen in the kitchen. And why had he stayed hidden for so long, letting them believe he was dead? He wasn't much of a bodyguard if he allowed Zohar to risk his life repeatedly without getting involved. Did he have his own agenda?

"Zohar and I got attacked by pfrells." Nira studied Askr, suspicion written all over her face.

"Where was this?" Askr demanded, his expression impassive.

"On the island where we met you. They dove at us on the beach. We escaped inland, where we stumbled across some temple ruins. I found a pillar with runic writing similar to the inscription on my watch."

"What did it say?"

Did Zohar imagine Askr's quick indrawn breath of air?

"I don't know. We didn't get the chance to copy it down. But I did drink from the Fountain of Wisdom as you advised. This symbol on my watch reads, One of Six. Does this mean I have five sisters? Real sisters by blood, or women with powers like mine?"

Askr straightened his robe, avoiding her probing gaze. "The others you speak of will need your guidance." He pointed to her wristwatch. "That can help you find them."

"What do you mean? And you didn't answer my question—"

"There's something else you should know." Askr pushed to his feet with the slowness of age. "The Trolleks are not your only enemy. They are merely pawns in a scheme hatched by a greater evil. Be warned. You must…"

A loud crash sounded from the master suite. Glass shattered. Askr glanced at the doorway, and his jaw dropped.

A sharp-beaked creature hurtled inside the dining room.

"Pfrells!" Nira leapt to her feet.

More winged beasts flew in, diving at them. One swooped at Askr, whose hand caught in the flaps of his robe when he went for his weapon. A talon slashed his throat, leaving a broad gash. Blood arched as he slumped over.

Zohar, gun in hand, fired but missed.

Nira shrieked again as a pfrell swiped at her. Zohar switched his aim, at the same time dodging a swinging tail aimed to knock him down. He twisted sideways and fired again. At his side, Lord Magnor fought a savage beast off with his blade.

One creature's loud cawing brought the pfrells to a pause. With a flutter of wings, they crowded the smashed window in the bedroom and flew away.

"What was that all about?" Zohar wiped sweat from his brow. His shoulder throbbed, but he was luckier than Askr.

"The Gatekeeper has been injured." Lord Magnor dropped to his knee, feeling for a pulse. "I am sorry. He is dead."

"Maybe that was their intent." Zohar battled his need to comfort Nira. Her pale face and wide eyes indicated shock. "They killed him, and then they left."

"You mean the pfrells meant to finish the job they'd started in eliminating the Gatekeepers?" Magnor's mouth thinned in a grim line.

"Askr was just about to tell us something important, too." Nira spoke in a hushed tone, her sad gaze falling on the old man.

How did his enemy—and at this point, Zohar wasn't even sure who they were—know the old man would show up here? Askr claimed he'd crawled inside the house as a lizard. Could more than one shapeshifter be at work, or had someone else leaked the news? Someone, say, like Lord Magnor?

The doorbell rang, then a heavy pounding ensued on the front door.

"Police. We know you're inside. Open up."

Nira gasped. "You've got to be kidding."

"We must leave." Zohar prodded her. "Take what you need."

He sped through the house, snatching the bag of cookies from the kitchen, the laptop computer from the study, and his equipment from the master suite. Nira stuffed their essential clothing and toiletries into a couple of pillowcases. Lord Magnor vanished. Did he use his so-called invisibility shield, or could he shift forms like Askr? Primer Pedar had vouched for him, Zohar reminded himself. Gorgie would only send someone who'd earned his trust.

"I am here."

The Tsuran's deep voice startled him, and he jumped. "I wish you would not do that."

"How do you intend to escape?"

He looked in the direction of Magnor's voice. "Nira acquired a pair of magic shoes that act like a transport device. Hold onto her and pray this works."

"Wait, what about Askr?" Nira slung their pillowcases over one shoulder and her handbag over the other. "We can't leave his body here. I know this sounds cold, but the cops already have enough dirt on us."

The pounding on the front door intensified. In another minute, the police would kick it in.

"You are correct." Zohar set his phase gun to vaporize.

Nira followed him into the next room. He did the deed then grabbed her hand. "Magnor, take hold of Nira."

"Where are we going?" she asked.

"To my shuttle." He named a popular tourist attraction. "I parked it among the props in the backstage studio lot. I thought it prudent to hide the shuttle in plain sight rather than cloak it on a residential street where someone might run into it. I hired a taxicab to get to our rendezvous."

"Clever. Hold on tight, here we go."

A familiar whirling sensation accosted him. When his vision cleared, they stood in front of the shuttle, parked between a vintage aircraft and a flying saucer replica. Noise assaulted him: race car engines revving from a nearby show, people chattering, music blaring on loudspeakers. A sweet confectionary scent pervaded the air from a snack stand in the environs.

Lord Magnor materialized alongside them, fortunately after a tourist tram rattled past and rounded a corner. Zohar's mouth curved as he regarded Nira. She stared at his shuttle with a wide-eyed look of wonder.

He dropped her hand and activated his comm unit to signal Paz. Time to regroup with his team to discuss their next move. They still hadn't located the jamming device, although an idea had come to mind that excited him.

"Sire, are you all right?" Paz answered on his first chime.

"I am here with Nira and Lord Magnor."

"Magnor? I thought he'd been—"

"Wounded in the fight. He used some kind of personal cloaking device to make himself invisible while he healed. What's the status with the others?"

Paz sighed. "Dal isn't responding to treatment. It's baffling the doctors. Yaron continues to guard him and he, too, doesn't understand why Dal continues to resist the appropriate therapy."

Zohar compressed his lips. He hated to do what came next, but he needed whichever members of his team he could salvage.

"Tell Yaron to set up a defensive perimeter in Dal's room. He can tell the nursing staff it is some religious ritual. Then have Yaron meet us on the ship along with Borius. Any word on Kaj?"

"No, sir." Paz sounded discouraged.

"That leaves you, me, Borius, and Yaron. Four of us, when there should have been seven."

"Don't forget me." Lord Magnor jerked a thumb at his chest.

"Oh, right. That makes five." When would Dal return to his senses? The prophecy said six sons of Thor were needed. Or maybe Kaj would show up soon. Worry for his engineer's safety gnawed at him, making his stomach churn.

"You have some messages." Paz's voice lowered. "One of them is marked urgent from Primer Pedar. He requests an immediate response."

Zohar gritted his teeth. "It will have to wait. I have enough on my mind."

After signing off, he keyed in the entry code for his shuttle. The hatch swung open.

"I'm not going." Nira stood her ground.

He spun. "What?" He didn't have time for women's tantrums.

"My place is here." Her fiery gaze bored into his. "Your men are your responsibility. Grace is mine. You may not think she's important, but I do. I won't give up my search for her."

"She is one cog in a wheel. Your world will be destroyed if we fail in our mission."

"Family matters more to me." Her eyes hardened into two brown stones. "Remember the prophecy? I have to find my five sisters if we are to prevent the coming disaster."

"We can prevent that disaster if we locate the Trollek jamming device, deactivate it, and locate their portals."

"And then what?"

"Then we seal the rifts."

"It may not be as easy as you think."

"Is that a prediction or a warning?"

Distrust seeped into his mind, along with a sense of betrayal. How dare she think of leaving him at a time like this? Obviously, she didn't care about his goals. She'd just said her earthly concerns mattered more to her. *Fool, you should have known better than to rely on her. That's what you get for opening your heart.*

"I'm just repeating what Askr and Edith told me." Her clipped tone matched the frost on her face. "It'll take more than you warriors to save the world this time around."

"Believe what you want. Every minute we waste arguing, the dimensional drift widens, and the buildup of cors particles approaches the point of no return."

Especially when he had an idea of where the jamming device might be hidden, Zohar didn't have time to spare. His duty precluded him from following forecasts by mystical oracles or from rescuing missing persons. That included Kaj, and while it grieved him to delay a thorough search, Kaj would understand their original directive came first.

From the corner of his eye, Zohar saw Magnor climbing the boarding ramp into the shuttle.

"Guess I'll be seeing you." Nira jutted her chin. "Good luck." She handed him the sack with his belongings.

"You, too." His chest hurt as though an arrow had pierced him. "You still have the ring I gave you, and that pendant may offer some protection," he said in a stiff tone. "Just be aware we will be busy fighting our own battles. If you need assistance, no one may be able to respond."

Chapter Twenty-Six

As she turned away, Nira heard the hiss of the hatch door shutting from behind. She should have known Zohar would abandon her. His parting words had cut deeply, as though she mattered to him as little as an ant.

She kicked at one crawling on the ground, her vision blurring with tears. Leaves scattered and wind smacked her in the face as the shuttle cloaked and took off. Zohar might as well have struck her himself. Pain bit into her at his desertion. She understood his devotion to his mission, so why didn't he realize her vow to rescue Grace was just as important?

Nira fingered the pendant he'd given her, considering how the Trolleks had been mysteriously quiet regarding her movements. Algie couldn't have finished with her so quickly. What of the blood sample taken from her in the lab? Had Paz learned anything through his analysis?

If he did, likely Zohar wouldn't share the news with her. Too single-minded to care about her problems, he'd left her in the lurch. Hadn't she anticipated this from the very start?

Dodging parents pushing strollers and gangs of teens as she maneuvered toward the theme park exit, she felt a deep sense of loss. How could the man make love to her, soar with her to that wondrous spiritual plane, and not think there was more to their relationship than sex?

Captain Thorald, my ass. He's more like Captain Kirk.

Bypassing a little girl wearing a pink princess dress and a rhinestone tiara, she paused to get her bearings. The boom of explosions from a nearby stunt show shook the air.

She followed the path as it curved past a small lake and an old-time diner, one of her favorite restaurants in the park. Her mouth watered for their meatloaf and macaroni and cheese. People gave her strange looks, doubtless wondering why she lugged around a stuffed pillowcase.

Turning right at the next intersection, she pushed against the stream of traffic, aiming for the lockers near the exit. Best to leave her sack here with her pitiful stash of clothes. Was this what her life had come down to: one bag of goods?

She still had her makeup kit in the car, but the cops would be on top of that by now. She couldn't go near her vehicle without being nailed.

After obtaining a locker, she stashed her sack inside and locked the door. Unable to part with her handbag, she slung the strap over her shoulder.

A vendor stand outside sold candy, drinks, and souvenirs. Nira walked over and perused the wares, considering that Grace might be weak and dehydrated. The older woman would need sustenance for their escape.

So will I. Her stomach rumbled. Grace wasn't the only one who might need refueling.

Backtracking to a fast-food place, Nira ordered a burger and fries while wishing her life could be as carefree as the happy, cheerful park guests. Contrast this place to Drift World, the Trollek theme park. She shuddered, envisioning the zombie-like mien of those visitors.

Worry about it later. Her first task was to find Grace, then she'd think about how to join Zohar in his battle against the nasty beasts. She had to find the other five women in the prophecy first.

She swallowed her last gulp of cola, discarded her trash, and visited the restroom before finishing her preparations.

At a gift shop on the main street, she bought a windbreaker and backpack. She tied the jacket around her waist and stuffed her Coach bag into the backpack for security. A couple of granola bars and water bottles completed her supplies.

Outdoors in the hot afternoon sunlight, she watched the crowd while an attack of nerves paralyzed her. Was she doing the right thing by plopping herself smack inside the enemy camp?

She'd soon find out.

Music blared from an elevated stage at the far end of the street, where costumed dancers gyrated to moves from a popular teen musical. Bystanders, enthralled by the performance, gathered along the street, waiting for the daily parade. People jostled by in their rush to gain a spot.

Now would be the perfect time for her to vanish, when everyone's attention was distracted.

Taking a deep breath to fortify herself, she squeezed her eyes shut and ordered the shoes to take her to Grace.

Her head swirled, and she felt her feet lift as though she were flying. When the disorienting sensation subsided, she opened her eyes.

She stood on solid ground before a quaint village with stone buildings. Her heart thundered in her chest. It looked as though she'd dropped into a scene from merry old England.

Peat smoke rose from blackened chimneys, its pungent aroma mingled with the scent of freshly plowed earth. A church stood on a promontory, its stone façade weathered from the erosion of time. The hilly terrain whistled with a chill wind that slashed into her bones.

Twilight approached, the horizon hazy. She shook her head. That infernal buzzing afflicted her ears again. Was it the result of her spatial shift, or were Trolleks nearby?

A shout sounded, followed by a sharp crack. The cry of distress came from her left, where a field stretched toward an edge of woods. People dug in the dirt; human slaves from the looks of the Trolleks prodding them with shock sticks. Was that where she'd find Grace, or would her landlady be in the village?

She didn't think an old woman would be sent to do physical labor, so she turned toward the town. A shiver racked her. She pulled on her windbreaker just as an elongated shriek raised the hairs on her arms. Good God, what was that?

It came from the innocuous looking village.

Adjusting her backpack, she neared a stone bridge spanning a stream. Voices sounded ahead. She ducked out of sight and flattened herself against a retaining wall.

"There goes another one squealing like a pig," a male said with a chortle of laughter.

"These puny humans don't last long. What do you really think goes on in Tent Ten, Nim? I've heard rumors."

Tent Ten? Nira's blood curdled. Wasn't that the hut in the Trollek village by Turkey Lake Park where she'd seen the woman strapped to a table?

"I dunno, but why else would Lege Morbus be here?" Nim replied. "Our Kaptein should be the one questioning prisoners, not a scientist from home."

"I'd like to work inside there. Ain't much else to do for fun in this maug place."

"You should join us in the tavern for a game of Kash, Toros."

"Maybe later. I pulled sentry duty at the dig."

"Waste of time, in my opinion. Whaddar those old tablets gonna tell us?" Nim said.

"Lege Morbus says they're important."

"He's just taking orders from someone else."

"I hear Algie is running the show. Only a clan chieftain's daughter would have the gall to lead an operation this big."

Their footsteps moved away, while Nira quaked beside the bridge. Algie was in charge of the horrific experiments being conducted on humans? Her feet remained glued to the pavement while uncertainty beset her. How would she find Grace, let alone the answers to all her questions?

If anyone spied her, she risked detection. Was that such a bad thing, though? She'd demand to speak to Algie, offering harmless information on the Drift Lords as bait. She still had her magic shoes for a trump card should she need to escape.

She wondered if Zohar was having any success but told

herself that wasn't her problem anymore. He'd gone his separate way, so why should she care? Nonetheless, she hoped he could rally his team and accomplish his objective. As for the prophecy, she'd worry about it later.

Focusing her attention, she surveyed the town. Many of the timbered buildings had upper levels leaning over the main street.

Careful to watch her footing over the cracked and uneven pavement, she sped past a tavern from which raucous laughter and the smell of ale emanated.

She dodged aside as a woman emerged from a doorway ahead. Her face expressionless, the slave walked with robotic precision, scraggly gray hair hanging in dirty clumps about her head. From the older women laboring in their villages, Nira wondered if Trollek females discouraged competition. Did they resent it when their mates took human women to bed? Then again, that could work in reverse. With their beauty, Trollek females easily ensnared men of her kind. How did their mates feel about this diversion?

She wished Zohar had told her more about their culture. The more she understood them, the better prepared she'd be for her next encounter. Algie may hold a high rank, for example, but was that common for members of her gender in Trollek society?

The weak sunlight barely penetrated into the gloomy interiors of the buildings. She crept along, peering into grimy windows, hoping to catch sight of Grace. At one residence, a slave served dinner to her kabak. The gaunt woman moved about with vacant eyes.

Her heart saddened, Nira peeked into the next few houses. This appeared to be a quiet hour, with Trolleks eating dinner, being groomed by servants, or engaging in dice games.

Berating herself for her ignorance of their customs, she didn't pay attention when she rounded a corner. Something hard as a rock bumped into her.

Her glance rose to meet the furious glare of an armed Trollek guard.

****

"She still has her emergency ring," Paz reassured Zohar as they stood on the bridge of the *Protector*.

"True, but will she use it? The Earthling can be damn stubborn. She does not comprehend how searching for her friend would distract us from our mission. I have wasted enough time already in pursuit of her goals rather than mine."

And that troubled him. Had she caused delays on purpose? What had they actually accomplished, other than hearing repetitions of the same mystical prophecy? He dealt with facts, not magic. His job was to squash the Trollek invasion before their foothold grew stronger.

Uneasiness clawed at him, and he rubbed his neck. Had he made the right decision? He felt like a worm, leaving Nira to her own devices, but he'd had no choice.

"We can track her locator beacon." Paz's voice held a hopeful note. His stringy hair, stubbled jaw, and shadowed eyes reminded Zohar he'd been at his station for hours.

"Unless she goes out of range. Or unless someone deactivates it." *Was that what happened to Kaj?* Zohar clenched his jaw. "What is the ETA for Borius and Yaron?"

"Ninety minutes."

"Very well. I will take messages in my cabin while we wait for them. You should go rest. Lord Magnor is having something to eat. I can send him to the bridge."

Paz gave a furtive glance toward the hatchway. "Is that wise?"

"I trust him as well as the rest of you." Zohar's lip curled in irony. At the moment, he trusted no one. That made the messages in his queue all the more imperative.

If only he could rely on Nira. Having someone to confide in would ease the burden of command, but he couldn't be certain of her motives.

Nor did she understand his viewpoint. He'd gone along on

263

her mythological quest, helped her find answers, but what had she done for him? Just when he needed her the most, she'd fled.

"Before you go, I've completed my data analysis. You'll want to hear the results." Paz strode to the science module and tapped in some commands.

Zohar compressed his mouth. Again, thoughts of Nira flooded his mind and stole his reason. What was the matter with him? He should have inquired about the lab reports beforehand.

"Go ahead." He braced himself for more bad news.

Paz gestured for him to take a look at the display. "I studied Nira's file on the crystal you obtained from Drift World and cross-referenced it with my analysis of her hair sample. She shows traces of Trollek DNA."

"What?" His gut clenched as though he'd been punched.

"It's a specific strand, quite identifiable when you know what to look for."

"Does that mean…?" Too choked to speak, Zohar clamped his lips.

"She is still human," Paz said quickly, as though aware of his concern. "This could date back to her ancestry, a genetic marker passed down through the generations."

"Perhaps."

No wonder she resisted confounding. It appeared Nira knew nothing about this unique trait she possessed. She'd been just as puzzled as he by Algie's interest in her.

Or had she been acting as their pawn all along?

Chariots of the gods, he had mated with her. He'd allowed himself to be seduced just like his father.

"What about the crystals from the Trollek village?" He barely got the words past the lump in his throat.

"I'm not finished looking at those yet."

Zohar turned away, the urge to vomit overwhelming him. This proved his unfitness to rule and supported his decision to appoint Primer Pedar as regent in his stead.

After requesting Lord Magnor to take the helm, Zohar

headed to his cabin. He listened to his messages before putting through an encoded call to the palace.

"What news do you have that is so urgent?" he asked Primer Pedar.

"You must return home, rageesh. The empire crumples in your absence."

He sighed. "What has happened now?"

"We have captured a rebel leader. You need to hear what he has to say."

"Put him on the comm. I do not have time for this."

"You will make time." Zohar had never heard the Primer sound so much like his father. "Your presence is desperately needed. What good will it do to defeat the Trolleks if you have no empire left? If civil war kills everyone while you are gone?"

"You told me the enforcers could handle things."

"Not anymore. Return at once, sire, or I will resign my post."

Alarm frissoned up his spine. "Come now, Gorgie, are you not being overly dramatic?"

"Nay, I have failed you." The older man's voice clogged with grief. "You will know the full extent when you arrive."

"Nonsense. We can resolve this crisis, if you tell me calmly what is wrong."

"I will only brief you in person. How fast can you get here?"

Zohar's mouth curved down. Torn between his current mission to prevent annihilation, or serving his people, he made his choice. Should he fail and Ragnarok occur, he'd at least like to be known as the king who cared.

"If I burn the engines at hyperspeed, I can be there within three days." He stiffened, his voice deepening. "But this has to be quick. Every minute I lose, we are one step closer to disaster."

Chapter Twenty-Seven

"I'm Kaptein Rolstoff. Who are you, and how did you get here?" The military officer squinted at Nira from behind his desk in command headquarters, a squat stone building at the end of the lane. His hook-like nose and oversized ears reminded her of a malformed owl. He smelled like something a cat might drag in.

"I'm Nira Larsen, and I demand to see Algie." She'd decided her best defense should be an offense. Her knees quivering, she resisted the urge to whisk herself elsewhere using her magic shoes. This was still her best chance to find Grace.

"She does not obey orders?" The Kaptein's narrow gaze skewered the guard who'd nabbed her.

"The woman appears to be resistant to confounding, *min drott.*"

"Curious." He turned his beady eyes on her. "We'll see what the Grand Marshal has to say. His Eminence prefers to interrogate prisoners personally."

I'll bet. Nira repressed a shudder but then his words hit home. Did that mean the Grand Marshal held rank above the military commander? That nugget could be useful.

"If you harm me, you'll be sorry." She thrust out her chin. "I have vital information for Algie. Notify her I'm here."

The sentry, eyes flashing, slapped her. "Show some respect, human. You are not in a position to make demands."

She stood tall, bringing a hand to her stinging cheek. "The Drift Lords will raze this place to the ground when they find me. You're making a mistake."

"The Drift Lords?" Kaptein Rolstoff pushed to his feet and strode around the desk to confront her directly. Spiky whiskers, tinged with gray, dotted his jaw.

"You got it. I'm valuable to them and to your leaders as well. A bonus might be in this for you if you handle it right."

The military commander studied her while she fought the urge to puke. Glancing away from his flabby ripples of skin, she surveyed the room. It wasn't only the cold wind whistling through cracks in the stone walls that made icy fingers of fear tickle her spine, but the general miasma blanketing the town. This entire place resonated with the stamp of evil, as though it had been the site for ancient pagan rites and human sacrifices.

"I suspect you're a spy sent by our enemy." The Kaptein swiped at a dribble of drool on his pudgy chin. "Confounding doesn't work on the Drift Lords, either."

"Algie wanted me to find out why. We're working together. I told you to contact her."

The Kaptein directed an oblique glance at the sentry. "Wait outside. I will question the human myself before we take her to His Eminence."

After the soldier left, Rolstoff shut the door before turning to her. "Tell me about Algie Morar. I've heard things about the general's wife but don't credit gossip."

Algie has a husband? Nira smiled with a confidence she didn't feel. "She reports directly to the Council of Elders."

"Tell me something I don't know. What does she want with you?" His cheese-scented breath wafted her way.

"It's classified, unless you're privy to what goes on in Tent Ten." Maybe she could gain some info here.

His glacial eyes perused her. "The Council is aware of her collusion with a human?"

She shrugged. "I imagine so."

Conflicting emotions crossed his face. "Come, I will take you to His Eminence myself." He gripped her shoulder. "He will decide if you speak the truth, or if you should have your tongue cut out for lying."

Nira swallowed past a lump in her throat as he led her outside. Flanked by a troop of four soldiers, they marched toward the largest residence, with fresh sealant between the stones and a thick thatched roof. Smoke poured from the chimney, adding a pungent odor to the chilly evening air.

Glad she'd donned her jacket, Nira shivered. She hoped this Grand Marshal didn't have the same sexual predilection as the previous one she'd met. Hopefully, this guy hadn't heard what happened to the other official.

A blast of hearth-warmed heat greeted her inside the structure, brightly lit and decorated with colorful tapestries, upholstered furniture, and polished wood tables.

Nothing but the best for the village tyrant.

Nira, accompanied by Rolstoff, followed a blank-eyed serving woman into a rear parlor. A bulky Trollek sat in a wing chair stuffing grapes into his mouth. At their entrance, he discarded a pile of vine remnants onto the wood floor.

"Clean it up, human." He kicked the slave bowing before him then swung his lazy gaze toward his visitors. "Rolstoff, why do you bring me this skinny redhead? I have my quota of house slaves. Do you wish her for yourself?"

"No, Your Eminence. She wandered in from the outskirts of town. She is resistant to our spell and claims she works for General Morar's wife, Algie."

The Grand Marshal looked her over as he might a spider on the wall. "Does she now? Come closer, woman. What's your name?"

"Nira Larsen." Shoved forward, Nira stumbled to a halt in front of him.

If he dared to lay a finger on her, she couldn't vouch for the consequences. Unable to control the mental power she barely understood, she might harm everyone in the vicinity. She needed to train herself, so she could deploy her talent at will rather than under emotional stress. Hoping she wouldn't have to test her ability, she swallowed.

The Grand Marshal's eyes narrowed to slits as he studied

her. "So, you are one of Algie's protégés? How is this, when you are human?" He eased himself upright, a generous paunch showing under his uniform tunic.

Relief bowled through her. "You know Algie, then?"

"The doktor is chief scientific advisor to King Jorg." He snickered. "Everyone knows she got her position through her father, chieftain of the Jarvik clan. She itches for a place on the Council of Elders. Imagine!" Snorting with laughter, he swatted Rolstoff on the shoulder.

"Do females not serve on your ruling body?" Nira asked.

The two beasts chortled. "Only males are permitted to enter the competition to become a chieftain." Rolstoff puffed out his chest, his biceps bulging. "And council members are elected from among the chieftains."

So Algie was a scientist with the ear of her king, Nira thought, *but she also had political ambitions. Interesting.*

The Grand Marshall dismissed the slave sweeping the floor, then he spoke to Rolstoff in a hushed tone. "Doktor Morar is in charge of that special research project involving the Tent Tens in each village. You'd think that would keep her busy enough."

Kaptein Rolstoff hunched his shoulders, his brow perplexed. "The General serves on the Council of Elders. Does she seek to upstage her own mate? Perhaps that's why the king granted her a position of authority, to keep her under control."

The Grand Marshal's gaze darted toward the doorway. "Take precautions if she comes here. There are some who question her loyalty to the Crown. She has her league of supporters."

Rolstoff raised his caterpillar-thick eyebrows. "Then you will summon her?"

"We can't risk her anger should this human speak the truth."

"Excuse me." Nira, who'd been absorbing their exchange, interrupted. "Can you tell me if you have a slave named Grace in the village? She's an older lady, thin with gray hair."

The Grand Marshal sneered at her. "Be silent, woman. I haven't given you permission to speak. Take her away until Algie's arrival," he ordered Rolstoff.

"Where do you want her? In the pen with the slaves marked for Tent Ten or bunking with the labor force?"

"Put her in an isolation cell. Feed her, but don't allow her to have contact with anyone else."

"As you wish, Your Eminence." Rolstoff clicked his heels together and bowed.

"How are people marked for Tent Ten?" Nira tried one last time to get some answers. "What makes them different from the other folks you capture?"

Rolstoff pushed her toward the exit. "Doktor Morbus checks everyone's health when they get here. He decides which slaves become house staff, who will work in the field, and who should be set aside for Tent Ten."

"Wait." The Grand Marshal's command made them both freeze. "One more thing. Remove her shoes and give them to me. My third wife has a collection."

****

Zohar paced back and forth in a parlor at the Grand Palace on Karrell. A visitor might be dazzled by the gilt trim, silk wallpaper, and crystal chandeliers, but he'd grown up here and took them for granted. Instead, he considered Primer Pedar's concerns.

Unhappy with harsh economic conditions, dissenters fomented rebellion. Leaders among them organized terrorist cells to engage royalist forces in bloody skirmishes.

"A republic isn't such a bad idea," Zohar told his prime minister, who sat slumped in an armchair with his permission.

He didn't stand on protocol with his old friend. Wearing a scarlet coat of office and a feathered hat, Gorgie appeared an anachronism to Zohar's eyes.

"Your Highness has no faith in himself. You can fuse the empire back together, but only if you take action. You have shirked your duty for too long. It is time for you to assume the throne."

"I am the worst person to lead the people. My father's weakness taints my blood."

The Primer's keen gaze studied him. "What makes you say that, sire?"

Zohar, who always felt like a child under the older man's scrutiny, glanced away. "I have fallen for an Earthling."

"Ah."

"You do not understand." Zohar raised his agonized glance. "She invades my mind and dominates my dreams. It must be a spell. I have no other explanation for this obsession."

"You think you are confounded? Is she a Trollek?"

His mouth curved into a twisted grin. "She possesses a strand of Trollek DNA. It gives her unusual abilities. How can I trust her?"

"I think you do not trust yourself, my liege."

"No… yes. I am confused."

Primer Pedar uncrossed his legs and stood with a muttered curse at his arthritis. "Does she command, and you obey?"

"How would I know? Confounded individuals are not aware they have been compromised."

"Your father knew. It destroyed him. That's what made him go insane."

Zohar's brow creased. "I believe I have free will when we are together. She wanted me to find her missing friend but instead I left to pursue my mission."

"You walked away from her?" Pedar gaped at him.

He nodded, misery pitting his stomach. "Nira's mentor and landlady was taken by the Trolleks. What if our positions had been reversed, and you were the one missing? I'd tear up the universe to save you."

"You'd do your duty. It is your task to defeat the Trolleks and seal the dimensional rifts." Pedar squared his shoulders like an old soldier. "You have no choice. Personal feelings must be put aside in your role as Drift Lord captain."

"And as king of Karrell and emperor of the Star Empire?"

"Put to rest your fears about her being like your stepmother. Has she ever made you do anything contrary to your nature?"

"Nay. She has protected me against the Trolleks, but that could be a ruse."

"How so?"

"To trick me while she uses divide and conquer tactics. Kaj is missing and Dal is ill. Our team is gravely diminished." Hanging his head, he despaired at their future. While he languished at home, the Trolleks would gain the upper hand. Success seemed a distant dream.

"Taking a queen would bolster your position."

Zohar bristled at the twinkle in Gorgie's eyes. "Then let the Assembly choose a bride for me. Besides, there's the Edict to consider."

"Ah. I presume you mean the Edict against inter-species marriage?"

"Exactly. The Assembly meant to prevent our people from falling into the same trap as my father."

"Bah." Pedar waved a hand. "Prejudice ran rife after the old king's death. You will be emperor. You can repeal it."

Zohar shook his head. "And risk being accused of tyranny? I will not cause the empire's descent into the same abyss as before."

"You care what happens to your subjects?"

His eyes blazed. "Of course, I care. But the empire is a behemoth better off without me at its head."

"You are wrong. Listen to the rebel leader we caught. He may change your mind. This is why I wanted you to come home."

Zohar strode inside the formal throne room while Primer Pedar summoned the prisoner. Approaching the cushioned chair on the dais situated under a silk draped canopy, he hesitated. He hadn't sat here since his father died.

Destiny pulled him onto its worn upholstery.

He stiffened when guards threw open the doors and dragged inside a shackled man.

"Bow before the Crown Prince," Pedar told the unfortunate fellow, who sported an unkempt beard, cracked lips, and defiant eyes. Beneath a soiled tunic, his muscles outlined a firm body.

"I don't bow to anyone, least of all to a tyrant. Put me on display for public torture if you will, but I refuse to obey."

A guard poised to strike him with a staff, but Zohar held up his hand. "I will hear your complaints. What is your name?"

"Ungar Quinn. Your people are starving, sire." The man's voice rang with boldness. "Taxes take what little we have, and high prices take the rest. But that is not the worst of it. The punishments maim our children, sterilize our women, and kill our men. We hoped for change when you took your father's place, but all you have done is reinforce the evils he brought upon us."

Zohar stood, fists clenched at his side. His face flushed. Chills ran up and down his spine. "What taxes? Why are people going hungry? Our warehouses reported surpluses last year."

"Surpluses that went straight to your officials."

Zohar's eyes widened, and he skewed a glance toward his prime minister. "Is this true?"

Pedar steepled his hands. "The High Exchequer assured me we had a positive balance sheet. I am not skilled in finance, sire, so I did not question his report. The failure is mine."

Zohar thinned his lips. If anything, the oversight was his own. "You spoke of punishments. Explain."

The rebel cocked his head. "Your father enacted severe penalties during his oppressive regime. He decreed that thievery was punishable by cutting off the right hand of the culprit. Adultery resulted in hysterectomy for the woman involved. Speaking out against the monarchy and its injustices brought death by public torture. These laws are still in effect today."

Redness invaded his vision. "No… that cannot be true. I repealed those measures." He spoke in a choked rasp.

Primer Pedar's bleak gaze met his. "This abomination is my fault. You instructed me to reverse those edicts. Apparently, since the Emperor signed the decrees, only you have the authority to stamp the revised documents. Again, I should not have relied on the word of others that matters were well in hand. With my sincere regrets, I tender my resignation."

"You will do nothing of the kind." Zohar tugged on his uniform tunic. He'd refused to wear the robe and crown of office. "We shall rectify this at once. Draft the relevant declarations and bring them to us for immediate approval. Quinn, we wish you to take word to your people."

He swallowed, finding it difficult to force the words from his throat. "We regret the, uh, neglect that caused this sad state of affairs. The laws will be amended and people compensated for their losses."

Realizing he'd lapsed into the royal plurality, he plowed on. "In addition, we will initiate further reforms. Our Assembly is run by hereditary nobles who fail to represent the majority of their constituency. They have been lax in keeping us informed. Therefore, we wish to establish a People's Electorate, with representatives chosen from each district in the Empire."

Nira would approve of his decrees, he thought with an ache in his chest. If only she were here to offer advice.

Quinn sank to his knees. "Bless you, Your Highness. You have answered our prayers. I will carry forth your message."

Zohar gestured impatiently. "Guards, release this man's shackles and set him free. Keep in mind, Ungar Quinn, we have not been crowned yet. Let us call for a referendum after the Trolleks are defeated. We shall yield to the people's will."

"Long live Prince Zohar!" Despite his reverent tone, a wary gleam remained in Quinn's eyes, as though he were afraid to trust Zohar's intent.

Realizing he had yet to prove himself, Zohar's first order of business was to reverse those terrible edicts. After Quinn departed, Pedar hastily drew up a series of documents for him to sign and stamp with the Royal Seal. Then Zohar called a brief meeting with his top advisers to issue further orders.

Proclamations would go forth announcing reform, but they

needed a better system of delivery. News media, for example. Mass communications had been forbidden since his father's era. That would have to change.

Chariots of the gods, he could use Nira's input in bringing his empire into the modern age. How could he survive without her? She made him feel worthy, as though the mantle of authority suited his shoulders. And for the first time, he wanted to lead his people into the future. A future that wouldn't exist if the dimensional drift kept widening.

With a heavy heart, he left the reins of office in Gorgie's chastened hands, strode through a portrait-lined corridor, and climbed upstairs to the royal suite. There he had a call to make on his private comm unit.

"Tog, what news?" He'd encrypted the channel to his friend in State Security. Leaning forward at his desk, he tensed in readiness for more bad tidings.

"I followed through on your requests, rageesh." Tog's crisp voice reminded Zohar of their youth. "Regarding the military grade armaments, I found a discrepancy in munitions inventory and traced it to a military base on Cavendii Two. Several suppliers make regular stops there. One company happens to be owned by Colonel Yaloom's brother."

"Yaloom?" Zohar's pulse accelerated. "Was he not the officer disciplined after the fiasco at Alamir?" Yaloom's division had mistakenly fired upon friendly troops during the border dispute with the Morano Confederation. The fallout had caused an uproar at home.

"Aye, the Major General was demoted to Colonel."

"You say his brother has a contract with the base at Cavendii Two? For what?"

"Machinery parts. Their company lost money in the economic downturn, but recently they have been doing quite well. Too well, in fact, for the income they report to the tax collectors."

"Hmm. An unreported profit indicates they may be engaged in illicit trade."

"I agree. Their ship, the *Hedery*, follows a route that takes them to the Osmer asteroid facility for refueling. I pulled in a favor and got hold of their docking manifest."

"And?"

"Another ship, the *Mariner*, always shows up at the same time."

"You believe the brother is stealing munitions from the depot on Cavendii Two and transferring them to the *Mariner* at Osmer Station?"

"Yes, sire." Zohar pictured him nodding his head of wiry black hair. "Next stop is a private storage facility on Earth."

Zohar reached for a drink of water. He'd filled a glass before making the call. His mouth had suddenly gone dry.

"Who is masterminding this trade? Colonel Yaloom?" That could account for the inventory discrepancy under his command, which no one might have noticed if Tog hadn't gone looking for it. Tog's answer surprised him.

"I don't believe so. Connecting the dots, I followed the trail to—get this—Timerus Halston."

"W-What, the High Exchequer?" He choked, spitting water down his chin.

"The *Mariner* is registered under a front company that I backtracked to your royal treasurer."

"But Halston… why?" The betrayal stunned him, and yet why should it, after what he'd just learned from the rebel leader?

Tog coughed. "He's been losing money on gambling debts. Besides smuggling arms, he's also been skimming the tax rolls and stealing from the grain warehouses. I'll have enough evidence to indict him when you're ready."

"Not yet." Zohar drummed his fingers on the desk. "Keep your investigation discreet for now. Were you able to determine where the Mariner offloads her goods on Earth? They must be using a cloaked shuttle to make the transfer."

"Sorry, but I lost the trail there. If I had to guess, I'd say someone on that planet is acting as middleman, arranging for arms sales from the traitors in the Empire to the Trolleks."

"Obviously. The question is, did this person hire the thugs who ambushed me? And if so, why?"

"Chances are Halston wouldn't want you assuming the throne and discovering his secrets." Tog's voice deepened. "This middleman is smart. Probably he gets paid both ways, from Halston and from the Trolleks."

"Any ideas on his identity?"

Zohar held his breath, dreading the answer. Despite what the Gatekeeper had said, Rayne couldn't be the guilty party. The ambush on Magnor and himself had come after Rayne's death. Did that mean the Gatekeeper had lied about Rayne sabotaging his equipment? If so, who had really killed Rayne and why?

"About that, you asked for a background check on your team." Tog cleared his throat. "Regarding Lord Magnor, it took some persuasion to get information. As you know, the Tsuran are a reclusive tribe from the mountain region. Magnor had a sterling reputation as one of their top warriors, until he screwed up. He got cast out in disgrace."

"That is bad?"

"Being shunned is the worst punishment for a Tsuran, worse than death. I assume your primer hired him as bodyguard because of his famed skills. But I wouldn't worry about him. The Tsuran warriors hold honor in high regard."

"What of the others?" Anxiety nibbled at his gut.

"Borius frequents bars that cater to *kags*."

"Borius? You cannot be serious. He may be bashful about his virginity, but he is quite open about it."

"Perhaps because he's never done it with a lady."

"But we did a stringent background check before accepting him into the corps."

"Yes, but as you said earlier, things could have changed since then. Listen to this."

Zohar's heart plummeted. "What?"

"Two years ago, when the Drift Lords had leave, he disappeared for an entire moon cycle. His spacecraft logged enough hours for a round-trip to Earth."

Chapter Twenty-Eight

Nira paused in the midst of doing sit-ups on the packed dirt floor in her cell. Her chest heaved from the exertion. She'd been in this hole for days with little to eat or drink. Refusing to let herself go weak, she entertained herself by exercising and reciting mental math problems.

Located in the basement of the Grand Marshal's house, the detention area held eight cells at a glance, with no windows and only one bare electric bulb in a central corridor. She'd noted that much before being incarcerated. Left in total darkness, she had no way of knowing how much time had passed.

A bolted wooden door sealed her inside. At regular intervals, a guard opened the top grating, peered at her, and then closed it silently. Once a day, he brought her a tray with bread and water. A metal toilet was the only furnishing in her cell. Dehydration made her visits there infrequent.

Feeling her way by touch, she splayed her fingers on the cold stone wall. Leaning against it, she sat and let her head droop. A chill stole into her limbs and penetrated her bones.

The Kaptein had confiscated her backpack, shoes, and diamond ring. He had tried to pry the watch off her wrist, too, but it wouldn't yield. He'd allowed her to keep the precious timepiece for now.

Nira thought about which loss she mourned more: her Coach purse, which had been the first luxury item she'd ever purchased, or the shoes, her only means of escape. She might languish here forever, and Zohar would never know.

Zohar. Had he located the jamming device? Was he even now planting explosives to destroy it? Did he care what happened to her? Or had she fled his mind like he'd flee her planet once his mission was done?

The threat of imminent death didn't hurt as much as his abandonment. She'd always known he would leave someday, but he'd just turned his back on her as though she meant nothing. How could their fates be entwined when she might never see him again?

Doubts assailed her. Maybe she'd been wrong about the whole mythological thing. Maybe she just wanted it to be true to explain why her parents had left her on a church doorstep.

Images swam before her eyes. She must be delusional, imagining Mimir's magic well and mischievous elves and a ferocious shapeshifting wolf.

A vibration shook the walls as the outer door burst open. Her heartbeat accelerated. It wasn't time for the guard's next visit, so who? Could it be the Kaptein returning to interrogate her? Or the Grand Marshal coming to amuse himself?

She shot to her feet, summoning strength to defy them.

A key rattled the lock, then the door swung wide. She threw up an arm, the light from the corridor blinding her.

Her eyes adjusted while an old woman hobbled inside carrying a tray. Nira sniffed chicken, and her gaze zeroed in on a plate of food and a pitcher of orange juice. Was this a mirage? She ran her tongue around the inside of her sore mouth.

Restraining herself from pouncing on the meal, she wondered what strings were attached to this gift.

She licked her dry lips, unaccustomed to speaking. "Thank you," she croaked.

The gray-haired slave shrugged in such a characteristic manner that Nira did a double take.

"Grace, is that you?" Her pulse raced. When the woman knelt to leave the tray but failed to respond, Nira corralled the muted buzzing in her head and pushed against it. "Stand up straight and let me see your face." Her faith restored, she spoke in a firm voice.

"As you command." Grace's blank eyes lifted. She wore a coarse cotton sheath that looked several sizes too big and a pair of dirty sandals. Her bones had grown more prominent, her wrinkles deeper.

Unable to help herself, Nira flung her arms around the older lady. Grace didn't move a muscle. After a few moments where she clung to Grace's frail body, Nira stepped back. Her resolve hardened. She'd found Grace. Now they had to escape so she could fulfill her part in the prophecy.

She straightened her shoulders. "You are no longer under Trollek mind control. You have free will. Look at me and see me for who I am."

Astonishment blossomed on Grace's face along with clarity.

"Nira. My word, what are you doing here? What's happened?"

Nira embraced her again, tears leaking from her eyes. She parted with reluctance only because the guard might return.

She gave Grace a brief explanation. "You'll have to keep pretending you're confounded. Find out how many guards patrol the house upstairs. Now that I've found you, I don't have to linger here any longer. Algie probably doesn't even know that I'm here."

Grace's expression brightened. "Actually, that's the woman who ordered you to be fed. She was furious when she arrived and learned how you'd been treated."

With renewed hope, Nira fell upon the food and drink, sharing her repast with Grace. They ate quickly, afraid of being interrupted by the sentry.

Once they'd finished, Nira swiped her mouth on a sleeve. Then she considered how to spirit the old lady away.

This is what it's all for, to preserve our families, our way of life, and our worlds. Zohar and I share a common goal. Why wasn't I kinder to him, less selfish, and more supportive of his mission?

She'd sacrificed their relationship to rescue Grace, but

squeezing the older woman's fragile hand, she decided the choice had been right.

Grace left silently, acting docile and carrying the empty tray. The guard came to escort Nira up the cellar stairs and into the brightly lit residence. Herded into a parlor, she stopped in front of Algie.

The Trollek scientist looked svelte in a slate wool suit, her blond hair styled in wavy layers. Red lipstick made a bright slash across her mouth.

"You smell as though you've just come from the stables." She raked Nira over, her lips curving in disapproval.

"My accommodations were rather sparse."

"Yes, I'm sorry for that." The regret didn't extend to her glacial blue eyes. "Why did you want to see me?"

"The Drift Lords turned their backs on me. I'm ready to deal."

"Is that so?" Algie paced, her long legs enhanced by two-inch heels. "How did you find this place?"

"I have my ways." Nira lifted her chin, unwilling to provide information unless she gained something in exchange.

Algie gave her a sly glance. "Did you sneak through another portal, like you did to reach our screened village in the park?"

"You heard about that?"

"I got a report. What did you do to the Grand Marshal?"

Nira raised an eyebrow. "I'll tell you under one condition. You let Grace go. Send her home and provide confirmation that she has arrived safely in Orlando."

"I may do so, but only if you do something for me first."

"What's that?"

Voices murmured out in the hallway. She wondered where the Grand Marshal had gone. Algie must have dismissed him to conduct their interview in private.

"We're excavating an archaeological site. You may have seen the workers out in the field. I'd like you to read the rune stones."

"I'm not a rune caster."

"No, but you can decipher the inscriptions. Why else do you think we left you alone for a while? So you could gain the knowledge." She must have seen Nira's expression falter. "Oh yes, our spies are everywhere. We've been keeping tabs on your movements. Nothing escapes our notice."

Nothing? Algie may not know about the magic shoes. She could be bluffing.

"Why are these runes so important?" Without waiting for an invitation, Nira sank into a nearby chair. Her knees wobbled. She still needed to regain her full strength.

"We're searching for a certain incantation."

"That does what exactly?"

"It unleashes an ancient and terrible power."

"And you want to bring forth this entity, why?" Nira's blood chilled. Was this the deeper evil she'd been warned against?

Algie sat opposite from her, crossing her legs. She clasped her hands together, averting her gaze. "I am under direct orders from his Majesty, King Jorg."

"Yes, I heard you're the chief scientific advisor to the king, but I thought you reported directly to the Council of Elders."

"That is true."

"Is it also true that your father is a clan chieftain and your husband is a council member?"

Algie straightened. "Where did you hear this gossip?"

Nira smirked. "I understand there aren't any females on this ruling council. For a woman of your intelligence, that must be irksome."

The blonde grimaced. "I plan to change that. In the meantime, it serves my purpose to please the king."

"Your purpose?" Nira leaned forward in her chair. "Does that have anything to do with my blood sample?"

Algie rose and paced the carpet. "Your genome contains a strand of our DNA. Somewhere in your ancestry, you're descended from a Trollek."

Nira lurched to her feet. Trollek DNA? Was that why their spell had no effect on her, because *she was one of them*?

Algie continued as though she hadn't just dropped a bombshell. "Our females have mated with human men before, but their progeny have never exhibited your talents. You're different. I want to know why."

I'm a daughter of Odin, whatever that means.

"I can understand why you'd want to examine me, but what about the test samples you're taking from other people? What's going on in Tent Ten?"

"You read the runes, then I'll explain." Algie glanced at a clock on the mantel. "It's nearly eight o'clock. The sun should have risen enough for us to see outside."

"Wait. About Grace—"

"Come now, Nira, or I'll question your sincerity."

Algie escorted Nira toward the front door, guards in tow. In the hallway, the Grand Marshal accosted them.

"I have reported this situation to my chieftain." His jowls quivered like a bowl of Jell-O. "He insists we offer you our cooperation. Be aware though, the Kaptein and I know your game. Our loyalty will not be compromised."

"This dig is important to the king, you idiot. And while I'm here, I'll see how my pet project is progressing." She pointed to Nira's bare feet. "Get this woman some sandals. I don't want her stepping on a nail outside."

Once he'd complied, Nira followed Algie outdoors where an early morning mist shrouded the fields. Her flip-flops sank into the soft turf as they headed toward the dig site. A faint scent of manure drifted on the wind.

"You must be proud of your project," she told Algie, fishing for information. "It has to be important for you to have the support of your king."

Algie's chest expanded. Her hair swayed as she picked her way over clumps of freshly churned earth. "Maybe you'll be more helpful if I tell you about my work. Centuries after our people were expelled from this world, our reproduction rate began to decrease.

"Recently, we discovered the reason. The water we've been drinking has rendered many of our males sterile. While our females can mate with humans and bear children, our pure bloodline is in danger of extinction. If we hope to continue as a species, we must correct this problem."

"Is that why you invaded our dimension?"

"Earth has a fresh water supply. The Jorgonauts, King Jorg's loyal subjects, believe military might is the solution. My colleagues, or the Videns as we call ourselves, feel science can protect the future."

"How so?" Nira's feet grew cold and damp from dew. She tread her way carefully, skirting holes in the ground. Shapes rose ahead that looked like crumpled stone ruins.

"If we can repair the damaged genetic sequence in our males, we wouldn't need your contaminated world. You've poisoned the atmosphere and polluted the soil. Who's to say the water here wouldn't be worse?"

"How can you repair the genes, and what does that have to do with your human test subjects?" The pungent aroma of peat smoke blew her way along with the scent of richly turned earth.

Algie smoothed her hair, lifted by the breeze. "I am attempting to splice our DNA into humans to find a compatible combination. Once a stable string is identified, we can adapt it to fix the damage to our genome."

This is why you're torturing our people? No wonder they scream in agony when their cells reject the foreign material.

"Did you take on this project yourself or because your king ordered you to work on it?"

Algie took a deep breath. "My father married me to Igor without telling me he was sterile. I'd always wanted children, and this came as a bitter blow, especially when I learned the extent of the problem."

Nira felt a surge of sympathy. Her plight in society wasn't

so different from some cultures on Earth. "So you applied yourself to finding a solution."

"That's right, and until I discover one that's satisfactory, I have to maintain my position. Hence I do the king's bidding."

"Why wouldn't the king accept your method rather than military conquest? And why torture humans in the process? We could offer you the help of our best scientists, if you ask. Raging war won't be profitable for either side."

Algie gave a furtive glance at the guards walking a decent pace behind them. "His Majesty hears voices that tell him what to do. Some say he is mad. Others don't care, believing his leadership is the only way to regain what we've lost."

They arrived at the excavation, where Nira noticed standing stones like the one on the island.

"See that tall pillar?" Algie gestured. "Interpret the carvings on it."

Zipping her windbreaker tighter to ward off the chill, Nira padded closer. At a signal from the guards, the human labor force backed off, giving them a wide swath.

She crouched down to examine the stone, its top worn smooth from erosion. Her fingers touched the cool surface, tracing the angular marks. The letters had faded, and in the oblique sunlight, they became harder to distinguish.

"Where are we?" She thought of the island. How many sites were there like this around the globe, and who had established them?

"We're in Cobbleton in northwestern England. What do you make of those markings?"

She peered closer. The symbols were like a pictograph in a cave, difficult to understand without knowing the context.

"It relates a story about an evil being who was shut away. When a great cataclysm occurs, this force will be liberated."

Was this referring to Ragnarnok, the doom that would follow the expanding dimensional drifts? Icicles of fear pricked her spine. What was this greater evil that would be released when the universe imploded?

Algie knelt beside her, invading the air with her honeyed scent that had the power to seduce men. "What else does it say?"

Nira related the next bit slowly, trying to understand. "There's a spell that can release this entity sooner."

And another incantation might banish it forever. She didn't say that part aloud, keeping it to herself. Were those the words meant for the sons of Thor and the daughters of Odin to utter together?

Algie's nostrils flared, her eyes glistening in the morning light. "The king has ordered me to find this spell. Are the words written here?"

"What do you know of this evil force?" Nira countered.

"King Jorg calls his unseen companion by the name Loki."

Nira sucked in a sharp breath. Loki. An evil trickster, companion to the Norse gods, shut away forever because of his treachery.

They *did* have worse things to deal with than the Trolleks.

Loki's power might be limited now, but once he emerged from exile, he'd be unstoppable.

No, that wasn't true.

According to the prophecy, she and five other women with abilities like hers must join forces with the Drift Lords. Together, they could beat back the evil spirit known as Loki. However, Zohar's team was being decimated. Soon there wouldn't be enough of them left. Did Loki know this spell existed, and if so, was he behind a plot to get rid of them?

She had to warn Zohar.

The sun rose overhead while she scribbled notes on a tablet Algie provided.

It looked to be around noon when she pressed a hand to her stomach. "I don't feel well. Being locked in that cell made me weak. I can't think straight until I rest."

"We're not done." Algie sat on a nearby rock, her face weary. She looked out of her element in her fine clothes among the turf. Sweat beaded her brow, and she kept running a finger under her jacket collar.

"I need something to eat." Nira put down her tablet.

In the distance, a squad of slaves turned fresh dirt. One of them stumbled and got jolted by a guard. Her heart went out to the poor soul, but she wasn't here to free anyone except Grace. Zohar had to make difficult choices too. She should have been more sympathetic to his cause.

"I must know what those inscriptions say." Algie stood, brushing smudges off her skirt. "The king is waiting for my report. He'll stop my research if he suspects I have my own agenda."

You've certainly told me an earful. That means you have no intention of letting me go.

"We don't want that to happen," Nira said agreeably. "I'm sure most of your people would prefer a scientific solution to their problems rather than warfare." *Never mind torturing innocent slaves in the name of research.*

Algie's face softened. "I'm glad you understand my viewpoint, Nira. So do my supporters. Our numbers are growing. All I need is one breakthrough." She paused, taking a deep breath. "Let's go eat, and then we'll continue our efforts."

As they strode toward the village, Nira searched for a way to nab Grace and escape. A stalling tactic would be necessary.

"I may want certain textbooks." She scratched her head, doing her best to look befuddled. "The runic words don't always mean what they say. I'll need the proper references."

"I'll get whatever you require. You can rest after lunch. I have to check on another matter, but it won't take long."

Algie tapped her armband, one which Nira realized every other Trollek wore as well.

Her eyes widened. Could it really be that simple?

She gave a surreptitious glance at her watch. All this time… she never would have figured it out on her own. But now, knowing her own connection to the Trolleks, the timepiece's purpose revealed itself. This gift from her birth mother held more than a runic symbol.

If her theory was correct, the escape hatch stared right at her.

The camp military commander accosted them before they reached the Grand Marshal's residence.

"May I have a word?" Rolstoff said to Algie in a snippy tone.

They moved aside, and Nira pressed to hear over the low buzzing in her head.

Algie leaned inward toward the Kaptein and spoke in a hushed tone. "Be assured, she won't be allowed to go free. Once I'm finished with her at the ruins, she'll become my guest in Tent Ten."

Nira's blood fired, and she clenched her fists to keep from slamming shut that mental door and leveling everyone in sight. Did Algie lie to save face, or did she mean it?

Nira wouldn't stick around to find out. Time to locate Grace and depart.

Algie led her upstairs to a private bedchamber in the Grand Marshal's house.

The blond's eyes glimmered as she waved Nira inside. "Refresh yourself. I'll have clean clothes and a lunch tray brought up. And make a list of any reference books you want."

"May I have my belongings back?"

Algie pursed her lips. "I'll see what hasn't been taken as spoils yet."

"Can you send Grace here? I could use her help getting changed." Counting on Algie's reliance on servants, she held her breath.

"Why not? Being with her might ease your mind." Algie's eyes turned cold as ice chips. "Don't try anything foolish. A guard will be right outside the room."

"Why would I?" Nira gave a crocodile smile. "After all, we share a common desire for peace just like we share a common ancestry."

Algie turned away, leaving Nira alone to use the facilities. When she emerged from the bathroom, she squealed with joy.

Her backpack lay on the bed, her Coach purse peeking out from inside.

Nira slung the straps over her shoulders just as Grace shuffled into the room.

"I am ordered to obey your commands, mistress," the older woman said in a loud tone, keeping her eyes downcast for the benefit of the guard outside.

Nira slammed the door shut and whisked her into the room. "Prepare yourself. We're outta here."

Chapter Twenty-Nine

Nira fiddled with her wristwatch, pressing on its face and twirling the hour hand. When nothing happened, she held on tight to Grace and wished herself back at the safe house.

A whirling sensation stole her vision as they hurtled through the spatial dimension. When her sight cleared, she recognized the parking lot by the café where it all started.

"My word, Nira, how did you do that?" Grace brushed a shaky hand over her haggard face.

"My watch acts as a vector shift device. The Trolleks use an armband for the same purpose. It's how they jump in and out of places."

"I'll be darned. You had this watch from your birth parents all along, and we never knew." Grace shook her head. Stalwart to the end, the feisty landlady had accepted Nira's explanation of events as though such things happened every day.

"I still don't know how it works." Letting go of Grace, she glanced around. Unlike the magic shoes, the watch didn't whisk her where she wanted to go. Maybe it opened a path on some sort of dimensional grid, in which case she could only jump from one node to another. Or maybe she just didn't know how to operate it, because the Trolleks vectored wherever they wanted.

Thoughts played some influence, though, because they'd ended up here and not halfway across the globe.

Worry about it later.

She added another item for her mental to-do list. Number one was to train her powers. Number two was to figure out how to use the Trollek transport device. Maybe Zohar's tech expert could reverse engineer it. That would be Kaj. Had Zohar located him yet? Were they safe?

Anxiety gnawed at her. She had to contact them but her first order of business was to take care of Grace.

She pulled her cell phone from her purse, but when she turned it on, the battery was dead.

"Let's go over to the Doubletree Castle Hotel. We need to get you somewhere safe."

Grace gave her a weary smile. "I can call my friend Evelyn. She'll pick me up, but what about you, dear? Will you phone your sisters?"

"No, I need to steer clear of them until this is over. I'll ask Evelyn to drop me off somewhere."

They trekked to the hotel lobby. Watching a family at the concierge desk buy theme park tickets, Nira stood by while Grace phoned her friend.

"Evelyn? This is Grace. Yes, I'm okay. Of course, I'll fill you in on the details, but first, Nira and I need a ride. Are you available?"

When Evelyn arrived in her dented Cadillac, Nira gave the address for the safe house just in case the Drift Lords were home. But as they cruised down the block, she spotted a hive of activity. Men in suits scoured the yard and invaded the house.

"Keep driving." She ducked down until they'd passed. "Drat, now I have no way to call the guys to find out where they've gone. Let's hope they haven't been arrested."

Grace twisted to face her from the front passenger seat. "Do the cops think your cousins blew up my house?"

"Not necessarily. The police want to question them, and that would interfere with their mission." A giggle bubbled into her throat. After all that happened, Grace still thought Zohar and his men were related to her.

"You can use my cell phone, dearie." Evelyn, a vibrant woman in her seventies with tinted blond hair, nodded at her purse. "Get it for her, Grace. It's in my bag."

Nira's eyebrows shot up when Paz answered on the emergency number Zohar had given her. She'd half expected to be ignored or find the number disconnected.

"Nira, where are you? Your signal went offline. Wait, I am getting a trace now. I have a fix on your location."

"What signal?"

"Zohar implanted a tracking beacon under your skin."

"Did he now? Let me talk to him."

Paz's voice softened. "Sorry, he's not available."

Of course not. I might be back on your radar, but I'm not on his.

"Can you come and get me? I have news." At his affirmation, she hung up. "Evelyn, would you mind taking Grace home with you? She's been through an ordeal and needs to rest before dealing with the insurance company and the cops." She handed Grace the phone to put back into Evelyn's bag.

"What should I tell people?" Grace's voice wavered.

"Your house exploded from a gas leak. You had just left through the back door and were out in the yard pulling weeds. That's why I didn't see you when I came home. The explosion left you stunned. You wandered around confused for a few days, then came to your senses and called Evelyn. Don't forget to notify your son that you're okay."

Grace's eyes sparked with fond affection. "Thank you for coming after me. I don't know how much longer I would have lasted in that awful place."

"What place?" Evelyn asked in a shrill tone.

Nira waggled her eyebrows at Grace to go along with her story. "Like I said, she stayed with some street people. It took me a while to find her. There, Evelyn, you can drop me off at the next corner. Thanks so much for coming to get us."

Nira waited by the curb for her lift. Traffic picked up with the rush to work. The temperature rose along with the sun. Her shoulders slumped under the weight of her backpack, but since it was all she possessed at the moment, she didn't mind.

Yaron showed up in a black sedan. "Looking for a ride, lady?"

"You bet. Take me to your leader."

"That would be Paz for now."

She slid into the passenger seat and shut the door. They lurched forward, his foot heavy on the accelerator.

"What do you mean? Did something happen to Zohar?" Maybe that's why Paz had said he wasn't available. The thought hadn't even occurred to her. Her heart thudded against her rib cage.

Yaron kept his eyes on the road. His knuckles tightened on the wheel. "The *rageesh* was recalled to Karrell. He left days ago with no immediate plans to return."

Nira's jaw dropped. He'd gone home? In the middle of a crisis?

So much for him. She'd known their relationship wouldn't last, but this just brought home her foolishness in believing they might have a chance. She blinked rapidly against a sudden wellspring of tears.

As for the prophecy, perhaps he wasn't the legendary descendant of Thor after all. But then why did she feel his necklace heating her skin as though her doubts angered the gods? And speaking of the pendant, it hadn't done anything for her in the Trollek camp. Was its fabled protective value nothing but fancy, too?

Sinking into silence, she decided that her people's only salvation would be up to her.

****

Zohar didn't break radio silence until he came out of hyperspace within Earth's range. But when he put in a ship-to-ship call to the *Protector*, he got an automated reply.

Tapping out a different code, he pinged Paz's personal comm unit. Relieved when the warrior answered, his spirits soared to hear Nira's voice arguing in the background.

"*Rageesh*, what news? Are things under control at home?"

"They will be. I am just entering Earth's orbit. Is that Nira with you?"

"Aye, sire. She has critical information to share."

"Have her wait until I get there." His pulse accelerated. He couldn't wait to see her pleasing smile, to look into her perceptive eyes, to plunder her rich mouth.

He docked his smaller craft inside the *Protector*'s hangar bay and took a shuttle. Cloaking the ship, he landed at the same theme park backlot attraction where he'd parked before. After sealing the hatch, he called for pickup.

"We paid cash to rent an apartment," Yaron explained on the way to their newly designated safe house. He gave Zohar a quick update.

Kaj was still missing.

Dal remained in the hospital but was finally awake, expected to make a full recovery but with some troubling memory loss.

Nira had spent time in the enemy camp with her nemesis, Algie.

Zohar pressed his lips together at this news. If he hadn't deserted her, she wouldn't have turned to Algie for answers. Desperate to find Grace, she'd offered herself once again as bait. Only this time, he hadn't been there to catch her if she fell. Now that he'd returned, he wouldn't leave her again. He'd let her know how much she meant to him and how desperately he needed her at his side.

The redhead held council in the dining room with Paz, Borius, and Magnor. She looked magnificent, her slim figure encased in tight black jeans and a patterned tee shirt that outlined her curves. Her brown eyes swept him a cool glance.

"Zohar, how nice of you to join us. I thought you'd left for good."

He stiffened in response to her chilly greeting. "And I thought you had gone your own way. How did you end up back here?"

"I found Grace and brought her home, with no thanks to you."

He stalked closer and confronted her face-to-face. "By deliberately placing yourself in jeopardy? Dumb move, considering you could have gotten yourself killed."

"Better than no move at all and abandoning Grace. Unlike you, I don't leave my friends behind."

"I had no choice. Urgent problems called me home. Now that I have dealt with them, I am free to resume command."

He clenched his jaw, studying her. Wisps of red hair feathered her face like threads of silk. Her chin, jutting out with its usual stubbornness, made him want to kiss her into a state of pliant bliss. His loins stirred, providing the very distraction he couldn't afford.

Paz cleared his throat. "Did you learn anything of the assassin while on Karrell, *rageesh*?"

He drew in a deep, stabilizing breath. "The Gatekeeper spoke the truth. Rayne plotted against us." It wasn't in his game plan to tell them what he'd learned.

"Nira suggests a change in strategy." Paz gave her an admiring grin, his dimples deepening. "She doesn't believe a frontal assault would be our best option."

"Is that right?" Zohar had supplied his team with a projected target before his arrival. He needed to show her who was in charge, and he could do that best in the bedroom.

He'd make her plead with him, beg for satisfaction. In his mind's eye, he saw her lying naked and felt his hand skim up her thigh. He'd stroke her soft flesh until she moaned with pleasure.

Her breath hitched, and he realized he'd been ogling her. What was wrong with him? They had a dire mission to complete, and all he could imagine was bedding her.

Her eyes softened, and her mouth parted, as though the same notion had entered her head.

Wrenching his attention away, he gestured for his mates to gather around.

"The coordinates I gave you pinpoint the jamming device." He took a metallic ball from his sack of equipment and placed it on the table. At the push of a button, a holographic map sprang into view.

"Awesome." Her eyes gleaming, Nira leaned forward.

"The signal for the jammer radiates from this region known as the Bermuda Triangle." He circled the area with his finger. "Its exact point of origin is in Drift World."

"I can't believe it's been under our nose the entire time." Paz's mouth curved down.

"Our noses were unable to detect it because the nearby portal obscured it. When I smelled cors particles, I figured they came from the gateway to the village. But then I thought of my shuttle, parked in a tourist attraction among other spacecraft models. In a similar manner, perhaps the Trolleks had hidden the jammer in plain view among like objects."

He adjusted his projector and it zoomed in, narrowing the focus. "The jamming device requires a powerful energy source. When I searched for any unusual spikes in the area, I found what I was looking for in the warehouses directly behind Drift World. No big surprise there."

What had surprised him was to learn the supply depot for the theme park also served as the storehouse for the illegal arms shipments from the *Mariner*. Cloaked while in orbit, the *Mariner* crew would have to send down a shuttle for the transfer of weapons to the surface. After resetting his sensors, Zohar had been able to trace its ion signature.

Not only were the Trolleks powering their jamming device from the warehouses behind Drift World, but they stored their smuggled weapons there, too. He surmised the beasts transferred these arms via their portal to locations around the globe.

He omitted any mention of the armament stockpile or smuggling scheme to his crew while distributing a series of printouts. Nonetheless, he figured they could take out two targets at once: the jammer and the munitions depot.

"I agree with Nira that a frontal assault would be inappropriate. We shall use SDI tactics."

"What's that?" Nira asked.

"Surprise, Diversion, Infiltration." He drummed his fingers on the table. "We have only five team members left: me, Paz, Yaron, Borius, and Magnor." He included Magnor, even if he wasn't an official Drift Lord. "Should even one of us be taken out, it will compromise the mission."

"Hey, what am I, chopped liver?" Nira folded her arms across her chest.

He skewed a glance her way. "Liver? What does a body organ signify?"

"You're forgetting that I'm a bonafide member of your team, buddy. Count on six of us. I have a weapon or two of my own, if you recall."

"Do not fret, little one. I have plans for you."

The way he said it brought a flush to her cheeks. They locked gazes for a brief instant before he focused on his men.

"Listen up. Here are your assignments." He rattled off his instructions. "Any questions?" When no one responded, he nodded, his face grim. "All right, then. Get ready to roll."

Chapter Thirty

Nira swallowed as she glanced at the impossibly high ladder scaling the six-story tall warehouse. Was she nuts for coming along on this raid? She hadn't protested her assignment, which was to neutralize any confounded humans that might oppose them, but she'd have liked to discuss things first with Zohar.

Damn him, she'd wanted to discuss *their* situation with him before they risked their lives.

How did he feel about her? Other than the lust she felt oozing from his pores every time he glanced at her, did he have any serious intentions? Had his trip to Karrell confirmed his duty as royal prince to take an approved bride, one considered suitable by his government? Regardless of their opinion, had he missed her? Did he even care what happened to her?

Biting her lip to keep from blurting out her questions, she stood beside the ladder while Zohar conferred with Yaron. Their task was to set explosives while Borius and Paz created a diversion. Magnor, assigned to watch duty, deployed his invisibility shield to avoid detection.

The warehouse stood in a construction center behind Drift World. They'd found a private entrance for cast members and had boldly driven inside. Blending in with the parked trucks, trailers, and buses had been easy, especially at night. Spotlights illuminated the various buildings, either other warehouses or temporary trailers with noisy air-conditioners, while a half moon brightened the night sky.

The jamming device was located on a singular tower with multiple saucers and antennae. Its energy source came from this flat-roofed building, labeled Facilities and Operations Services. Loading platforms made up the rear, while the front had a simple staircase leading to the main entrance. No windows graced the building which bordered a thick woodland.

The team's main objective was to eliminate the power source. The explosion should kill the jammer, topple the tower, and destroy its infrastructure.

Unfortunately, Dal, their demolition expert, was out of commission in the hospital. Fortunately, the team cross-trained in various skills so his absence wouldn't prove an obstacle.

Stomping her feet to rid her sneakers of sand, Nira tugged on the ebony shirt she wore over dark pants. Zohar's team wore all black plus vests with multiple pockets.

Her glance met his. Something burned bright in his expression, then extinguished. He tightened his lips, giving the hand signal for them to move.

Following Zohar, who took point, she placed one foot above the other on the ladder, praying the rusty metal rungs would hold. The air smelled like moisture and rich earth. She focused her gaze upward, amusing herself by watching Zohar's butt as he climbed.

She hoped he'd interpreted the aerial view correctly, that a door on the roof would provide entrance into the complex. So far security had been lax. There didn't appear to be any guards, just cameras aimed at the main entrance.

Like ants, they crawled up the ladder. Their labored breathing broke the night, along with sounds of aircraft engines droning overhead, thunder rumbling in the distance, and the chorus of crickets.

"You are doing well." Yaron's voice came from below. He held the rear-guard position.

"Thanks." Her muscles trembled from exertion. Vowing to start working out once things returned to normal, she gritted her teeth as she strained to reach the roof.

Never would she have imagined herself in this role. Her goal was to teach mythology and share her fascination of the subject with her students. Now it seemed so mundane to be stuck in one place doing the same thing year after year. What would happen once they defeated the Trolleks? She couldn't conceive of returning to a normal life knowing what she did now.

That is, assuming they survived. Oh, man. Her ankles would kill her tomorrow, but it would be worth the price if they put the Trollek jamming device out of action. Then Zohar's team could locate the rifts between dimensions, shut them down, and end the hostile incursion.

Finally, she scrambled over the top and rolled onto the roof in utter exhaustion. Yaron tumbled over the edge next. He sprang into a crouch with his phase gun at hand, while Zohar scanned the area with his mobile PIP.

"It is too quiet." Zohar's eyes glimmered in the moonlight.

Nira agreed. Why hadn't they run into any patrols? Were the Trolleks so confident no one would locate their jammer?

The Drift Lord captain led them to a door beyond a series of ventilation stacks. When his PIP beeped, he held up his arm in warning.

"Stand back. There's a defense grid." He ran a pen-like device around the door's edge until its light changed from red to green. "All clear."

He stuck the tool back in its pouch, then slid the door open. His weapon held in one hand and his PIP in the other, he motioned for them to follow.

A musty odor inside made Nira wrinkle her nose. Dim overhead lighting illuminated dismal gray walls and a concrete floor. The heavy clank of machinery sounded in the distance, and underfoot, the floor shook with a faint vibration.

"Remember the plan." The whites of Zohar's eyes shone in the low light. "We take out the power source. The transmitter on the tower is a secondary target."

"How will we recognize the generator?" Nira asked.

"My PIP will identify the energy signature." He inclined his head. "There should be stairs around the next corner."

Nira padded after him down a utility staircase, gripping a metal rail with peeling paint. She felt like a heroine in an action film. Surely this scenario was surreal. Yet here she stood, undeniably a member of Zohar's team. Pride swelled within her chest as she watched his broad back. Even if he cast her aside when they completed their mission, she'd savor the memories.

The vibration grew as they descended levels and so did her sense of unease. The rumbling noise increased at the same time. At the bottom floor, Zohar cracked open the door and peered out.

"No one is about." His voice strung taut.

"Maybe it's their off-shift." Although possible, she doubted that's why they hadn't run into any opposition. Her nape prickled. Something was afoot.

Her cohorts aimed their weapons as they proceeded cautiously into a huge warehouse.

Crates and cartons lined the walls several rows deep, but that wasn't what drew Nira's attention. The machinery noise clattered from a wide depression in the center of the cavernous hall. A bright glow emanated from this pit.

Zohar squinted at his PIP. "The energy signature comes from that mechanism."

Nira strode over and glanced down, wincing at the racket. A spinning thing at its core whirled in a blur of speed. Pistons stamped up and down around it, and water flowed in a river far below. Conduits, pipes, and cables twisted in all directions. As they approached, a beam of light in the center shot toward space through a skylight above.

"Congratulations," a female voice crooned from the shadows. "You've found our jammer. But we have found you. Throw down your weapons. The game is over."

Algie emerged from the surrounding gloom, accompanied by a horde of armed humans. Zohar cursed, while Nira's heartbeat raced in a fast staccato. He knelt and placed his weapon on the floor. Yaron followed suit. They straightened slowly, facing Algie. Nira stepped back to stand at their side.

"How did you know we would find this place?" Zohar held his chin high, every inch the commander even when outnumbered.

"Simple, we let Nira escape with the old woman. We'd planted a tracking device on her, just like you did. Our signal piggybacked onto yours so you wouldn't detect it. We wanted to get all of you in one swoop." Algie beamed at them. "And so we did."

Nira broke in. "But we're missing—" She caught Zohar's intense glare and stopped.

"Two other team members?" Algie finished for her. "Your friend Dal is no threat in his condition. As for Kaj, he's been our guest for a while."

"You have Kaj?" Zohar lunged forward but two guards grabbed his arms to restrain him.

"Drift Lords are tough to crack, but we have our methods. He'll tell us what we want to know."

Zohar's jaw clenched. "What is that? I thought you wanted us all dead."

"Yes, but he can supply us with some data critical to our objectives before he dies." She addressed the guards. "Secure the men and leave the girl for me."

Nira watched helplessly as Zohar and Yaron had their wrists bound behind their backs. She could use her power to free the slaves from mind control. Did Zohar want her to do it now?

Zohar caught her eye and gave a subtle shake of his head.

Standing straight and tall, he addressed Algie. "I do not believe your story about tracking Nira here. If you meant this as a trap, how did you know we would discover this place?" His gaze swung toward Nira. "You have Trollek DNA. Have you been spying on us from the start?"

Nira's jaw dropped. He knew about her inherited gene?

"Surely you don't think… you can't believe… Algie told me I have a string of Trollek DNA, but it could be from interbreeding in the past. It doesn't mean I'm one of them."

Zohar looked down his nose at her. "You resist

confounding. You have other gifts. How else can you explain your powers?"

Nira gaped at him, speechless. Did he mean his accusation, or was it a ruse to help her escape? She could claim she'd been working for Algie all along.

"You've heard the prophecy." Her voice came out as a hoarse rasp. "Remember what Askr told us."

"That old man who called himself the Gatekeeper?" Algie snickered. "The Dark Lord possessed him."

"Who?" Zohar's nostrils flared. He looked like an ancient god himself with his proud bearing and commanding tone.

"The one who will rise again at the great cataclysm." Algie's mouth turned down.

Loki. The trickster who conned the gods of Aesir.

Nira moistened her dry lips. "I thought you served science. Now you're telling me you believe in Loki, an evil spirit who appeared in the myths of old?"

"I serve my king." Algie cast a furtive glance behind her.

Right, Nira thought, and according to what Algie had told her earlier, King Jorg hears Loki speaking to him. Was Algie afraid the cunning Loki might even now be eavesdropping, or was she loathe to voice her doubts in public?

His brow creased, Zohar peered back and forth between them. "What do you mean, this evil being possessed the Gate-keeper?"

"The old man lied." Nira waved her hand. "Askr didn't catch Rayne tampering with your equipment. Rayne was innocent."

"Then who killed him?"

A figure broke from the shadows. Borius. What was he doing here? He should be outside, creating a diversion with Paz.

Her face blanched when Paz stumbled into the light after him, hands tied behind his back, an armed guard prodding him forward.

"I can answer that question." Borius's face lit with a triumphant smirk. "People back home do not want you to assume the throne, Captain. They paid me to enlist the Trolleks to their cause. I killed Rayne."

To Nira's surprise, Zohar didn't look in the least shocked by this revelation. Instead, his glance glittered with rage.

"You lied about talking to Rayne on the comm unit that day in front of Grace's house. He was already dead. And you set up that ambush in the alley to take out Lord Magnor and myself."

"You knew?" Borius looked chagrined. "How?"

Zohar's lips thinned. "I traced your connection to the Royal Exchequer. Halston's greed stemmed from his gambling debts, but what prompted you to betray us?"

Borius shrugged. "My boyfriend has expensive tastes."

"What did you tell the Trolleks about our mission?"

"Nothing. My job was to maintain our arms trade. Halston was afraid you'd interfere when you came to Earth. He ordered you to be terminated. I merely supplied the opportunity."

"Were you responsible for the tainted juice that sickened Dal?" A muscle twitched in the side of Zohar's jaw.

"That was easy." Borius smiled, his eyes cold. "I had hoped more of you would drink it."

Nira, appalled by his treachery, glanced around for signs of their other friend. Had Borius forgotten about Lord Magnor, or was he already dead?

Hoping they still had an ace up their sleeve, she tilted her head at Zohar. When did he want her to neutralize the guards?

"Ow." She clapped a hand to her head. That infernal buzzing increased in volume. More Trolleks must be vectoring in.

Sure enough, a squad blinked into view, an ugly bunch with stout bodies, bulbous noses, and large prickly ears. The burliest of the bunch wore a row of medals on his uniform.

"Quig! What are you doing here?" Algie's face registered shock at the sight of him.

"Stand down, wife. You have been summoned by the Council. My task is to escort you home." His hand swept in a circle. "Major Zune will take charge of the prisoners."

"Not the woman. She's mine." Algie's eyes blazed.

"You overstep your bounds, *teecaht*. Do as you are told. I do not wish to punish you." He cast her a fierce look.

Lord Magnor, now would be a good time to show yourself. That is, Nira thought, if Borius hadn't betrayed him too. Better he should wait, though, or he'd be outnumbered. Same for her power. She wouldn't use it until Zohar gave the signal. Hopefully, she could limit its destructive force.

"I'm sorry, Nira." Algie's voice held genuine regret. "I had great plans for you. My husband will regret his actions."

"Be careful what you say, wife, or you'll be accused of aiding the Viden cause. Come, we go now."

"Yes, General." Algie's mouth twisted into a sly smile. "Nira, perhaps we'll meet again. Your talents are too valuable to waste."

She knows, Nira thought. *Is she telling me to use my ability?*

Nira didn't get the chance to ask, because in another instant, Algie and the General vanished in a shimmer of light.

"Guards, seize him." Major Zune pointed to Borius.

"Me? But I've been supplying you with energy weapons. We have a deal!" Borius struggled as sentries grabbed his arms and secured his wrists behind his back.

"Not anymore. You've served your purpose. We can produce the weapons ourselves now. Die with honor." Major Zune grinned as he aimed his disruptor.

Borius shouted at him. "Colonel Yaloom will hear of this. He'll stop the shipments. You still need our heavy artillery."

"To use against whom? The Drift Lords are finished. The humans are our slaves. And after the great cataclysm, this world will be ours."

"How will your people survive a global disaster?" Nira tucked a strand of hair behind her ear. "You'll be destroyed along with everyone else. The dimensional shock wave will leave nothing unscathed."

Major Zune shook his head. "The Dark Lord will protect us."

"Not true. If a massive energy flux disrupts the space-time continuum, it will affect everything in the multiverse. Loki knows this. Before creation, or what we call the Big Bang, there existed a great void. Loki plans to destroy everything and rule over this void in vengeance to the gods who banished him. He's just using you."

Algie had spoken of the Videns, a subversive group who opposed the Trollek king and his invisible demon. But would she gain enough allies to make a difference among her people?

"No more talk." The Trollek officer scrunched his eyes. "It is time for you to die. Move them to the pit."

Dragged by his soldiers, Nira cringed as the mechanical clamor increased in decibels. Grinding and chopping noises competed with the buzzing in her head, making her temples throb.

Two confounded humans took a stance directly behind her. One push, and she'd go tumbling into that hellhole to be crushed by those chopping pistons or whirled into mush by that spinning thing. Looking at it made her dizzy.

The Major puffed out his chest. "Our jamming signal is so strong that it blinds your sensors to the rift generators."

Zohar tensed where he stood beside her. "How does it work?"

"Hydrosolar energy. That's why we picked this location. The strong Florida sun, combined with a confluence of currents from the Gulf of Mexico and the Atlantic Ocean, produces the power we need."

Nira glanced at Yaron and Paz facing her from the opposite side of the circular rim. Their eyes focused on Zohar as though awaiting his signal. Was Zohar hoping Lord Magnor would show, or did he plan for her to neutralize the human slaves? That would still leave the Trolleks, a formidable force.

Borius shifted uncomfortably where he stood next to Paz. A soldier stood behind him, aiming a disruptor at his spine. Evidently, he'd been acting purely out of self-interest, not because he had been spellbound. Zohar hadn't said what he'd learned on his home world, but he must have suspected something.

"It's amazing how a single tower can block our sensors. You came up with this technology all on your own?" Zohar's voice held grudging respect as he addressed the Trollek commander.

The major gave a contemptuous snort. "We are not the backwoods troop you met on our last encounter, Captain. This jamming signal hooks into the global satellite network."

What would happen if their team destroyed the transmitter alone? With no outlet for that energy beam, would the disruption in flow cause a massive power surge?

Was that the predicted catastrophe? Were they meant to create the very disaster they sought to prevent?

Zohar must have considered the dangers. That's probably why he wanted to take out the generator first.

The major sauntered from captive to captive, tapping each one on the shoulder. He stopped behind Paz, whose grim face stayed fixed on his commander.

"The Drift Lords have caused enough trouble for us, Captain Thorald. That ends here."

Major Zune swept his foot at Paz's ankles, tipping him off balance. He pushed him over the edge.

"No-o-o-o!" Nira screamed, restrained from rushing forward by the Trolleks gripping her arms.

Paz's cry of surprise reached them as his body tumbled downward, bounced against a metal wall, hit the spinning thing, and disappeared from sight into the rushing current below.

While Nira stared, frozen in horror, several things happened at once.

Bumping Yaron away from the brim, Borius lunged at the major. "I'll have no further part in this." Fury contorted his face as he butted Zune in the stomach.

Lord Magnor whisked into view, an avenging caped figure assaulting the troops from behind. His sword flashed, cutting down soldier after soldier as he dodged their fire.

Zohar spun and kicked at the humans who had no one to tell them what to do.

Nira summoned her reserves to force the buzzing noise behind a mental door and blasted a message for them to stand down.

They dropped their arms, while she turned her wrath on the Trolleks.

Borius fought the major, who'd lost his disruptor but now slashed at him with a dagger. Being bound, Borius held the disadvantage. He'd just dodged one blow when Zune stabbed him in the thigh.

Blood spurting from the wound, Borius slid to the floor. Then Major Zune turned toward Yaron, who already had his hands full against two Trolleks. Bound as the others, he used his feet and body to battle his foes.

That did it. Nira pictured the major in a closet. She slowly closed the door in her mind's eye.

Zune halted, opened his mouth, but no sound came out.

Against rising pressure, Nira forced the door shut. Sweat popped on her brow. Her pulse raced. Guilt assailed her, but if she didn't end this, more people would die. Spots danced before her vision. She swayed on her feet, but she finally slammed the door closed.

Zune slumped to the ground.

His troops reacted in unity. In the next instant, they pressed their armbands and vectored from sight. The air shimmered in their wake.

"Magnor, cut us loose," Zohar commanded.

The swordsman complied while slaves stood about like robots who'd been switched off. Slain Trolleks littered the ground.

"See to Borius," Zohar ordered the Tsuran. Freed from his restraints, he rushed to Nira's side. "Are you all right?"

"Yes, I think so." Her voice came out as a high-pitched squeak. Her knees shook, but his grip steadied her.

"You fought well. Now we must finish what we started and lay the explosives."

"Borius is dead, *rageesh*." Magnor's solemn tone rang out in the cavernous hall. "The knife must have hit an artery."

"He saved my life." Yaron's eyes were as dark as his beard. "I was next in line to be pushed into the pit, and he knocked me out of the way."

"Give him the credit he deserves." Nira knew he'd betrayed them, but in the end, his heart had prevailed. "As for Paz… I'm so sorry." Her throat clogged. She'd miss the dimpled warrior with the sexy drawl.

Zohar's expression shuttered. "We shall mourn those we have lost later. Yaron, you and I will set the charges. Nira, free these people from their mind set and send them home. Lord Magnor, open some of these crates and verify what is inside."

He checked his chronometer and set a time for extraction.

Nira fulfilled her duty amidst a glorious sense of comradery. No matter how Zohar felt about their future together, she'd proven herself a worthy member of his team.

Now if only the Crown Prince of the Star Empire would accept that he needed her by his side on a permanent basis.

Chapter Thirty-One

Zohar, stretched naked beside Nira on his bunk on the *Protector*, kissed her neck while she lay like a milk-fed cat, satiated and curled on her side toward him.

"You continue to amaze me." He stroked her cheek and then trailed his hand to her breast.

Her mouth widened in an alluring smile that roused his ardor once more. He liked how her gaze ignited when he touched her. He liked how she gave herself so generously, making him feel as though he'd come home to the family he'd always wanted.

The fear had evaporated that he'd be weak like his father. She empowered him and bolstered his confidence, asking for nothing in return except respect and affection.

If he wed her, he could be a great ruler. However, military ops suited him more than diplomacy, and if he became Emperor, he had to establish reforms to win over his opponents. Nira would be a great spokesperson for the Crown.

How would his people feel about an Earth woman as their empress, let alone one who possessed the Trollek gene?

If necessary, he'd abdicate the throne for her. How ironic, that now, when he had made the decision to take his rightful place, his choice might end the monarchy.

But he was jumping the gun, as they said on her world. He didn't even know if Nira would have him. She hoped to continue her studies, plus her family and friends meant a great deal to her. Did she care enough for him to sacrifice these things and become his bride?

Maybe she didn't have to give up her passion for mythology, he thought as an exciting idea popped into his brain.

"Have I commended you yet on your performance yesterday?" He slid his palm over the curve of her hip.

She made a small sound of pleasure. "Many times. I'm glad I could release those confounded humans from their mind control, but it's too bad they lost part of their memory. I still don't understand how my power works." Her voice lowered. "So far I've only killed one Trollek at a time. Major Zune had it coming, but what if I snap one day and snuff out more lives?"

He smoothed his fingers along her tender inner thigh, while she squirmed under his ministrations. "You are not a killer at heart, Nira Larsen. I doubt that would happen. Your lethal power only seems to work against a target in response to a direct threat."

"I hope you're right."

Hearing the doubt in her tone, he sought to provide reassurance. "In the meantime, you can train your talent so you have more control over it. And your blood may provide a way for us to synthesize a vaccine against the Trollek spell."

"True." Her face brightened. "Let's hope the cops buy your story of an underground gas pocket causing all those explosions. I still can't believe the way that munitions stash went up."

He grinned broadly, proud of their accomplishments. The explosion had caused a fireball that destroyed Drift World along with the jamming device. Fortunately, the park had been closed so no guests were present.

She rolled onto her back, folding her hands under her head. "What about Kaj? Algie said the Trolleks have him."

"Kaj is strong. He will survive until we find him."

His jaw clenched. Unfortunately, finding Kaj wouldn't be their top priority. Now that they'd located the gateways through which the Trolleks entered this dimension, his team had to seal them shut. The beasts used some sort of generators to keep the portals open. His next order of business was to determine how they worked and to destroy them.

He could just imagine the Trolleks opening rifts on other worlds and expanding their conquest on multiple fronts. He must vanquish their spearhead on Earth before their influence spread.

"I wonder if we'll see Algie again." Nira stared at the ceiling. "Maybe we can contact her friends, the Videns, who believe in science rather than military conquest."

"We could use more allies, but don't forget their experiments. Paz analyzed the data from those crystals I obtained. They hold information on Tent Ten subjects."

Nira grimaced. "What sort of information?"

"Remember you wondered why the Trolleks marked certain people for their village? They have a distinctive protein in their blood."

"Maybe like me, they share a genetic component with the Trolleks from interbreeding in the past. I told you Algie is attempting to splice Trollek DNA into the human genome. She might think this protein makes those people more compatible. I suppose this means we'll have to look elsewhere for allies. Her supporters will continue their trials." Nira pursed her lips in thought. "Edith said there were others like her to guide us."

"Such as Sylvia?" Zohar winced. "Did not Algie say it had been their plan for you to acquire the knowledge to read runes? Sylvia's shoes took you to the Fountain of Wisdom, and if you recall Mimir's words, those shoes once belonged to Loki."

"You think Sylvia could be a vessel for Loki's spirit like Askr?" Nira's eyes glistened in the soft cabin lighting. "Or maybe she's another Gatekeeper. Askr said he was the last of his kind, but he could have been lying under Loki's direction."

"Too bad you lost the shoes and the golden ribbon, but at least we still have the amulet."

Nira had given the charm back to him, claiming it did nothing for her benefit. Perhaps it had to be worn by a descendant of Thor. He had yet to discover its protective power, unless Askr had lied about that as well.

"Anyway, what do we do now?" Nira tapped his chest,

making him long to capture her finger and suckle it. "You said you lost Dal's signal."

"I do not understand how he could have checked himself out of the hospital in his condition. He must have awakened and wandered off confused. That does not explain what happened to his tracking beacon, however."

"I guess you're stuck here for a while, huh? You wouldn't leave your men behind, plus the rifts still have to be sealed shut." A seductive smile curled her lips.

"Correct." He planted a kiss on her nose. "I have a theory about how the rift generators might work. Remember those solar calculators and mirrors the Trolleks were collecting? I believe those may play a role."

Her face softened. "So the mission continues."

"Aye, the mission continues. We stay until the Trolleks are a threat no more."

****

She wasn't losing him yet. A sigh of relief escaped her lips. It would be impossible to say goodbye after Paz's loss, Borius's betrayal, and Dal and Kaj's disappearances.

Propping herself on an elbow, she regarded him with concern. "What about the prophecy? That heaviness you felt when falling through the spontaneous rift, now we know the cause. Loki inhabits the underground prison into which he was exiled by the gods. He grows stronger. Ragnarok will herald his return."

"Not if we seal the rifts and stop the dimensional drift from widening."

"Will that stop him? He may have other ways of causing Armageddon, now that he has a foothold here."

"Armageddon? What is this?" His brow wrinkled.

"A biblical reference to the end of days. I think it'll take more than sealing the rifts to stop Loki. According to the legend, the six daughters of Odin and the six sons of Thor must chant a spell together to repel him."

"If you can count," Zohar said in a sardonic tone, "you will realize there are only two Drift Lords left plus Lord Magnor."

"The prophecy doesn't say you all have to be Drift Lords."

His eyebrows lifted. "Indeed."

"Perhaps when I find the other women like me, these other sons will become evident. Magnor isn't a Drift Lord."

"He is one now. We have to change our criteria if our league is to survive. Sniffing cors particles does not have to be a prerequisite. We can use our sensors to detect them." His gaze darkened. "Is that your plan, to search for these other women?"

"It's what I'm meant to do."

"We go our separate ways? I do not like this, my *carona*. As you once told me, our destiny is to be together."

He kissed her soundly. The kiss deepened, while his hands roamed her body. His mouth slanted over hers, claiming her with a hunger that she returned. Then they were all over each other, a tangle of limbs, making fast and furious love as though there would be no tomorrow.

When it was over, and she lay in bliss at his side, she dared to venture what was on her mind.

"What did you mean about us being together? After the prophecy is fulfilled, what then? You won't kick me off your team, will you?"

He laughed, a happy sound from deep in his soul, while his turquoise eyes captured hers. "We belong together… forever, my heart's mate. I need you to make me whole. My people need you to unify our lands and bring a breath of fresh air to our old ways."

"You've decided to accept your birthright?" She swallowed her disappointment. Surely then he'd leave her behind.

His grin transformed his face. He looked lighter, freer, somehow. "Indeed, I have. I am not my father. I will be a just and fair ruler who recognizes the right of his subjects to have a voice. But I cannot do it alone. I lack the experience in democracy, diplomacy, and history."

"History? What does that have to do with anything?"

"We have much to learn from our past mistakes. Moreover, as you taught me, we have much to gain from studying the different mythologies of our peoples. We need someone with your training and background to guide us."

"I see. Are you offering me a job?" Dismay clogged her throat. Was this the future he saw for them?

"Not in the manner you are thinking, little one." Tilting her chin, he brushed her lips in a light caress. "Will you marry me and become my Empress? I have fallen under your spell and cannot live without you."

Her eyes widened. "You're asking me to… but what about your advisors? Wouldn't they object?"

"If they do, I will gladly give up my throne for you. I love you madly. Say yes and make me the happiest man in the multiverse."

Oh, heck. She still had to finish her graduate degree, locate her prophesied sisters, make sure Grace was okay and her adopted siblings all right. So many things to do, but they didn't compare to the tasks Zohar's team had yet to accomplish.

Worry about it later.

Today, at this hour, she had Zohar. He needed her. He wanted her. He meant to stay with her always.

How could she refuse an offer like that?

Her eyes misted. "Yes, I'm ready for new adventures. We'll face them together, my love."

THE END

Author's Note

The idea for the Drift Lords Series came from a ride at Disney's Epcot theme park. In the Norway pavilion used to be a ride called Maelstrom. Your boat entered a dark tunnel and rose up a steep incline. At the top were three trolls who cast a spell for guests to disappear. Suddenly, the boat sped backward through time into Norwegian history. I loved the idea of evil trolls and Norse mythology. For my series, I decided to mix magic and myth into modern times.

Norse myths provided the basis for the Drift Lords' mission and the threat to our planet. These stories are a blend of science fiction, fantasy, and romance. I hope they sweep you to a world beyond your imagination and provide an escape from reality. Follow up with *Warrior Rogue* and *Warrior Lord*, the next books in the series.

****

For updates on my new releases, giveaways, special offers and events, join my reader list at https://nancyjcohen.com/newsletter. Free Book Sampler for new subscribers.

Thank you for taking the time to read my book. If you enjoyed the story, please consider writing a review at your favorite online bookstore. Reader recommendations are critically important in helping new readers find my work.

Reader Discussion Guide

- Do you believe Nira had any option other than joining Zohar's team?

- How well did she handle the revelations about Zohar's origins and the Trolleks?

- What did you think was happening in the Drift World theme park?

- Why might the Trolleks be collecting solar calculators and mirrors?

- Do you think Nira should have allowed Algie to take her blood sample?

- What kind of experiments did you believe the Trolleks were conducting on humans?

- Should Zohar have gone with Nira to find Grace rather than follow his own pursuits?

- Which do you think is the greater evil, the demon Loki or the Trollek king?

- How do you think the prophecy will play out?

- Do you want to read more in this series? Why or why not?

- Do you like the blend of magic and myth in a modern-day setting?

Warrior Rogue Excerpt

Here's a peek at Book #2 in the Drift Lords Series

"If he doesn't show up in the next ten minutes, I'll kill him." Jennifer Dyhr paced back and forth on the Tokyo film set for a video game commercial. Their lead actor, Keith Monroe, was more than an hour overdue. What could have happened to him?

"I called his hotel room." Sandi tapped her pen on the clipboard cradled in her arm. Dressed in a prim suit, she looked more like a schoolteacher than a fashion designer's assistant. "He didn't answer, so I left a message. Ditto for his cell."

"The jerk. You'd think he would be more reliable." Jen tucked a stray hair behind her ear. Her twist was coming undone, same as her composure.

"It's the producer's problem, not yours."

"Oh, yeah? Who else could we get to look the part of a vengeful Norse god?" She waved a hand. "If you recall, I'm the one who recommended Keith for the role. I wouldn't have won this project without him."

"Don't be so hard on yourself. Like, your costumes have nothing to do with Keith's no show."

Sandi's calm tone failed to reassure her. "The producer might not see it that way. He'll lump us Americans together and blame me for Keith's behavior."

"Oh, come on, Jen. He's lucky to have you. You're the best in the field."

"True." Jen squared her shoulders. Inspired by visions from

the past, she'd made her mark on the fashion industry and garnered numerous awards for her designs based on Viking influence. She'd become as much a celebrity as the stars who wore her garments.

Nonetheless, Jen had yet to introduce her line overseas. If she wanted her company to expand, she needed gigs like this one to show she could compete in the global marketplace.

"I hope Keith wasn't in an accident." Her heart raced at the thought. "Maybe we should call the hospitals."

"You can suggest that to Mr. Nakamura." Sandi bobbed her head in a warning nod.

Jen braced herself as the director hurried over. A lanky man with black hair, Mr. Nakamura wore a perpetual scowl and his tense posture like a seasoned samurai.

"Keith Monroe is passed out drunk in his hotel room," the translator interpreted after a rapid-fire dialogue by the director. A boyish-faced youth, Akeno had confided to Jen his wish to work on the film crew someday.

"You're kidding," Jen blurted before remembering her place. "I mean, I'm so sorry. Please accept my apologies for Keith's irresponsible behavior."

She bowed her head in deference, expecting a tongue-lashing in response. Her Japanese associates would need someone to take the blame. Jen only hoped this snag wouldn't damage the reputation she'd worked so hard to build.

"The producer has already called the casting office for a replacement," Akeno said after another spate of dialogue from his employer, whose irate tone matched his angry eyes.

"We need a guy with the right build," she reminded them. "Blond hair and blue eyes would be a bonus."

While they waited for the stand-in actor to arrive, Jen inspected the stitching on her costumes.

"Jen, this woman's seam is splitting." Sandi indicated one of the extras portraying a villager.

Jen cursed under her breath. "Did she sit down? I told her not to bend. This shift barely fits around her hips."

She grabbed a needle and thread from her kit as the director herded everyone to take their places on set. The storyline involved a barbarian ravaging a peaceful village until a Norse god appeared to battle him.

It amazed her how the sound stage looked like a real Viking town with thatched roof houses spewing smoke from holes in the roofs, vendors lining a busy market street, and wood planked walkways leading toward a fake pier rimmed with barrels of wine.

The village street bustled with action as actors walked through their paces and chatted amongst themselves. She could almost smell the sheep dung and wood smoke.

Uh-oh. Her visions often started with a sensory impression. Quickly, Jen wrapped up her repair and stashed away her kit. Reality receded as a white haze swept into her mind.

When her eyes focused again, she was strolling down the village street in the distant past.

Her gown swished against her leather boots as she beamed a friendly smile to the blacksmith. Across the road, the fur peddler waved. She nodded him a greeting, her nose wrinkling at the smell of fish emanating from the wharf. Shivering, she drew the edges of her shawl closer together, as a stiff breeze blew off the sea.

Shrieks of surprise made her vision evaporate. A man charged into view from around the corner onto the studio set.

A naked man.

Jen stared at him, aghast. What kind of joke was this?

Lacerations marred his body, and heavens above, what a magnificent body the man had. Her glance dropped from his massive shoulders to his muscled chest and then down to his very masculine package. The glory of him stole her breath.

"Where am I? What's happened?" His wild-eyed look and combative stance froze the actors on set.

His American accent startled Jen. *Brilliant, just brilliant.* Who else but their stand-in for Keith Monroe would show up with such melodrama? She should have recognized him at once from his wheat blond hair and blue eyes, but she'd been too focused on his, ah, other parts.

She fought an urge to fan herself, the heat from the spotlights raising her temperature. Or maybe that wasn't what caused her to feel so hot all over.

The man's gaze slammed into hers, and time stood still. The distance between them shrunk, blotting out their surroundings, until only the two of them stood facing each other on a plain where mist swirled at their feet. Their heartbeats pounded a sensual rhythm in harmony.

In her mind's eye, she shed her clothes as a hunger she'd never known swept through her. A hunger for him.

Shaking her head, she reoriented herself. Much as she'd like to admire his physique all day long, they had to get moving. Time was money as far as the producer was concerned. This guy needed to be clothed, fast.

"Sandi, get me Keith's costume and tell the makeup artist we need her." Jen's voice came out as a high-pitched squeak. She cleared her throat. "Our new stand-in has done a great job on those fake wounds, so he shouldn't need more than a touch-up."

Mr. Nakamura hustled over with the translator in tow. He jabbed his finger at the new guy. "You there, what is your name?"

The actor stiffened but didn't respond. He glanced at the other crewmembers who had stopped to watch. A look of confusion spread over his face. His jaw tightened, a day's growth of bristle adding authenticity to his role.

"What's your name?" Jen spoke in a loud tone like people did to foreigners who could hear perfectly well but didn't understand.

"I am Paz Hadar." His dimples deepened as he regarded her. "Who are you?"

His slow, lazy perusal generated warmth throughout her body. Those devilish eyes roamed from her hair, to her rayon maxi dress, to her low-heeled sandals. A gleam of appreciation entered his expression, making her heart beat faster.

"I'm Jennifer Dyhr, the costume designer." Jen pronounced her last name like deer. "You are inappropriately dressed, Mr. Hadar. Or undressed, I should say."

Mr. Nakamura's lips compressed. "Tell him he has ten minutes to get ready. I am not amused by his dramatic entrance. He is only a substitute for our star."

"*Hai*, Mr. Nakamura-san."

Jen gave him a deferential bow. After he walked away, she signaled to Paz. The man sauntered over as though strolling about naked was a normal occurrence. Had he meant to disrupt the set and attract everyone's attention?

No matter. She had to make him look like a vengeful Norse god. Standing before her, the man towered over her five-foot eight frame by at least six inches.

Moisture glistened on his skin. His hair hung in damp clumps, as if he'd just come from a swim. He must have been near the studio to rush over, disrobe, and apply his makeup.

However, he'd forgotten to remove his watch. Having been so focused on his other *attributes*, she hadn't noticed the fancy dial before. Further up his forearm was a broad gash. When she touched the edge, he winced as though it hurt for real. Unable to help herself, she let her fingers slide up his arm, outlining his firm bicep. He drew in a sharp breath but didn't move.

Her glance roamed to his chest, where a tangle of golden hair tempted her to feel its texture. His scent entered her nostrils, a strange mixture of sea air and salt.

Her temples pounded. Oh, no. Afraid she'd segue into another vision, she grabbed the trousers Sandi brought over and thrust them at him.

When he just stood there, she clucked her tongue. "What's the matter with you? Put these on. And take your watch off. It doesn't belong in this scene."

He plucked the pants from her fingers and pulled them on while she averted her gaze. When he muttered under his breath, she dared to look again. Poor fellow fumbled with the drawstring ties at his waist as though he didn't know what to do with them. Good God, what planet did he come from?

She grabbed the ends, pulled tight, and tied a bow, all the while conscious of his proximity and powerful musculature.

Standing so close, she had a terrible urge to feast her eyes on him. He was quite the man, and it had been a while since she'd split with her last boyfriend.

Resolutely looking into his crystalline eyes, she moistened her lips. Her throat had gone dry when she touched his skin. "I hope you've been briefed on your role."

His brow furrowed. "Of course. I know what to do."

His deep voice resonated through her like warm honey, turning her bones fluid and making her belly flip-flop.

Best to finish this as fast as possible.

She offered him a linen shirt next followed by a brick red tunic. When she'd studied what Vikings had worn, she had been pleased to learn they dyed their fabrics in bold shades. Wealthy people wore clothing trimmed in silk with gold or silver threads. These styles became the inspiration for her unique designs.

Paz donned the garments and stuffed his watch into a pants pocket. After he secured a leather belt around his waist, she gave him a cloak to fasten at his shoulder with a faux gold brooch. The cobalt color brought out the ocean blue of his eyes. He glanced at her, and she blushed to be caught staring.

She stepped away as he tugged on his boots. The makeup artist bustled over to bring some order to his unruly hair and to dab cover-up on the dark shadows under his eyes. Odd that he hadn't fixed that problem when he'd applied his fake lacerations. And was that scratch on his cheekbone starting to smear?

The director called for everyone to take their places. Jen retreated with Sandi to a spot off to the side where they could observe. Ready for any wardrobe disasters, she prayed they'd get this done in as few takes as possible.

Mr. Nakamura issued instructions, but the new guy wasn't listening. He tensed as the pace picked up. Jen swallowed. Did he understand what his role required?

"Action," the director yelled in the equivalent Japanese.

Lars Anderson, the Scandinavian actor hired to play the bad guy, charged onto the set wearing what accounted for full battle armor in those days: a chain mail tunic and conical helmet complete with metal eye and nose guards. He looked ferocious with his full beard, blazing eyes, and feral grin. Swinging a long-handled battle-axe, he gave a chilling war whoop.

Fake blood sprayed as he attacked the villagers. Carnage resulted. Or rather, what would appear to be carnage on screen. While the other actors screamed in mock fright, the man called Paz reached behind his back. A startled look crossed his face as though he expected to find a weapon there.

Chaos broke around him. Jen hoped he knew his moves. He was supposed to use his magical power to stop the villain dead in his tracks.

That didn't appear to be his intention. Instead, Paz launched himself at Lars as though the hounds of hell were on his heels.

Pow, thunk, thud.

His fists and feet aimed practiced blows at his opponent.

Lars didn't even have time to feign a defense. He raised his arms, but Paz's punches hit home with unswerving accuracy.

Along with the cast and crew, Jen watched in fascinated horror. Were the cameras getting this? The director observed in stunned silence as his cameramen kept filming.

Paz smashed the hapless actor on the jaw. With a howl of pain mingled with surprise, Lars wheeled around. Jen's heart leapt into her throat when Paz lunged for a stick on the ground.

Her eyes widened. Was that a yardstick? Someone must have left it there by mistake. What did Paz want with it?

Stop, she wanted to say but her mouth wouldn't form the word. *Wrong prop. And you're playing a Norse god. You don't need a weapon.*

Paz twirled the yardstick like a staff before striking Lars at mid-thigh. The stick snapped, but Paz kept his motion flowing, following through with a kick to the same spot. Lars cried out, his legs crumpling. He went down, flat on his back.

Immediately, Paz planted a foot on Lars's chest and pointed the broken yardstick at his throat. His arms tensed.

In another instant, he'd put a lethal vent into the guy's trachea. What was the matter with him?

"Don't move," Jen hollered, recovering her voice.

Paz hesitated, stick poised in the air.

"You're hurting him. Haven't you filmed a fight scene before?"

"Fight scene?" Paz's brow creased, as he regarded her with puzzlement.

Meanwhile, crew members rushed forward to break the men apart. One man put out an arm to hold Paz back, while another helped Lars to his feet.

"Where's the first aid station? Ow, my leg." Lars cast Paz a scathing glance. "What's wrong with you, mate? You cudda killed me."

Blood oozed from a cut on his bottom lip. He yanked the helmet off his head and swiped his mouth. "I'm bleeding, you idiot. If I have any marks on my face, my career is ruined. Ruined! You'll hear from my lawyer." With a growl, he limped backstage and out of sight.

Jen scuttled over. Could this day get any worse?

She gripped Paz's arm. "Didn't you study fight scene choreography when you took acting classes? You could have seriously injured Mr. Anderson."

Across the room, the director spouted a torrent of words at the crew. Jen was sure he must be chewing them out. It wasn't their fault, for heaven's sake.

"What do you mean?" Paz shook her off. "He was butchering those villagers. I couldn't stand by and let that beast murder people."

She stared into his confused blue eyes. "Paz, they were acting. You know, pretending," she explained when he shook his head in bewilderment. "This set, all that blood, it's fake."

"I don't understand. People were screaming, fleeing in

panic." He lifted his chin. "It is my duty as a Drift Lord to protect them."

"You're playing a Norse god. You were supposed to use magic to defeat your enemy and not pick up a stick on the ground. A yardstick, no less! Didn't you get a script?"

"Your words have no meaning for me." He rubbed a hand over his weary face. His fingers came back stained with crimson. "Is this fake, too? My head pounds as though hit by a hammer."

"Good Lord, you're really bleeding." Jen examined the gash on the side of his head. "These wounds are real. No wonder you're so out of it. What happened to you?"

"I remember an impact, and then… nothing."

Her mind somersaulted on what she knew about the guy. He showed up here naked and confused, and everyone assumed he'd prepared for his role. Had the poor fellow been in such a rush to take the job that he'd had an accident along the way? A concussion would explain his strange behavior.

She crooked her finger, signaling Sandi who'd been consulting with the makeup artist.

"Yuki says she didn't touch the cuts on this man's face because he had done such a good job of applying paint." Sandi squinted at him. "That stuff is smearing, but she's afraid to come any closer to fix it."

"That's because his wounds are real." Jen turned to Paz. "This is my assistant, Sandi. We're both concerned about you. Tell us what happened on the way here. You must have been in an accident."

"Accident… yes. No. The images are—how do you say it? My mind is unclear."

Mr. Nakamura broke off from his conversation and strode in their direction. From his taut posture and pinched face, Jen expected a reprimand.

"Security said no one drove through the studio entrance." Poor Akeno looked as though he had swallowed a lemon pit as he translated the director's words. "How did this man get here?"

"I think he may have been in an accident." Jen glanced at Paz. His lips were clamped together, his complexion pale. *Don't pass out*, she pleaded silently. *We need to get you to a doctor.* "He could have left his car behind, walked the rest of the way, and stumbled through the gate. A head injury would account for his confusion."

Sandi's eyebrows lifted. "I've known a lot of desperate actors in my time, but this? If he really got whacked on the head, he belongs in the hospital."

"You're right. I'll take him."

For some reason, she felt drawn to the newcomer. Maybe it was the lost look in his eyes, or perhaps his unstable state of health. Being ill in a foreign country could be terrifying, and he could use her support.

Sandi drew her aside. "Are you nuts? You don't know anything about this guy. Like, he could get violent again."

"I'll be all right. He seems to respond to me, so I can get him through the hospital hoopla. In the meantime, check on Keith and see if he's on his way yet. I'm counting on you for damage control."

The translator gestured to her. "Miss Dyhr, the director wants this actor's contact information."

Did he plan to press charges against the poor guy, too? She shouldn't be surprised. Mr. Nakamura would need to save face in the producer's view. Forget their opinion of her—it must be blown to hell by this incident.

Jen had been completely unaware Norse mythology interested video gamers until Sandi pointed out a couple of games titled *Viking Warrior: Bridge to Asgard* and *Valkyrie Knights*. This revelation had opened a whole realm of possibility for her. She'd designed wardrobes for feature films and magazine shoots galore, but never an ad for a video game company.

She'd been so excited when her hairstylist brought the Japanese producer into her Manhattan showroom, and he'd called afterward to offer a job. It gave her the perfect opportunity to extend her brand.

"Mr. Nakamura, this man needs medical attention." She thrust her chin forward, determined to salvage her reputation by assuming responsibility. "With your permission, I'll take him to the hospital. If Keith still isn't here by the time I return, I promise to call the casting office myself for a replacement. I'm so sorry for the delay."

After giving him another respectful bow, she turned to Sandi. "I'll order my driver to bring the car around. Try to appease the big wigs while I'm gone. We have to find some way to salvage this situation."

Jen led Paz backstage to change into some borrowed street clothes. Then she herded the newcomer out the exit and into the busy midday traffic.

For more details, visit https://nancyjcohen.com/warrior-rogue/

Meet the Drift Lords

Who are the Drift Lords?

The Drift Lords are galactic warriors sent to Earth to seal a dimensional rift opened by an ancient enemy. To defeat the invaders, they must join forces with a special group of Earth women, whose legendary powers are just awakening. Like the Trolleks, the Drift Lords descended from the Originals who inhabited Earth. Legend says they're the prophesied sons of Thor.

The Drift Lords are born with a special trait that becomes evident at puberty when they gain a heightened sense of smell. They are able to sniff cors particles, meaning they can tell when a portal is open. Medical tests confirm this unique ability. Since it's a rare trait, enlistment in the League is mandatory throughout the Star Empire for anyone who possesses it. Their job is to repel the Trollek incursions and seal the rifts.

During the seventeen years of The Great Purge, the Drift Lords were persecuted and outlawed. They had to train in secret on various non-aligned worlds, but still their numbers were drastically reduced. Seven years ago, they were reinstated, and the training academy reopened. Zohar's warriors are the only remaining hope to save mankind. Their ship is the *Protector*.

How Do They Operate?

The Drift Lords work in teams of seven. The Sacred Seven represent earth, fire, water, air, time, space, and the Wise One, creator of all. The team trains at a mountain retreat on the planet Karrell for four weeks per year. When they are not engaged in training or off on a mission, the warriors follow their own careers.

Their uniform consists of a belted black tunic and tailored black pants with a utility belt. The fabric has protective properties similar to lightweight armor. It protects against projectile weapons and light laser fire. They carry a PIP or Portable Intel Platform, with capabilities ranging from scanning to sensors to a levitator beam.

The Drift Lords polarize themselves against the Trollek mind touch, called confounding. Each day after bathing, they shock themselves with a painful pulse emitter. Coating themselves with a permeable oil helps to mitigate the discomfort. The effects last twenty-four hours. They also use a nose numbing spray to ward off the alluring scent of a Trollek female. But the best method of protection is the immunity transferred by physical contact with their destined mate.

The Team Members

ZOHAR THORALD is Captain of the Drift Lords and Crown Prince of the Star Empire. He's the military strategist. Reluctant to be crowned emperor, Zohar has to learn to accept his destiny.

BORIUS MORAINE is the anthropologist and cultural expert. This young man is afraid he'll lose his strength along with his virginity.

DAL FIZORE is the demolitions expert. He's a sinewy, muscled fighter who likes to blow things up for fun.

KAJ DURET is the team's engineer. He prefers working with machines rather than people, as they can't hurt him. In his spare time, he puts together old spacecraft engines.

LORD MAGNOR is an expert swordsman who likes to whittle wood carvings of animals and watch crime shows on TV in his free time. Initially hired as Zohar's bodyguard and lacking the genetic trait that defines a Drift Lord, he becomes a full-fledged member of the team.

PAZ HADAR is the communications and linguistics specialist. When not deployed as a Drift Lord, he repairs space telecom relays. He can say, "Come to bed with me" in numerous languages.

RAYNE is the procurement officer. He secures supplies, lodging and meals.

YARON OF THE GLADE is a medic and science officer. When off duty, he plays melancholy music on his larp, a stringed instrument, and he enjoys the serenity of nature.

Meet the Trolleks

Who are the Trolleks?

The earliest sentient people on Earth were humanoids called the Originals. Descendants of the Originals took different paths. Some of them fled to the stars and seeded other worlds. One group lived close to nature on this planet until mankind encroached on their territory. Humans persecuted them until they were no longer comfortable here. During a natural rift between dimensions, they passed through to another world with pristine forests and fertile fields. These people became known as the Trolleks.

They're invading Earth because their race is dying. Over the years, the water on their world has made the males go sterile. Trollek females are able to mate with human men and have children but these offspring are considered tainted. Their home world is called Jak'Tar.

Their Politics

The Trolleks are divided into two factions.

The Jorgonauts, followers of King Jorg the Terrible, believe the invasion is justified on the basis of survival. They pursue revenge for being banished from Earth many eons ago, plus they seek a clean water supply. They aim to subjugate humanity and use human women as breeders.

The Videns believe their best hope for continuation as a species is through science. They aim to correct the damaged genetic sequence in the male. Their scientists, led by Dokter Algie Morar, are attempting to splice their male Trollek DNA into humans to find a compatible string. Once a stable sequence is identified, it can be used to correct the damage to the Trollek male genome. The SARB project means Stabilize and Reboot.

Algie, a clan chieftain's daughter, was married to General Morar before being told her husband couldn't conceive. She resents that men make the laws on her world and hold the positions of power, and she is determined to change this status.

The Videns think King Jorg is being manipulated by a malevolent force with its own agenda. Otherwise, their liege must be insane, responding to voices no one else can hear. The demon, Loki, has promised King Jorg that Trolleks will rule Earth after a great cataclysm. But is the king being fed a lie, or will Loki truly provide for his people?

Special Abilities

Trolleks can micro-maneuver vectors within the space-time continuum. Using an armband device, they can "parallel shift" themselves and inanimate objects from one location to another. Cors particles are produced when they shift. The Drift Lords can detect this smell that's like burnt wiring. In battle, the Trolleks micro-jump to dodge enemy fire and to fling objects at their foes. The vector disintegrates along with the Trolleks' departure.

Trollek males are super strong. They move with unusual speed and agility. Females lure victims with their beauty and compelling scent. All Trolleks secrete a chemical substance that directly alters the human brain. They transmit it through touch, via their palm. The confounded person follows orders from the Trollek who touched them. Confounding is irreversible and eventually causes amnesia or madness.

The Trolleks have few weaknesses. They are prone to territorial disputes. They don't like loud noises, such as church bells, because it reminds them of Thor's Hammer. And legend says there's a magic weapon that can defeat them.

Glossary

ACTUATORS: Engine parts.

AESIR: The warrior gods in Norse mythology.

ALAMIR: A battle during the border dispute with the Morano Confederation.

ANRIAT: A planet with an unsavory underworld of criminals and desperadoes.

ASGARD: The celestial abode of the Aesir gods.

BERMUDA TRIANGLE: Also called the Devil's Triangle, this area in the Atlantic Ocean ranges from Bermuda to Puerto Rico to Miami. It is the site of anomalies where ships and planes disappear, and radios and compasses stop working.

BOGGER: Derogatory Trollek term for a female.

BORATUS WORMS: Creatures that bore into nerve ganglia.

CARONA: Karrellian term of endearment.

CAVENDII TWO: A military base of the Star Empire under command of Colonel Yaloom.

CORS PARTICLES: Matter produced at the event horizon of a dimensional rift.

DAZLITE: A thumb-sized pocket light.

DISRUPTOR: A hand weapon with two settings—stun and kill. Disrupts neural pathways. Used by planetary patrols and local military units for crowd control. May be assigned as a secondary weapon to ground troops, more often to officers. Class One military use restricted armament. Blue beam.

DOKTER: Trollek word for doctor.

DONIK: Curse word equivalent to bastard.

DONJON: Tower.

DRAGON'S TRIANGLE: Also called the Devil's Sea, this is an area in the Pacific basin southeast of Japan between Iwo Jima and Marcus Island that is the site of anomalies where ships and planes disappear, and radios and compasses stop working.

DRIFT LORD: A warrior who has the special ability to sniff cors particles and who is trained to fight Trollek incursions.

DRIFT WORLD: An adult role-playing theme park in Orlando, FL. "A place where your fantasy job becomes reality. Whatever part you want to play, it's yours for a day."

DROTT: Trollek military form of address for superior officer.

DWARFS: Short-statured men who live underground. They have pale faces and long beards. Skilled metalworkers and goldsmiths who craft magical items for the gods. Greedy fellows, they can make themselves invisible. Weakness: Their power is woven into their hair.

DYTHIUM CHARGES: Explosive compound.

EDDA: An epic of Germanic origin.

ELVES: Nocturnal beings that live in wooded areas. They enjoy dancing and gambling, but people who dance with them must be wary.

EMP GRENADE: A grenade that emits an electromagnetic pulse of a high intensity, short duration burst of electromagnetic energy.

EVENT HORIZON: Rift caused when dimensional plates grind against each other.

FAFNIR: A giant disguised as a dragon to guard his treasure.

FARARRA: A pleasure planet with resorts, emporiums, eateries, and entertainment complexes.

FENRIR: A son of Loki and a fire giant disguised as a wolf. He killed Odin at Ragnarok.

FOUNTAIN OF WISDOM: A source of water under the roots of the giant World Tree. Guarded by the god, Mimir.

GATEKEEPERS: Allies of the Drift Lords, these shapeshifters help protect humanity during Trollek incursions on Earth.

GIANT: According to Norse mythology, giants were the first living creatures. They have the gift of disguise. Two types: Fire Giants and Frost Giants.

GJOLL: A river in the underworld that souls must cross to reach Helheim.

GLITTER BUG: A lightning bug type insect on Paz's home world.

GRAND MARSHAL: Governor of Trollek towns. Addressed as "Your Eminence".

GRIMSHAW: Lord Magnor's name for his sword.

HAGRET: A bird with outstretched wings.

HAS'PUTE: A Karrellian curse word.

HEL: Goddess ruler of Helheim and Loki's daughter.

HELHEIM: The realm of the dead ruled by the goddess, Hel.

HERIS: Form of address for a Trollek landowner, second in rank to a Grand Marshal.

HYPERSPACE: Faster than speed of light travel via a distortion of the space-time continuum.

IMMOBILIZER: Stun weapon used by Star Empire military units in covert ops. Class Two restricted armament.

JADLOK: Elven liege of the lake's region.

JAK'TAR: The Trollek home world.

JAWANI: A standard universal language.

JORG: King of the Trolleks.

JORGONAUTS: Followers of the Trollek ruler, King Jorg.

KABAK: Trollek who commands a confounded human.

KAG: Man who likes boys.

KARRELL: Home world of Zohar Thorald and training ground for the Drift Lords.

KASH: A Trollek dice game.

KEWA STONES: Diamonds.

KIMMLEBUSH: A curse word in Dwarf language.

KLICK: A kilometer or approximately .6213 miles.

KNESTA: "Beloved" in Lord Magnor's tongue; a term of endearment.

LASER CARBINE: RAD-4 Rifle with enhanced infrared scanner; used by military troops.

LAVA BOMB: Explosive device, similar to a grenade.

LEERA: A term of endearment in Paz's native language.

LIEMA: A long-necked animal that moves with grace, native to Paz's home world.

LEY LINES: An energy grid intersects Earth at twelve distinct geographic points called Vile Vortices. Ley lines are the lines connecting these points of the electromagnetic field.

LEYTNANT: Officer in Trollek military force.

LOKI: Loki is a mischievous trickster and shapeshifter who was banished to an underground prison by the Norse gods. He is a malevolent being bent on revenge and galactic domination.

LOXOTAN: A painkiller.

LYTHIX SERUM: Truth serum used by the Trolleks.

MALNATIUM: A volatile but powerful energy producing compound.

MAUG: A curse word used as an adjective; a derogatory term.

MENIG: Lowest enlisted rank in Trollek military force.

MIDGARD: The middle land occupied by mankind in Norse mythology.

MIMIR: God who guards the Fountain of Wisdom.

MIMIR'S WELL: The Fountain of Wisdom guarded by the god, Mimir. This water supplies one of the roots of the great World Tree.

MIN DROTT: Trollek form of address for superior officer.

MINGLING: Sexual intimacy.

MJOLLNIR: Thor's magic hammer, forged by the dwarves. When thrown, it returns like a boomerang.

MODGUD: Giantess guardian of the bridge over the river Gjoll leading to Helheim.

MORABI NERVE JAB: A hand chop to a sensitive bundle of nerves.

MORANO CONFEDERATION: An alliance bordering the Star Empire.

MORATA: Paz's home world, a desert planet in the Zood System.

NEUTRINO: A small elementary particle that carries no electric charge.

NIDHOG: Dragon who gnaws on a root of the World Tree and guards the spring Hvergelmir.

NID RUNE: A curse.

NIFLHEL: A lower level of Helheim where the evil dead suffer endless torment.

NORNS: Three Goddesses of Fate who guard the Urd Well.

ODIN: Ruler of the Norse gods.

ORIGINALS: Early sentient beings who inhabited Earth.

PAMADORE: A type of poultry consumed on Karrell.

PFRELL: Flying creatures with sharp talons and spear-like beaks; a hunter species native to the Trollek world.

PHASE GUN: Type of energy weapon. The Drift Lords carry Monix T-6 laser pistols. Three settings—stun, kill, vaporize. Spare power packs (miniature energy cells) are carried in utility belt pouches. Older model: T-4, has to be reloaded more often.

PHASE RIFLE: Long-range version of above. Powered by portable energy converter.

PIP: Portable Intel Platform; handheld data unit with sensors and scanning capability. This device also has a levitator beam to move heavy objects.

POLARIZE: The means by which Drift Lords protect themselves from the Trollek spell.

PURPURA BLOSSOMS: A sweet scented flower on Karrell.

RAGEESH: Honorary form of address for the Crown Prince of the Star Empire.

RAGNAROK: End of the world and destruction of the multi-verse.

RIFF: Karrellian term for lowlife or thug.

SCREEN (verb): To hide from sight.

SHAPESHIFTER: Beings who can alter their form.

SHELL SHEDDER: Old-fashioned projectile weapons favored by the Trolleks. Drift Lords' lightweight clothing armor protects against these projectiles.

SHIRAJO MANOR: Trollek stronghold on Togura Island.

SHOCK STICK: Rod-like punishment device used by the Trolleks for slave control. It delivers a painful electric shock.

SIRE: Honorary form of address for royalty on Karrell.

SIRA: Honorary form of address for noble ladies on Karrell.

SKAP: Slang term for a Viden.

SLOGG: Trollek word for slave.

SMARK: A curse word in Paz's native tongue.

SNIPELING: A reptilian creature that lives in rock crevices. Poisonous venom.

SONIC GRENADE: Weapon used by Star Empire troops. It causes a blast of sonic waves.

SPATIAL SHIFT: Instantaneous transport from one place to another.

STAR EMPIRE: An alliance of sentient planets ruled by a hereditary Emperor.

TEECAHT: A derogatory name for a Trollek woman who steps out of bounds.

TENT TEN: Site of Trollek medical experiments on humans.

THOR: Warrior god of Norse legend who carries Mjollnir, a magic hammer.

THOR'S HAMMER: Thor's magical weapon, Mjollnir, returns to its thrower.

TROLLEK: Intelligent creatures derived from the Originals, the Trolleks revere nature, despise humans for chasing them from their land, and believe in taking by force what suits their needs.

UGRON: A grizzly bear-like creature.

URD WELL: Fountain of Youth protected by the Norns, its spring feeds the root on the World Tree that supports Midgard.

VALHALLA: Odin's hall where dead warriors reside and prepare for Ragnarok.

VALKYRIES: Warrior maidens of the god Odin, these women carry warriors who die in battle to Valhalla. Also called Shield Maidens.

VANIR: Norse gods who were farmers and merchants.

VECTOR: An invisible line on the time-space continuum.

VECTOR SHIFT: See spatial shift.

VEILED: Shielded from view.

VIDENS: Faction of Trolleks who support science instead of conquest as a solution to their problems.

VILE VORTICES: An energy grid beneath the earth's crust intersects the globe at twelve distinct geographic points called Vile Vortices. These are often sites of anomalous activity. Five each of these vortices are at an equal distance above and below the equator. Two are located at the north and south poles.

WAGMIRE: A type of rodent.

WIGONK: A domesticated canine on Karrell.

WONK: Trollek slang term for male appendage.

WORLD TREE: The great ash tree that connects all nine realms of the universe. Also called Yggdrasil.

YMIR: The first Giant in Norse mythology.

About the Author

Nancy J. Cohen writes the Bad Hair Day Mysteries featuring South Florida hairstylist Marla Vail. Titles in this series have been named Best Cozy Mystery by *Suspense Magazine*, won Readers' Favorite gold medals and the RONE Award, placed first in the Chanticleer International Book Awards and third in the Arizona Literary Awards.

Her nonfiction titles, *Writing the Cozy Mystery* and *A Bad Hair Day Cookbook*, have also garnered numerous awards. These include gold medals in the FAPA President's Book Awards and the Royal Palm Literary Awards, First Place in the IAN Book of the Year Awards and the *Topshelf Magazine* Book Awards. *Writing the Cozy Mystery* was also an Agatha Award Finalist.

Nancy's imaginative romances have proven popular with fans as well. These books have won the HOLT Medallion and Best Book in Romantic SciFi/Fantasy at *The Romance Reviews*.

A featured speaker at libraries, conferences, and community events, Nancy is listed in *Contemporary Authors, Poets & Writers*, and *Who's Who in U.S. Writers, Editors, & Poets*. She is a past president of Florida Romance Writers and the Florida Chapter of Mystery Writers of America. When not busy writing, she enjoys reading, fine dining, cruising, and visiting Disney World.

Follow Nancy Online

Website – https://nancyjcohen.com
Blog – https://nancyjcohen.com/blog
Twitter – https://www.twitter.com/nancyjcohen
Facebook – https://www.facebook.com/NancyJCohenAuthor
LinkedIn – https://www.linkedin.com/in/nancyjcohen
Goodreads – https://www.goodreads.com/nancyjcohen
Pinterest – https://pinterest.com/njcohen/
Instagram – https://instagram.com/nancyjcohen
BookBub – https://www.bookbub.com/authors/nancy-j-cohen

Books by Nancy J. Cohen

The Bad Hair Day Mysteries
Permed to Death
Hair Raiser
Murder by Manicure
Body Wave
Highlights to Heaven
Died Blonde
Dead Roots
Perish by Pedicure
Killer Knots
Shear Murder
Hanging by a Hair
Peril by Ponytail
Haunted Hair Nights (Novella)
Facials Can Be Fatal
Hair Brained
Hairball Hijinks (Short Story)
Trimmed to Death
Easter Hair Hunt
Styled for Murder
Star Tangled Murder

The Drift Lords Series
Warrior Prince
Warrior Rogue
Warrior Lord

Nancy J. Cohen

Science Fiction Romances
Keeper of the Rings
Silver Serenade

The Light-Years Series
Circle of Light
Moonlight Rhapsody
Starlight Child

Nonfiction
Writing the Cozy Mystery
A Bad Hair Day Cookbook

Order Now at https://nancyjcohen.com/books/

#